They're beautiful.
They're socially desirable. They're destitute.
*INTRODUCING THE DESPERATE
DEBUTANTES . . .*

"You are to France, my lord?" Ava asked her stepfather. "And we are to remain here, the same as before?"

"Aha!" he said, lifting a finger. "Not *precisely* the same as before. The endless days of shopping and ordering gowns and shoes and whatnot have come to a most desired end."

Ava and Greer gasped. Phoebe looked as if she actually might be ill.

"Furthermore, I see no reason to pay for servants now that you are in mourning. There will be no traipsing about this Season's assemblies. You are three industrious young women. I should think you are quite capable of making a bed and sweeping a carpet."

"Oh dear God," Ava moaned, and closed her eyes. "I beg your pardon, sir, but our mother was quite wealthy. If I may be so indecorous as to inquire . . . surely she left *something* for our care?"

"Of course she did," he said pleasantly. "A modest dowry for each of you. The rest is left to me to look after as I see fit."

"We're doomed!" Phoebe whispered to the ceiling.

**National bestselling author Julia London creates a
world of daring passions, witty repartee, and
powerful emotions in her unforgettable novels.**

"Heel-kickingly fun and high-spirited."
—*Publishers Weekly* on *Highlander in Love*

"Exquisitely romantic, lusciously sensual."
—*Booklist* on *Highlander Unbound*

ALSO BY JULIA LONDON

Highlander in Love
Highlander in Disguise
Highlander Unbound

JULIA LONDON

The HAZARDS of HUNTING A DUKE

POCKET STAR BOOKS

New York   London   Toronto   Sydney

An *Original* Publication of POCKET BOOKS

 A Pocket Star Book published by
POCKET BOOKS, a division of Simon & Schuster, Inc.
1230 Avenue of the Americas, New York, NY 10020

ISBN 13: 978-1-4165-1615-6
ISBN 10:   1-4165-1615-8

This Pocket Star Books paperback edition June 2006

10 9 8 7 6 5 4 3 2 1

POCKET STAR BOOKS and colophon are registered trademarks of Simon & Schuster, Inc.

Front cover hand-lettering by David Gatti
Front cover illustration by Jim Griffin

Manufactured in the United States of America

For information regarding special discounts for bulk purchases, please contact Simon & Schuster Special Sales at 1-800-456-6798 or business@simonandschuster.com

For the Whine Sisters, who help me rise and whine
every day without fail.

The HAZARDS of HUNTING A DUKE

One

~~~~~

The Marquis of Middleton, who was the sole heir to the powerful Redford duchy, had an air about him, a palpable energy that exuded power and wealth. There was also the potent sexuality of a very masculine man that was felt by most women—and perhaps a few men. It was indeed a *potent* sexuality.

The marquis, Jared Broderick, said or did nothing to provoke such feelings in others, for in all honesty, he was quite unaware of his remarkable power. Had someone suggested that he caused women to feel weak at the knees with just a look, he might have laughed and unabashedly confessed to adoring all women, for he did. Poor women, rich women, daughters of Quality or commoners, he cared not—just as long as they were completely and unapologetically female. That meant they must have a scent of sweet waters about them, be soft, occasionally silly, vexing, enticing, and inspiring—both in the boudoir and beyond.

With his darkly golden brown hair, square jaw, broad shoulders, and hazel eyes flecked with gold, he was considered dangerously handsome among the *haute ton,* the elite society of London. He was tall and broad and lean, possessed of an athletic build. His rakish habits had a slightly sinister side, too, for a man who enjoyed both gaming and women was bound to run into a spot of trouble from time to time. Whispered rumors of a duel persisted, a duel in which he had purportedly proceeded fearlessly and had emerged victorious.

The most recent tale of his recklessness had to do with his performance during the course of a stag hunt last autumn. The stag had sensed the hunters and had broken through the forest to escape. It was said that Middleton risked his neck and that of his big bay horse to catch the stag, leaping over rock walls, storming through dangerous gullies and thickets, racing far ahead of the other riders. But when Middleton had cornered the stag, he reined up, turned his mount around, and returned to the estate. They said it seemed as if it wasn't the hunt that mattered but the ride.

In the posh interiors of London's gentlemen's clubs, more than one man remarked that the marquis rode so hard that day not because he was in pursuit of a prize stag, but because his own demons were in pursuit of him.

Whatever his habits, they were routinely reported, thinly disguised, in the London morning newspapers, and surely none endured around the elite Mayfair district of London as well as the tales of his exploits in the beds of some of the most important women in town. What made these rakish tales even more scintillating was that he was heir to one of the most powerful duchies in England and Wales, and the thought of him siring bastards about town was cause for great distress to his father, the current Duke of Redford.

It was well known that many lords desired that their daughters be groomed for a match with Redford's son, and the odds-on favorite was thought to be Lady Elizabeth Robertson. Lady Elizabeth's father was a dear boyhood friend of the duke's, and it was agreed by all wagging tongues that her pedigree for becoming a duchess was unparalleled.

What the gossips didn't know, however, was that the marquis and the duke had engaged in many loud arguments about Lady Elizabeth in which the marquis had steadfastly refused to entertain the idea of a match with her and the duke insisted he would approve of no other match.

It was, in fact, another *on dit* in this morning's newspaper that had prompted the duke to summon the marquis like a servant once again.

Jared came, but he sat carelessly as his father paced. The duke was gripping the latest edition of the *Times* in his hand, too angry to speak for several moments. " 'A certain *widow*,' " he read, and threw the paper down as he pinned Jared with a cold glare. "I know very well to whom they allude—everyone in town knows of your affair with Lady Waterstone."

Jared shrugged. So he'd been visiting the widow's bed—he was a man, and he'd developed a certain corporeal fondness for Miranda, Lady Waterstone.

"Have you no care for your reputation? What if Lady Elizabeth should read this?" the duke asked him through gritted teeth.

"What if she should?" Jared responded irreverently. He owed no measure to Lady Elizabeth that he could see, and frankly, if his father was so keen to see the woman married, Jared thought, perhaps *he*, a widower for many years, should do the marrying. Jared was completely unrepentant about his refusal—he thought nothing of living every day as if it were his last, and no fatherly desire to see him wed a woman with the face of a horse would keep him from it.

But as Jared's refusal became more entrenched, the greater umbrage his father took with him, today notwithstanding. "I have suffered the indignity of hearing of your association with this woman at my club—and now I must read it as well?"

"I am not responsible for what is printed," Jared said.

The duke's face turned dark. "Yet you are responsible for the contemptible behavior that ignites such rubbish to be printed, are you not? I demand that you not debase our name and title with the likes of that woman, do you quite understand me? You will not lie with a harlot who married above herself," he snapped. "Now that she is widowed, she would sink her talons in the heir to the Redford title, and I will not have it! Lady Elizabeth is perfectly suited to carry a legitimate heir, and as soon as is possible within the bounds of propriety!"

Jared bristled with indignation. "Is that all that I am, your grace? Breeding stock for your vast realm of influence?"

His father's dark brown eyes narrowed. "You are vile."

"Very well," Jared said, quietly seething, "if the price for having been born to your exalted house is to produce a bloody heir, I shall do so. But I shall do so at my leisure and with whom I please."

"You will *not* produce an heir with whomever you please!" his father thundered. "There is much more at stake here than your lustful cravings! I should think you would have learned as much from the ugly consequences of your previous libertine habits!" he said, piercing old wounds. "I warn you, Lord Middleton, if you think to dishonor me further, I will see you disinherited by order of the king!"

Jared threw his arms wide with a shout of incredulous laughter. "By all means, my lord! I will not stop you—I would *welcome* it, for at least I'd be free of the yoke you have put on me!" He meant that sincerely. Granted, he'd made his fair share of mistakes—but so had the duke. Let him disinherit—Jared was a marquis in his own right; he had no need of the title of duke and frankly, he did not want it.

But his father suddenly sank into his ornate mahogany chair behind an even grander desk and covered his face with his thin hands for a moment. "For the love of Christ, Jared," he said, his voice hoarse. "For the love of *Christ*, please do as I ask." He lifted his head from his hands and looked at his son. "You cannot forget that our family was once steeped in debauchery and made bed with whores and bastards. It took *years* for our name to be recognized by the monarchy. For you to debase that good name now with your slut is unconscionable. Marry a woman of proper standing and put a son in her, then whore with whomever you please!"

"Just as you did?" Jared asked evenly.

The duke paled. He leaned back in his chair, gripped the edge of his desk, every muscle in his body quivering with rage. "Get out of my sight," he said quietly.

Jared gained his feet. "Your grace," he said with a nod, and strode out of the massive town house on Park Lane bound for White's, desperately angry with his father, and even angrier with the two footmen who had been ordered to follow him.

All his life, he had chafed under the absurdity of his supposed responsibility. His was a dishearteningly simple and primal function—he was breeding stock to the ducal Redfords, valued for nothing more than his ability to procreate. Honestly, he really remembered little else from his childhood, particularly after his mother had died in his fourteenth year. His memory of her was fading, and he could scarcely recall her softness, or the warmth of her breath, or the smell of lilacs on her skin. He remembered that she would laugh when she was with him, but in truth, he saw her only occasionally. His parents resided in London or the country, wherever his father's mistress resided.

Jared, on the other hand, resided elsewhere, with the nursemaids and governesses and tutors who would sculpt him to be a duke one day.

Even when he'd gone off to school, his acquaintances were closely watched, his schooling carefully monitored. He never felt close to anyone, really, save his two good friends, Lords Stanhope and Harrison, who had been schooled alongside him.

The talk of producing an heir began the moment he'd come of age, the demands growing louder each passing year. Now, on the eve of his thirtieth birthday, the demands were deafening.

More than once Jared had wished he'd been born the son of a crofter, a merchant, a banker—any occupation his father might have esteemed above his cock. But he'd been born the son of a duke, and from the time he could remember, his father had sought to control his destiny, whom he befriended, whom he loved.

As a result, Jared loved no one.

He made his way to White's, the gentlemen's club to which he belonged, and moped about, refusing to even hold a hand in a game of whist when his friends pressed him. When the game ended, his oldest friend, Geoffrey Godwin, Viscount Harrison, insisted he accompany him to the Fontaine ball. "I can't let you drink alone," he'd said, clapping Jared on the back. "You may very well harm someone."

"I don't want to go to any bloody ball," Jared muttered. "I despise the vapidity of the social season. It's scarcely begun and already there is a parade of debutantes and their mothers before me, all hungry for a spectacular match and unparalleled fortune."

"Oh now, don't be so harsh on the poor birds and their mothers," Harrison said, touching Jared's glass with his before swallowing the last of his whiskey. "Don't let the fathers off so easily—there is nothing more bloody stilted than the conversation of a man with an unmarried daughter."

"*Ach,*" William Danvers, Lord Stanhope scoffed, waving a hand at them. "Walk in my shoes, will you? Have your fortune entailed for generations to come so that *you* must be the one to hope for a spectacular match with a *woman* of unparalleled fortune."

"Impossible," Jared snorted. "Women don't have fortunes—men do."

"That, sir, is precisely my problem," Stanhope said, and with a sound of disgust, pushed a hand through his blond hair.

"Come on, then," Harrison said. "Stanhope is headed for the gaming hells to increase his paltry fortune. But I have it on good authority that there will be a high-stakes table at the Fontaine ball for the wealthy gentlemen who do not enjoy dancing."

Jared glanced at Harrison. "High-stakes?"

"*Very* high-stakes," Harrison confirmed with a smile.

Jared shrugged. "I would prefer the warmth of Miranda's body to a damn card game."

"But Miranda is not about, she is in the country. What else shall you do but drink until they carry you home? Come along, then, my good Lord Middleton— come and win a tidy little sum to take your mind from your troubles."

Perhaps a bit of friendly wagering would serve as a useful diversion from his dark thoughts about his father. "Very well," he said with a sigh, and scowled when Harrison and Stanhope applauded his decision.

And when he and Harrison stood at the door of the Fontaine ballroom, both of them a head taller than most, Jared felt a familiar bit of happiness at seeing so many agreeable and attractive women. He missed Miranda in his own way, but Harrison was right, she was not about. Therefore, the sporting man in him determined that he should give the night his best effort.

Across the room, Ava Fairchild nudged her sister and cousin and nodded at the two impeccably dressed gentlemen standing at the entrance, both of whom were clad in black tails, white silk waistcoats, and expertly tied neckcloths. The only distinguishable difference was that Middleton wore a badge on his breast that marked his title superior to that of Harrison.

"Oh *my*," Phoebe sighed appreciatively as they gazed at the two men. "I should very much like to make their acquaintance one day, if only for the pleasure of a single dance."

"A dance? I had in mind something far more exciting," Ava said. Her sister and cousin looked at her expectantly, and Ava winked at them. "A torrid love affair. With Middleton."

It was a game the three of them played, a bit of lustful wondering about the opposite sex. But Ava's choice caused Phoebe to snort indelicately. "Darling, I do believe you have gone completely daft. You've not a hope for a proper introduction to Middleton, much less a love affair, not with every breathing debutante queuing before him . . . unless, of course, you are willing to offer up your good virtue."

"Perhaps even your life," Greer added. "He's got a recklessness in him that borders on madness. And when he does deign to dance, it is only to seduce. That is how his affair with Lady Waterstone began, you know."

Ava smiled with surprise. "You seem to be uncommonly well informed about him, Greer."

"I've overheard quite a lot about him, and none of it good," she said with a shrug. "Have your affair with Harrison, Ava, for he's every bit as handsome. Really . . . every bit," she said wistfully.

The three young women looked at Harrison for a moment. With his dark hair and clear blue eyes, he was quite handsome—but Ava's gaze slid back to Middleton, who was smiling alluringly at a woman near him.

She could imagine he seduced women all the time, which was, frankly, part of his allure. But she was not so foolish that she didn't know Middleton was just a dream to mere mortals such as themselves. While on paper their standing in society was quite respectable—their late father had been an earl—their real social standing did not meet the standards that would be expected for a future duke. Middleton's title and income—not to mention his fine looks and charming manner—were such that he could attract any woman he desired. Surely all women desired him—the words he uttered in the course of his casual flirtations were legendary, known to most women through the excited whispers in ladies' retiring rooms about Mayfair.

Ava had no expectation of ever being noticed by a man of his stature, much less engaged in any sort of affair. Nevertheless, she found the fantasy delightful. "Then perhaps I shall just marry him," she said gaily, startling her sister and cousin. "Why shouldn't I?" she said to their twin expressions of shock. "I am the daughter of an earl, and I'm at *least* as desirable as Lady Elizabeth."

The three of them glanced to their left, where Lady Elizabeth, wearing a drab yellow gown, was holding court with a coterie of debutantes who flocked around her like so many geese. Unfortunately, she stood next to Miss Grace Holcomb, the daughter of a very wealthy merchant who had just arrived in London, from as far away as Leeds. Miss Holcomb, an amiable young woman by all accounts, was quite eager to take her place in a society that valued birthright as much as fortune, and had made the grave mistake of attaching herself to the humorless Lady Elizabeth. Perhaps as a testament to her wealth, Miss Holcomb was wearing a very bright rose-colored gown and lots of glittering jewelry. Elizabeth faded quite from sight next to Miss Holcomb, a situation Ava was certain Elizabeth would remedy in short order.

"Well, then?" Ava asked. "Am I not at least as desirable?"

"Obviously, you exceed her in looks and bearing," Greer said thoughtfully, receiving a small but grateful nod of acknowledgment from Ava, for Elizabeth did indeed have a rather spectacular nose, "but everyone expects her to be the Season's favorite. And *you*, dearest, have been out for three years now and remain quite unmarried." She wiggled three gloved fingers at Ava to press home her point.

Ava grabbed those fingers and squeezed playfully. "Not from a lack of opportunity," she said. "I've had more than my fair share of offers, just like you, *dearest*."

She did not look at Phoebe, who'd not had an offer since her coming out last year—the poor dear was painfully shy around gentlemen. Greer, on the other hand, was so clever that gentlemen always sought her partnership in parlor games. And Ava—well, Ava was quite happy to enjoy the courtly attentions of a variety of gentlemen, and in fact, encouraged it. "I happen to enjoy being unmarried. Life is far more exciting with the attention of many handsome men and I suspect exceedingly dull with the attention of only one."

"Then you and Lord Middleton must be very much alike," Phoebe opined. Greer laughed roundly at that, and Ava inadvertently glanced at the entrance of the ballroom again. Unfortunately, her fantasy had disappeared along with Harrison into the crowd. Worse, Sir Garrett was closing in on her, striding as quickly as his corseted girth would allow.

"Oh how divine," Greer said cheerfully. "Now you may enjoy the attention of Sir Garrett."

Ava groaned; Sir Garrett was a very large and gregarious man with thick lips and a tuft of hair on the crown of his head. He had, over the course of two Seasons, developed great affection for her. Lately, he'd begun to make a nuisance of himself—he sought her out at every opportunity and had begun to monopolize her at every event.

Yet Ava took pity on the man. He'd never married

and seemed to be rather lonely. She could hardly deny him a dance now and again, but the poor thing was rather thick when it came to her gentle rebuffs. He did not seem to understand that agreeing to dance with him was her way of being polite.

As he arrived at her side, Ava heard Phoebe giggle and felt her elbow at her waist, yet she smiled graciously as Sir Garrett reached for her hand. "Lady Ava," he said, bending over it.

"Sir Garrett, what a pleasure," she said, dipping into a curtsy.

He grinned broadly, bumped the back of her hand with his lips, then turned his grin to Phoebe and Greer as Ava pulled her hand free of his bearlike grasp.

"If I may be so bold," he said, turning his attention to Ava once more, "I would remark that you are by *far* the *fairest* of *all* the many ladies in attendance tonight," he said, sweeping his arm wide to indicate all the ladies, and obviously forgetting Greer and Phoebe.

Ava reminded him with a small inclination of her head.

Sir Garrett instantly realized his faux pas; his florid face flushed even more. "That is to say . . . the *three* of you, ah . . . Fairchilds, all of you . . . are quite . . . *fair*," he stammered, turning hopelessly redder.

Phoebe and Greer smiled demurely and thanked him for his kind words, as they had on at least two previous occasions.

He removed a kerchief from his pocket and dabbed at his forehead, his gaze on Ava again. "Miss Fairchild, would you do me the honor of standing up with me on the next dance?" he asked, dabbing at his temple. "I believe it will be a quadrille, and I assure you, I have endeavored to learn the steps in the correct sequence so there will not be another incident as you had the misfortune to endure at the Beltrose ball."

The misfortune being that Sir Garrett had mashed her poor toes quite flat on a quadrille. But Ava felt that old tug of sorrow for the hapless knight and smiled. At least she would get the dance over and done with. "I'd be delighted, sir."

His face lit up with his pleasure. "*Oh!*" he exclaimed, and clapped an arm across his barrel chest, the kerchief waving like a little flag between his fingers, "you do me *such* honor, Lady Ava!" He quickly stuffed the kerchief in his pocket and offered his hand, broad palm up.

Ava reluctantly slipped her hand into the paw he offered and shot a look of helplessness at Phoebe and Greer as Sir Garrett marched her toward the dance floor.

On the opposite side of the ballroom, Harrison had kicked Jared onto the dance floor so that he might have a moment with a young woman who seemed more interested in Jared than him. Jared had obliged Harrison's interest in the woman by asking Mrs. Honeycutt, a woman whose personal company he had enjoyed for three full weeks one summer while her husband was in Scotland, to stand up with him for a quadrille. He preferred the quadrille for old lovers, as the dance was performed with four in a square, which meant there was really no place with sufficient privacy to talk about hurt feelings over old news, as women were wont to do.

A waltz, on the other hand, was a very private dance and lent itself to the whispering of amorous suggestions to women he had not yet had the pleasure of knowing.

Mrs. Honeycutt was determined, however, to tell him what she thought. "I have missed you," she whispered as he took her arm and twirled her around. Jared said nothing, just smiled, let her go, and moved around the square to Lady Williamson. But when he turned to face Mrs. Honeycutt again, she looked at him like a sad little puppy that was not permitted to go abroad with its master.

Jared smiled charmingly, bowed his head, and stepped forward, took her hands in his, went round, and let her go. And when he stepped back to his position, he collided hard with someone at his back.

"Oh dear!" Lady Williamson exclaimed, looking over his shoulder.

Jared quickly pivoted about; the person who had collided with him was an attractive young woman with dark blond hair and startlingly pale green eyes. She was, unfortunately, in the hands of Sir Garrett.

"I do beg your pardon, my lord," Garrett blustered, and groped awkwardly for the hands of his dance partner as a bead of perspiration ran down his temple.

The woman glanced over her shoulder and smiled at Jared in a funny way, as if she was perhaps a bit mortified, but far more amused to have been swung so violently into him. And if he wasn't mistaken, she gave him an apologetic shrug of her shoulders before turning her full attention to Sir Garrett again.

As well she should have. Her very life was at stake.

Jared turned back to his square and fell easily into step once again. But as he passed around the circle, he caught the eye of the woman again. She smiled fully at him, and it struck him that there was no vanity or guile—or perhaps more important, no avarice—in that smile. So many women looked at him with the gleam of want in their eyes.

But this one had green eyes full of laughter, and he realized, watching her be manhandled by Garrett again, that she was not attempting to gain his attention as he might have expected, but was genuinely amused by the clumsy dancing she was being forced to endure.

That, he thought, was refreshingly different. He knew far too many members of the fairer sex who would have been quite appalled by Garrett's handling and would have said as much. The man was a war veteran and fiercely loyal to the crown, and what he lacked in social finesse he made up tenfold in courage. Jared respected the woman's ability to see beyond her partner's bumbling dance.

He had no notion of who this woman was, but he was mildly intrigued.

When he came around to the side where he might see her again, Sir Garrett's body shielded her from view, and he did not have occasion to catch sight of her again on the dance floor, and for that he was sorry.

$\mathcal{T}\!wo$

Some time later, at the back of the ballroom, partially hidden by a massive palm, Ava, Phoebe, and Greer frowned at the slipper Ava held in her hand.

"It's hopelessly broken," Phoebe declared, flicking the heel with her finger. The offending piece clung to the rest of the shoe by an alarmingly small sliver of silk. "And I worked so hard to *bead* it," she added with a bit of a pout.

What Phoebe lacked in self-confidence she made up in creative endeavors. She was a master at taking their purchased gowns and shoes and accoutrements and enhancing them with embroidery and beading to make them truly original. She had beaded the slippers Ava was wearing over a fortnight this winter, painstakingly creating tiny suns that matched the dark gold embroidery she'd done on the blue silk gown Ava was wearing. She'd also strung small, glittering beads together that the three of them wore wrapped in their hair.

"Clumsy Sir Garrett," Ava sighed. "He hadn't the slightest notion of the steps, and he moved forward instead of backward as he ought to have done, and pushed me right off the edge of the dance floor."

"Poor man," Greer said. "To be so hopelessly besotted with a woman who shall not have him."

"Of course I shall not have him," Ava muttered as she studied her shoe. "If he were to offer, I'd politely decline and suggest he set his sights on Miss Holcomb. She would be delighted to receive an offer from a knight."

"Aunt Cassandra said you really must begin to consider all serious offers," Greer reminded her.

Phoebe and Ava stopped in their examination of the slipper and looked at Greer. Greer raised a brow.

"Did she indeed? And pray tell, what did she say of you?" Ava asked. "You are only a year younger than me, and you've had one serious offer this young Season that *you* refused."

"My circumstance is quite different from yours," Greer said calmly. "I cannot possibly consent to marry a man who will not read as much as a newspaper, and Lord Winston, by his own admission, does not enjoy reading at all. In fact, he admitted quite plainly that he believes books are a frivolous expense."

"There, you see?" Ava asked as she slipped her foot into the offending shoe. "You have made my point. We are not bound to accept offers from gentlemen we cannot abide every day for the rest of our lives. It is the same reason I cannot accept Sir Garrett's offer."

"No . . . but Lord Downey might," Greer suggested, referring to her aunt Cassandra's current husband, Ava and Phoebe's stepfather.

Ava frowned at her cousin. "Fortunately, Mother is not bound to agree with Lord Downey's preferences. If Mother wasn't feeling unwell and was in attendance tonight, she would remind you that she would never marry me away to Sir Garrett, as a match with him would be 'neither convenient nor inspired,' " she said, mimicking her mother.

Greer smiled—Lady Downey had told them many times that marriage was strictly a matter of convenience and fortune, and rarely inspired.

Privately, Ava thought her mother's second marriage to Lord Downey was neither very convenient nor inspired, and really did not see the allure of such an arrangement at all. At two and twenty, Ava was one of the oldest unmarried women among the Quality still considered to be marriageable, and yet she saw no reason to rush into a match—her mother's fortune was more than enough to keep them all quite happy. Why shouldn't one hope for compatibility and affection above fortune? What purpose was there in a marriage of convenience if a young lady already had a suitable fortune to provide for her? Ava preferred to wait for an offer from a man she might love.

"I do not think Sir Garrett will offer for you tonight," Phoebe said. "Nor do I think you will dance another set this evening, as your shoe cannot be repaired. You'd best sit with Lady Purnam until she's ready to see us home."

Lady Purnam was their mother's closest and dearest friend, and had instantly offered to see the three young women to the ball when Lady Downey began to feel unwell. The offer was met with some reluctance by Ava, Phoebe, and Greer, for Lady Purnam believed, by virtue of her close association with their mother, that she had a duty to insinuate herself into their lives and instruct them on all matters to do with propriety. She could be very tiresome in that regard, and the suggestion that Ava might have to sit an entire evening with her was more than she could possibly endure. "Sit alongside Lady Purnam and listen to her chatter all evening while I suffer the undying attention of Sir Garrett? Thank you, but I'd rather walk home."

"Ava, don't be silly, you can't possibly walk. The rain is turning to sleet and your shoe is *broken*," Phoebe reminded her.

"I can think of nothing worse than sitting in a chair at a ball while everyone dances past me," Ava said. "I'll ask Lady Fontaine to send a footman to attend me," she said, and suddenly smiled. "Did you see the one with the golden hair and lovely brown eyes?"

Phoebe snorted. "A *footman*? Now I am convinced more than ever you are daft," she said, and held out her arm. "Come on, then. To Lady Purnam's side."

With a groan of capitulation, Ava took Phoebe's arm, and listing a little to the left, allowed Phoebe and Greer to escort her across the room.

Lady Purnam was seated in a thronelike chair near the dance floor, closely peering through her lorgnette and studying each pair of dancers that waltzed by. She was delighted to have Ava's company and waved at a footman to have a chair brought over.

Ava sat, but a little petulantly and frowning at the departing backs of her sister and cousin as they joined Miss Holcomb at the punch bowl.

"A broken shoe, eh?" Lady Purnam said, directing her lorgnette at Ava's feet. "Happened to me once, at Ascot. The heel broke and I couldn't possibly make my way to the railing to see the end of the horse race."

"How unfortunate."

"It was *terribly* unfortunate. Lord Purnam was in quite a dither, for his horse held the lead until it was bumped by the king's horse and faltered." She turned suddenly toward Ava and said dramatically, "He *never* recovered."

"The horse? Or Lord Purnam?" Ava asked innocently.

Lady Purnam clucked her tongue. "The horse, of course!" She turned back to the dancing and picked up a fan, and began to fan her bosom. "To have a broken shoe at a ball is inconvenient, isn't it? You cannot dance, and you dare not say whyever not when a gentleman inquires. Gentlemen should not hear of such things as flawed garments, shoes, and other personal articles."

Ava glanced curiously at Lady Purnam. "I cannot mention a broken shoe?"

"No," Lady Purnam said, shaking her head. "It is uncouth to mention a broken shoe. A gentleman will want to repair it, which would put him in direct contact with your foot, which is connected to your leg, of course, and it will turn his thoughts to forbidden things."

Ava failed to see how a broken shoe could bring to mind anything other than a broken shoe. "But I—"

"You may politely decline," Lady Purnam said sternly, with a pointed look at Ava. "But you must *never* give a gentleman such a personal reason for your decline."

Dear God. Lady Purnam's idea of propriety seemed positively medieval and all too meddlesome. But Lady Downey had trained Ava to be nothing if not exceedingly polite, and with a slight sigh, she resigned herself and leaned back in her chair.

"Up, dear," Lady Purnam said, tapping her knee with her fan. "Up, up, up," she said with each subsequent tap to her knee.

Ava sat up, her back straight and stiff, her feet tucked carefully under the hem of her gown, her hands folded in her lap. After a moment, however, she was already beginning to feel mad with tedium. She could not sit like a duck on a pond all night, so Ava carefully began to persuade Lady Purnam to have her new barouche plucked from the stream of carriages outside to drive Ava home.

Across the ballroom, near the French doors leading to the terrace, Middleton and Harrison stood near a small side cart that held various spirits. They'd just come from the gaming room, where they had both been successful. Harrison was two hundred pounds richer for his trumping of Lord Haverty, a notorious gambler, and Jared had wagered—and won—a private ride around Hyde Park in his coach in the company of Lady Tremayne. It was an assignation Lady Tremayne had spent several months pursuing, and with a bit of whiskey in him, Jared was happy to oblige her.

As he gave Lady Tremayne the requested half hour to extract herself from her friends and, more important, her husband, Jared joined Harrison in the ballroom to have a drink before Harrison returned to the gaming tables and Jared escaped this affair altogether. As he sipped his whiskey and idly watched the dancing, his gaze inadvertently landed on the woman he'd seen dancing with Sir Garrett. She was seated next to Lady Purnam, looking very bothered by something or someone.

He nudged Harrison and nodded in her direction. "Who is she?" he asked. "The woman in the blue, seated next to Lady Purnam."

"Lady Ava Fairchild," Harrison said instantly. The man surprised Jared at times with his knowledge of what seemed to be virtually everyone in the *ton*. "One of Lord Downey's stepdaughters."

That was mildly interesting. Lord Downey was not the sort of man Jared could ever call friend.

"She's been out two, perhaps three years now. Rather remarked for being a bit of a coquette." He glanced at Jared sidelong. "Why the interest? It's not as if you have an eye for debutantes."

Jared shrugged. "I have no particular eye for her or anyone else." He shifted his gaze past Lady Ava, scanning the crowd, and unfortunately, caught Lady Elizabeth's eye. She smiled brightly, as did several birds in her little flock. "Bloody hell," he muttered.

Harrison followed his gaze and chuckled. "Go on, then, have a dance with anyone but her," he suggested. "Nothing will turn a woman away as quickly as one dancing with another partner. They can't abide being ignored, you know."

That sounded like sage advice to Jared, and he handed his glass to Harrison. "Thank you, sir, for a most excellent idea," he said, and without thought, started in the direction of Lady Ava Fairchild.

He reached Lady Purnam first, a woman he'd known for years. "My lady," he said, taking up her hand and bowing over it, "your beauty continues to astound."

"Middleton, you rogue!" Lady Purnam cried happily. "I've not seen you about in ages and ages. I rather began to believe the rumors that you were no longer amused by debutantes and balls, but only poor widows."

"How heartening to know that the *ton*'s good opinion of me is still intact," he responded cheerfully, and Lady Purnam tittered.

He clasped his hands behind his back and glanced at the young woman to Lady Purnam's left, who remained seated, serenely watching the dance floor.

"Oh," Lady Purnam said, following his gaze. "Do please forgive me, Lord Middleton. May I introduce to you Lady Ava Fairchild?"

"Indeed you may," he said, and cast a warm smile in the young woman's direction.

Lady Ava turned her head toward him and smiled demurely as she gracefully held out her hand. "It is a pleasure, my lord."

"The pleasure," Jared said, taking her hand and bowing over it, touching his lips to her knuckles, "is most assuredly mine."

She smiled shyly, then glanced away.

Jared smiled, too. He was quite practiced with young debutantes—knew how to charm the stockings right off of them. "Forgive me, Lady Ava, but did I see you at the Season's opening ball? I am certain that I did, for my eye is naturally drawn to the rarest of beauties."

One of Lady Ava's fine brows rose above the other. She smiled and shook her head and said, "I think you must have seen someone else, my lord, for I did not attend."

"Didn't you?"

"I can assure you I did not."

"But surely you *did*, Ava," Lady Purnam said anxiously.

"Surely I did *not*, Lady Purnam," she said, and smiled up at Jared with such a serene countenance that, for a brief moment, he felt a bit off balance.

"Forgive me, you are quite right," he said. "For I could not have forgotten a single detail of you."

Her smiled widened and she blushed a bit as she gently pulled her hand from his grasp.

"Ah, they are playing a waltz now. Lady Ava, would you do me the honor of standing up with me?"

Lady Purnam practically levitated out of her chair as she looked at Lady Ava, but Lady Ava lifted her gaze and said sweetly, "Thank you, my lord . . . but regrettably, I must decline."

"Must you? If a waltz is not to your liking—"

"Oh no, sir, it is very much to my liking."

Lady Purnam looked like a large fish, opening and closing her mouth as if she intended to speak but could not find the words. "You mean that you are not feeling well, don't you, my dear?" she asked with a slightly menacing look in her eye for the young woman.

Lady Ava smiled sweetly at the older woman. "Oh no. I am feeling perfectly fine."

Frankly, Jared was speechless. He couldn't remember a time that a woman declined to dance with him. Particularly not in front of an audience. He was, he was starting to realize, suffering a direct cut. For the first time in his memory, he was being directly *cut*, before half of the *ton*.

"Perhaps another time, then," he said, and bowed again. "It has been a delight to make your acquaintance."

"Thank you."

"Lady Purnam."

Lady Purnam twisted about in her chair, looking quite distressed. "My lord, I do believe there has been a tragic misunderstanding—"

"I assure you, Lady Purnam, there has not," he said politely, and with a curt nod for the two of them, he walked on, feeling, frankly, a little deflated. Yet in an odd way, it was the most interesting thing to have happened to him in a crowded ballroom in the years since he'd come of age.

He'd had enough of ballrooms, however, and

decided to await Lady Tremayne in the comfort of his coach. Now *there* was a woman who would appreciate his attention.

Lady Purnam glared at Ava. "What is the matter with you?" she hissed as Middleton disappeared into the crowd.

"My shoe is broken—"

"Yes, yes, I *know* your shoe is broken, you little ninny, but you just refused the Marquis of Middleton!"

"But I can't possibly dance!"

"No, but you might have offered more explanation!"

Of course she might have, and she really wasn't sure why she hadn't, other than the things Greer had said about Middleton and Lady Purnam's edict rambling about her head. "I beg your pardon, Lady Purnam, but you *told* me—"

"Dear God," Lady Purnam said, fanning herself so violently that it was a wonder the feathers in her hair didn't take flight. "It is exactly as I told your mother— you can be entirely too obtuse at times, Ava. Yes indeed, I told you not to be so carelessly personal with the gentlemen in this room, but I did not intend for you to insult the Marquis of Middleton!"

"I did nothing to insult him!" Ava protested. "At least I didn't *mean* to insult him. Honestly, I would have preferred to dance with him, to kick my shoes off and dance, but you quite clearly told me I could not."

"*Oh!*" Lady Purnam said with much exasperation. "You know very well what I meant! As I live and breathe," she sighed irritably. "To have witnessed your tragic dismissal of a fine lord, one who is unquestionably the best catch in all of London— Have you any idea of his *fortune*?"

No, but Lady Purnam would enlighten her, Ava was very certain. Before she did so, however, Ava saw her opportunity in this so-called tragedy. "*Now* will you allow your carriage to take me home? I cannot possibly bear to see him again after my gaffe," she insisted.

"Yes, dear, do go home at once and tell your mother what you did, and hope for your sake that she can see a way to repair it, for I certainly cannot!" she said, signaling a footman.

Ava would indeed go home and tell her mother. In fact, she couldn't *wait* to tell her mother that while Lady Purnam might be her dearest friend, she was far too easily excited by the smallest things. She had not *insulted* Middleton. She simply had refused to fall at his feet just because he'd tried to seduce her with a smile. Admittedly, it was a knee-shaking smile, but that was neither here nor there.

And so it was, a quarter of an hour later that, having announced to Phoebe and Greer that Lady Purnam was sending her home in the coach, Ava stood in the foyer, her cloak gathered tightly about her, waiting for the footman to return and tell her that Lady Purnam's new barouche had been brought round.

The footman entered the foyer a moment later, along with a cold gust of wind that hit Ava squarely in the face. "Weather's taken a turn, milady," the footman said apologetically. "Unusual for this time of year."

"So it is," Ava said, and peered out. There were no fewer than three crested carriages in front of the house, all of them shiny testaments to the caliber of guest Lady Fontaine had in her house.

Unfortunately, Lady Purnam's grand new carriage

looked exactly like the other two, save the crest, and for the life of her, Ava could not remember the Purnam crest.

"Which one is Lady Purnam's?" she asked.

"That one there," the footman said, pointing to the three carriages. "The one with the bird in its crest."

"Oh, yes, of course," Ava mumbled, and took an uncertain step outside. The sleet had turned to snow, and fat, wet flakes were making it very hard to see.

Another footman appeared holding a lantern high. "Milady," he said, indicating she should come now.

Ava stepped out and hurried forward as best she could with her broken shoe. As they neared the carriages, a coachman swung down from the bench of the first carriage to open the door. Ava had only a moment to see the crest, but she saw an eagle carrying a branch in its talons. The coachman held his hand out to Ava, which she took and quickly ducked inside, landing on a thickly padded velvet squab, the same deep red color of the silk covered walls. The shades—likewise made of silk—were drawn.

"There's a rug beneath the seat, milady," the coachman said hurriedly, and shut the door, obviously anxious to be under his pelts and leaving her in total darkness in his haste.

"*Drat*," Ava muttered, and bent over to find the lap rug when she heard men's voices calling out and the carriage suddenly lurched forward, pitching Ava off balance. She put a hand out to the bench opposite to steady herself, but instead of touching velvet, she touched a living, breathing thing.

With a shriek, Ava shot up, flinging herself back against the squabs at the same moment the flare of a match lit the interior of the carriage and illuminated the Marquis of Middleton. She gasped loudly and for the air she needed to breathe; he was stretched across the opposite bench, his shoulder against the silk wall, one foot planted firmly on the floor of the coach, but one leg cocked at the knee, his foot perched irreverently on the velvet squab as he reached up and lit the interior lamp.

It took another moment for Ava to find her voice. "What . . . what are you doing in Lady Purnam's carriage?" she asked, pressing a hand to her rapidly beating heart.

"I'm not in Lady Purnam's carriage. I'm in *my* carriage."

How slowly the meaning of those words penetrated her consciousness. After what seemed like minutes, Ava finally realized she was in the wrong carriage. "Oh my *God*," she exclaimed, mortified, and instantly moved for the door—but Middleton stopped her with a well-placed boot to the handle of the same door.

"If you have stolen inside my coach to apologize for delivering a direct cut to me in front of all of London, I accept."

She blinked. "I didn't come to apologize." Middleton lifted a brow. "Dear God," she muttered. "My lord, I have made a horrible mistake."

He smiled smugly.

"I mean that I was to be in Lady *Purnam*'s carriage and the footman said there was a bird in the crest, but as I hadn't paid the slightest bit of attention to Lady Purnam's crest I was uncertain about *any* bird until I saw the eagle . . ." she said, gesturing vaguely to the door of his coach. "Although now I seem to remember a nightingale . . ." She shook her head, unclear about what she remembered. "I have broken my shoe," she added quickly, sliding her foot out for him to see.

He glanced down at her foot.

"And Lady Purnam said that her carriage would see me home. So you see it's all a very unfortunate mistake."

"*Very*," he said low as his dark gaze skated over her to the hem of her gown and back.

Ava swallowed hard. The coach lurched again, only this time, it kept moving. "Oh dear," she said, gripping the squabs. "Will you please have your driver stop so that I may step out?"

He said nothing, but remained there, sprawled carelessly on the bench, his foot braced against the door handle.

"My lord—"

"Appease my curiosity, will you? Why did you cut me?" he asked idly. "Have I harmed you in some way? Displeased you? Ignored you?"

Ava opened her mouth to assure him he had not, but she was struck with the notion that he was, incredibly, wounded by her refusal. Lord Middleton, who had scads of women flinging themselves at his coattails whenever he walked by, was wounded because she had refused to dance with him.

She wanted to savor that thought, but the coach was picking up speed, and suddenly all she could think of was what Greer had said about him. She lunged again for the door, but Middleton steadfastly refused to move his boot. "Do you intend to jump from a moving carriage?"

"If I must," she said firmly. "I am to be in Lady Purnam's carriage."

"First you refuse to stand up with me before the *ton*, and now you would jump from a moving carriage. Lady Ava, I am beginning to believe you do not esteem my good company."

"I do not know you, my lord, so I have no opinion of your company, either good or bad. This is not what you must think."

"No? Then what exactly is it?"

"My shoe is quite broken, as I showed you. I couldn't possibly dance."

"Why did you not merely say so?"

He had her there. She couldn't confess it was because Lady Purnam had decreed that she should not, or that she knew of his reputation . . . or that there was something strangely empowering in eliciting his displeasure. "I suppose I thought a polite decline was all that was necessary," she said pertly. "Now will you please have your driver stop?"

"I wouldn't advise it," he said, almost cheerfully. "I reckon hordes of Lady Fontaine's guests saw you cut me in the ballroom. Now I reckon hordes more are standing under the portico watching the snow fall and wondering together if they should leave now before the roads become impassable. Imagine the endless speculation were they to see you vault from my carriage with your maidenly virtue scarcely intact and run for Lady Purnam's coach."

Oh dear God, he was right. Ava bit her lip and glanced at the door. When she turned her gaze to him again, Middleton was smiling with an expression that was entirely too self-satisfied.

He was enjoying the scandalous lies that were certainly being spread at this very moment, the *roué*. "I shall, of course, take you home at once," he said, graciously inclining his head. "To protect your chaste reputation."

The way he said it made her think that he had in mind the exact opposite. Lord in heaven, she could imagine what Lord Downey or her mother would say!

Undoubtedly, they would have expected her to remove herself from his carriage by now.

"Or perhaps the crowds will be gone by the time we have circled Hyde Park," he suggested. "And then you will be quite safe in changing coaches."

"Hyde Park?" she echoed weakly.

He grinned wolfishly. "I do beg your pardon, Lady Ava, but I was expecting someone else. My driver wasn't told there'd be *two* handsome callers."

Her face flushed hot, but at the same time, Ava felt a shiver of anticipation.

Or perhaps it was fear.

Honestly, she wasn't quite certain what she felt, really, other than an overwhelming curiosity that collided with foolishness as all the dangerous, devilish things she'd ever heard about Middleton crowded into her brain.

And then he picked up the edge of her cloak as casually as he might pick up his own and rubbed it between his fingers. "Have you a direction? Or do you intend to come home with me?" he asked, watching her.

Heat flooded her face again. "Fourteen Clifford Street. Thank you."

He smiled as if he'd expected her to give in and reached up, opened the small door beneath the driver's seat that allowed him to communicate, and said, "Fourteen Clifford Street."

Ava smiled thinly, clasped her hands tightly in her lap.

He shut the trap and then suddenly sat upright, boxing her legs between his. In fact, his legs were so close to hers that she squeezed hers together and rearranged her skirts so there was no danger of their touching.

The skin around his eyes crinkled with a smile and

he leaned forward, looking into her eyes. "Do you want to know why I think you declined my invitation to dance?"

No. *Yes. No, no*— "Why?"

"Because you meant to trifle with me. You do like to flirt, do you not, Lady Ava? You enjoy being a bit of a coquette, hmm?"

She choked on a small laugh of surprise. This man, possibly the most sought after man in all of England, believed she had declined to dance so that she might *flirt* with him? It was apparent that his ego was as large as it was fragile, and that knowledge put her on solid footing. "I suppose I do flirt a bit . . . with some people," she said, smiling.

"Which people?"

She shrugged. "Friends."

"But not me, is that what you would imply?"

"Oh *no*, not you."

"Why not?"

"Because . . . were I to flirt with you, my lord, I have no doubt you would presume a better acquaintance."

He chuckled a little and leaned in closer. "Would I indeed?"

Ava shifted backward, away from the pull of his smile. "Of course you would. You are far too accustomed to flirting with the gentler sex in her entirety . . . if one can believe what is printed in the newspaper or whispered in drawing rooms. My unfavorable response would surely disappoint you."

"And you have this from the gentler sex in her *entirety*, eh?" He chuckled. "That's rather a lot, isn't it?"

"Not in her *entirety*, for you cannot count me in that number."

He smiled as if they played some sort of game. "Is my reputation as randy as all that?"

His dark hazel eyes, she decided, were the very color of the hills in autumn around Bingley Hall, where she'd spent her childhood. Quite attractive eyes, really. "I think you are being coy, sir. I suspect you know your reputation far better than I could ever hope to know it."

His grin broadened and he inclined his head. "All right, I will concede that point. But I should like to know—if it is true I have such an effect on the gentler sex in all her entirety . . . then why aren't *you* counted in that number?"

"I suppose I prefer the admiration to be bestowed upon me . . . as opposed to being the one who must bestow the admiration."

He laughed; the rich, deep timbre of it gave Ava another little shiver of delight. "How very rich and how very honest of you."

"I am indeed honest, my lord."

"Then I must bestow my admiration on you, Lady Ava, so that you will not cut me so openly again. But first you must tell me," he said, leaning forward again, his face only inches from hers, "how do you prefer to receive your admiration?"

"I beg your pardon?"

He leaned even closer, so that now Ava could see the curl of his dark lashes as his eyes casually took in her features. "Do you prefer to be admired in word . . . or in deed?"

The question, posed with such a sinfully delicious smile, caused her pulse to quicken, and Ava sank back into the squabs, regretting her brash flirting. "I can't possibly know what you mean."

Middleton playfully bumped her knee with his. "Now who is being coy?"

Before she could respond, before she could even

think of a response, Middleton suddenly moved forward, close enough to kiss her. Ava reflexively gasped
with surprise, to which he gave her a boyish smile as
his gaze dipped to her lips and caused her belly to
sink a little.

"I did not hear your honest answer, madam. Do
you prefer your admiration in word . . . or in deed?"

Her body was melting ahead of her brain. She
could certainly understand why women fell under the
man's spell—those eyes were overpowering and the
smile on his lips was so alluring that she feared she
might very well expose herself to any number of
potential scandals, right here, right now.

She looked at his mouth, but found no relief there,
and madly wondered if he did indeed intend to kiss
her. *A kiss from Middleton!* There was only one way to
achieve such dizzying heights of trifling sport, wasn't
there? "*In deed,*" she said in a near whisper, then
caught her breath and held it.

"Good girl," he muttered, and moved until his lips
were just a hairsbreadth from hers. He hovered there,
and Ava prepared herself to be kissed by lifting her
chin slightly.

But the man surprised her by licking her lips, and
he could not have been more sensuous in doing so.
With the tip of his tongue, he traced a slow path
across the seam of her lips. Ava froze. It was the
most sensual, *decadent* thing anyone had ever done
to her, and it was so deeply stirring that she inadvertently released a small sigh of pleasure when
he'd done it.

When she did, he lifted his hand to her jaw and
gently angled her head just so, catching the sigh with
his mouth as it passed through her lips. He drew her
bottom lip lightly between his teeth and teased her

body forward by slipping his free hand to the small of her back, persuading her forward while his tongue slipped into her mouth.

She felt as if she were falling toward him. She let him draw her into his embrace, opening her mouth to him, finding his waist with her hand. He was kissing her so thoroughly that she began to feel uncomfortably hot in her cloak, and with her free hand, she fumbled with the clasp and pulled it carelessly from her shoulders. He moved a hand to her shoulder, ran his palm down her arm, then across the bare skin of her bosom, and down, cupping her breast, squeezing it, his fingers brushing across the tip.

Ava gasped in his mouth; he moved her easily, pushing her down, so that she was on her back with her head propped against the side of his carriage. As his hands roamed her body, his mouth traced a wet path to her bosom, his tongue flicking between her breasts, his mouth pressing against the mound of flesh while his hand kneaded her.

When he lifted one breast free of the confines of her gown, Ava panicked and tried to sit up—but then he took the tip of her breast in his mouth, and she was falling again, sinking back into the squabs, her eyes closed to the storm brewing in her, her body on fire.

And then suddenly the coach came to a halt.

Middleton paused in his attention to her breast and glanced at the door. He sighed, calmly put her breast back into her gown as best he could, and kissed the hollow of her throat. He moved up, nipped at her lips once more as he pulled her to an upright position and draped her cloak around her shoulders, before lazily fading into the squabs of his bench across from her.

Ava was sitting in the same spot he'd left her, still leaning toward him, still feeling his lips on hers. As the door of the coach swung open, she looked out into the snowy night, then at Middleton.

He smiled, grabbed her hand, brought it to his mouth and pressed his lips to her knuckles, then let her go. "Have a care when you refuse a man's offer to dance, Lady Ava," he said with a wink.

Her mind had obviously deserted her, for all Ava could mutter in return was, "Thank you." And then she concentrated on making her jelly legs move. With the considerable help of Middleton's coachman, who caught her when she landed awkwardly, having forgotten her blasted shoe, she managed to exit the carriage without making a fool of herself. Once she was firmly on the ground, she pulled her cloak over her head and glanced back at the coach.

The marquis leaned forward and smiled through the open carriage door. "Good night, Lady Ava. It has indeed been a pleasure." He glanced at the coachman. "See her safely to the door, Phillip," he said, and then leaned back, all but his long legs disappearing from her sight.

The coachman shut the door and held out his arm to her. "If you please, milady."

She pleased. Ava put her hand on the man's arm and walked forward, bouncing unevenly to her right, her mind a million miles away from her shoe.

And when she was safely inside, and his carriage had gone on into the night, Ava removed the offending shoe and smiled softly. She couldn't *wait* to tell her mother what had happened. Well, *almost* everything that had happened—she was not as foolish as that.

But that dreamy smile would be her last for some time, however, for her stepfather rushed into the foyer before she could divest herself of her cloak, his expression unusually serious. For a moment, Ava thought he somehow knew of her ride in Middleton's carriage and meant to take her to task for it. But he uncharacteristically reached out his hand to her.

"*Ava,*" he said.

"Yes, sir?" she asked, surprised and a little frightened by the gesture.

"Your dear mother suffered a seizure of some sort just after supper. I regret to tell you that the physician is not hopeful."

Three

Cassandra Reemes Fairchild Pennebacker, Lady Downey, died suddenly at the age of five and forty years.

While it may have seemed to some that scarcely had the last clump of dirt been shoveled onto her grave when her husband, Egbert Pennebacker, Viscount Downey, left for France, in truth a month had passed. One long, interminable month during which Egbert suffered the tears of Cassandra's daughters and niece while he fretted that his longtime mistress, Violet, had perhaps found another benefactor. He could not possibly know, for she was in France.

Frankly, Cassandra could not have picked a more inopportune time to die. Egbert, who had never been one to partake in the whirl of the social season, had been set to sail for France the very morning they buried his wife. Naturally, he'd sent a letter to Violet straightaway relaying the sad news and sending along sufficient funds for her safe voyage to England so that she might help him through a very trying time.

He'd yet to hear a word, not a solitary word. Not a note, not even a whisper of condolence in a month.

The uncertainty of what was happening drove him quite mad, and he paced his study more often than not, his stout legs and small feet taking him round and round the room while he nervously soothed the few strands of hair remaining on the crown of his head. In this state of acute anxiety, he could scarcely bear the company of the grieving girls. They moped about, rarely went out, and had covered everything in black. At supper just a few nights past, when he'd casually mentioned he'd not enjoyed asparagus soup in many years because Cassandra did not care for it, Phoebe burst into tears.

He'd lost his temper altogether.

"For Christ's *sake*!" he'd bellowed with such force that his monocle popped right from his eye. "How long must I endure the incessant wailing in this house?"

"She's not *wailing*, sir." Ava quickly intervened as Greer handed Phoebe a handkerchief. "Surely you can understand the deep sense of loss my sister feels—indeed, we *all* feel. Our mother has only recently passed."

Honestly, as if he needed to be reminded of that.

Egbert stared hard at a spoonful of soup for a moment before quickly stuffing it in his mouth and spooning more. Of course he didn't begrudge them the time to grieve their mother properly—he, too, was sorry for her demise. After all, she'd been his wife for ten years and a tolerable one at that. He just wished they would do it in their chambers and not muddy his thoughts any more than his thoughts were already muddied. While her passing was sad, life did indeed go on, did it not?

He'd finished his meal in silence, but his mood had grown darker and darker as he eyed the three of them. They looked at him as if he were the one being unreasonable.

After supper, Ava had ushered Phoebe and Greer up to their suite of rooms and left him alone with his port and his cigar, but not before bestowing a disapproving look on him. That one was just like her mother. Egbert imagined they all despised him, and truly, he wasn't so heartless, but Violet had been his little flower for nearly eight years. He could not bear the thought of losing her, too, and was desperate for an excuse to quit this endless mourning and leave London to learn for himself why Violet had forsaken him.

And that night, with the help of his port and a cigar, he landed on his excuse. Joy filled him, and he sprang from his chair and hurried to his study, his legs working hard to carry his rotund body as quickly as possible. Once there, he took pen and paper in hand and dashed a quick letter to Violet, filled with various declarations of adoration and devotion, and informing her that he would arrive in Paris in a fortnight.

The second letter he wrote was addressed to his spinster sister, Lucille Pennebacker, at the Lake District family estate, Troutbeck. In that letter, he insisted his sister come to London straightaway.

A week later, Egbert summoned his stepdaughters to the main salon. As he watched them enter his study swathed head to toe in the black bombazine of mourning, he mentally congratulated himself on being a charitable man, for what he would do for these three orphans was far and away the most charitable act they could expect from anyone. Certainly he would never turn out three orphaned debutantes, and he wished them no harm—but he wasn't their father, was he? It did not, therefore, fall to him to ensure they found their way in this life. No, *that* responsibility had been Cassandra's and now belonged to the girls' kin, whoever that might be. That was precisely why he had urged Cassandra to marry them off before it was too late.

Alas, as with everything else, Cassandra had scarcely listened to him at all.

Pity that she hadn't, for it would have spared them all a great deal of anxiety. Here were her precious girls, completely dependent upon his charity as they took their seats. They sat properly and smiled uncertainly at his sister, Lucille, who had arrived just this morning and who had, judging from the thin smile on her doughy face, already found her charges quite in need of her guidance.

Ava, the oldest and boldest of the three, looked from Lucille to Egbert and to Lucille again. She'd never really warmed to him, and he could see myriad thoughts and suspicions flashing in her green eyes. This one thought too highly of herself to his way of thinking, for she'd never agreed to any of the acceptable offers they'd received for her hand.

Egbert had wanted to accept the very generous offer Lord Villanois had made last Season, but Cassandra wouldn't hear of it. "His fortune is hardly the sort I should want for our Ava," she'd said with a sniff. "And he is far too fond of his drink. I shall not waste a perfectly good dowry on the likes of him."

Egbert did not believe that Villanois was more or less fond of his drink than any other man, but Cassandra continued to make excuses, just as she had done when other men had come forward, for no man was good enough for her dear Ava.

Egbert rather supposed any offer would be good enough for her now that he was the final authority.

Her carefree ways were a luxury Ava would know no more—she was well past a suitable age for flitting from ballroom to ballroom. She was of an age that she should have a child on her hip and one in her belly.

Ava seemed to sense his disgruntlement and glanced at Phoebe.

But Phoebe did not possess her sister's intuitive sensibilities, and merely smiled at him. He'd always thought Phoebe was too trusting of mankind in general, really.

"May I introduce my sister, Miss Pennebacker," he said, gesturing lamely to Lucille.

The three young women nodded politely; Lucille actually stood and curtsied as if they were royalty, saying, "It is a pleasure to make your acquaintance."

"Thank you," Ava said.

"I've rung for tea," Egbert said, and impatiently gestured for Lucille to sit. She sat. "It shouldn't be a moment." He idly watched Phoebe as she situated her gown just so. She was similar to her sister in size and shape, but her pale blond tresses were lighter, her eyes a bluish green. Privately, Egbert always thought her the most handsome of the three and had believed her time on the marriage market would be quite short. Unfortunately, Phoebe was too shy for her own good, and to make matters worse, she had a propensity for dreaming—her head was always in the clouds, or in a book, or in some sort of artistic endeavor—and he rather supposed that was why she hadn't received any offers.

When he'd expressed his concern about the lack of offers for Phoebe to his wife, Cassandra had brushed his concern aside with the ridiculous excuse that Phoebe had a special talent for art, and to marry would rob her of the freedom to express herself. "If she were forced to marry, any husband would keep her pregnant and in the nursery before he would allow her to paint, mark me," she'd said with much superiority.

Egbert didn't understand his wife's reasoning, for that was exactly where they all belonged.

A commotion at the door startled him from his thoughts.

"The tea has come," Lucille announced, and bustled forward with her big hips bouncing along behind her to meet Richard, the butler, as he brought in the tea service.

Ava and Phoebe turned to see what she was about, but Greer sat still, looking curiously at Egbert. That was because Greer was inherently a rather clever and curious girl. She was dark where her cousins were light, her hair the color of coal and her eyes dark blue. She was as handsome as her cousins but in a subtler way—a man had to look twice to see the beauty in her.

When Greer's mother, Cassandra's baby sister, had died, her father was quick to remarry, hoping to gain the son he'd been deprived of with his first wife's death. Cassandra had taken Greer in, and as far as Egbert knew, Greer's father had never taken an interest in her. Therefore, Greer was what he considered the poor relation. Yet Egbert was perhaps fondest of her, for she shared his practical, intelligent nature.

Unfortunately, because Greer was a poor relation, Egbert's charity toward her had been overextended. Certainly there was another person in the illustrious Fairchild family who could bear her cost, or at the very least, see her married.

Greer had received offers, too, but by the time they

had been brought round, Egbert had realized Cassandra meant to keep them all with her, and had lost interest in the excuses she threw up in Greer's defense.

An inadvertent smile creased his lips as he looked at the three of them now. He intended to remedy their unmarried situations just as soon as he returned from Paris. They would be married to the highest bidder in turn, or, if they refused, sent to live with relatives. He had no desire to support them any longer than he must. For goodness' sake, he already had the burden of Lucille.

The three young women looked at him expectantly as Lucille poured tea.

Egbert sighed, pressed his fingers to his temples, and leaned back in his chair. "Very well, then, we are all settled and I shall not make preamble. The question is simply put: Now that Cassandra has died, what are we all to do? I shall tell you what *I* am to do. I have found it very difficult to mourn my wife properly, what with all her things and her children about. It's been very . . ." He racked his brain for a word, and finding none, repeated, ". . . *difficult.*"

"You poor dear!" Lucille said, and put her hand atop his, squeezing gently. "I had no idea you were so aggrieved."

Egbert glanced down at her pudgy hand, then glanced up at her face. Lucille promptly removed her hand.

"If I may, my lord," Ava said, leaning forward slightly in her seat. "Perhaps we might spare you the, ah . . . *difficulty.* We've discussed it, and we should like you to know that we'd be willing to reside elsewhere if it pleases you."

Oh? This was an interesting twist—something

completely unexpected. "Elsewhere? And where would that be?" he asked, almost gleefully.

"We thought a small house in Mayfair. Nothing too grand, of course. And we'd require only Beverly, our lady's maid. Oh, and a housekeeper, of course."

Egbert was taken aback—Cassandra had never mentioned that these three had funds of their own. He couldn't see how it might even be possible. Certainly if he'd known, he would have insisted on the details so that he could manage it for them, for really, what did three young women want with their own funds? "Your own residence," he repeated carefully.

Ava nodded.

"And I suppose you have sufficient funds?"

Ava exchanged a look with her sisters. "I'm rather certain that we do."

But she did not look entirely certain because she was, obviously, a woman, and women were not meant to handle finances. "Could you then, perhaps, *become* certain?"

Ava blinked. "I beg your pardon?"

"How can you possibly hope to lease a residence if you don't know how much money you've got?"

"Oh dear, Egbert! That's so vulgar!" Lucille chastised him, earning an impatient glance from her younger brother.

"It is a matter of necessity that it be discussed, Lucy," he said impatiently, "and I can think of no way to discuss it other than to utter the words aloud!"

"I beg your pardon, my lord," Ava quickly interjected, "but you are in a much better position to know about the, ah . . . money . . . than am I."

Now she was confusing him. "Me? How could I possibly know?"

"Well," Ava continued, looking just as confused,

"we . . . we don't know how . . . how *much* she had, but we rather supposed there is enough to take a modest residence."

It was suddenly clear to him, and Egbert, charitable man that he was, almost came out of his chair in his eagerness to lean across the desk and pin the bold one with a stern look. "Are you suggesting, miss, that *I* lease you a residence?"

Ava blinked. "I, ah . . . I just assumed that you would—"

"Then you assumed incorrectly!" he bellowed. "Clearly you do not understand what a financial and social burden the three of you present to me!"

"But we *do*," Ava hastily sought to assure him with Phoebe and Greer nodding furiously alongside her. "That is why we thought to offer to go elsewhere."

"You will remain here," he said sharply, sinking back in his chair. "I cannot possibly afford to put you up in a separate residence. Now. As I was saying before I was interrupted, I find it very difficult to mourn my wife properly with you and her things underfoot," he said, gesturing wildly to them and the furniture, which indeed had been purchased with his wife's money. "So I have decided to go to Paris for a time. You will remain here under the care and watchful eye of my sister."

The three of them looked at Lucille as if they were seeing her for the first time, but Ava quickly returned her attention to Egbert. "That is all, my lord? You are to France and we are to remain here, the same as before?"

"Aha!" he said, lifting a finger. "Not *precisely* the same as before. The endless days of shopping and ordering gowns and shoes and whatnot have come to a most desired end."

Ava and Greer gasped. Phoebe looked as if she actually might be ill.

"Furthermore, I see no reason to pay for a coterie of servants now that you are in mourning. There will be no traipsing about this Season's assemblies, will there? Moreover, you are three industrious young women. I should think you quite capable of making a bed and sweeping a carpet. I shall retain Cook for you, but as a daily."

"Oh dear God," Ava moaned, and closed her eyes. "I beg your pardon, sir, but our mother was quite wealthy. If I may be so indecorous as to inquire . . . surely she left *something* for our care?"

"Of course she did," he said pleasantly. "A modest dowry for each of you. The rest is left to me to look after as I see fit."

"We're doomed!" Phoebe whispered to the ceiling.

"Oh come now!" he scoffed at them. "It's not as if you've been turned out into the street! I shall see that you are properly cared for! You shall have a roof over your head and food in your belly. What more could you possibly need?"

"What *more*?" Phoebe echoed, a little too petulantly for his taste. "We can hardly go out into society without proper clothing!"

"At last glance, girl, you have more clothing than can be housed in a single room," he sharply reminded her. "I should think that will suffice until I return."

"How long will you be away?" Greer asked calmly.

He shrugged. "Until autumn at the earliest, I should think. Perhaps even as late as the start of the next Season."

"That is *months*!" Ava cried. "You will force us to live like paupers for *months*?"

"Do not raise your voice to me, Lady Ava! There is no call for a theatrical performance! I have provided for your needs—paupers indeed!"

Phoebe turned to Ava, who grasped her hand and held it tightly.

Greer was the only one to keep her composure, looking at Egbert with such cool intensity that he shuddered slightly. "If I may, my lord . . . what do you mean to do with us when you return?"

"Precisely what should have been done long ago. Next spring shall come a new social season, and I shall accept the offers for your hands that will undoubtedly be brought round," he said with a confident smile, and rose from his seat. "And I shall do so as expeditiously as possible, for it is long since time you were all properly married."

Ava opened her mouth, but he spoke before she could argue. "This interview is complete! I should like to review some items with my sister, and then I have the servants to contend with, so if you will excuse us?"

"My lord, you'll not release Beverly from service, surely," Phoebe begged.

"Won't I? Three young women in perfectly good health do not need the assistance of a woman to dress themselves each day!" he said sternly. "You may help one another. Come, now, I'll not have your despair! You shall manage quite well on your own and with Lucille's help, I assure you! Now, then, go on with you."

The three of them reluctantly gained their feet.

"Here, now, you mustn't look so downcast," Lucille said sternly. "Your face will bear the permanent lines of it if you continue to frown!"

They glanced uneasily at Lucille as they walked out, heads down, lips pressed firmly together.

"Oh dear," Lucille sighed when the door closed behind them. "That did not go very well at all, did it?"

"It went perfectly well, Lucy," Egbert muttered, but his mind had already moved on to how he might release the servants.

The servants were gone by the end of the week. Ava, Phoebe, and Greer stood in the foyer, fighting tears as they bid good-bye to servants who had been in their mother's employ for so long they were considered family—family who had been tossed out onto the street with nothing more than a fortnight's salary and the promise of a reference.

"But I ain't got nowhere to go, milady," Old Derreck, their gardener and horseman, said to Ava as he pushed a thick hand through a shock of gray hair. "I got nowhere to lay me head."

Ava caught a sob in her throat, threw her arms around him, and held him tightly to her. "I'm sorry, Derreck. I'm so very sorry."

"Here," Phoebe said, pulling Ava's arms from the old man and taking his hand in hers. "Take this." She pressed three gold crowns into his palm—the last three gold crowns Phoebe possessed. "It's hardly anything, but it will at least provide you with lodging for a time."

"Until I can send Lord Ramsey a note on your behalf," Ava interjected, thinking of one of her mother's friends. "He's always in need of a good gardener. I am certain he can find you a position in his household," she promised, cringing inwardly at her lie. She had no idea what Lord Ramsey needed or didn't need, but she would beg him to take Old Derreck in as a favor to her mother's memory if nothing else.

Beverly was the last to leave, and the three of them cried as they clung to the woman who had helped them bathe and dress for as long as they could remember. "There, now, wipe your tears," Beverly said bravely. "I'll not have you carrying on for me. I've been meaning to visit my mother in Derbyshire for ages. So wipe your tears, all of you. Lady Downey would not like you to cry. She'd ask what you would do to improve your lot, wouldn't she?"

Beverly was right, but it didn't hurt any less.

When she'd left, Ava closed the door behind her, feeling the weight of her sorrow and worry of what would become of the three of them like a heavy winter cloak about her shoulders.

"I hate him," Phoebe whispered.

Ava gathered Phoebe and Greer to her, and the three of them retreated to their rooms to grieve in private.

Lord Downey left two days after that, his step amazingly light for a man whose waist circumference seemed to equal his height. By the following Monday, a little *on dit* buried deep in the pages of the daily newspaper suggested that three young women known very well about town had lost their fortune to their stepfather and would undoubtedly be in search of another man's fortune as soon as they could put aside their mourning clothes.

That small mention was, as far as the three of them were concerned, a death knell for their social life. Fortune was everything to the *ton*, and those who did not possess at least a bit of one were not, as a rule, particularly welcome in the salons of those who had fortune in abundance.

They agonized for days what to do, and finally agreed on a course that was unconventional, and in some cases, ill-advised. They were a bit desperate, true, but they were far more determined to find their way in the wake of their mother's death.

Four

LONDON
MARCH 1820

It was Jared Broderick's bad luck to have returned to London after a particularly harsh winter a full fortnight after his father. It had given the old man time enough to meddle in his affairs, long enough for him to have arranged an interminable luncheon with Lord Robertson and his family. The duke had not, it would seem, mellowed over the winter months while Jared had remained at Broderick Abbey, managing to stay out of his father's sight and, he'd hoped, his mind. He'd entertained Miranda only thrice in an effort to maintain a low profile.

Yet if anything, the old man seemed even more determined in his mission to see his only son married to Lady Elizabeth Robertson.

Lady Elizabeth Robertson had not improved in looks or mien, as one might have expected after a full Season out. To be fair, Jared was basing his opinion on one exceedingly dull luncheon at which he was still engaged. The woman had said very little and eaten much less, which was not, he supposed, sufficient information by which to judge a person's entire character.

But his opinion of her had not changed.

He thought he would crawl out of his skin if he was forced to endure one moment more of this luncheon, and as he watched Lady Elizabeth take precisely measured bites of her whitefish, his mind wandered again to his father's most recent threats.

It was his own fault—he should have held his tongue yesterday when his father asked him if, after a winter of contemplation, he realized he must put Miranda aside for the sake of the dukedom.

"No," Jared had said wearily.

"No? That is all you will say?" the duke had asked incredulously. "I do not think you understand me, sir. If you refuse to put her aside, then I am prepared to expose your greatest mistake and all those associated with it."

At first, Jared thought he'd misheard him, but when he saw the look of triumph in his father's eye, he was stunned. "Are you *threatening* me, your grace?"

"*Threaten* is perhaps too harsh a word. I am trying to impart the depth of my conviction," the duke responded evenly.

"You have a rather cold way of imparting your conviction."

"I do what I must to ensure the sanctity of the name Redford."

Jared had scoffed at that. "Can you truly say that in the same breath you use to threaten me? My God, I don't believe you care for anyone or anything other than your blessed name!"

"That's ridiculous," his father had said, waving a bony hand at him. "I care for *you*, but you are too bloody stubborn to see it. Yet I care for your honor more, which you have so carelessly squandered. Do as I ask, Jared," the duke continued at Jared's groan of exasperation. "Marry Lady Elizabeth. Her family is awaiting your offer. Perhaps you will speak to her father at luncheon tomorrow."

"I will not speak to him," Jared said calmly. "I will not be forced into marrying her."

The duke sighed, and he looked, Jared thought, older than he had at their last meeting, four months ago. "I am warning you—don't push me to do something you will regret."

"I don't *push* you to do anything, your grace. I have only asked that you leave me to live my life as I see fit. It is a request any man might make of his father," he snapped, and walked out, ignoring the duke's shouted warning that he would do what it took to keep his name from being tarnished.

Jared had left Redford House feeling as he always felt after these interminable interviews—as if his father had placed an invisible vise around him and was slowly turning the screws, torturing him with his demands, forcing his hand.

London was swelling with the Quality as they began to make the trek from the country to town in anticipation of the Season, and he rather supposed yesterday's row had already spilled across Mayfair, for his father's servants, he believed, were amazingly fast in their ability to spread untoward gossip among the *ton*.

To stave off any more gossip—and for deeper, more complex reasons that he did not fully understand—Jared had come to the Robertson luncheon as commanded. He'd come to keep the peace, he supposed, fearful that his father would make good on his threat and hurt more people than just Jared. It had pained him to do so, for the day was lovely and quite warm for an early March day.

But here he was—stuck in a drafty mansion, seated

across from a demure Lady Elizabeth while her mother spoke of their winter—imagining days and weeks and months and even years of such tedium stretching before him.

"We had a repair done on the east wing," Lady Robertson was saying, as if he might possibly care what they did. "But what with all the rain and snow, the work was not completed."

"Ah," he said, forcing himself to look away from Elizabeth's deliberate chewing.

"Once we have completed the work, we shall host a weekend affair for all of our good acquaintances. We've a dozen bedrooms in that wing alone."

"Very good," he said idly, and glanced at Elizabeth again. She smiled shyly. He smiled very thinly, trying to think of one thing—anything!—that would be more excruciatingly painful than to spend an entire weekend in the country with this family.

He could think of nothing.

Elizabeth carefully folded her linen and put it on her lap. She was so proper he was certain the slightest breach in etiquette would break her in two. He shifted his gaze away, caught his father glaring at him, and shifted his gaze to his plate.

Fortunately, Lady Robertson turned her attention to the Season's social calendar, noting—for his benefit, he supposed—the number of balls to which Elizabeth had received invitations. Jared scarcely heard a word she said, for her endless monotone gave him ample opportunity to relive the spat he'd had with Miranda last evening.

Miranda was growing weary of the ongoing disagreement with his father, which seemed to have grown more vitriolic since they had returned to London. "I can't possibly imagine why you won't do what he asks to appease him," she'd said as she sat prettily on her chaise in her silk dressing gown. "Once you put a child on some girl, then we might continue on, shan't we, and it won't be the least bit different than your father's affair with Lady Sullivan, will it?"

At the mention of his father's long-standing affair with a woman who had survived his mother, Jared flinched inwardly. He was never really certain why, but the notion of his father bedding someone other than his late mother had always pricked him. He supposed it was because it was done so openly. He could remember a time when he was a boy, the servants discussing before him the need to send linens up to Lady Sullivan's house, for the duke did not care for her coarse sheets. Even then, it had seemed insupportable for his father to take vows of fidelity before God and then forsake them.

Yet here he was, contemplating that very thing.

It wasn't unusual, really. In some circles—his, to be exact—it was expected. Marry one woman for pedigree and fortune; make love to another. It was, for better or worse, the way of many couples among the Quality.

"For God's sake, just do as he asks, Jared," Miranda said again with great exasperation as she began to brush her long dark red hair. "It is the only way we shall ever be together in any measure of peace—of that I am convinced."

"We might be together in peace if we were to marry," he said, surprising himself as much as Miranda. He was fond of Miranda in a lover's way, and in that moment, it occurred to him that if he would be forced to marry, why not marry Miranda? "My father might disown me, but at least we would live as man and wife and bring our legitimate children into the world."

Miranda made a cry of alarm and dropped her brush. "I think all that clean country air has made you mad, darling. Of course he would disown you, for I will never possess the credentials necessary to appease your father. And if he disowned you, you could not give our children the things *you* had as a child. I daresay you would never forgive yourself." She'd turned and looked at him pointedly. "And I daresay, neither would I."

Her response had stung him. He understood how women were taught to think of marriage—power and wealth meant everything, apparently even to Miranda. Yet the confirmation that his title and fortune meant more to her than he did cut like a knife.

Now, as the Robertson meal was ending—just before he feared he would be driven to leap from the table and fling himself out of the windows onto Audley Street below—Lord Robertson suggested the ladies take their ices in the solarium with the duke. "I thought perhaps Lord Middleton and I might enjoy a cheroot. You do enjoy a good cheroot, do you not, my lord?"

Jared glanced at his father, whose expression was so full of expectation that he wanted to scream. He shifted his gaze to Lord Robertson and smiled. "Thank you, my lord, but I must beg your leave."

No one said anything for a moment until Elizabeth made a small sound of despair, and the duke . . . well, the duke turned dark. A very unpleasant shade of red.

"Please do forgive me, but I have another engagement I simply cannot miss," he added, almost cheerfully. "It is a parliamentary matter."

"Middleton—" his father started, but Jared was already rising from his chair.

"I had quite forgotten it until this morning, your grace," he said pleasantly, and smiled at his host. "You will forgive me?"

"Of course," Robertson said, looking confused.

Jared quickly went to the mother and took her hand in his. "Thank you, Lady Robertson, for a lovely luncheon," he said, and turned to Elizabeth. "Lady Elizabeth, I have thoroughly enjoyed your company. I look forward to the time we might dine again," he said, and took her hand, brought it to his lips, kissed her cold knuckles, and quickly let go.

Elizabeth looked at her mother, her eyes wide with consternation, but Jared walked on, to the head of the table, passing a string of footmen who had, no doubt, been brought out to impress him. He offered his hand to a stunned Lord Robertson. "Thank you again, my lord."

"But I thought . . . I thought we were to have the afternoon," he said weakly.

"Another time, perhaps," Jared said, and bowed low. He scarcely looked at his father. "Your grace," he said before he walked out of the room.

Let his father make good on his threats. Jared was beyond caring at the moment, for he could not possibly endure another moment in that dining room. If he had to marry, so be it. But he would not, under any circumstance, marry Lady Elizabeth Robertson.

He went directly to his club and sent word for Harrison to join him if he was able. When Harrison appeared an hour later, Jared felt restless, and given that the day was bright and unusually warm, he convinced his old friend that they should ride in Hyde Park.

Naturally, he gave Harrison a brief account of the latest argument with his father and the luncheon he'd ruined.

"Sounds frightfully tedious," Harrison agreed. "Does he still threaten to disown you?"

Jared laughed wryly. "Not only does he threaten it, I would suspect that as we are speaking, he is drawing up the order for the king's signature."

Harrison smiled a little, then looked at his friend. "What if he carries through with his threat? Have you determined your course?"

Oh, he'd considered it. Through many sleepless nights, he had wandered Broderick Abbey's halls, considering it. He had his own title, his own seat. Granted, he did not have nearly the wealth his father had, and would lose the substantial stipend he received as the son of the Duke of Redford. But he was ready to face it—he had studied agriculture and was brimming with ideas for improvements to his estate. And besides, what he valued and wanted more than anything on earth was not a fortune, but the freedom to be who he was.

Yet the duke had raised the stakes with his latest threat.

"I have considered it," he said simply, and meant to say something more, but a sound brought his head up—a laugh, a word, he wasn't certain what—but his gaze landed squarely on the woman with blond hair and pale green eyes.

Fair . . . Fair . . . Fair-something.

He could not bring her name to mind, but he remembered her quite clearly. She was in the company of two young women who resembled her, and all three of them were dressed in the black bombazine of mourning.

"Her name," Jared said, taking in their black gowns. "I don't recall it."

"Fairchild," Harrison offered.

Fairchild, of course. Lady Ava Fairchild. "Who passed?"

"Her mother, Lady Downey," Harrison replied, and glanced at Jared from the corner of his eye. "You should pay more attention to the society pages, Middleton. Occasionally, there is an interesting *on dit* about someone other than you."

"Astonishing."

Harrison chuckled and looked again at the three young women walking toward them. "I have heard that Lady Downey died suddenly and without provision for the fortune she'd brought to the marriage. By law, it reverted to Lord Downey. Unfortunately, that has left the three of them somewhat destitute, save a small dowry for each of them. It's a pity, really, for they seem to be agreeable young women—yet I daresay the lack of fortune won't help them in the marriage mart this Season."

"Perhaps," Jared said thoughtfully. "But there are some men among us who don't care a whit for fortune—yourself included," he remarked, glancing at his friend.

Harrison laughed. "Ah, but I've neither a father pushing me to wed a fortune nor a fortune so entailed that I must wed for money, as Stanhope will likely do one day," he said, referring to the fact that Stanhope's fortune was entailed to the hilt, leaving to him very little real income. "As my circumstances stand, I have the luxury of time to wait for the perfect wife."

The perfect wife. Jared snorted. The perfect wife, to his way of thinking, had little to do with fortune. The perfect wife would be a comely woman with an agreeable personality and a lusty appetite in his bed. She would have a sufficiently high birth to satisfy his father, but for God's sake, without a fortune so large as Lady Elizabeth as to necessitate what felt like the joining of nations. And she would be an orphan if he had his way, so that she would not have dreadfully dull parents who could fill an entire hour of conversation with talk of repairs made to the east wing—

A jarring thought suddenly occurred to Jared and he looked at Ava Fairchild again. A moment later, he abruptly swung off his horse.

"What are you about?" Harrison asked.

"Bloody hell if I know," Jared muttered, and stepped into the path as the women came upon them.

Ava Fairchild, deep in conversation with her companions, glanced briefly at him, then jerked her gaze up again, the surprise of recognition glimmering in her eyes. He was instantly and rather warmly reminded of those lovely green eyes in far more intimate circumstances.

That sultry, seductive kiss in his carriage—what had it been, almost a year ago?—had been an impetuous act just like dozens before it, nothing more than a bit of harmless flirtation. But looking at her now—the faint blush in her cheeks, the clear green eyes, the blond hair peeking out from beneath her black bonnet, he recalled that the kiss had stayed with him well into the next day because she'd been so . . . delightfully *fervent* about it.

He bowed. She blinked and looked nervously about. He lifted a quizzical brow as he put his hand out to receive hers. She managed to gather her wits and stepped forward to give him her hand.

"Good afternoon, my lord," she said, curtsying.

"It is a pleasure to see you again, Lady Ava," he said, and noted that her companions looked at her with great astonishment as he bowed over her hand. He deduced, judging by the way she closely watched him as if she expected him to confess how he'd made her acquaintance, that she had not told anyone about their carriage ride together—an encounter that was now playing itself out in his mind's eye.

When he let go of her hand, she gave him a brief and anxious smile. "I, ah . . . may I introduce you to my sister, Phoebe, and my cousin, Greer?" she asked, gesturing to each companion in turn, her eyes never leaving him.

The two curtsied politely but peered at him suspiciously.

"How do you do," he said, and turned back to Ava. "I offer you my condolences for the loss of your mother."

"Oh," Lady Ava said, her lovely face falling. "Thank you. It's been almost a year since she left us, yet she is still greatly missed."

"Lady Ava." Harrison had come down off his horse and stepped up to greet her. "How do you do?"

"Lord Harrison," she said, smiling warmly. "So good to see you again."

"Is Lord Downey still in France?" he asked. "When we last spoke, you rather thought he'd return for the Season."

"At present, he is still in France, but we do expect him in the near future."

Not thinking clearly and terribly uncertain what he was about, Jared asked, "Will you attend the Season's events?"

Ava Fairchild blinked. "We are in mourning."

"For one month more," her cousin hastily interjected. "When we come out of mourning, we shall be pleased to accept invitations."

Lady Ava jerked her gaze to her cousin.

"Then I shall very much look forward to seeing

you again in a ballroom, Lady Ava," he said with a smile. "I recall that you enjoy dancing."

Her eyes widened slightly, then narrowed. "I do indeed, my lord—particularly a waltz."

He almost laughed. "Then perhaps you will allow me the honor of reserving a waltz now?"

"How very kind of you to ask," she said, and the corners of her mouth turned up in a beguiling little smile. He understood, of course, that she did not necessarily agree to his request. He smiled with amusement, and noticed that she was indeed quite fair. He hadn't really recalled just how fair.

Lady Ava's cheeks flushed an appealing shade of pink at his scrutiny; she glanced at the timepiece pinned to her breast. "Oh dear, we really must be on our way." She lifted her gaze to him, her green eyes shining with some delight. "If you will pardon us?"

"Of course," Jared said, stepping back to allow them room to pass. "I look forward to seeing you during the course of the Season—and to the dance you have promised me."

"Good day, my lord," she said, smiling coyly. She shifted her gaze to Harrison and curtsied, as did her sister and cousin. "Good day."

"Good day, ladies," Harrison said, lifting his hat. He and Jared watched as the three of them walked on, their heads together, their arms linked.

Jared's mind was whirling around the improbable, inconceivable idea that had popped into his head without warning and now refused to dislodge itself.

As if he were reading Jared's mind, Harrison sighed playfully. "Well," he said, glancing sidelong at Jared. "She *is* an earl's daughter. I suppose you could do worse."

Jared smiled.

"Have you considered, old chum, what a certain widow will make of it?"

"I've not considered a blessed thing," he said truthfully. But as he admired Lady Ava's derriere as she moved away, he was struck by the peculiar feeling of being particularly intrigued, just as he had been the first time he'd met her. He glanced at Harrison and winked. "Miranda . . ." He shook his head, reaching for his horse. "I will speak with Miranda."

Five

~~~~~~

"But how did you meet him?" Phoebe demanded for the hundredth time since they'd arrived home yesterday afternoon. "I don't recall your being introduced."

"Don't you? I suppose it happened before Mother died," Ava said as she quickly dressed to go out, her mind on an extremely urgent matter.

"No, I *don't*," Phoebe insisted. "I am *certain* I would have recalled it. And why should he ask for a place on your dance card now? It's not as if you are out in society, and even if you were, he rarely attends the balls. I don't quite understand it."

"There is nothing to understand," Ava said. "He was just being kind. And really, we have far more important things to think about than that."

"Perhaps *you* do, but I am rather curious," Phoebe said, and looked up from her sewing. "It seemed as if he knew you."

"Dear lord, will you please think of something else?" Ava said. "Think of a *butler*. We *must* have a butler if we are to reenter society."

No one argued, for the three of them were perfectly aware that every fine house in Mayfair had a full coterie of servants, and if a house did *not* have them, it was a foregone conclusion that the house no longer had its fortune. And if the poor souls of a house were thought to be *without fortune*, they were thought to be *without prospects*.

As it happened, they had reached the most desperate of moments several months ago, one that called for the most unthinkable actions, but nevertheless, Ava and Greer had begun to slowly and steadily fill the house with servants. They had done it by joining the Ladies' Beneficent Society, their only escape during their long months of mourning suffered under Lucy Pennebacker's watchful eye. She was never far from their side, hovering about them like a vulture, taking her charge to look after them very much to heart—she was fiercely determined to see after them and their virtues.

Their only way out was through charitable works, for even Lucy couldn't object to that. The society was a group of women formed under the auspices of St. George's parish church, whose function was to help those less fortunate than themselves. Each week, the ladies assembled to visit a small parish workhouse, where they took fruit and sweetmeats to the poor souls who had come from what the ladies assumed were wretched dens of iniquity. In exchange for the fruit and sweetmeats, the parish wards were asked to listen to the ladies' recitation of select Bible verses, and at the conclusion of the readings, to affirm that they had dedicated themselves to leading proper, God-fearing lives.

Lady Downey used to laughingly say that this practice was the least the good church ladies could ask, being so astoundingly free of sin and poverty themselves.

The members of the Ladies' Beneficent Society

were delighted to see Ava and Greer among their number, and spoke fondly of Lady Downey and her wonderful sense of charity. It was something the girls had never really known about their mother. Honestly, Ava had believed it to be a social club.

At the parish workhouse—which was, surprisingly, situated behind the public stables on Portland Street, near the fashionable Regent Street—Ava and Greer handed fruit to the residents, read aloud the Bible verses, and shrewdly studied the inhabitants when they weren't working to appear very pious.

Through a series of visits to the parish poorhouse, they managed to convince a few carefully chosen inhabitants to come to the Downey house on Clifford Street, where they would be given food and shelter in exchange for their service.

The lack of wages, however, made it a difficult proposition to even the poorest of the workhouse's denizens. Ava and Greer had managed to coax only three into their home. Sally Pierce, a reformed harlot, had become their lady's maid.

"But what if she is not entirely reformed?" Phoebe had fretted the first night Sally was in their employ.

"Best hope that she is, darling, for we shall all be completely ruined if she is not," Ava had whispered.

They had also managed to retain Mr. William Pell and his son, Mr. Samuel Pell, who had both been injured in a horrible carriage accident. Mr. Pell the senior had lost a leg and therefore could no longer light lamps, as was his profession. His son, an apprentice, had a mangled arm that hung at a strange angle on his left side. But between the two of them, they managed to make one fairly decent footman.

The Fairchilds did not, however, have the services of a butler, and Ava could imagine nothing worse than if someone were to call and be greeted at their door by Lucille Pennebacker. She was determined to pluck a suitable butler from the ranks of the poorhouse at once, so that she might teach the lucky man a bit about butlering before they reentered society.

She was preparing to do just that when Greer stood. "Ava. Before you go, there is something I must tell you."

Both Ava and Phoebe, who was working to hem a gown—she was altering old gowns to make them look new for their reentry—turned and looked at her.

"I've been doing quite a lot of thinking about our situation, and . . . well, here it is: I've an uncle on my father's side to whom I believe my father's fortune was bequeathed when he passed," she said, clasping her hands tightly together. "Uncle might be of some use to us, for if I am correct, there are no other male heirs to whom the family fortune would naturally go. There is a good chance that *I* may be the sole heir. Therefore, I have written my uncle requesting an audience and I intend to make a plea that he advance a bit of my inheritance now. An annuity or something very near to it, to help us make our own way. What do you think?"

"It's a marvelous idea!" Phoebe exclaimed at the same moment Lucy bustled in carrying an armful of freshly laundered linens. "Where is he, then? Berkeley Square, I should think—there are scads of elderly folk milling about there."

"Who is at Berkeley Square?" Lucy instantly asked.

"*Berkeley Square?*" Greer asked incredulously, ignoring Lucy. "That's not as much as a mile from here, Phoebe! Wouldn't you suppose that were he in Berkeley Square, I might have *called* on him? No, no—he's in the Marches, silly!"

"The *Marches*?" Phoebe cried, clearly taken aback. "Greer! You cannot possibly think to go there! It's practically all the way to America!"

"No . . . but it is Wales," Greer said with a thoughtful frown. "I've not seen it in some time."

"You've not seen it since you were *eight*, Greer," Ava reminded her as Lucy dropped the linens and gaped at Greer.

"But I've not forgotten it," Greer said quickly. "I have rather a good memory of it, actually, and a letter with a direction in my mother's things. I can make my way about."

"Dear God, she is *serious*," Phoebe said, aghast.

"I shall be away for only a few months," Greer doggedly continued. "Perhaps three at the utmost. How long could it possibly take to reach Wales and then convince my uncle to loan me a bit of my own inheritance? I think it should be very tidy, really."

"*Tidy*? Don't be absurd!" Ava cried. "How do you think to even *get* to the Marches?"

"In a public coach . . . with Mrs. Smithington. She asked Lady Purnam for recommendations of a good traveling companion, and Lady Purnam thought of me."

"Oh, I am *certain* she did!" Ava exclaimed with great exasperation. Lady Purnam's meddling in their lives had not abated in the least since their mother's death.

"But it's so far away!" Phoebe said.

"Don't be a ninny, girl," Lucy said harshly. "Let her go if she wants. She's got a proper traveling companion and it's one less mouth to feed, isn't it?"

"*Lucy!*" Phoebe cried.

"What, then, you think it is easy to feed you and the poorhouse rats underfoot on what Egbert allots?"

"Lucy, please," Ava said irritably. "The parish pays us five pounds per person to take them off the poor-house rolls, yet you won't allow them to eat more than a few potatoes—"

"I suppose I should give them *your* food, should I?" she responded, just as irritably. "Let her go," she said again. "When Egbert returns, you'll all be gone," she added ominously, and turned on her heel, quitting the room.

Her words sobered them all. No one spoke—they just looked at each other as the truth of Lucy's words closed in around them.

"I leave on the morrow," Greer said quietly. "Mrs. Smithington desires to begin in Hertfordshire and leisurely make our way west."

"Oh *no*," Phoebe said, and a tear slid down her cheek. "I won't be able to bear your absence."

"Dear God," Ava sighed, giving in, and moved to embrace her sister. Greer joined them, and the three of them held each other tightly for some time, whispering that they would reunite, that this would all one day be behind them like a bad dream.

That afternoon, as Ava walked across town to the parish poorhouse, she struggled to hold on to her belief that these were only temporary circumstances for them, that there would come a day again, perhaps soon, when their lives would return to what they had always known. Ava had to believe it, for she had nothing else in which to believe.

And besides, she'd had another idea, something she'd been mulling over for several weeks now.

No one could possibly understand the weight of the responsibility she felt along with her grief of losing her mother, but she was keenly aware that as the oldest, she was the one who should look after Phoebe and

Greer. She felt alarmingly unprepared to do that and terribly anxious about it—she fully expected Lucy was right, that her stepfather would want to rid himself of the three of them quickly. Worse, she had no doubt that *she* would be the first to be offered up in marriage.

It was inevitable. It had been inevitable from the moment of her birth. But it had occurred to her—late one night as she lay awake worrying, as had become her habit—that if marriage was indeed inevitable, then wouldn't she be wise to take advantage of her stepfather's absence and shape her own destiny?

In other words, if she secured an offer for her hand—a *proper* offer—before her stepfather presented one to her, she could provide for Greer and Phoebe and thereby prevent them from suffering the same fate as she, of having to marry before they were fully prepared to do so.

She really had no other recourse. She was a woman. It wasn't as if she could suddenly take up a trade and earn their keep, for God's sake—or buy a commission in the Royal Navy, or inherit her mother's estate, or invest the thirty pounds she kept hidden in a porcelain box.

Yet *marriage*! It seemed such an astonishingly huge proposition.

Lord God, how she missed her mother! Her mother would know precisely what to do.

Life had been so gay when she was alive—Mother embraced life and relished the soirées and dinners she attended, loved more than anything else to shop along Bond Street for clothing and accessories and linens and furnishings for her house. She was always laughing, delighting in the tales the girls would bring back to her from the many assemblies they attended, matching them with tales of her own.

She'd been a good mother to them. She'd taken Greer in when she was eight, and while Ava's father was alive, they had all lived at Bingley Hall.

In the summer, the girls would play in the meadow amid wildflowers and grazing horses. During the long cold winters, Mother would organize plays for them to perform, and they would dance and sing for Father, who always clapped enthusiastically for each and every performance. If they did their schoolwork, they were rewarded with a trip to Mother's closets to play among her many gowns and hats and shoes.

"Mind your manners and be a proper young lady, and one day you shall have as many gowns as this," she'd told them all, twirling around in the latest fashion to arrive from London.

"I shall make my own," Phoebe would insist. Even at the age of six she'd had a love of needlework.

"Shall we all go to balls?" chubby little Greer would ask, and Mother would catch her by the hands and twirl her around and reply in a singsong voice, "You shall attend balls and soirées and assemblies, of course! You shall be the toast of London, my darlings, and every man shall desire to marry you!"

But then she would grow sober and sink to her knees so that she could look them square in the eye. "But you will promise me, won't you, my dear lambs, that you will not be silly and fall in love, for marriage is an act of combining money and convenience. *Love* comes afterward," she'd add with a wink.

Of course they'd all dutifully promised, but Ava never really understood her mother's reasoning. She believed her mother had truly loved her father—the days at Bingley Hall were halcyon days. Surely her father's fortune hadn't mattered to her mother. But Ava harbored no illusions about her mother's second marriage. There was perhaps a bit of affection between her and Lord Downey, but love? All-consuming, heart-stopping love? No, never.

It wasn't until Ava came out into society that she understood what her mother had meant—several debutantes had married men who had matched them more in fortune and standing than in temperament. She could think of only two debutantes who had purportedly married for love, and their standing in society had not profited from their unions. If anything, their status had been somewhat reduced.

But was that so terribly wrong? Was social standing more important than love? Ava couldn't help wondering if a person's life was not dramatically improved with a bit of genuine affection for one's bedmate, regardless of wealth.

Her confusion on the matter was one of the reasons why Ava had never really settled on a particular suitor. Now she was regretting her carefree life. Now she was worried what would become of them and feared the worst. She could almost hear her mother: *"Now it is a matter of convenience, darling. Now it is time for you to have a husband and the security of his fortune."*

All right, then, she'd marry, but she'd not marry the likes of Sir Garrett. No, she'd decided she would hunt for someone better suited to her tastes, and she had in mind someone far more handsome and far more dangerous: Lord Middleton.

Since she'd experienced that illicit kiss, which she still remembered with shining clarity, she could think of no one else. As long as she was to be married, she would like to know more of that sort of kiss—and beyond. And if she had to marry for convenience and fortune, what better fortune than that of a man who would one day be a duke?

She had thought about it long and hard and had concluded that she had nothing to lose by trying to win an offer from him.

Her only dilemma was, how exactly did one go about hunting a duke?

Six

⎯⎯⎯⎯⎯⎯~⎯⎯⎯⎯⎯⎯

One week later, Ava had her butler. Mr. Morris, an elderly jeweler's assistant who had been dismissed because his eyesight had become so bad he could no longer clearly see the jewels on which he worked, and without income of any sort, had ended up in the parish poorhouse.

He came to the house on Clifford Street but was quite apprehensive. He seemed to think that having never butlered before might be a hindrance to his performance.

"Of course not," Ava assured him, in spite of having no practical knowledge of a butler's duties. "It's all very simple, really. You open and shut doors, mainly."

That had seemed to appease him somewhat, but nothing could appease Lucille Pennebacker. "He's not a butler, he's a clerk, and he smells of sulfur and rotten eggs!"

"You must remember that we are doing a good deed, Lucy."

"A good deed!" she spat. "You are up to no good, Ava Fairchild. Wait until Egbert hears of it. He'll not have a man smelling of sulfur in his house!"

Ava rather imagined that was true, but she nevertheless made her way to the parish poorhouse to have Mr. Morris's name removed from the rolls and to collect the five pounds the parish would pay her for having removed him from their responsibility. It was not an ideal situation to be sure, but she was hopeful that he could be properly trained.

She was so lost in thought that she didn't notice the three gentlemen emerging from a club on Regent Street, or that one of them paused to look at her. She didn't notice him at all until he suddenly started walking away from his companions in her direction.

"Come on, Middleton!" one of the other men called.

Ava's breath caught in her throat. It *was* Middleton. She couldn't believe her opportunity after several nights lying sleepless in her bed, wondering how she might insinuate herself into his lofty sphere. But as she had assumed she would do so *after* she had come out of mourning, she couldn't think exactly what to do with the opportunity that was presenting itself as Middleton came to a halt before her.

"Lady Ava?" he said, looking at her curiously.

Three years of honing her skills in ballrooms and salons across Mayfair suddenly bubbled up. "My lord Middleton!" she said, and curtsied deeply, shifting the empty basket in which she had carried fruit to the poorhouse.

"*Middleton!*" one of the companions—whom she recognized as Lord Harrison—shouted laughingly. "We'll be late!"

He seemed not to hear him. "You're walking alone?" he asked, peering behind her. "Rather far from home at an odd hour, aren't you?" he asked as his two companions started back toward her, too.

"I, ah . . . why, no, my lord," she said as Lords

Stanhope and Harrison joined them. Now there were three gentlemen eyeing her curiously.

"Come on, then, Middleton," Stanhope said with a grin. "You'll incite a certain friend to jealousy if we are late."

"Stanhope, do you not see Lady Ava Fairchild and her basket before us?" Middleton asked grandly, gesturing toward Ava. The three of them peered at the empty basket she'd forgotten she was carrying.

"Oh," she said, glancing at the basket. "I've just come from the parish poorhouse."

"Dear God," Stanhope muttered.

"All right, then, you've seen the lady's basket," Harrison said. "Forgive us, Lady Ava, but we really must go on. We are late for an important engagement."

Stanhope laughed.

"You must ignore them, Lady Ava," Middleton said with a charming smile. "They've had far too much whiskey and have quite forgotten their manners." He said it with an easy, captivating smile that made Ava begin to feel rather warm in her black crape gown.

"*Ach*, I cannot wait any longer," Harrison said, putting a hand on Middleton's shoulder. "Someone awaits my appearance," he added with a wink.

"Go, then," Middleton responded, flicking his wrist at the two of them. "I shall be along directly, but at present I should like to know what Lady Ava Fairchild is about with her big . . . *basket*."

"As you wish," Harrison said.

"But . . . but I thought—" Stanhope stammered, but Harrison slung his arm around his shoulder, pulled him aside, and said something low. Whatever he said caused Lord Stanhope to jerk his head up and peer closely at Ava before smiling broadly.

"Good *day*, Lady Ava," he said politely, and he and Harrison strode away, laughing at some private jest.

Middleton put his hand on his waist, revealing a strong figure in form-fitting dove-gray trousers, a striped waistcoat, and a coat of navy superfine. "Pay them no mind," he said breezily. "But you, my lady, *you* are very curious."

"I'm hardly curious, my lord," she said, trying very hard not to notice his muscular form. "I am a member of the Ladies' Beneficent Society. Perhaps you have heard of it?"

"I can't say that I have," he said, his smile turning brighter.

"We are employed in charitable works."

"What sort?"

"What *sort*?"

"What sort of charitable works?" he asked as his gaze casually moved down the length of her.

Really, it was very warm beneath her cloak. "Ah . . . the usual sort."

Middleton lifted his gaze from his casual perusal of her and grinned as if that amused him. "The usual sort . . . feeding poor foundlings? Tending to the infirm?"

Looking for a butler. "Ah . . . reading the Bible," she said, and focused on smoothing a wrinkle in her sleeve. "To . . . to the, ah, poor people."

"Aha!" he exclaimed. "A worthy endeavor, to be sure!"

Was that laughter she heard in his voice? She glanced up from her sleeve. He was grinning. For the sake of argument, suppose she *were* reading the Bible to poor people. What on earth was the matter with that? "Are you . . . are you *laughing* at me, my lord?"

"Not in the least," he said instantly. "I mean to compliment you on your good works." He inclined his head.

"It's quite true, you know," she lied indignantly. "I am in the midst of an important charitable endeavor."

He smiled fully at that, and Ava felt the force of it all the way to her toes. "Not just a single act, but an entire endeavor. Bravo, Lady Ava. And where are you off to now? To spread more goodness about? You must allow me the honor of seeing you to it."

"Thank you, but that is not necessary," she said. "Your friends are waiting." *Not to mention a certain friend who would be incited to jealousy. What a rogue he was!*

"What friends?" he asked, and before she could respond, he said, "Come, then, let me see you home."

The very suggestion alarmed her. If she was to lure him to her, the *last* place she wanted Lord Middleton was at the door of her home when a jeweler's clerk and Lucille were vying for the chance to open it. There would be the usual introductions, and Lucille would wonder aloud who he was, and Middleton would undoubtedly wonder aloud why there was no butler, to which Mr. Morris would correct him and say *he* was the butler, and the rest was too awful to imagine. "It's really not necessary, my lord."

"Perhaps it is not necessary, but it is my pleasure and my duty. It is dusk, madam. I cannot think of letting you walk alone after dark. Don't you know that wicked men roam these streets at night?" he asked with a wink.

She had a sense of that, yes, and eyed him suspiciously. His soft chuckle made the hair on the back of her neck stand—not from fright, she realized, but from the expectation of something pleasurable.

"Please do allow me, Lady Ava. It is not often I am in the company of such goodness," he said, crossing one arm over his heart.

He was flirting with her. The Marquis of Middleton was actually *flirting* with her. Ava suddenly smiled. "Well, then, I suppose one might consider this as doing a small bit of the Lord's work, mightn't one?"

He laughed, a deliciously deep laugh that put crinkles at the corners of his eyes, and held out his hand to her. "I am in your debt," he said, and gestured for her basket. "To your home, then?"

"Ah, no," she said quickly. "To the, ah . . . the church."

"The church?"

"It's just over there," she said, gesturing down the road as she handed him her empty basket.

"Thank you, but I can at least claim to know where St. George's church is located. It just seems rather late to find anyone there."

"*Au contraire*," she said pertly. "Charity can be performed at all hours, my lord." She put her hand on the arm that he offered her.

"Then you are to be commended on your devotion, Lady Ava."

She glanced at him from the corner of her eye. "You seem surprised," she remarked as they began to walk.

"It is a bit surprising, for I had not noticed you at church services, and one would think a pious person would attend services regularly."

"Hadn't you?" she asked airily, in spite of the fact that she hadn't attended Sunday services in quite some time. "Perhaps if you were to turn your head to the left and right and say good morning to those around you instead of staring solemnly forward, you might see me."

"Ah. But that would take my attention away from the sermons of our vicar," he said, and looked at her with hazel eyes that had gone dark. "And were I to see you, Lady Ava, I would be tempted . . . *quite* tempted . . . to forget the good vicar entirely. Until, of course, should come the moment I would beg him for salvation for thinking improper thoughts," he said, taking in her figure once more. "In truth, I might be in need of salvation this very evening," he added softly, and lifted a dark gaze to her eyes once again, regarding her with an expression she could only term ravenous.

Ava's stomach dipped to her toes.

She was no stranger to flirting—she rather fancied herself a veteran at it. But there was something different about Middleton's gaze—it seemed so intense that she had the feeling she was standing before him without a stitch of clothing.

She struggled to think clearly. "In need of salvation, truly?" she asked softly.

He smiled a little. "You should know better than most. I'm in constant need of salvation—you've read the newspapers, I trust?"

He was walking so close to her, his head inclined in her direction, and she couldn't help but think of that kiss for perhaps the thousandth time. "Indeed I have, my lord," she said slowly, her thoughts growing muddled as she looked into his dark hazel eyes. "In passing, of course . . . when I am searching out the news of Parliament."

"Charity and politics, too?" One corner of his mouth tipped up; a smile danced in his eyes. "Most ladies seem to be interested only in dancing and poetry and rumors of who has offered for whom."

"I assure you, sir, a woman's interests are wide and varied and go well past the dancing and poetry and . . . gossip."

"Not in my experience. Many of the remarks made to me by the fairer sex lead me to believe that females think of little more than gowns and shoes and which gentleman stood up with which lady more than twice in the course of one evening."

"Oh," she said with a nonchalant shrug. "I wouldn't know, really. I can scarcely abide ballroom gossip."

He laughed softly. "You are indeed a paragon of virtue, Lady Ava. Perhaps your interests would extend to a charitable auction to benefit the Foundling Hospital? I am lending it my name and I know the effort is in need of good volunteers. I should very much appreciate your assistance."

His suggestion surprised and elated her. The thought of working alongside him on some important charitable event was almost too good to be true—it was precisely the opportunity she needed to gain an offer from him.

"May I impose on you?" he asked. "It's rather a large event, one to which the full ranks of the aristocracy will be invited to donate goods to be auctioned. I will host it at Vauxhall Gardens in June, before too many of the *ton* have escaped to the country."

"I should be delighted," she said earnestly. "Anything to further a good cause," she added, thinking of her own cause. "Ah, here we are," she said, nodding to the cross street down which the parish church was located.

He glanced around, looking a bit confused.

Ava laughed. "The church, my lord. Have you forgotten where it is located?" she teased him.

He smiled and took her hand in his. "Thank you for allowing me to escort you," he said. His eyes were shining as he brought her hand to his mouth and pressed his mouth to her gloved knuckles. His gaze was intent, his lips warm through her glove, and a flood of heat raced up her arm and swirled around inside her.

He lifted his head, his eyes never leaving hers. "And thank you for agreeing to help my charity," he added softly, and slowly turned her hand over, and pressed his lips to her palm. "But thank you most of all," he said, as his hand caressed her arm, "for agreeing to dance with me at your next opportunity." He bent over her arm and kissed the flesh on her wrist that peeked out between the buttonholes of her glove.

She felt positively overheated now. "D-did I agree?"

He smiled. "I am certain that you did."

"I don't recall," she said breathlessly.

His smile broadened, and with the authority of a marquis, he whispered, *"You will,"* and pressed his lips to the bare patch of flesh between her glove and her sleeve on the inside of her elbow.

Ava drew a steadying breath. His lips, warm and wet, seemed to burn her skin.

He lifted his head and slid his hand down her arm, his fingers tangling with hers as he let her hand fall away. "Will you be all right from here?"

"The church is only a stone's throw, sir."

"Then I bid you good evening, Lady Ava. Do have a care not to astonish the entire town with your virtue," he added with a wink, and handed her the empty basket. He stepped away, pausing once to look at her again before striking out, striding purposefully in the opposite direction.

Ava fussed with her basket and reticule as she surreptitiously watched him until he disappeared around the corner. Only then did she turn and march after him, turning right where he turned left, her step amazingly light, her hand still tingling from his kiss.

Was it possible? she giddily asked herself. Could she possibly lure a man like Middleton away from a woman like Lady Waterstone? Could *she* be the one to gain an offer from the highly desirable and unmarried marquis?

Why ever not? she silently responded, and with a happy smile of hope, she quickened her step.

Alone in his study the following morning, Jared held a letter he'd received from his butler at Broderick Abbey. The contents of the letter disturbed him, and made him think of Ava Fairchild again.

His father was clearly determined to carry out his threat, and with that weighing heavily on his mind, Jared had privately conceded that he would have to marry to keep his father from it. Not Lady Elizabeth, however, no matter how hard the duke pushed him. But someone vibrant, someone whom he would at least enjoy impregnating.

And that someone, he had decided, was Lady Ava. She was the perfect wife. She had the proper pedigree, but no parents or fortune of her own and was therefore in need of a fortune. She was vibrant and merry and quite pretty. He could do his duty by her, then continue on as he always had, avoiding any ugly obligations or entanglements with family.

With that in mind, he pocketed the letter from Broderick Abbey and picked up a pen. On a piece of vellum emblazoned with the family crest and exquis-

itely engraved with his name—THE HONORABLE
MARQUIS OF MIDDLETON, ESQ.—he wrote:

> *Dearest Lady Ava,*
>
> *Thank you for allowing me to see you safely to
> church. Hearing of your efforts to read the Bible to
> the poor was as pleasurable as it was inspiring. I am
> delighted that amid the many parish works in which
> you are engaged you are able to find the time to
> assist us in the auction for the Foundling Hospital.
> Your good work is ever appreciated, my lady, but I
> would be remiss if I did not point out to you that
> St. George's parish church is on Maddox Street, and
> not Burgh Street, as you seem to believe.*
>
> *Sincerely, M.*

Satisfied, Jared rang for a servant. When a footman
appeared, he handed him the note. "Have this deliv-
ered at once with a bouquet of the best hothouse roses
you can find," he said. As the footman quit the room,
Jared leaned back in his chair and put his hand in the
pocket that held the letter from Broderick Abbey.

Seven

That very afternoon, Ava and Phoebe were suffering another of Lady Purnam's calls. She had taken it upon herself to look in on them at least once weekly, if not more often.

She was seated in an overstuffed chair, sipping the tea Lucy had made. "You've one more full week of mourning," she said when Ava remarked she would be glad to put away her black bombazine gowns. "I know you will be tempted to enter society as soon as possible, but I would advise a period of half mourning. Perhaps three months." She put aside her teacup, clasped her hands in her lap and looked pointedly at the two of them.

"Half mourning?" Phoebe asked, exchanging an anxious glance with Ava. "Is it customary? We have been in deep mourning for a full year."

"I am aware of that," Lady Purnam said, shifting uncomfortably in her seat. "But you would do your mother's memory a great honor to continue in half mourning for a period of time. It is the proper thing to do."

"But . . . is it prescribed?" Ava asked carefully.

"Not in so many words," Lady Purnam sniffed. "Yet society would certainly think the better of you for it. My advice to you is to observe three months. Oh, don't look so glum! You can go abroad in half mourning."

"But we can't go to balls," Ava pointed out.

"Certainly not. Who can dance when a dear mother has passed?"

"I beg your pardon, your ladyship," Lucy said. "I'm not one to ever disagree with the need for propriety, but I believe they should be allowed in society."

Ava and Phoebe exchanged a wary glance. If anyone was more rigid in following the rules of proper society than Lady Purnam, it was Lucille Pennebacker.

Even Lady Purnam seemed surprised. "I daresay it may be customary to enter society after one year where *you* hail from, Miss Pennebacker," she said imperiously as she shifted again in her seat. "But I believe I am better suited to judge what is proper here in town."

"Perhaps," Lucy said with a sniff of her own. "But the girl's stepfather will return in April, and I daresay *he* won't abide a longer period of mourning. It is well past the time they were married, their poor dear mother's death notwithstanding."

"Oh, Lucy, please—" Ava started.

"I assure you, Miss Pennebacker," Lady Purnam interrupted, "that when I have had occasion to speak with Lord Downey, he will not force the issue of marriage before the period of mourning has been duly observed."

"Speak to him all you like," Lucy said, and picked up the tea service. "But I believe I know my brother very well. If you will excuse me?"

"By all means," Lady Purnam said, and smiled so thinly that it seemed more like a sneer.

When Lucy had left the room, Lady Purnam shook her head. "She is the *most* disagreeable woman to ever grace a proper salon! I suppose *she* is responsible for the hiring of your Mr. Morris, that fool! Do you know that he kept me waiting on the stoop while he announced me?"

"I shall speak to him at once," Ava said.

Lady Purnam sighed and stood up. "You might suggest to Lord Downey that he look after the upholstering of Cassandra's furniture when he returns. It's in desperate need of repair. Well, then, darlings, I must be off. Shall I have a modiste sent round to measure you for half mourning?"

"That won't be necessary," Phoebe said quickly. "I'll do it."

"Now, Phoebe," Lady Purnam said as she moved as slowly as a barge toward the door, "have a care that you don't do so much needlework that you mark your hands. A gentleman does not care for a lady's hands to show the signs of toil."

"Yes, madam," Phoebe said politely, and she and Ava dipped identical curtsies as Lady Purnam said good day and promised to call again in a week.

"We will look forward to it," Ava lied beautifully.

When the door shut behind the departing battle-ax, Ava groaned with exasperation as Phoebe rushed to the chair in which Lady Purnam had been sitting and picked up the cushion.

"Oh dear God," she sighed, and pulled a crumpled linen day dress from beneath the cushion.

"What is it?" Ava asked.

"A trial of sorts," Phoebe said wearily. She dropped the gown and walked to the windows overlooking the courtyard, reached behind the long, heavy burgundy drapes, and withdrew a basket that was spilling over with fabric.

In anticipation of their coming out of mourning, Phoebe had been taking their late mother's gowns and cutting them down to fit herself or Ava. In some instances, she took two gowns and combined them into one.

"Are those gowns?" Ava asked as Phoebe picked up a green silk she had combined with gold brocade. She quickly took it from Phoebe's hand and held it up to her body. "What on earth will you do with so many? There are more here than we could possibly wear in a Season."

Phoebe shrugged. "I find needlework comforting," she muttered, and turned away.

Ava believed her, but at the same time, she was highly suspicious, for when Lucy or Sally would enter their rooms, Phoebe would quickly shove the gown she was working on under the bed, behind a cushion, or now, it would seem, in a basket behind the drapery.

"All right, let's have it, shall we?" Ava demanded as she turned and looked at the other gowns piled in the basket. "What on earth are you doing, hiding these gowns?"

"I am not *doing* anything at all. I am only sewing," Phoebe insisted.

"Yes, darling, I can plainly *see* that you are sewing. But why are you hiding it?"

Phoebe looked at her sister, chewed her bottom lip a moment, then glanced at the door of the salon. She suddenly rushed across the room and pushed a heavy ottoman against it and fell onto it, as if she were exhausted.

"What are you about?" Ava demanded.

"All right, if you must drag it out of me, I'll tell you." She lifted her chin. "I fancy myself a decent seamstress."

"Phoebe, you are an extraordinarily talented seamstress! Just look at this!' Ava exclaimed, holding the green and gold gown up to her again. "I always rely on you to take the gown from our modiste and alter it to make it more flattering."

"That's just it, Ava. I can *do* that. I can make my own creations. Therefore, I decided I should make them for purchase."

Ava blanched. "For *purchase*? Oh dear heart, you can't *sell* them. Where would they be purchased?"

"On Bond Street."

"*Bond* Street?" Ava cried. "Are you mad? A trade? A *trade*, Phoebe? You cannot possibly think to entertain a trade, not after all the work we've done to maintain appearances! If you were to take up a trade, it would relegate us to the very bowels of the *ton*, for no one will tolerate a loss of fortune *and* a trade! No," Ava said firmly, shaking her head and throwing up a hand when Phoebe opened her mouth to speak. "Your idea is not without some merit, but it is absolutely insupportable." And with that, she tossed the gown aside and folded her arms implacably.

"If you are *quite* finished," Phoebe said with a snort, "you've not yet heard the brilliance of my plan. No one, save you—and Greer, when she returns, naturally—shall know that *I* have made gowns to be sold."

"Indeed? And just how do you propose to perform this bit of magic?"

"You may laugh if you will," Phoebe said indignantly, "but I know which Bond Street shops would be happy to sell such fine gowns!" She suddenly stood up. "Just imagine it, Ava: Suppose *you* were to wear *my* gown and patronize one such shop," she said, sweeping up the green and gold gown Ava had tossed aside and holding it up to her sister. "After many compliments are made—and how can they not be made, for this is beautiful, if I do say so myself— then you might casually mention to the shopkeeper that you happen to know the very reclusive and exclusive French modiste who has made the gown."

Phoebe thrust the gown toward Ava, forcing her to take it, then began to pace, her hands clasped behind her back, her brow furrowed. "There certainly will be gossip of a new modiste in London, a very *eccentric* modiste, one who refuses to be seen. One who refuses to create gowns for just anyone." She stopped pacing a moment and looked at Ava. "You will make that claim. You will say that had it not been for a very good friend of our dearly departed mother, who convinced the modiste to take pity on you, you would not have such a beautiful gown."

Ava blinked and looked down at the gown she held.

"Ava, don't you see?" Phoebe cried with great excitement. "You shall pretend to be an agent for this reclusive modiste, who is, in truth, *I*! You know as well as I that there is not a single woman among the Quality who can bear to be left behind when it comes to the latest fashions. They shall all descend on the shop to be measured for gowns!"

"How can you possibly accomplish so many fittings for gowns without being seen?"

"The shopkeeper will take the measurements. The shopkeeper must be our unwitting partner, or it will never work. *You* must convince her of it."

"I don't know," Ava said uncertainly, but Phoebe gripped her shoulders tightly and shook her lightly.

"*Think* of it, Ava! With the money we make, we shall continue to purchase our gowns in the finest shops on Bond Street, so that everyone will see us and never suspect we are behind the creation of the gowns!" She smiled brightly, clearly convinced of the brilliance of her plan.

Ava said nothing for a long moment, mulling it over as Phoebe watched her anxiously. There was something to be said for her plan—particularly the part about being able to afford to shop on Bond Street themselves. At last she shook her head and said incredulously, "Blast it all if I can find a single thing wrong with it, Phoebe."

Phoebe squealed with delight. "Just wait until you see the gown I am making. It is *exquisite*—"

"But how will I wear it out of this house?" Ava exclaimed. "I rather think I'd be remarked upon were I to walk into a Bond Street shop wearing a ball gown."

"We must be creative. You will take the gown and don it discreetly in the shop, and simply explain that you are commissioning gowns like this one for when your period of mourning is over."

"I don't know . . ."

"You *must* do it! The Season has already started, and the shops will be taking orders for the balls as we approach warmer weather. If you don't do it within the fortnight, our opportunity shall be lost!"

Ava had no opportunity to respond, for there was a loud and somewhat uneven knock at the door of the salon. In a flurry of satin and silk, she and Phoebe quickly hid the gowns. With Phoebe seated, Ava moved the ottoman and calmly opened the door to a very large bouquet of roses, behind which Mr. Morris stood.

"I beg your pardon, mu'um," he said behind the flowers. "Flowers have come."

"Mr. Morris! Come in, come in!" Ava said, and helped direct him to a table. The flowers were gorgeous—at least three dozen roses in a large crystal vase, the scent of them divine, the color of them as brilliantly red as rubies.

Mr. Morris carefully situated the vase on the table, then wiped his sleeve across his forehead before handing Ava a note. "If I may, mu'um . . . is a footman to stand *in* the foyer or *out* of the foyer when he comes calling?"

"If he is awaiting a reply, he is to stand in," Ava said. "Is there a footman awaiting a reply?"

"Oh no," Mr. Morris said with a firm shake of his head. "I sent him on his way."

Ava suppressed a groan. "Very well. And in the *future*, sir, a lady should never be left to wait on the stoop. Do please bring her in."

He nodded very slowly, as if committing her instructions to memory.

"Thank you, Mr. Morris."

He bowed, turned sharply on his heel as the two Mr. Pells had taught him to do, and quit the room.

Phoebe jumped up from her chair. "Who sent them?" she exclaimed, delighted. "It is Greer! Oh yes, they *must* be from Greer."

Ava opened the note, saw the flourish of an *M* and felt her heart swell. She turned her back to Phoebe and quickly read the note. She laughed; a smile spread across her face. A deep, brilliant smile. She hadn't been wrong about what she'd felt in his presence. He *did* esteem her!

"*Who?*" Phoebe demanded.

Ava glanced at her sister, held the note coyly to her

chest, and leaned over to inhale the scent of the roses. "I do believe they are the most beautiful roses I have ever seen."

"Who are they from?" Phoebe demanded again, her hands going to her hips.

"We must decide which gowns you can make ready for me, for I am coming out of mourning next week."

Phoebe gasped. "Lady Purnam will be beside herself!"

"I don't care," Ava said, smelling the roses again. "You heard what Lucy said. We haven't much time, Phoebe. We have mourned our mother properly for one full year and the Season has already begun. We must reenter society before Lord Downey returns."

"Not before I know *who*—" Phoebe abruptly snatched the note from Ava's hand. Ava grinned as her sister read the note with widening eyes. When she finished, she whirled around and gaped at Ava, her expression full of consternation. "Dear God . . . Ava, what have you done?"

Ava laughed, snatching the note back. "Nothing . . . *yet*," she said, and grabbed Phoebe's hand and sat her down to tell her everything.

By the next morning, they had determined their new course of action.

First, as Ava had no intention of coming out of mourning without the latest fashions, she allowed Phoebe to send her to Bond Street with a blue satin gown embroidered in pale gold and lavender.

Phoebe was right—the shop mistress was awed by the gown, and really, of Ava in that gown. It went exactly as Phoebe had said it would—the shop mistress complimented the gown so profusely that Ava had reason to mention an exclusive modiste who had, unfortunately, suffered a horrible accident that left her disfigured and missing one leg. Phoebe wouldn't like that particular description, but it was the only viable reason Ava could think to explain the modiste's reluctance to come out herself.

At the end of her ridiculous tale, she had an order for three gowns to be fashioned like the blue satin.

And she had a lovely blue satin to wear to the first ball to which she could secure an invitation.

Eight

~~~~~~~

During the evening of the Duke of Clarence's highly anticipated mid-Season grand ball at St. James's Palace, Lord Stanhope was divested of a considerable sum of cash in a card game while at Brooks, a gentlemen's club only a short walk from the ball's main entrance.

Stanhope became enraged by his loss and accused the winner, Sir William of Gosford, of cheating. Sir William took great umbrage to the accusation and lunged across the table at Stanhope. Were it not for Lord Middleton, who fearlessly threw himself into the melee without hesitation, someone might have been seriously injured, if not killed.

But by the time the survivors had made their way to the ball, the crookedness of Middleton's pristine white silk neckcloth and the scratch on his cheek were rumored to be the result of a spat with his lover, Lady Waterstone.

Yet it was not Stanhope's misguided accusation and subsequent fight that explained the dark look in Middleton's eye or the unyielding set of his jaw—it was that his father had conspired to keep him from Miranda and in Lady Elizabeth's company.

He'd only come to the ball because of his good

acquaintance with the Duke of Clarence and because Miranda had wanted to attend what was considered to be one of the most important social events of the Season. Certainly no expense had been spared for it— hundreds of white lilies in magnificent porcelain vases graced small consoles along the walls. Beeswax candles lit the ten crystal chandeliers that hung over the ballroom, the innumerable sconces along the walls in the passageways, and the dozens of candelabra that lit a dozen or more sitting rooms. The ballroom floor had been polished with beeswax to provide the smoothest of dancing surfaces, and music was provided by a ten-piece orchestra set in a balcony above the dance floor.

A dozen palace rooms full of expensive French and Russian furnishings were open to an enormous number of guests—four hundred by some counts, as much as five hundred by others.

And in that crush of people, the Duke of Redford kept a steady stream of gentlemen dancers at Miranda's side. Perhaps even more annoying, the duke stood up with Miranda himself—she could hardly refuse his request—and had instantly set tongues wagging across the palace.

What was said between the two of them Jared had no idea, for at the conclusion of the dance, his father had escorted Miranda to the opposite side of the ballroom from where he stood and then into an adjoining room.

In the meantime, Lord Robertson had brought Lady Elizabeth round, and there she stood like a silly little girl, her hands clasped before her, her wistful gaze on the dancers. "Which dance pleases you the most, my lord?" she asked Jared after a time of silence.

He looked at her and tried to imagine her as his wife. "I don't care for one more than another."

She lifted her chin—a bit imperiously, he thought. "I am most delighted by the quadrille." How convenient for her—the dancers were setting up for a quadrille at that very moment.

Jared swallowed a sigh of tedium and forced a polite smile. "Would you care to dance, Lady Elizabeth?"

Her face lit up. "I should like that very much, my lord." She was still beaming as he led her to the dance floor so they could assume their places. He hardly noticed her, however, because he was watching the door through which Miranda and his father had disappeared.

But as the music started, he turned his gaze to Elizabeth and bowed as he'd been trained to do since he was a small boy, then began the steps, taking her hand and crossing over, changing hands and crossing again, stepping forward, stepping back, and turning to his right as Elizabeth turned to her right, which left him to face the woman of the couple that formed the other half of their square.

He smiled with surprise upon seeing Lady Ava before him.

She smiled and took his hand. "Good evening, my lord," she said as she crossed him.

"A very good evening indeed," he said as they crossed again.

She smiled again as she stepped up, and then back, and then moved to her left to take the hand of her partner, Lord Angelsy.

Dear God, how had he missed her? She was breathtaking in an exquisitely embroidered blue satin gown that hugged her frame to its utmost advantage. Her golden hair was done up with a string of pearls that matched the teardrops at her ear lobes and her throat, and her eyes, her pale green eyes, seemed almost gray.

He hadn't realized she'd come out of mourning.

Jared went round with Elizabeth again, who said, "I've very much enjoyed the work in the charity auction."

"I'm very glad to hear it." He'd left the work on the auction to his good friend Lady Bellingham, and knew only what he received in reports from his secretary, Mr. Bean. "I understand things are progressing," he added, and looked again to Lady Ava, letting go of Elizabeth's hand, turning left, and facing Lady Ava once again. As he took her hand he said, "I didn't know you'd come out of mourning."

She said nothing, just smiled up at him with sparkling greenish gray eyes as she crossed him. He took her hand again. "You have not danced a waltz, have you?" he asked as they crossed. "For you have promised it to me," he reminded her as they stepped forward.

"Did I?" she asked airily as she stepped back. "I don't recall."

He grinned at her and turned to his right to meet Elizabeth again, who said, "His grace the duke has said that you might expect as many as four hundred."

"I beg your pardon?"

"Four hundred persons at the auction on Friday," she clarified as he let her go and she turned right.

"As many as that?" he asked, and turned right, facing Lady Ava. He took her hand and squeezed it playfully. "If you've promised the waltz away, I shall have to fight the gentleman for the right," he said as they crossed, "for it is mine, fairly bargained and won."

She laughed, her teeth flashing white between rose-colored lips, turned around, and offered her hand again. "Is that how you scratched your cheek? Fighting for a waltz?"

He chuckled, stepped forward, then back, and turned left, to a stoic Elizabeth. She said nothing—just stared hurtfully at him as he took her hand. *Would that this dance end!* "You must forgive me, Lady Elizabeth. I am all at sixes and sevens trying to remember where to step."

She nodded slightly as she crossed him.

Jared finished the dance without speaking to Lady Ava again, but he couldn't help overhearing her laugh of pleasure at something Angelsy said. He could well imagine the flirting between them—she was especially beautiful tonight, and any man with even a bit of a brain would realize the woman needed to make a match.

He really had no time to squander—for that and other more pressing reasons.

When the dance ended, he escorted Elizabeth to the side of the dance floor and excused himself, making some mention of gaming. As he walked from the room, he scanned the crowd, looking for Lady Ava, but she had disappeared from view. He was, he realized, surprisingly disappointed. There was something about the woman that continued to intrigue him.

But it was just as well—he really needed to find Miranda and assure himself that his father hadn't done anything to harm or upset her.

Ava found Phoebe in the company of Lady Purnam and her two friends, Lady Botswick and Lady Hogan. Predictably, Lady Purnam had been quite upset by Ava and Phoebe's decision to reenter society, and had insisted on accompanying them to the Clarence mid-Season ball when they received the invitation.

"Ah, there you are," Lady Hogan said, reaching for Ava's hand. "Oh my, how lovely you are. Was that your mother's gown?"

"No, I—"

"Phoebe was just telling us that your cousin, Greer, is Mrs. Smithington's traveling companion! What an agreeable occupation for her!"

"Yes, I think she enjoys it very much," Ava said.

"I remarked to Lady Purnam that I thought it was something that perhaps the two of you might consider likewise," Lady Botswick said.

Ava looked at Phoebe, then at Lady Botswick. "Traveling companion?"

"Yes, of course," Lady Botswick said, nodding her head so that the corkscrew curls at her ears bounced up and down. "Traveling companion, or perhaps governess. Have you considered the position of governess?"

"I . . . No, we have not considered it," Ava said. "*Ever.*"

"Oh well," Lady Botswick said, exchanging a look with Lady Purnam. "I just assumed, what with your circumstances, you might have considered it."

"Our circumstances?" Ava echoed, and looked at Lady Purnam. The woman turned a curious shade of pink, and Ava understood instantly that she had betrayed their confidence and had told her friends of their lack of fortune. "I can't imagine we'd have opportunity," Ava said, turning her attention to Lady Botswick again. "Phoebe and I hope to marry soon."

For some reason that made Lady Hogan smile and Lady Purnam begin a very serious study of her shoes. "Ooh, I am certain that you *do*," Lady Botswick said sympathetically.

Her patronizing tone made Ava bristle. Apparently, she and Lady Hogan assumed—no doubt along with the rest of the bloody *ton*—that she and Phoebe were no longer particularly marriageable.

"How lovely your gown," Lady Botswick said, changing the subject. "I think I should like a glass of wine. Lady Hogan, would you care for a glass of wine?"

"I would indeed."

The two ladies excused themselves, leaving Phoebe and Ava to glare at Lady Purnam. "You told them of our situation?" Ava asked. "How could you?"

"I did no such thing!" Lady Purnam said, looking quite uncomfortable. "When the subject came up, it was clear that they already knew. I am guilty in that I did not *deny* it."

"*Really*, Lady Purnam." Phoebe sighed.

"I wouldn't ask that you deny what is true, Lady Purnam, but I should hope that as our mother's dearest friend you would not confirm it," Ava said sternly.

Lady Purnam looked very chagrined, and she grabbed Ava's wrist before she could turn away. "You mustn't be so cross, dear. In truth, your situation seemed to be well understood by most long before even *I* knew of it."

"I see," Ava said coldly. "The vultures gathered as soon as Mother died, did they? If you will please excuse us."

"Ava, darling, please—"

"I really must speak with my sister."

Lady Purnam sighed and dropped her hand from Ava's wrist. "Very well. But you harm only yourself in pretending your situation is rosier than it is," she said, assuming a high-handed tone. "It does you not a bit of good to flit about society as if things were the same as they were before your mother died, for they are not. Your situation has been drastically altered, and the sooner you accept it, the sooner you may find a proper situation."

"Thank you for your unsolicited advice," Ava said tightly, and grabbed Phoebe's hand, pulling her away from the stunned and meddlesome old woman.

"We are *doomed*," Phoebe said, resigned.

"No we aren't, Phoebe," Ava insisted. "You will not believe that. We are *not* doomed!"

"What will save us, Ava? Your grand scheme of marrying a marquis hasn't quite come about, has it?"

It was true that Ava had heard nothing from Middleton since the delivery of the flowers. Even the work on his charity auction, which she had so foolishly assumed would include only him and her, had been a disaster. The good souls working on the event seemed to be a string of women he'd been associated with at one time or another, including Elizabeth Robertson. The only saving grace for Ava was that Grace Holcomb had volunteered to help so that she had at least one friend among the group.

"You'd best hope Sir Garrett doesn't greet Lord Downey when his ship docks," Phoebe snapped irritably.

Ava's stomach clenched. She'd had such high hopes for tonight, but then Middleton had arrived looking a bit disheveled, and the rumor had circulated he'd had a spat with his lover. He'd had his eyes on Lady Waterstone all evening, had danced with her, and even now, Ava could plainly see the two of them, not fifteen feet away, deep in conversation with Lord Harrison.

Worse, when he wasn't dancing with Lady Waterstone or admiring her from a distance, he was in the company of Elizabeth Robertson.

Ava turned her back on the sight so that she wouldn't have to see him smiling so charmingly at Lady Waterstone.

She'd all but given up hope before the quadrille, but she had been heartened by his expression upon first seeing her, as if he was genuinely surprised and delighted to encounter her there.

"It's not working, Ava," Phoebe said morosely. "Your marquis is obviously in love with Lady Waterstone and about to offer for Elizabeth Robertson. I hardly think there is room for a third woman. You must think of someone else—or perhaps Lady Botswick is right. Perhaps we should consider taking positions as governesses—"

"Don't be ridiculous," Ava said irritably, stung by the notion that Phoebe could be right, that they could very well be striving toward nothing more than a fantasy. "I won't give up so easily. What of your gowns?"

"It's scarcely enough to see us through."

"Then Greer will help us—"

Phoebe sighed with exasperation. "We haven't heard from Greer since she left!"

"But we *will*," Ava said, growing angry with her sister. "And besides, there is any number of gentlemen who might offer for one of us."

Phoebe shook her head. "The only man who will offer without regard for fortune or connections is Sir Garrett."

Ava snorted.

"I know how hard you have tried, Ava," Phoebe said earnestly. "But it is clearly hopeless."

"It's *not* hope—"

"I beg your pardon, Lady Ava."

She closed her eyes, took a breath, and turned around to face Sir Garrett. He was smiling broadly, his hands wringing his ever-present kerchief. "I . . . I thank you for the dance earlier this evening, and I agree that I should not ask again, as your dance card is quite full," he said, bobbing his head at her.

"Thank you for understanding, sir," she said.

"I only meant to inquire if you know . . ." He paused, dabbed his forehead, and then glanced at the ground. "That is to say, if you are aware of when your stepfather shall make his return to London."

Her heart began to pound, and Ava looked at Phoebe. "Ah . . ."

"We do not know, sir," Phoebe said quickly. "It might be as long as a month. Perhaps even longer."

"Oh," Sir Garrett replied, grimacing a little. "That is rather unfortunate, for there is a matter I should like to discuss with him at once." He glanced up, put his kerchief to his temple, and smiled hopefully. "I think you know what matter that is, Lady Ava."

Ava could only gape at him as she groped for Phoebe's hand.

"Good evening, Sir Garrett," a deep voice intoned, reverberating throughout Ava's body, flooding her with an enormous sense of relief and reprieve. She closed her eyes for a moment, then opened them, turned her head, and saw his brilliant hazel eyes and warm smile. She smiled, too, and curtsied. "Good evening, Lord Middleton."

"Lady Ava," he said politely. "Lady Phoebe," he said, inclining his head to Phoebe before shifting his gaze to Ava again. "I hope you haven't promised all your dances to Sir Garrett, madam, for you had promised me the next dance."

"Oh," Sir Garrett said, looking very surprised. "Oh, yes, of course." He looked at Phoebe. "Lady Phoebe, would you do me the honor?"

Phoebe blinked, then managed to smile as she glanced at Ava. "Thank you," she said, and put her hand carefully in Sir Garrett's paw so he could lead her onto the dance floor.

Middleton held out his arm to Ava. "You promised," he said with a wink.

"I never *promised*, my lord," she said, smiling up at him, "but I should be delighted." She put her hand on his arm.

He instantly covered it with his own, squeezing it as if they had an intimate friendship. "If I may, you are beautiful in blue, madam."

The compliment thrilled her. She had spent quite a lot of time on her appearance, making Lucy redo her hair twice. "How kind of you to say so."

"When we last met, I hadn't realized that your period of mourning was nearing its end," he remarked as he led her onto the dance floor.

"Ah, but you might have known it were you to attend the meetings for the auction," Ava said, and sank into perhaps the best curtsy of her life as they took their positions.

He laughed and bowed, then took her hand and lifted her up. "It seemed as if there were enough good souls—far better than mine—to plan the event. I didn't think that more than my name was needed," he said, and as the orchestra began the first strains of the waltz, he slipped his arm around her waist and took her hand in his.

"I suppose you are right," Ava said as she put her hand on his unpadded shoulder. "Your presence might have incited a brawl."

He laughed as he gracefully led her into the music.

Ava glanced around them as they began to waltz—she could see more than one head swiveled in their direction, the looks of blatant curiosity. The marquis could do nothing without its being remarked upon by a host of people, she realized. That should have made her more circumspect, but Ava didn't have the luxury of time to be coy or demure. If he'd heard of her plight and found her unsuitable, she would prefer to know it sooner rather than later so that she might devise another plan for her and Phoebe and Greer.

Unfortunately, while Ava had always enjoyed the attention of gentlemen, she'd never been as bold as she thought she must be now if she were to gain the marquis' undivided attention.

She glanced up at him. He was smiling down at her, a lock of his golden brown hair skating over his eye as they moved. He was an excellent dancer, his movement fluid, his hand firm on her back, gently guiding her one way, then another. He seemed amused by her perusal and raised a brow, and Ava felt the burn of inexperience in her cheeks.

"Thank you for the roses," she said. "They were beautiful."

"Ah. I am glad you enjoyed them. There is an unwritten rule among men, you know—beautiful roses must be given to beautiful women."

She blushed. How odd, but it felt as if her feet were moving on air. "You are too kind, sir."

"I trust my direction helped you find the church?" he asked with a subtle wink.

She laughed. "All right, it's true. I've been horribly remiss in my attendance." She looked up at him. "I have yet another confession to make."

"I am always keen to hear a woman's confession." His gaze drifted down to her bosom.

"Well, then, steel yourself," she said, and took a

breath. "I'm really not very good at all. I gave myself far too much credit the evening we met."

"Oh dear." He grinned a little lopsidedly. "Do you mean to say that you don't read the Bible to the poor?"

"On occasion . . . but I could not claim it is a habit."

"And what of the Ladies' Beneficent Society? Are you a member?"

"Only recently."

He grinned and twirled her round, deftly pulling her closer to him. "Then should I surmise that your assistance with my charitable auction is an imposition?"

"No," she said quickly. His eyes were mesmerizing, lulling her into a feeling of bliss in his arms. She could waltz all night, round and round, for as long as he looked at her like that. "No, my lord," she said, shaking her head sheepishly. "I wanted to lend my help to the auction. I hoped it would give me an opportunity to be . . ."

Her voice trailed away, and she looked uneasily at his shoulder. She wasn't exactly a courtesan—she didn't know how to take flirtation much further than she already had.

"To be?" he softly prodded her, pulling her even closer.

She didn't care that he held her too close for propriety, or that everyone was looking at them. "To be . . . *admired.*"

That made Middleton laugh. He threw back his head and laughed as he twirled her round the edge of the dance floor, and then again, so that the lights above her were spinning in a fantastical display and she could focus on nothing but his face, his handsome face and eyes that seemed as deep as a river.

She didn't get her wish to waltz all night, unfortunately, and it ended far too soon. She was still feeling heady, still feeling the strength of his arms around her, the pleasure of his smile. Middleton led her off the dance floor and continued on, through the crowd, oblivious to the curious looks cast in their direction.

It took Ava several moments to get her wits about her, several moments before she realized he was guiding her out of the ballroom in full view of everyone. "Wait! . . . Where are we going?"

"You look flushed," he said, and led her down a brightly lit corridor, then turned in a darker corridor and kept walking, but dropped his arm from beneath her hand and put his hand on the small of her back. Possessively. Securely.

"What are you doing?" she asked again, the good girl in her growing alarmed, sensing danger.

"I should like to admire you," he said, and smiled down at her. *"Properly."*

Those words and his smile made her heart race. If she'd been possessed of the least amount of common sense, she would have stopped there. But she suddenly didn't care where he led her, she didn't care that half the world had seen them disappear. She didn't care about the propriety of it or what would be said, cared about nothing but being with him, feeling his tall, powerful body next to hers, experiencing the beauty of his smile.

They reached a pair of doors, which Middleton threw open with the confidence of a man who was familiar with the palace. The doors led to a private, moon-drenched terrace that overlooked St. James's Park.

Ava leaned her head back and filled her lungs with cool night air in an effort to still her heart. Middleton dropped his hand from her and walked to the balustrade, standing with his hands on his waist, his back to her, staring into the night.

The slightly dizzy feeling began to abate, and Ava resumed a mannerly stance. Middleton turned around, leaned up against the balustrade, folded his arms across his chest, and quietly observed her, his eyes dark and unreadable. Something in him had changed. The *roué*, the charmer, was gone, and in his place was a darker man, his thoughts private, his gaze searching for . . . *what*?

"You still seem flushed," he said.

"It was rather warm inside the ballroom."

"Do you suppose it was the warmth of the ballroom that put such color in your cheeks? Or perhaps something far more incendiary, such as the warmth between us?"

She didn't answer; her silence was her admission of the truth.

"Come here," he said low. When Ava didn't move immediately, he said again, "*Come.*"

Her feet moved. As she neared him, he held out his hand to her. Unquestioningly, she slipped her hand into his and didn't resist when he pulled her in between his legs. His hands caressed her arms, his eyes caressed her face, her hair, her neck, lingering a moment on her breasts. His gaze didn't seem so wolfish now, but rather sadly thoughtful.

"You're shivering," he said, and slipped his hands behind her back, pulling her to him. Ava was close enough to see the red line of the scratch on his face, and the unwelcome image of Lady Waterstone came to mind. The image of a more sophisticated, experienced, and beautiful woman with a fortune of her own.

"What is your age?" Middleton asked, his gaze on her collarbone.

"I just turned three and twenty."

"Hmm," he said, nodding a little.

He probably thought she was far too old to be unmarried and still acting the debutante. She *was* too old. "What is *your* age?" she asked.

He smiled a little. "I will be thirty years in a matter of weeks. You are the oldest of the Fairchilds, are you not?"

She nodded.

He brushed a strand of hair from her shoulder, his fingers leaving a tingling trail on her skin. "Whom do you love?" he asked softly.

Ava swallowed and glanced at the stars overhead. "My sister and my cousin."

"Only them?" he asked, and tenderly kissed her shoulder.

Ava didn't know what game they played, but felt a little desperate as she glanced down at his dark head. "Whom do *you* love?"

He hesitated slightly, then moved his mouth to the hollow of her throat. "No one," he uttered, and traced a path to the top of her cleavage. "Shall I admire you, Ava Fairchild?" he asked as he kissed the top of her breast. "Shall I admire you in deed?" His hand slid down her hip, cupping it.

She sucked in her breath and put her hands on his shoulders for support. "You are bold with my person, sir."

"I am a bold man," he said, and kissed the top of her other breast. "I generally take what I want." He paused, and looked up. "And I want you." He straightened suddenly, his body brushing hers as he rose, and then leaned down, and kissed her temple.

"Dear God," Ava whispered, but he caught her whimper by covering her mouth with his. She made another small sound of alarm at the wave of sensual hysteria his words and the touch of his lips shot through her. He lifted his hand to her face, touching the corner of her mouth with his finger as he kissed her. Everything in her screamed to push away, to obey at least *some* level of decorum, but she couldn't, even if she'd tried. She'd already fallen, had plummeted into that cloud of pleasure and desire, and in fact, her hand had wrapped around his wrist, holding tightly so that she didn't float away.

He slipped his tongue between her lips as he pressed his body against hers, pressed against her the evidence of his growing desire for her. Ava had never felt anything like it, and it stirred something very deep and primal inside of her. His hand drifted to her breast, cupping it, squeezing it. She answered him by running her hands down his shoulder, then up his chest, the hard, muscular plane of him.

Her body strained for air. Her breasts pressed against his chest, her heart slammed fitfully against her ribs as his lips moved expertly, smoothly on her hers, his tongue tangling with hers, sweeping her teeth, the valleys of her cheeks, his hand reverently cupping her face while his thumb stroked her cheek.

A pressure was building in her, a need for air or to scream or to fling herself headlong down whatever path he was taking her. He pressed tightly against her—or perhaps she pressed tightly to him—but it was an incredible sensation, the feeling of being swept under by a tide, of rolling and spinning weightlessly into an ocean of pleasure.

But then the tiny mewl of a woman's cry of surprise brought reality crashing in like the tide crashes against the rocks on shore. Ava gasped, tried to pull away, but he held her fast with one arm.

His hand fell away from her face and he looked over her shoulder. "Ah. Miranda," he said, as if he was expecting her.

Mortified, Ava cried out and forcibly pushed away from him. She was ruined now, completely ruined. Yet Middleton wasn't as quick to let her go—he seemed to have no care for her or her virtue. He smiled reassuringly, swept his thumb over her bottom lip, and then for some inexplicable reason, he kissed her tenderly on her forehead. "Your sister will wonder what has become of you," he said softly, and let her go.

Ava stumbled away, took a moment to get her breath, then turned reluctantly to face Lady Waterstone, who stood in front of the door.

The woman was glaring at her. "Go on, then," she said curtly, gesturing toward the door. "Run to your sister."

Ava needed no more encouragement—she walked quickly past Lady Waterstone, through the doors, into the darkened corridor, where she flung herself up against the wall, gripped her hands together and pressed them to the roiling in the pit of her belly as her chest heaved with each frantic breath.

She couldn't seem to catch her breath, couldn't seem to think anything except, *God in heaven, what had she done?*

If Lady Waterstone, or Middleton for that matter, dared to breathe a word, she'd be ruined.

Nine

————

Two days after her astounding lapse of judgment, Ava was still waiting for the ax to fall. She wondered what Mother would have done in her shoes—if she would have given in to passion, if she'd have taken what fate handed her and made do. Ava would have given the world to talk to her mother today.

She didn't tell Phoebe what had happened, although Phoebe suspected something was amiss. But Phoebe was completely occupied with her plan to clothe the entire *ton*, and was toiling away, hand-beading two of her mother's gowns, cut and sewn together to make a new one. Every time someone knocked on the door, Phoebe went into apoplexy, jumping about and shoving fabric and thread here and there, and kicking sewing baskets beneath the bed or table, while Ava rushed to see who was invading.

It all served to increase Ava's anxiety.

On the third day, the day before the charitable auction, Ava missed a meeting of the auction committee by claiming she had a headache.

"But the auction is on the morrow," Phoebe said, looking askance at her.

Ava said nothing. She couldn't face the expressions

of women who might have heard about her scandalous behavior.

The afternoon was particularly gloomy, both inside and out.

The post, which Mr. Morris brought Ava, included a handful of letters and the *Times*. Ava sorted through the letters, and felt a surge of happiness at the sight of familiar handwriting.

"At last!" she exclaimed. "It's from Greer!"

"Greer!" Phoebe cried, putting aside her work of repairing Ava's camisole. "What does it say?"

Ava handed the rest of the letters to Lucy, broke the seal and unfolded the vellum. "It is written from Ledbury. Where is Ledbury?"

"I don't know—read the letter!" Phoebe urged her.

"*Dearest Ava and Phoebe,*" Ava read. "*I am writing to you from Ledbury. The weather has been quite dreary and wet, and the public coach was forced to stop, as the roads are presently impassable with all the rain. But Mr. Percy assures me it is not usually given to rain quite as much as this, and it should clear any day now, at which time we shall resume our journey.*"

"Mr. *Percy*? Who is Mr. Percy?" Phoebe demanded.

"I haven't the slightest idea," Ava said, and continued to read. "*I must deliver the most peculiar piece of news. In discussing my family history with Mr. Percy, I learned that my good Uncle Randolph passed just last spring. He was kicked by a horse he was gelding. The injury was quite severe, and though he apparently lingered for days, he did indeed succumb to it. Naturally, I was saddened to hear such distressing news, but Mr. Percy took great pains to assure me that there is still plenty of the Vaughan family about in these parts.*"

"What?" Phoebe cried, hurrying to Ava's side to read over her shoulder. "Her uncle has passed and yet she goes on? *Who* is this Mr. Percy? What if he is diabolical?"

"Listen to this," Ava said, reading on. *"I have very much enjoyed the journey, although Mrs. Smithington does poorly in the carriage and remarked that Wales is rather far from London. However, Mr. Percy kindly soothed her nerves by assuring her that should the weather hold, we shall arrive in Bredwardine by Monday of next week. I shall write you then. I apologize for not writing ere now, but this has been a rather bumpy ride, making it quite difficult to pen a letter. My love to you both. Fondly, Greer."*

Ava lifted her gaze from the letter and looked at Phoebe, who returned her gaze with a wide-eyed look of horror. "Who in God's name is Mr. Percy?"

"I don't know," Ava said, and folded the letter. "We can do nothing but wait for her next missive. But I assure you, if there is a level head among us, it is on Greer's shoulders."

"That is very true," Lucy said with a firm nod. "She's very bright, that one."

Ava smiled thinly at Lucy. "She is."

"You might find this interesting," Lucy said, holding up another letter. "It is from Egbert. He says he shall be home within the month."

Ava's heart sank. "Does he say aught else?"

"Just that he's looking forward to tidying up here. Would you like to read it?"

"No, thank you," Ava said quietly. She couldn't bear to look at Phoebe, who had grown so still that Ava could almost hear her heartbeat.

She picked up the newspaper and tried to focus on the words printed there, and when she could find nothing of the parliamentary news to interest her, she turned the page.

"Shouldn't pay that wretched thing a bit of mind,"

Lucy piped up. Ava glanced over the top of the newspaper to look at her. "Gossip is the work of the devil."

"I shall do my best to keep the devil from your ears," Ava said, and raised the newspaper again, as she had no such tender sensibilities about gossip.

The door swung open and Sally struggled through, carrying a bucket of coal. "Mr. Morris says you're to have this," she said, awkwardly lugging it to the hearth.

"If Mr. Morris says we are to have it, then why doesn't *he* bring it in?" Lucy demanded.

"Dunno, mu'um," Sally said, huffing and puffing. She put the coal down, then braced herself against the mantel and wiped her brow with her apron. "Had a caller, mu'um," she said to Ava. "But Mr. Morris turned him away."

"Who?" Ava asked, her hopes rising for one spectacular moment.

"Sir Something or such," Sally said, and Ava's hopes were dashed to pieces. "Came to call on your stepfather, but Mr. Morris says he ain't within. So the gent asked for you, and Mr. Morris told him he wasn't permitted to change his call. The gent said that wasn't the rule at all, but Mr. Morris said it was, and besides, it was too early to call on ladies—"

"That blockhead!" Lucy cried, and came to her feet, storming out of the room as quickly as her girth would allow.

"Oh dear Lord," Phoebe muttered. "Ava . . ."

"I know," Ava whispered, and looked again at the newspaper. Her eye caught a particular *on dit* halfway down the page.

Few have had the privilege to view the beauty of St. James's Park from the private terraces of the palace, by the light of the sun or the moon, but one good lord was inspired to gather orphans under his wing to see it. The viewing, however, was met by some disdain from certain widows who believe the park is not a proper place for poor orphans.

She felt the burn of shame in her cheeks and the race of her pulse. It was only a matter of time before names were put to the *on dit*, if they hadn't been already, and she'd be the object of much untoward speculation. If she wasn't already.

Sally put her hands on her waist and bent backward slightly. "What's got you so glum, mu'um?"

Ava started. "Me?" She forced a smile, folded the paper and tucked it into the seat next to her. "Nothing at all. I was thinking of a charity auction I must attend on the morrow." And yes, she *had* to attend it. Her absence would cause even more speculation.

"Oh? Who's the auction to benefit?" Sally asked innocently.

Ava looked at her lap. "Poor orphans."

Ten

The day of his auction dawned cold and wet, matching Jared's mien in general. He wasn't surprised by the weather, really—as of late, it seemed as if the universe was conspiring against him. He stood at the window of his town house that overlooked Grosvenor Square, watching the rivulets of rain run down the paned glass, the letter he'd received from his gamekeeper at Broderick Abbey crumpled in his hand.

He didn't know what to do with the information in the letter. He didn't know how to make things right anymore. His entire life, he'd believed himself invincible, above the earthly bonds so many men felt. Now he felt at sea. He was drifting, his direction unknown, unable to see a harbor on any horizon.

With a weary sigh, he put the letter into the pocket of his dressing gown and returned to his desk, where another letter sat, awaiting another answer he did not have.

He'd first read it last night when he'd arrived home. But he'd been a little in his cups and had tossed it aside. This morning, however, he scarcely had the heart to pick it up again.

Dearest, the letter began.

Please forgive me! I cannot bear to be without you—I cannot sleep for dreams of you, and each day seems endless without you in it. I was wrong—I know you must do the prudent thing for the sake of your family, but please, I beg of you, do not abandon me for it. I shall wait for you, darling, my every breath a hope for you.

Yours forever, M.

He crumpled the letter and threw it in the fire behind him, then fell back in his chair, his face in his hand. He was sorry for her, but it didn't sway his thinking—there had never been an understanding between them, particularly not since Miranda had made her feelings known that she valued his title above him.

And now he had to face his destiny, but he was like a blind man, stumbling toward it through darkness. He wasn't ready for matrimony, but it seemed that the holy state of matrimony was ready for him.

Lord God, what a remarkably mixed-up world he lived in.

He glanced at the gold clock on the mantel. In a few hours, he would be expected at the Prince's Pavilion in Vauxhall Gardens to auction off the accoutrements of the *ton*, the proceeds of which would go to support the Foundling Hospital. He stood up and walked numbly through his study and up to his suite of rooms to prepare for the day, for this event was, as everything else in his life, his duty.

Rain did not deter the ranks of the Quality, for it would be remarked if one of their member was not in attendance when everyone else had braved the weather to donate to a worthy cause. Jared groaned when he saw the throng crowded inside the Prince's Pavilion to avoid the rain instead of the main promenade around the orchestra tower, which had been the planners' intent. It was so crowded that there was not a breath of air to be had.

Jared paused just inside the entrance, surveying the finely dressed crowd. It was an excellent turnout given the weather, and everyone seemed in fine spirits—no doubt with help from the ale he had suggested be made available. He had noted through the years that on average, men tended to be more generous with their purses when they'd been drinking.

He entered the room with an easy smile on his face, practiced in dozens upon dozens of such gatherings in his life. He greeted and thanked the patrons who had braved miserable weather to support the Foundling Hospital, and accepted their congratulations on the success of the auction.

As he smiled and laughed and spoke to God knew who, he wondered if she'd come, or if she'd seen the morning *Times* and had decided against attending an event with so many who would whisper of a new, titillating scandal.

He was speaking with Lord Valmont when he saw her—she was at the podium where he would stand to auction the items, wearing pale green muslin that was the very shade of her eyes, embroidered with tiny cherries and tied with a sash just below her bosom. She'd wrapped her hair up in an identical strip of green cloth, but a few golden strands had escaped the wrap and reached her shoulders.

She was marking items, he noted, but she stood alone. While the other women involved in the auction worked together in pairs or groups of three or four, Lady Ava Fairchild worked alone, either by choice or as a result of the scandal that was beginning to brew and swirl around her.

As he spoke with Lord Valmont, she suddenly looked up from her work, her gaze catching his. His smile went a little deeper, and he lifted his chin just slightly, almost indiscernibly, to acknowledge her.

But Lady Ava quickly turned away, first right, then left, and without looking at him again, she hurried off the dais and through a door Jared knew, from previous events at the prince's private pavilion, led to a private receiving room.

He excused himself from Lord Valmont as soon as he could and continued on toward the dais. He could see Lady Elizabeth, off to his left, modestly dressed, holding court with several young women around her. His father also was in attendance, speaking with the Duke of York. And naturally, Harrison and Stanhope, who had both donated far above what he might have hoped, sharing a bit of ale—and, of course, a pair of debutantes.

At the dais, he inquired of Lady Bellingham and Mr. Bean how long it would be before the auction started.

"Oh, my lord, the donations have been so very generous," Lady Bellingham said, beaming.

"We are still in the process of cataloguing some of the late arrivals," Mr. Bean said, perfunctory as usual. "I would estimate another hour is needed."

"Thank you. Please see to it that there is ale and food for the guests."

"Of course," Mr. Bean said with a curt nod of his head.

Jared moved on through the crowd, smiling, greeting, trading small talk, until he reached the door Ava Fairchild had slipped through. With one last look at the crowd to assure himself no one seemed the wiser, he stepped through it.

He walked down a narrow corridor to the private receiving room, opened the door, and stepped inside. It was dark, save for the light of the gray day that filtered in around the drapes.

There was a burst of loud laughter from a group in the pavilion that caused her to move. He saw her then, standing with her back against the wall, her chest rising with each anxious breath, her golden hair visible in the dim light. Jared quietly closed the door behind him. "Lady Ava? Are you all right?"

From where he stood he could see her swallow deeply. "Perfectly fine," she said softly.

He moved slowly toward her, taking in her lovely face and neck. She anxiously pressed her lips together and looked away from him. She seemed, he thought, to feel trapped. He closed the distance between them and touched his hand to her temple, brushing a strand of silky hair behind her ear. His hand drifted to her shoulder. "Where is your sunny smile, Lady Ava? I have missed it these last two days."

She turned her head to look at him with pale green eyes that were full of an emotion he could not fathom. "I cannot smile"—she sucked in her breath when he touched his fingers to the smooth ridge of her bare collarbone and continued breathlessly—"when such wretched things are printed. I may very well be ruined."

"No," he said as his gaze slipped to the swell of her breasts. He'd always considered her a shapely woman, very appealing in her looks, but he had not, until this very moment, desired her so completely. "No, not ruined."

She gave him a skeptical look, at which Jared

smiled, and she visibly shivered. He was not the only one affected by the close proximity of their bodies in a darkened room.

His gaze fell to her lips as he caressed her collarbone and her neck with the back of his hand, enjoying the warmth of velvet-soft skin, detecting the scent of rose petal soap. He caressed her as if he possessed her, which, for all intents and purposes, he did in that moment.

"You cannot be ruined if I am an honest man. And, madam, I am nothing if not an honest man."

Her pulse leapt beneath his hand; she lifted her face, eyeing him intently, her eyes glimmering in the dim light. "What do you mean?"

Her husky voice and her glimmering eyes were all working on the man in him. He leaned down so that his lips were just a moment from her temple. "*Ssh* . . . this is a delectable moment and I would not lose it to words." And then he kissed her temple, so lightly, so breathlessly that she shivered again, only more violently than before. His hand fell to her shoulder to steady her; the other he slipped around her waist, pulling her into his body as he slid his mouth across her cheek to her lips. She moved slightly, angling her head toward him, and Jared nipped at her plump lips.

But when he slipped his tongue into her mouth, a harder, more powerful desire began to possess him. He wanted her. He hadn't felt a woman in his arms like this—not like this, not like he felt her in his arms—and he wanted to touch all of her body, to smell it, taste it, feel it. She was pulsing beneath his hands, her body coming alive, responding to his touch. He slid his lips to her chin, then to the hollow of her throat, sliding down farther, to her bosom, his hand on her hip, kneading the soft flesh, the other finding her breast.

When he squeezed the flesh of her breast, she gasped with pleasure above him, and it stoked him like the flames of a fire.

Jared rose up again, covered her open mouth with his, her breast with his hand. He tangled the fingers of his other hand in her hair, pulling her head back and lifting her face to him.

He held her so tightly to him that he could feel the pounding of her heart against his body and the palm of his hand. It was an exquisite sensation, building a fever inside him and spreading like liquid fire to his limbs. He groaned with desire, pressing his body tightly against her, and Ava curved into him. He dipped his hand into the bodice of her gown and filled his palm with her bare breast. She gasped again, and her head fell back against the wall behind her, but he hardly noticed, for he had freed her breast from the confines of the gown and dipped his head to it, taking it eagerly into his mouth.

Ava grabbed his head, her fingers raking through his hair as he devoured her breast. Her hands fluttered to his shoulders and down his arms, gripping him as her body rose up to meet his mouth, pressing into him for more. He let go of her breast and raised his mouth to hers as his hand swept down her side, around to her hip, squeezing her, then down her leg, and around to the apex of her legs at the same moment a roar of laughter, followed by a collective shriek, went up outside.

The noise seemed to waken her from his attention to her, and she dragged her mouth from his, choking and pushing him away from her. "This is *madness!*" she cried. "I am on the precipice of ruin and I am throwing myself into the abyss of it by being here with you now!"

"No, you don't understand—"

"I understand completely, and I—"

"I want to marry you," he quickly interjected.

It took a moment for his words to find their place in her mind, and when they did, they clearly shocked her. She reared back as if he'd burned her, her expression hurtful, as if she believed he was jesting somehow.

"Did . . . did you . . ."

"I did just express my desire to marry you."

She still seemed unconvinced, still looked at him distrustfully, and he suddenly realized that he'd gone about this all wrong. What an idiot he had been! He abruptly went down on one knee and took her hand in his. "Lady Ava—"

She gasped, and covered her mouth with her hand.

He didn't smile, but looked directly into her eyes as he covered her hand with both of his. As peculiar as it was to him, he realized he suddenly needed her answer. "Lady Ava, would you do me the honor of being my wife?"

She gasped again, only heavenward, then slid down the wall to her haunches, so that she was eye level with him. She cupped his face in her hands, her gaze intent. "Do you sincerely mean this?" she asked him earnestly.

"Would I ask this, the answer to which will shape the rest of my life, if I did not sincerely mean it?"

"But we hardly know one another!"

"We know that it would be a good match of fortune, standing, and compatibility, do we not?"

"Yes . . . with the possible exception of fortune, my lord, for I have none."

"I don't care."

She drew several breaths as she studied his face, her eyes full of confusion and mistrust, but also a glimmer of hope.

"Lady Ava, you must end my agony," he said quietly. "Will you accept my offer of marriage?"

For a moment, he feared she would reject him, and the swell of bitter disappointment filled his throat, surprising him. But then she smiled brilliantly, illuminating the dimly lit room. "Yes," she said. "*Yes!*" She lurched forward, kissing his face, almost knocking them off balance in the process, their fall stopped by his stength.

He kissed her, aware that he was, remarkably, relieved and even a bit happy that she had consented. He lifted his head and grinned. "I should very much like to continue this happy moment, but I must go now and do my duty."

She nodded, her eyes still full of astonishment. He leapt to his feet, reached for her hand, and pulled her up, then helped her arrange her gown. When he was satisfied that her gown was properly arranged, he smiled at her. "You want this, don't you?"

She laughed a little, her smile beaming up at him. "More than you could possibly know, my lord."

He kissed her cheek, then opened the door for her.

When the Marquis of Middleton and Lady Ava Fairchild emerged from the private receiving room, the assembled crowd went mad with titillation. But their excitement at being present for a piece of delicious scandal was nothing like the small riot of gossip that quickly spread throughout their ranks.

The marquis, they said, had asked for Lady Ava's hand in marriage and she had accepted.

Men wondered if he knew she had no money. Women, their feelings bruised by this sudden pairing, wondered if she knew he was having a love affair with Lady Waterstone.

And as the auction proceeded—Lady Ava handing the items to be auctioned to Lord Middleton (who raised a record sum for the hospital)—only three people were not gossiping excitedly about the extraordinary news: Lady Elizabeth Robertson, who took the news quite hard; Sir Garrett, who perhaps took the news even harder; and the Duke of Redford.

Several people standing near the duke said that, in fact, he looked furious.

Eleven

〜🙠🙢〜

Early the next morning, Jared was summoned, as he fully expected he would be, to Redford House, the massive town house on Park Lane where his father held court. He strode ahead of the butler who announced him into the large study where his father was standing at the massive hearth, warming his hands.

The duke did not offer a hand to his son—he barely spared him a glance at all. "How dare you," he said calmly, "make an offer of marriage without my consent."

There were times such as this that Jared absolutely despised his father. He'd expected questions, but he had at least hoped his father would acknowledge that he had, at last, done as he wanted. "You have cajoled me, threatened me, and you have won. I thought you would be pleased that I have decided to marry as you have been so keen to see me do."

"*Yes,* I am keen to see you married!" the duke suddenly exploded. "But I was keen to see you marry someone of acceptable lineage!"

"Lady Ava Fairchild is the eldest daughter of the late Earl of Bingley," Jared said, working hard to maintain his composure.

"And she is also the stepdaughter of Lord Downey," he said acidly. "A man who would be nothing more than a commoner had it not been for his uncle's generous connections. He's not even come to me to propose the *possibility* of a match with my son! Perhaps he is wise enough to know that this woman cannot be better suited to you than Lady Elizabeth."

"You insult me by implying that someone other than I must speak to you before I am permitted to make an offer of marriage!" Jared spat.

"It is not only customary, it is necessary. You're no common smithy's son!"

Jared choked on a bark of bitter laughter. "No, your grace, I am not. Would that I were."

The duke snorted with disdain. "You've done quite well as the son of a duke. What are the terms?"

Jared shrugged insouciantly. "I have not inquired."

His father's gaze narrowed to little beads of sheer disgust. "Do you mean to tell me that you have made an offer of marriage to a woman who will one day be a duchess without discussing the *terms*?"

The question infuriated Jared. "The terms are rather simple, your grace. I chose a virgin of good standing who is capable of providing an heir," he snapped. "All else is immaterial."

"Don't be coy," his father shot back, striding away from the mantel to the bellpull. "You know perfectly well that a match of such importance requires a certain appraisal of her suitability."

And here it went, their singular inability to speak to one another without harm. "It is not my intent to be *coy*," Jared said tightly. "But it is plain that her *suitability* has more to do with her womb than her fortune."

His father gasped. "How dare you be so vulgar with me?"

"Are you any less vulgar with me? You have told me on more than one occasion that you must have your heir. I have brought you a *suitable* vessel to provide just that, and now you would know her *worth*?"

"As usual, you have no concept of what you say," his father said angrily. "You are so very careless with this family's responsibility." His gaze raked over Jared. "You are a disappointment to me."

"I can be no more a disappointment as a son than you are a father. And frankly, I should rather be careless than heartless. You have interfered with every aspect of my life. Could you not at least allow me the courtesy of choosing the woman with whom I shall spend the rest of my days on this earth? I intend to marry Ava Fairchild, sir. The offer has been made. If that does not please you, there is nothing more I can do."

The duke paled; his gray eyes turned wintery. "Nothing more you can do?" he managed, his laugh sour. "You could be the son I raised you to be. You could make a better effort to understand what honor and duty and pride mean before you drag our name through the mud with a woman like that whore Waterstone! You could heed my advice instead of turning your back to me time and again! And now you have only made this situation worse by offering without thought! I would advise you not to engage in any more talk of marriage until this woman has accepted our terms."

It was all Jared could do to keep from lunging at the old man. Or wringing his neck. "Her name is Lady Ava Fairchild. And they are not *our* terms," he managed to say, his voice full of dark anger. "They are *mine*. All else may be yours, but *this* marriage is mine." He turned and strode for the door before his father could speak, his hands aching to be around his father's gullet.

He should have gone to his club or home—somewhere quiet, somewhere he could take a deep breath and calm himself. His father was a difficult man, and Jared had learned when he was a boy that if he took the time to recover his composure, he could usually smash down the hurt and resentment into a compact, neat little box that he stuffed away somewhere deep inside himself.

But today was different, for he had let go of his pride and conceded to his father's wishes, had agreed to a perfectly acceptable match, yet his father still found fault. Jared's anger was so raw that he could scarcely think, much less calm himself. His first thought was to speak with his intended bride and set a wedding date as soon as was possible.

He barked at his driver to proceed directly to the Downey town house, where he sprang out of the carriage before the footman could descend and strode to the door, rapping hard with the brass handle.

A man dressed in an ill-fitting suit of black clothing opened the door almost instantly and peered curiously at him. "Aye?"

Aye? Jared was momentarily taken aback, but quickly recovered, reaching into his coat pocket for a card. "Lord Middleton calling for Lady Ava," he muttered, holding the card up between two fingers.

"A caller!" the butler said aloud, looking terribly pleased. "One moment, milord." He turned away from the door, walked across the foyer to a small console, and picked up a silver tray, with which he returned and held out to Jared. Jared impatiently dropped the card onto the tray.

"Right, then. Now I'm to take it up," the butler informed him.

"I am quite clear on the procedure, sir, so if you would hurry it along."

The butler smiled—one tooth missing, Jared couldn't help noticing—and stepped back. "You might come in, then."

Sweeping his hat from his head, Jared stepped across the threshold. He'd never been inside the Downey home, and while he found the décor tasteful, it seemed rather Spartan, the house small.

The butler held the silver tray out from his body, as if he were afraid to touch Jared's card. "This way, if you please, milord."

"Would you not deliver it first?" Jared asked as he removed his gloves.

The question seemed to confuse the butler. He wrinkled his brow, seemed to be lost in thought for a moment, then shook his head. "No, milord. You're to accompany me, I'm quite certain."

Rather odd, Jared thought, but he supposed they lived without the suffocating bonds of formality here, which, under different circumstances, he might appreciate. He followed the butler up a narrow staircase, then down an even narrower corridor to a pair of polished doors, which the butler instantly threw open without knocking.

Inside, three women gasped and jerked their gazes to the door. Ava was the first to react, practically leaping from her seat and rushing toward the butler. Her sister, seated beside her, jumped up and whirled about, and seemed to be stuffing something in a basket as she stole several furtive glances over her shoulder.

And the third woman—dressed in the gray of a

maid's uniform—smiled so lustfully at him that Jared feared for her employment.

Ava did not seem to notice her at all as she frantically grabbed the silver tray the butler held and pushed the man back toward the door. "Mr. Morris!" she exclaimed, smiling anxiously at Jared. "You're to *announce* the guests."

"I'd do so, mu'um, could I read his card."

That earned a furious blush from Ava. She glanced nervously at Jared, then the tray, and snatched up the snowy white card. "You should really wear your spectacles, sir," she gingerly chastised the butler. "It is Lord Middleton calling."

"Lord Middleton calling, mu'um," Morris said, bowing slightly.

"Thank you," Ava responded tightly. Behind her, Lady Phoebe clasped her hands demurely in front of her, but with her foot she pushed a basket out of Jared's sight.

"How do you do, my lord?" Ava said, curtsying.

"Very well, thank you." He glanced at the maid, who continued to smile wantonly.

Ava noticed his gaze and frowned at her maid. "Sally, will you kindly find Lucy and have tea brought up? My lord, please do come in," she said, motioning toward a settee. "Mr. Morris, that will be all."

"Aye," he said cheerfully, and walked out of the room.

Sally, however, was not so easily put off.

Ava's smile faded. "Sally, that will be *all*, thank you."

Surprisingly, at least to Jared, who often forgot his servants were even in the same room because they were so deadly quiet and inconspicuous, this maid frowned at Ava. "As you wish," she said petulantly.

He would have dismissed her from employment on the spot.

Ava, however, merely smiled, smoothed back a loose strand of honey blond hair that had fallen over her eye, and said uncertainly, "How . . . how good of you to call."

"Perhaps now is not a good—"

"It's *perfect*," she said, more securely, and reached out her hand to him. He took it and brought it to his lips. "Will you sit?"

"Thank you." With a flip of his tails, he settled into the seat she had indicated. Ava and her sister sat on an opposing settee at the same moment, side by side, and flashed twin, beaming smiles at him.

Ava had a fair face, he'd give her that, as did her sister. Both of them were pretty in an unconventional way, but it was the *joie de vivre* in Ava that he found most attractive. Attractive, perhaps . . . but *marriage*? He swallowed down a lump of sudden hesitation and looked at his hands.

"How good of you to call," Ava said again, forcing conversation.

Jared glanced up and saw that her hand was nervously clutching her knee. "Thank you," he said for want of anything better, and glanced at her sister. "I had hoped we might talk," he said softly.

Ava and her sister exchanged a quick look.

"If you will excuse me, my lord," Phoebe said, and stood up. "I was just, ah . . . just in the midst of writing a letter to our cousin, Greer." Her eyes flicked to the writing desk, as did Ava's. The desk was remarkably free of ink or paper. "I mean to say, I was in the midst of *thinking* of writing a letter—"

"The inkwell," Ava said evenly, "has been refilled.

It's just there, in the desk drawer. So you might attempt your letter, darling."

"Yes. A letter," Phoebe repeated, and stood up, marched to the writing desk, sat hard on the wooden chair, and spread her hands before her, looking at the desk as if she'd never seen it before. She was, Jared realized, doing her best to give them some privacy.

"In the drawer," Ava said again, smiling anxiously at Jared. "You will find ink *and* paper in the drawer. A pen as well." Her smile went brighter, as bright as it had been yesterday in the Prince's Pavilion at Vauxhall. Moreover, it was a smile that somehow made him feel better about what he was doing, more sure of himself.

He leaned forward, planted his arm on his knee, and said softly, so that Phoebe would not hear, "If you will forgive me . . . I would hope that we might see our way to the altar sooner rather than later."

"Oh!" Ava said, her eyes lighting up.

He glanced at Phoebe, who had yet to locate the ink, but was making a concerted effort to find it by opening all the drawers of the writing desk. "I thought perhaps we might marry at my seat, Broderick Abbey, under special license. I have taken the liberty of applying to the archbishop for it."

She blinked. Her smile faded.

"Lady Ava?"

She likewise stole a glimpse of her sister, who had not found the ink but a letter of some sort, which she was pretending to read very closely, then looked at him earnestly. "I must inquire, my lord—will this . . . *marriage*," she said, stammering a little on the word, "protect my sister and cousin from being bartered off in marriage to the first man who asks? My stepfather will want to see them married quickly and without regard for their preferences. I should like to offer them a haven, if you—"

"Of course."

"But . . . but Greer is in Wales just now—at least we *hope* she is in Wales—and Phoebe, well, Phoebe—"

"Madam, my home will be your home, and therefore, by extension, home to your sister and cousin."

"Really?" she asked hopefully, and straightened up, beaming at him.

"Then you will agree to travel to Broderick Abbey to marry?" he asked.

"I will. When do you propose?"

"Soon. I cannot bear the wait."

"Soon?" She suddenly leaned forward again, so that her face was close enough to kiss if he were so inclined. "How soon do you mean?" she whispered.

"As soon as is possible."

Her pale green eyes lit up and she smiled. "But you realize, my lord, that there will be all sorts of wretched speculation as to why we marry quickly, do you not?" she whispered.

"I don't care," he whispered back.

"What of a dowry? Shouldn't you know the details of my dowry? My mother left a modest amount—"

"A dowry is not necessary," he said quickly. "Leave it to your sister and cousin."

Ava straightened again and blinked. "But . . . but my dowry is the only fund left to me, in the event you, ah . . . in the event you, well, *perished*, to say it quite bluntly. Not that you would," she said hastily. "I mean, unless you were an old man. Which you will be one day, but then so shall I be an old woman, and I wouldn't have *need* of it—"

"Lady Ava," he calmly interrupted. "I shall ensure you are left with adequate pin money should I perish. I will even put it in a separate estate so that it is legally yours if you desire. But I would prefer that we forgo any negotiations with your stepfather about the dowry as well as forgo the posting of the marriage banns so that we might proceed as quickly as possible."

"All right," she said slowly. "Shall we say a month?"

"I had in mind a date sooner than that. I had in mind Friday next."

"Friday next?" Ava exclaimed.

"Friday next?" Phoebe echoed, startling Ava and Jared. "Are you quite mad, my lord? There's no time for a trousseau or a gown—"

Jared glanced at Ava. "I will provide whatever you need."

"No, Ava!" Phoebe cried. "What of Greer? You can't marry without Greer at your side!" she exclaimed just as the door flew open.

Any response Ava might have given was lost as a rather large woman bustled into the room, carrying a silver tea service and a plate piled dangerously high with scones.

Jared quickly gained his feet.

"Good afternoon, good afternoon!" she said as she hurried to the table between the settees and lay the service down. "I am Miss Lucille Pennebacker, Lord Downey's sister and guardian to these two young women." She thrust out her hand.

Jared took it. "Lord Middleton, at your service."

Lucille Pennebacker instantly dipped into a girth-defying curtsy. "It is indeed a pleasure, sir! Please do sit," she said as he helped her up, "and allow me to serve you tea." She was already pouring. "How kind of you to offer for our Ava. Now that she is of a certain age, my brother and I had despaired of receiving a proper offer."

"Miss Pennebacker!" Ava cried, clearly mortified.

The woman shrugged as she handed a china cup and saucer to Middleton first. "It's very well true!" she said, pouring another cup. "You're one foot on the shelf, my dear." She settled onto the settee next to Jared with her back ramrod straight and her cup balanced precariously on her knee as Ava rolled her eyes at her sister.

"My brother is expected within weeks," Miss Pennebacker said. "I suppose you'll want to speak to him as soon as he arrives?"

"Unfortunately, we haven't time to wait," Jared said politely. "Lady Ava and I have agreed we will not prolong this engagement. In fact, we will be leaving for Broderick Abbey by the end of the week."

The doughy woman's cup froze midway to her mouth and her little finger, properly extended for tea drinking, likewise froze. She did not move, did not speak, but could only blink big black eyes at him.

"*Ahem,*" Ava said, trying to draw Jared's attention.

He ignored Ava and smiled pleasantly at her chaperone. "Are you quite all right, Miss Pennebacker?"

Miss Pennebacker suddenly sounded as if she was strangling. She put down her teacup with a clatter and gaped at Ava. Then at Jared. "You cannot mean this!" she exclaimed as she pressed a chubby hand to her equally chubby bosom. "You cannot marry without Egbert's consent! It's just not done!"

"I beg your pardon, Miss Pennebacker, but have you any reason to believe Lord Downey would refuse my suit?" Jared asked.

"N-no," she said, shaking her head.

"Then we shall proceed." He smiled.

The woman's face turned red, her eyes filled with shock. "*Ava?*" she squealed.

Ava gave Jared a quick but murderous look, then smiled kindly at Miss Pennebacker. "I agree with Lord Middleton."

"Oh dear," Miss Pennebacker said again, and fell back against the settee, staring at the ceiling with shock.

"Oh my lord," Ava sighed, and handed her teacup to Phoebe as she moved to assist her keeper.

Twelve

~~~~~~

Lady Waterstone developed a very sour feeling in the pit of her stomach the day Lady Flynn called. Lady Flynn had been the first on Miranda's doorstep the day after the bloody charity auction with the news that Middleton had supposedly offered for a young bird. Lady Flynn prided herself on dispensing, posthaste, any and all news concerning Middleton. Miranda had no reason to think today was any different.

Having heard the extraordinary tale of what had transpired at the charity auction, Miranda had smiled and assured Lady Flynn that she was well aware of Middleton's intentions to marry, and thought nothing of it. "I shall remain his particular friend," she'd said with a coy smile.

But today, the sour feeling quickly turned to nausea, and she could not hide the bitter taste of it.

"They are to marry at once, at Broderick Abbey," Lady Flynn said as she picked over a basket of pastries. "What do you suppose that means?"

"I couldn't rightly say," Miranda said. "He has not taken me into his confidence."

"Well, I'll tell you what all of London thinks it means," Lady Flynn said pertly. "And it's scandalous."

Miranda rather imagined it was.

When Lady Flynn had taken her leave, she told her butler that she was not receiving any more callers, closed the door to her bedroom suite and locked it, then sat down on her chaise, her hands pressed against her abdomen and the uneasiness at the core of her.

He hadn't even told her he would marry. He hadn't responded to her letter, either. He hadn't spoken to her since the day he had come to tell her he was done.

Miranda's pulse had leapt dangerously when he said that he was ending their affair, and she'd quickly crossed the room to him, put her hand against his square jaw, and gazed up into his eyes. "Surely you cannot mean it, my love," she'd whispered in a sultry voice. "You can't possibly put me aside for long—not after all that we've shared."

He smiled coldly, his eyes raking over her as he wrapped long fingers around her wrist and pulled her hand from his face. "We shared nothing more than a mutual physical desire for one another. My situation and responsibility to the title are immutable. I have a duty to perform."

"Yes of course! But what has that to do with me? With *us*?"

He'd gazed into her face, his lips pressed firmly together. "Nothing," he said quietly. "That is why I am ending it. We really are nothing to one another."

She'd been stung by the easy way he said it and had gasped with grief. "How *cruel* of you."

"Do you deny it?"

"Of course I deny it! I love you!" she cried, but she didn't love him, not really. She was fond of him, fonder still of their physical relationship. What she truly loved about him was his position in society, his remarkable wealth and generosity, and suddenly she felt entirely too vulnerable. For the first time since their passionate affair had begun, she was fearful of losing him as a benefactor.

The queasiness of fear only intensified when he bid her farewell.

But Miranda was not defeated so easily. She would have him back in her bed, his favors filling her house, her closet. The moment he had done his duty by his sweet little bride, he'd want a woman.

To convince herself this was true, Miranda decided to have a look at his little bride.

Phoebe declared Ava had lost her mind. Ava agreed that it was entirely possible, but as everything was happening so quickly, she didn't have time to think— she had only three days to prepare for her departure, and then, once at Broderick Abbey, only three days to prepare for her wedding. There was no time at all to dwell on the thought that she would be the *wife* of a man who one day would be a duke.

A man she scarcely knew, really.

That thought occurred to her quite often.

As often as the thought that she had *nothing* to wear.

To make matters worse, as word spread around Mayfair, she was plagued with a sudden rush of callers. People she knew only casually were suddenly calling as if they were old friends, sniffing around about the details of her wedding and her courtship.

Lady Purnam was, naturally, the first to call, the tone of her voice as disapprovingly unpleasant as her mien. "How is it *possible*," she demanded without preamble, "that you could agree to something so indecorous?"

"I beg your pardon!" Ava protested.

"Don't behave so missishly with me, madam! This rush to obtain a special license so that you may marry within a fortnight is scandalous! The entire world will think you are with child!" she'd all but shouted, banging her parasol on the floor with each word.

"I hardly think the entire *world* will be concerned with my wedding, Lady Purnam, but in the event the entire world *is* concerned, I don't care!"

Lady Purnam gasped with shock. "Have you any idea how extremely disappointed your mother would be?" she shrieked.

"My mother would congratulate me on a match that was convenient *and* inspired!"

"Oh! You are incorrigible!" Lady Purnam cried. She did not stay long, so incensed was she that Ava would not listen to reason.

When Miss Molly Frederick and Miss Anne Williams called, Ava suspected that their mutual friend, Lady Elizabeth, had put them up to it. After the obligatory congratulations and talk of the wedding, Miss Frederick mused, "How do you suppose Lord Middleton came to his decision to offer for *you*? After all, there were so many debutantes for whom he might have offered."

"I suppose," Ava said airily, "that he was attracted by my inherent charm."

Phoebe, who was seated across from her, almost spit her tea as Miss Frederick and Miss Williams exchanged a look of astonishment at her cheek.

"You are indeed quite charming," Miss Williams lied solicitously. "But I should think you would not like to be married to someone who is known for reckless behavior."

"Reckless? Lord Middleton?" Ava responded with

a gay laugh. "My fiancé does indeed enjoy a good sporting event," she said, crafting her response from the things she had read or heard of him. "But I rather think he shall tame his ways once we are married."

Behind Miss Frederick's head, Phoebe rolled her eyes.

"I am certain he will," Miss Frederick said with a thin smile. "But nevertheless, I should not like to be married to a rogue."

"Indeed?" Ava said, and smiled wickedly. "I should think marriage to a rogue would be far more exciting than marriage to a vicar," she said, knowing full well that a parish vicar had made his intent to marry Miss Frederick well known.

And, in fact, Miss Frederick colored quite red and did not mention the rogue again.

When they had left, Phoebe folded her arms across her middle and shook her head. "You are shameless."

"Why?" Ava demanded. "Why should I explain my decision to the likes of *them*? Why is everyone so anxious to know how it is the Marquis of Middleton offered for *me*, poor Ava Fairchild? Why can't they just accept that he esteems me?"

"Oh, I don't know . . . perhaps because it happened so quickly without any sort of courtship?" Phoebe asked.

Ava ignored her. She ignored all the prying callers. She had her doubts, of course she did, but she found it insupportable for anyone to believe she was not as deserving of his esteem as anyone else. She was certainly as deserving as Lady Elizabeth. She met their prying questions with scorn—but none of them had prepared her for the arrival of the temptress herself, Lady Waterstone.

She called one day in the company of some of the

women from the Ladies' Beneficent Society. "How very happy you must be," she'd said, taking Ava's hands and smiling in a way that made Ava's blood run cold.

"Indeed I am," Ava said, perhaps a bit too forcefully.

"Do you think you'll prefer Broderick Abbey to town?" Lady Waterstone asked, her eyes glittering.

"I . . . I don't know," Ava answered honestly. "I've not seen Broderick Abbey."

"I think you will find it lovely and the country air divine. It's a wonderful place for children," she said. "I've seen it often," she continued as she took a seat Ava had not offered. "I particularly admire the master suite. The colors are very inviting." She looked up, saw Ava's look of horror, and smiled. "The house is open to the public when he is abroad, you know."

"No," Ava said weakly. "I did not know."

For the remainder of the call, Ava could hardly speak—she was completely obsessed with the question of just how *many* times Lady Waterstone had seen Broderick Abbey—and in particular, the master suite? How long had they been lovers? How was it he had left someone as worldly and beautiful as Lady Waterstone for her?

She despaired the visit would ever end, but when it did, she vowed she'd not accept another caller.

Of all the women who had called on her, only Miss Grace Holcomb was kind to her, and seemed truly excited that she was to marry a marquis. "He's quite handsome and so charming. I am so happy for your good fortune, Lady Ava. I hope I will know such fortune one day," she'd said sincerely.

Not even Phoebe was particularly kind—but then again, Phoebe was very exacerbated by the whole affair, as she was making Ava's wedding dress by sewing well into the night, as well as helping make arrangements to pick up Ava's life and move it to Broderick Abbey.

"I can't imagine what you must be thinking," Phoebe snapped at Ava the morning she was to meet Middleton's father, the duke. "Granted, you have made yourself a match, Ava, but to wed him in a *week*? There is no time to do anything properly!"

"And what will you do for a lady's maid?" Lucy demanded just as adamantly. "You cannot be a marchioness without a lady's maid! Everyone will talk!"

"That's very true," Ava said thoughtfully.

No one said anything for a moment, and then slowly, all eyes turned to Sally, who was sitting on the chaise.

Sally's eyes widened. "Me?"

"Yes!" Ava cried.

"Oh no!" Sally protested, gaining her feet. "I won't go off and live with country bumpkins!"

"That's a bit high and mighty if you ask me," Lucy said.

"Beggin' your pardon, mu'um, but I never met a country bloke who knew his arse—"

"I'll pay you handsomely," Ava quickly interjected before Sally could finish her sentence.

"Pay?" Sally said, relaxing a little. "How much?"

"One hundred and fifty pounds," Ava said, ignoring Lucy's squeal of shock and dismay. "You'll come to Broderick Abbey a week after I arrive there with as much of a trousseau as Phoebe can throw together."

Sally put her hands on her hips, puffed out her cheeks a moment, then exhaled and nodded. "Done. But I won't live in the country forever, mu'um. Six months is all I'll give you."

"Fair enough," Ava said.

"Well, if you *must* take her, I will show her the trunks and how to fill them properly, like a good lady's maid," Lucy said, seeming quite cheerful that Sally would be leaving, too. "Come along, then," she said imperiously.

"I'm coming. Don't lace your corset so tight," Sally groused, and proceeded to follow Lucille out.

"What of Greer?" Phoebe demanded when she and Ava were alone. "You can't go through this without Greer. It would hurt her so."

"Even if I were to send for Greer, she wouldn't come back," Ava said. "She is up to her elbows in trouble." Indeed, a letter had come from Greer just yesterday. She claimed to be quite surprised by the changes at her old family home, and, particularly, how impoverished it all seemed to be now.

Nothing is as I remember, she had written.

The estate is in disrepair. Mr. Percy believes that perhaps my uncle incurred a rather sizable debt as a result of his fondness for horses.

"Mr. Percy again!" Ava had exclaimed as they read it.

In spite of the many changes, however, I am confident that I can and will determine what has happened to the family estate and will return forthwith to you. Mr. Percy has urged me to call on a solicitor, who might be able to shed a bit of light on my family's affairs, such as they are.

"Who *is* this Mr. Percy?" Phoebe cried. "How can we possibly trust him?"

"We cannot. I don't like it at all," Ava said darkly.

"Write her straightaway and tell her that she *cannot* trust this mysterious Mr. Percy!"

"I will, after supper. At present, we have too much to do with your blasted nuptials to stop and write Greer," Phoebe said testily.

"All right, Phoebe, I know you are displeased, but what choice did I have?" Ava exclaimed. "You know as well as I that if I hadn't made this match, when Lord Downey returned, he would hand me off to Sir Garrett straightaway! At least this way, we shall rest assured that we shall not want!"

"Surely his fortune is not the only consideration! Do you esteem him? Do you have anything in common with him that might suggest you will live compatibly as man and wife? Isn't the point of a proper courtship to determine if you suit?"

Ava snorted at that. "Don't be naïve. This is about convenience and fortune, Phoebe—"

"And if it's not convenient? If it is about something entirely different than his fortune, what will you do then?"

"What do you mean?" Ava demanded. "This is a good match of fortune and standing! And if I displease him, then I suppose he shall go his way and I shall go mine!"

"He shall go his way, all right," Phoebe snapped. "Into the bed of Lady Waterstone."

Why that should sting so terribly, Ava could not say, but she glared at her sister. "You don't know him," she said quietly.

"And neither do you," Phoebe responded tightly. "So at least allow time for a proper courtship."

"No," Ava said stubbornly. "There is no need. He truly esteems me, I can see it."

She truly believed he *did* esteem her in some way. Certainly she had come to esteem *him*. He was kind. And playful in a way she found charming. And when he smiled . . . dear Lord, her insides turned to soup.

Phoebe sighed, shook her head, and sat. "You're mad. I don't care what you say," she said and refused to speak again as her needle moved in and out of the gown Ava would wear to marry Middleton.

That was just as well—Ava was preparing to meet the Duke of Redford and didn't have time for Phoebe's angst. She lifted her chin and looked at her reflection in the mirror. She was wearing a soft plum day gown Phoebe had made for her, trimmed in black. "What do you think?" she asked with her back to the mirror so that she might see the train that fell from between her shoulder blades to the floor.

Phoebe glanced up and frowned. "How will you explain to the duke that you are so quick to wed without your stepfather's consent?"

It was a very good question, and while Ava would never admit it, she was actually afraid of meeting the duke. She'd seen him only once or twice, usually across the room at a ball or gathering, and he'd always seemed so stern and tall and forbidding. "I don't know how I shall explain it," she muttered. "I can scarcely explain it to myself. Now do please tell me how I look!"

Phoebe's grim expression softened a little and she smiled. "Lovely, Ava. He cannot find fault with your appearance. You will give him beautiful heirs."

Heirs. Ava sighed. Yet something else she had not thought through entirely. *God*, she longed for her mother!

She had precious little time to long, however, because a few minutes later, there was a rap on the door, and Mr. Morris shouted from the other side, "A carriage awaits, milady!"

Just then the door flew open and Sally burst through, passing Mr. Morris. "And what a carriage it *is*," she squealed, grabbing Ava's hand and pulling her to the window to see. Below them on the street was a landau carriage so new that the gold Middleton crest emblazoned on the side glinted in the sunlight. It was pulled by a team of two huge grays, adorned with black and gold plumes.

"Dear God," Ava murmured as Phoebe pushed her aside to see.

"Oh *my*," Phoebe said, her voice full of wonder. "I've never been so close to a carriage as fine as that."

"I have," Sally said, peering down at it.

Ava and Phoebe looked at her, then at the carriage again. "Do you suppose the squabs are velvet?" Phoebe asked in a whisper.

"Oh, they'd be velvet, all right," Sally quickly assured them.

"If you don't mind, milady," Mr. Morris called from behind them. All three women whirled about. "The driver is waiting."

"The driver? Did not Lord Middleton come to escort me?" How could she possibly arrive on the duke's doorstep without her fiancé?

"I wouldn't know, mu'um. I only say what they tell me, I do."

"Tell the driver I shall be along momentarily."

As Mr. Morris went out, Phoebe looked at Ava suspiciously. "Where *is* he?"

"He's obviously waiting for me in the coach or at Redford House," Ava said firmly, and rather unconvincingly, as she picked up her reticule.

"Remember," Phoebe said kindly, "be very pleasant and smile often. The duke wants to know you are the pleasant sort and not one to give trouble."

"But—"

"On second thought," Phoebe quickly interrupted as she handed Ava the matching redingote she'd altered for her, "perhaps it is best you do not speak at all if you can avoid it."

Ava snorted as she shrugged into the coat. "Thank you, darling." She picked up her bonnet, kissed her sister, and waved to Sally on her way out.

She should feel happy, she thought, but she didn't feel happy at all. She'd never dreaded anything quite as badly as this in her life—it felt a little as if she were marching off to a funeral.

Thirteen

~~~⚬~~~

Middleton was not waiting for her in the carriage as she'd hoped, and, in fact, had sent no word at all. The driver said he was to see her to Redford House on Park Lane and no other instruction was given him.

When the carriage pulled into the small courtyard of the palatial Redford House and the footman opened the door, Ava's stomach clenched. What was she to do? Proceed without her betrothed?

Proceed, apparently, as the footman had put down a step for her and was holding up his gloved hand. Ava leaned forward and glanced out into the courtyard, where two more footmen had suddenly raced from the front door to stand attentively at the bottom of the steps.

"Ah . . ." she said, wincing a little, "is Lord Middleton about?"

The footman glanced over his shoulder. "I do not see him, my lady."

"Don't you?" she asked weakly, craning her neck to have a look about the courtyard. "I confess to being a bit at a loss. Are you quite certain his lordship did not send a message to me? Perhaps with instructions to wait somewhere other than the duke's drive?"

With the barest hint of a smile, the footman helped her down. "He did not, madam. Perhaps the duke's butler could be of some assistance."

"The butler, of course!" she exclaimed, relieved. "I should have thought of it myself. Thank you."

The footman was smiling fully now, and he touched the tip of his hat. "A pleasure," he said, stepped back, and looked straight ahead as she straightened her redingote and bonnet.

Once she was completely straightened out and had passed as much time as was possible without drawing attention to herself, Ava reluctantly proceeded to the steps leading up to the house and smiled at the two footmen there. It seemed entirely too late to turn back now—she supposed she was about to meet her future father-in-law without benefit of introduction from her future husband. And why was that? God forbid, had he changed his mind? Had he discovered he no longer wanted to marry her, but his letter explaining his change of heart had not yet arrived at her door?

No, that was ridiculous. He wouldn't have sent a carriage for her if he'd had a change of heart. Perhaps he did indeed intend to marry her but leave her fully to her own devices, beginning with the proper introduction to his father. Whatever the reason, this did not augur a particularly good beginning, did it?

As she stood pondering her predicament, the massive pair of entry doors opened, and a small, impeccably dressed man stepped out. "My lady? Might I be of assistance?"

"How do you do. I am . . ." *Waiting for my betrothed to do me the courtesy of introducing me to his father.*

The butler cocked his head to one side.

"I am Lady Ava Fairchild," she said, and lifting her chin, marched up the steps. If there was one thing the Fairchild women did fairly well, it was to stare down adversity and muddle through. It wasn't as if she'd never met a duke before—of course she had. This one was no different—he wore the seal of the royal order of something or other on his chest just like all the others.

When she reached the door, the butler stood to one side to allow her entry. She swept in as if she were queen of the castle, stopped directly in front of a console, and went about removing her bonnet.

"Shall I tell his grace what your call regards?" the butler politely inquired.

"Is he not expecting me?" she asked, and thrust her bonnet at him. "I don't believe I have come with a card—"

"It is not necessary. I shall tell him you have called." He bowed deep, put her bonnet aside on the console, and walked away.

His grace would think she was a loose woman, calling on him all alone. The more she thought of it, the angrier she became, and she jerked her gloves off, one finger at a time, and tossed them onto the console next to her bonnet. The footmen had returned, and she shrugged out of her redingote and held it up to one of them on the tip of her finger.

The footman rushed to take it.

As she stood there, lost in thought, the front entry opened again and Middleton swept in, his cloak snapping around his ankles as he strode across the marble foyer to the console. "Forgive me," he said, and leaned down and pressed his lips to her cheek. "I was unavoidably detained."

Detained? The man smelled of whiskey and smoke.

She could just imagine how he'd been detained and glared at him.

He did not seem to notice her expression as he impatiently shook off his cloak and handed it to a waiting footman. "Are you quite prepared then?" he asked, straightening his cuffs.

"Prepared?"

Middleton glanced at her sidelong. "To meet the Duke of Redford."

She was here, wasn't she? "I suppose I am," she said.

"Very well," he said briskly, and held out his arm. "Let us repair, then, to the lion's den."

Ava started to ask him what he meant by that, but he'd already picked up her hand, placed it squarely on his arm, and begun walking. "I would advise you to use an economy of words," he said flatly, his expression grim. "It will not do to prolong this conversation. Respond when spoken to, allow him to have a look at you, but otherwise, do not speak."

"I beg your pardon?" Ava asked indignantly, and yanked her hand from his arm.

Middleton stopped midstride and sighed irritably as he turned to face her. "Lady Ava," he said shortly, sounding terribly formal for a man who would marry her in a matter of days, "allow me this—I am well acquainted with the man. He is not a particularly congenial sort, and as he did not personally select you to be my wife, he is not in a particularly welcoming mood."

Ava gasped.

"Therefore," Middleton continued, ignoring her shock, "I advise you only so that this interview will be over quite rapidly and you emerge free of harm. Understood?"

"Free of harm?" she echoed, mortified. "You would

choose *this* moment to tell me your father is not happy with the match?" she exclaimed, and glanced frantically over her shoulder. "Really," she whispered loudly, rising up on her toes so that her lips were near his ear, "shouldn't you have said something before *now*?"

Middleton actually laughed. "Before *now*? Have you forgotten that I proposed marriage to you only this Friday past?"

Ava colored slightly. "It still seems you might have found time to mention it."

He smiled again, and touched his fingers to her jaw. "There was no time to tell you," he said. "And to have told you any sooner wouldn't have altered my father's feelings."

That was an excellent point, and really, when he smiled, she couldn't help but be charmed by him. Standing there in that wide, carpeted corridor, with the paintings of Middleton's ancestors staring down at her, Ava wished that he really did love her.

"Well then?" he asked, his gaze falling to her lips. "Shall we proceed? Or would you prefer to postpone the meeting?"

"No," she said softly. "On to the lion's den."

The Duke of Redford was a proud man, but if there was one thing that gave him pride above all else, it was his son, Jared. He loved him dearly, and wanted to see his son succeed him, to have the respect he was due.

But Charles worried that his son was too much like his mother in some respects. He was something of a dreamer, just as she'd been. Jared's blind spot had always been that he believed he was free to be like any man, free to come and go and do as he pleased, answering to no one. He'd never understood or would not accept that his responsibility tethered him. He was *not* free—in some respects, he was a prisoner to his life. Every move he made was watched by his peers, every smile he turned on a woman was reported. Every bit of business he transacted was discussed in gentlemen's clubs about town.

Of course there were many privileges to offset the immutable rules of the aristocracy. His wealth alone afforded him grand opportunities. His title and handsome appearance meant he could have any woman of proper pedigree that he desired. Why Jared couldn't see it this way, why he had to buck against the reins of his fate, his father simply could not understand.

But his son had never accepted it and had made some very foolish decisions in his life that had affected others as well as himself. Even as recently as a few months ago, Jared had made a rash decision Charles could scarcely believe. Whether his son did it to defy him or because he truly, if misguidedly, believed in what he was doing—he could not seem to understand how such decisions impacted the entire duchy.

As the sole heir, every misstep, every bit of disregard he showed for his birthright and the establishment weakened the Redfords. A man's duty was to his crown and his family. Not to himself.

And now this. After cavorting with the whore Lady Waterstone, Jared had bowed to pressure and offered for a woman whose pedigree did not match that of Lady Elizabeth Robertson. He'd gone and found compatibility with the daughter of a woman who had definitely married up when she snared the Earl of Bingley in her web, a young woman who was now the stepdaughter of Lord Downey. The duke shuddered just thinking of that man.

Even now, Charles did not consider himself to be a coldhearted man, and he did sincerely wish his son well. He was determined to make his peace with Jared—he'd done what Charles had asked of him, and while he didn't approve of the match, Charles was accepting of it.

He was therefore pleasantly surprised when the woman who would be his daughter made her entrance. He expected a mousy little thing, awed by her surroundings, frightened of his stature. Lady Ava was no such woman. She walked across the room, her chin high, her eyes bright, and extended her hand to him as she sank into a perfect curtsy. "Your grace, it is my great pleasure to make your acquaintance."

Surprised, Charles lifted her up. "Thank you," he said, looking into her face. Her large green eyes seemed to sparkle naturally with a winsome smile that curved into dimples on each cheek. Her hair, the color of honey, was artfully swept up and tied with ribbon.

"You have agreed to marry my son," he said, stating it aloud more for his own benefit than hers.

"I have," she said, smiling prettily.

"And your stepfather? What is his opinion? As he has not been to call, I can only surmise he is quite pleased."

"My stepfather is not as yet aware, your grace. He is in France and won't return for another week or so."

That was a bit startling, for he would have assumed Jared spoke to the man before speaking to Lady Ava. But then again, he knew that times were changing—the formality of these matches was not nearly as rigid as that of his youth. "Well," he said,

smiling charitably as he gestured for them to sit.
"There will be plenty of time to gain his permission,
won't there?"

"I don't know," she said uncertainly. "I don't think
he shall return before we are married."

Charles stopped in his move to a chair and stared
at the young woman. "I beg your pardon?"

"We are to be married next week," Jared said.

His chest constricted around his heart. "Next
week?" he echoed. "I haven't heard of this!"

"We have only just decided and have come to tell
you." Jared spoke so easily, so coolly, that it angered
Charles. His son smiled serenely, and the smile struck
Charles with a disquieting thought—his son hated
him.

"Might I inquire as to *why* the rush to the altar, as if
I can't already surmise?"

"There is nothing to surmise," Jared said, his smile
fading. "But we saw no reason to delay it . . . do you?"

"It's absolutely scandalous!" Charles said, barely
able to control his anger. "The entire *ton* will think
your fiancée is with child!"

"She is not, sir. And we will be at Broderick Abbey,
away from the gossips who feed such rumors."

"I hardly care *where* you will be, sir. There will be
talk," Charles said sharply.

"I beg your pardon, your grace . . ."

Startled by the interruption, Charles jerked his
gaze to Lady Ava.

"I . . . I wanted to go forth," she said uncertainly.

Jared looked at her with surprise and then chuckled, whether only to annoy his father or because she
amused him, Charles could not be sure. But he turned
fully to face his would-be daughter-in-law. "I scarcely
care, Lady Ava. To marry so quickly is *vulgar*."

She blinked her wide green eyes at him, then glanced at Jared. "My fiancée is being kind," he said. "It was entirely my idea and she has graciously agreed. It is best for us."

Charles angrily turned away from his irreverent son, frustrated, appalled, and furious. "I want this abomination *stopped.*"

He heard Lady Ava's soft gasp, but his son said clearly, "No, your grace. We are committed."

He jerked around and pinned Jared with a hot look. "How dare you flaunt your impertinence—"

"We are not flaunting," Jared said calmly. "We would keep this a private matter, with only family and a few dear friends attending. And you, if it pleases you."

That stopped him. As tumultuous as the subject of marriage and heirs had been between them, Charles was stirred by the prospect of seeing his only child marry. He glanced at the pretty young woman beside him, who had not collapsed with shock and dismay as he would have expected given the tender constitution of women in general, but looked rather hopeful.

He frowned. Looked her up and down. "Is there any reason to expect you are not capable of conceiving or giving birth?" he asked bluntly.

"Your grace!" Jared protested hotly, but Charles stopped him by lifting a hand.

"It is a legitimate question."

"No, your grace," Lady Ava said quickly, her hand going to Jared's to still him, her porcelain cheeks stained pink.

Charles sighed. "And when might I be subjected to this abomination of a wedding?"

"Next Friday morning," Jared said tightly.

A lump of something—regret, disappointment

perhaps—formed in Charles's gullet, but he swallowed it down. He looked at Lady Ava once more. She was a sturdy girl, not one given to vapors, he imagined. "Very well, then. I shall witness."

One of Jared's brows lifted above the other. "Thank you," he said quietly.

"Now go," Charles said irritably, and turned away from them again, unable to comprehend why he felt so utterly dejected at that moment.

He heard a bit of whispering, then heard them quit the room. For a long time after they'd gone, he stood at the window, looking out over Hyde Park. And then he retired to his desk, took a hand portrait of Jared's mother from the bottom drawer and gazed at it.

And he hoped, with every fiber of his being, that Jared would at least find the happiness that had eluded him with Jared's mother.

Fourteen

⌾～⌾

The morning Jared took his intended and her retinue to Broderick Abbey passed quickly—they were only a half hour away from his home when Jared realized it, he'd been so lost in thought.

He glanced at Ava and her sister, both of whom had slipped into naps when their idle chatter could no longer sustain the three of them, being the strangers they really were. It had occurred to him, on the long ride home, that he did hold some affection for Ava—but the thought of marrying her still shocked him. It seemed quite unreal to him that he was on the verge of committing himself for all time, and moreover, to a woman he scarcely knew. In spite of being attracted to her, in spite of the way she appealed to him in some primal way, he could not help feeling trapped. He was about to be chained forever to a life he did not want and had never sought until his father had forced it on him.

The carriage turned up a familiar, tree-lined road that led to the abbey entrance. This was the point in the journey Jared normally felt a sense of peace wash over him. His estate was the one place on earth he was free of his father's criticism, the one place he was free to live as he pleased. Today, however, he felt nothing but a sense of dread, almost as if his father had somehow managed to invade Broderick Abbey.

Another mile and the road widened beneath tall, towering oak trees, meticulously manicured, which provided a dramatic entrance to the abbey grounds. What was left of the medieval abbey had been swallowed up by Georgian architecture; his home stretched long on either side of what had been the abbey, four stories high and U-shaped around lawns and gardens that were the envy of many a nobleman.

Jared nudged Ava; her eyes fluttered open and she smiled sleepily, pushed herself up, and yawned as she stretched her back like a cat.

"We are home," he said, surreptitiously admiring her slender form as she stretched.

"Home," she repeated dreamily—but then her eyes sparked. "Broderick Abbey?" she asked excitedly, and leaned across her sister to see out the window.

The forest was thick along the road. It was a fact that Broderick Abbey had some of the finest hunting in all of England, and it was precisely because Jared had kept the forests as pristine as possible. The coach rounded a corner, and the lake came into view, stocked with trout and pike. On the far end of the lake, he could see a part of the herd of cattle he raised at Broderick Abbey. It was ironic, really, for the Broderick fortune had been made on sheep trading in Europe centuries ago.

His father still raised sheep on his estate; Jared raised cattle.

"What's that?" Ava asked as Phoebe roused from her nap and joined Ava in looking out the window. She was pointing at the old Bridget Castle ruins that still marked a hill on his estate.

"That was once the home of my mother's ancestors. They were ousted by the Yorks." He glanced at the ruins and saw a young boy atop a mound of rocks, waving as the coach sped by, and felt his heart skip a beat.

Ava laughed with the enthusiasm of a young girl at a circus as they rolled past fields where workers were cutting hay, stone cisterns used to store rainwater, more cattle, a few sheep, and stacks of hay. "Perhaps I should have asked after your family history, sir, for my father's family ancestors were on the side of the Lancasters," she said, referring to the medieval Wars of the Roses. "I hadn't—*oh!*" she exclaimed, losing her train of thought as the stone gates marking the entrance to the grounds of Broderick Abbey came into view.

He supposed that there were any number of things they should have asked one another before coming here.

"Oh, *Ava*," Phoebe said reverently. "It's beautiful." A few moments later, they sailed through the gates and around a stand of trees, pulling to a halt in front of the ivy-covered arched entry that led into a small garden courtyard before the main entry.

The carriage rumbled to a halt, then listed slightly as the footmen clambered down. Jared leaned forward to see through to the courtyard and the double oak doors of the entry as they swung open. As the footmen put a bench down and opened the door of the coach, a string of servants came running out of the house, the women in the familiar gray gowns and white aprons, the men in standard Broderick livery of black and gold. And of course, his butler, Dawson, who was quickly lining up the staff by rank to greet the marquis and the woman who would be his wife and their mistress.

A footman from the house stepped in front of one covered by the grime of the road and held up his hand to Ava. She hesitated slightly, glanced at Jared as Phoebe helped her on with her coat, then shifted her gaze to the assembled servants, who were all peering around one another to see her. With a noticeable draw of breath, she gave her hand to the footman and stepped down. And she proceeded to shake out the skirts of her traveling gown, avoiding the curious gazes of the staff as she waited for Jared.

He followed Phoebe out and offered Ava his arm. She glanced up, to his neckcloth, before lifting her gaze to his, where he could see the consternation in her eyes. He understood her uneasiness—it was a big house with a big staff, much larger than what he assumed she was accustomed to. He gave her what he hoped was a reassuring smile. "I have long admired your courage. Do not let it desert you now," he urged her, and dipped his head to see her better, nodding almost indiscernibly to the staff. "They will certainly respect you more if you show them no fear."

Lady Ava pressed her lips firmly together. "Right you are," she muttered, then gave him a resolute nod and put a hand on his arm. He led her into the courtyard, where he began the introductions to her new staff by introducing her to his butler. "Lady Ava Fairchild," he said, "please allow me to introduce you to my butler, Mr. Dawson."

Dawson instantly bowed at the waist, and Ava extended her hand. "I've heard quite a lot of good things about you, and it is my great pleasure to make your acquaintance."

Bloody hell if old Dawson didn't look a bit surprised. He was accustomed to people like Miranda, who had a bad habit of sweeping past him as if he did not exist. The butler smiled at Ava and inclined his head. "The pleasure, my lady, is most assuredly mine."

"You'll show me about, will you, Mr. Dawson? The abbey is overwhelmingly enormous, and I am certain I shall be lost."

"It shall be an honor," Dawson said, clearly pleased to be asked.

Jared next turned to Miss Hillier, his erstwhile housekeeper, and once, a long time ago, his nursemaid. Miss Hillier smiled warmly, as if she wanted to take him in her arms like a mother. In truth, she had been the only mother he'd known for the first ten years of his life. Unfortunately, Miss Hillier still had a tendency to be too motherly.

Jared put his hand on the small of Ava's back. "Lady Ava, my fiancée," he said, and to Ava, "Allow me to introduce Miss Hillier, our housekeeper."

Miss Hillier turned a beaming smile to her new mistress. "Oh my, how lovely you are, my lady."

Ava blushed self-consciously. "I am very pleased to make your acquaintance, Miss Hillier. I shall need your expert assistance to guide me through my duties as mistress of such a very grand house."

And on down the line they went, meeting the staff that kept Broderick Abbey functioning. The footmen, the housemaids. The cook and scullery maids. The groundsmen, including the gardener and his men, and the stable hands, the game manager. There were three dozen of them, a veritable army.

And Ava greeted each and every one with a word and what seemed like an honest expression of interest in what they did. Moreover, Jared noticed, she touched their hands, their elbows, their shoulders, looked them squarely in the eye and smiled. It was no wonder that the staff members were all gazing rather approvingly at his intended bride, for which, Jared realized, he was relieved and pleased. Broderick Abbey was his treasure; the staff and their satisfaction with their employment were important to him. He had not realized how important until this moment.

They proceeded inside, with several of the staff running ahead to open rooms for his inspection. Dawson instructed two footmen to have their trunks brought in, and the cook to have the tea readied.

"Miss Hillier, if you will please show the ladies to their suite of rooms," Jared said as they entered the foyer and he helped Ava remove her pelisse. "When they are ready, I shall meet them for luncheon in the west dining room."

"Very good, my lord." Miss Hillier gestured for Ava and Phoebe to come along.

With another anxious glance at Jared over her shoulder, Ava, in the company of her sister, who had yet to take her eyes from the walls and ceiling, dutifully followed Miss Hillier, taking in the surroundings as they went.

Jared handed his hat to Dawson.

"If I may, my lord?" Dawson asked.

"Yes?"

"Felicitations on your upcoming nuptials. She's bonny, if you don't mind me saying."

A small smile crept across Jared's mouth. "She is indeed. Thank you, Dawson. Have a mount saddled, will you?"

"At once, my lord," Dawson said, and with a glance to a footman, sent the man running.

Jared followed the footman out and down the drive, walking slowly to the stables. While he waited, he leaned heavily against a post and put his hand to his forehead. He was feeling this sea change in his life more acutely now that they were here, in his home. His decision was beginning to feel truly unalterable.

Perhaps he was only exhausted—the Lord knew he hadn't slept at all this week, his mind racing around his whirlwind marriage, those disturbing feelings of being trapped. But he was also feeling wildly empty, as if all his normal thoughts and emotions had deserted him, leaving a void for new, wild thoughts and unfamiliar emotions to fill.

What he wanted was for nothing to change with the singular exception of siring a legitimate son. Everything else he wished to remain the same. That was, he realized with sickening dread, an impossibility given the vows he would take in a matter of days.

A stableman appeared with a young mare. "I beg your pardon my lord, but she's not your usual—"

"She'll do," he said, reaching for the bridle.

"She's a bit green, sir," the stableman tried again.

Jared looked the young mare in the eye. The horse stared back at him with a wildness that mirrored what he felt deep inside himself. "Excellent," he said, and fit his foot in the stirrup and swung up. The horse reacted skittishly, pushing and pulling, trying to get out from beneath him. Jared squeezed his thighs against her. "Steady, old girl," he said soothingly, "steady."

The mare was in no mood to steady herself and bolted for the paddock gate, trying yet to dislodge him. It took all the strength Jared had to hold her, but the moment they cleared the paddock gate, he let her go and held on, every muscle tensed with the effort to keep his seat.

The horse was green, but she couldn't possibly be half as wild as he felt inside. As she raced along, he began to feel that perhaps he could outrun the invisible beast that was pursuing him. But as they approached a stone fence, Jared knew a moment of fear. He didn't know her, didn't know if she would clear the fence or balk. But it was too late to pull up, so he leaned low over her neck, gripped the reins, and closed his eyes.

She stumbled, and his heart dropped . . . but then he felt the horse rise up, and felt the two of them soar.

Miss Hillier gave Ava and Phoebe a quick tour of the main living area of the house before taking them up to what would be Ava's suite. "The ladies' rooms are just here," she said, moving through a grand sitting room and into a suite of rooms that consisted of a bedroom the size of the Downey salon, a sitting room full of silk-covered chaise longues and cherrywood furnishings, a dressing room, and a bathing room with porcelain fixtures. The walls in the suite were painted pale green and the elaborate crown moldings and paper friezes that adorned the ceilings were painted in creamy white.

Ava put aside her reticule and took in her grand surroundings as Miss Hillier walked around, pointing out various features. The bellpull. The brazier, should the fireplace not provide enough warmth. The linens storage, the vanity.

When two footmen appeared with their trunks, Miss Hillier chattered away, directing them left and right, and Ava wandered to one set of expansive windows overlooking a lush green lawn and a very large fountain. She'd never lived in anything so grand. Not even Bingley Hall, for all its splendor, could be counted in the class of Broderick Abbey, and that fact intimidated her on some level. When she'd set out to improve her family's station in life, she'd not imagined this sort of wealth.

As she stood there, gazing absently at the beautiful landscape, she noticed a movement—a lone rider.

"His lordship doesn't have a set time for supper. Would you care to set one, madam?" Miss Hillier asked.

"I don't know—I should speak with him, I suppose," Ava responded, distracted, as the rider rode full-bore for a stone fence.

"He's rather unconventional in that regard," Miss Hillier said with an airy laugh. "Always has been."

Ava didn't respond—her pulse quickened as she realized it was Middleton who rode so recklessly for the fence.

"Never been one to stand on custom, not since he was a wee lad."

"You've known him that long?" Phoebe asked as Middleton came to the fence. Ava felt his recklessness in her veins, felt the split second during which the horse might have balked, killing him. The horse stumbled; she closed her eyes, then quickly opened them in time to see the horse come down on the other side of the fence and crash into the forest, Middleton's riding coat waving out behind him.

"Oh yes, indeed. I was his nursemaid."

Ava drew a steadying breath. And another. *From what, or to what, do you run?*

"Very well, then, it looks as if all is in order. Is there something else I might do for you, Lady Ava?"

Hire a chaise, send me back to London. Ava turned and smiled at the housekeeper. "No . . . no, thank you."

Miss Hillier nodded and began to move.

"There is one thing," Ava said, stopping Miss Hillier's march.

"Yes, madam?"

"Where might the master's suite be?"

"Just in there," she said, nodding to her right. "His dressing room adjoins yours." Ava and Phoebe exchanged a look to which Miss Hillier clucked her tongue. "You needn't fret at the impropriety of it, my lady. His lordship will reside in another part of the house until you are wed."

"Ah," Ava said, surprisingly relieved. "Thank you."

"Will that be all?"

"Yes, thank you."

Miss Hillier gave them a happy smile and bustled out, pausing only to straighten some linen towels on an étagère before sailing through the door and closing it soundly behind her.

When she left, Phoebe turned around and fell on the bed with a squeal. "My God!" she exclaimed. "Have you ever seen a place so grand?"

Ava looked around the room and shook her head. "No. Never." She felt almost triumphant. She'd done it—she'd hunted and bagged one of the most sought after bachelors in all of England. Good Lord, she'd even be a *duchess* one day.

So why, then, did she feel so vulnerable? Was it because he rode so recklessly away from the house? Was it because she was on the verge of being wife to a man she knew so little about? And one day mother to his child? Ava longed for her mother—she would have laughed at Ava's fears and pushed her out the door with a reminder that after her wifely duties were all said and done, she might have any bauble she wished, and to certainly ask for an expensive one.

Ava lifted her head. She could almost hear her mother. *"You've made your bed, young lady. Now you shall lie in it. But what a scrumptious bed it is, darling."*

There was nothing to be done for it—Ava *had* made her bed, had connived and schemed to make it. So now it would seem she most definitely would lie in it.

It *was* a rather delicious bed.

"Come on," she said, playfully slapping Phoebe's knee. "Let us prepare ourselves for '*luncheon*,'" she said, mimicking Miss Hillier.

Fifteen

~~~~~~~~

Over the next two days, so many people arrived at Broderick Abbey that Ava rarely saw her betrothed, save at mealtime, and even then, they were surrounded by family and friends. After supper, the ladies would retire to a sitting room so that Lady Purnam might regale them with tales of what was to be expected of a good bride (deference at all times seemed to be the sum of it), and the men would retire all the way to the village of Broderick, from which they would return in the wee hours of the morning, well into their cups.

Ava knew this because Middleton and his two good friends, Stanhope and Harrison, were possessed of a desire to sing a song to her beneath her window, so loudly and so poorly that they woke the entire house.

Nevertheless, Ava was happy—Broderick Abbey was so elegant, and the grounds so beautiful. She would very much enjoy being mistress here, and more than once, she had to pinch herself to make sure it was real. What had once been fantasy was alarmingly real, and she was absolutely giddy about her accomplishment.

On the day before her wedding, Lucille Penne-backer arrived, and she and Lady Purnam immediately began to compete with one another in instructing Ava on the proper direction of her large household staff, much to Miss Hillier's considerable and obvious chagrin.

That did not dampen Ava's spirits. She and Phoebe privately laughed at the battle of three strong wills. Even the duke's arrival on the eve of her wedding, which cast a pall over the festive atmosphere, did nothing to sober her. In fact, nothing sobered her until the moment she was to take her vows.

The wedding ceremony took place promptly at nine o'clock Friday morning. Ava wore a gown of pale rose satin. It pleased her enormously that the man who would be her husband seemed suitably impressed with her appearance; as they gathered outside the chapel, one brow arched high above the other as he took her in, head to toe. He took her hand, kissed her lips to the delight of the servants and grounds people gathered, and said, "You are indeed the loveliest bride I've ever had the pleasure to see."

The compliment sent a shiver down Ava's back and made her feel a little flush with pride.

"Are you quite ready?" he asked.

She laughed. "Are *you*?"

He seemed to consider the question for a moment. "I suppose I am," he said, and smiled at her. "Shall we carry on, Lady Ava?"

"We shall," she said, and put her hand on the arm that he offered.

But as they walked into the church, her nerves began to fray and her thoughts got the best of her. Up until this morning, she'd been so blessedly busy that she hadn't really had time to think about the vows she would take. But now, standing before a parish vicar, everything seemed a little blurry. How was it, she wondered, as she promised to honor a man she really didn't know, that she had come to this point? She'd been so pleased with herself up until this moment—and now she couldn't quite discern why she suddenly felt so unsettled.

She glanced at Phoebe on her left. The small bouquet of peonies Phoebe held shook so badly that it was a miracle any of the blooms remained intact. Ava wanted to tell her sister that it was all right, that she'd done it, she'd married for convenience and fortune, and they never would need worry again. Only the vicar's words—the bits about honoring her husband, loving and comforting him—made her realize that what she really wanted was to marry for love.

Suddenly, she didn't feel victorious or particularly clever. She felt a bit disingenuous.

Ava glanced at Middleton from the corner of her eye as he repeated the vows the vicar put to him. "Wilt thou have this woman to thy wedded wife?"

Middleton hesitated a moment.

Wilt thou have this woman? Ava silently echoed.

His lids fluttered, but then he cleared his throat and said plainly, "I will." He glanced at her and gave her a slight wink.

What was he thinking? What thoughts crowded his head in this moment? she wondered as he slipped a plain gold ring on her finger. Did he, like her, find it strange to stand up and vow to commit to her for the rest of their natural lives, knowing so little about her? Or did he think that it was merely a matter of convenience and that his life would go on, unchanged, with possibly the exception of planting a child in her?

The vicar pronounced them man and wife before Ava could ever really focus on what was happening. She dutifully turned her face up to her husband, who put his arm around her shoulders and kissed her possessively.

There it was again—that strange, niggling feeling inside her, that tiny but fervent desire that he love her. If he loved her even only a little, then this would seem right somehow.

In spite of the morning hour, the champagne flowed freely at the wedding breakfast that followed the ceremony. Outside, the servants and groundsmen shared in the champagne and food that had been prepared with the help of villagers from Broderick. Family, friends, and local dignitaries were seated inside the terrace sitting room, which had been set up with tables to host the wedding breakfast.

Middleton and Ava made their way through the small crowd of servants gathered outside, smiling and nodding to their lusty calls of congratulations. As was customary, Middleton tossed coins to the children. One boy, Ava noticed, did not scramble for the coins with the other children, but looked at her curiously. She smiled at him. The boy returned a very bright and charming smile.

Inside, men happily clapped Middleton on the shoulder while the women professed happiness for Ava and eyed her beautiful dress. A trio of musicians, hired from the village, played lively music for them. The room was full of laughter and joyous celebration, save one person, who did not seem to enjoy the celebration in the least: the Duke of Redford.

Ava was standing near her new husband, who had been swallowed up by his friends, when Lady

Purnam sailed to her side, took her by the hand, and dragged her aside. "What are you waiting for?" she hissed.

"I beg your pardon?"

Lady Purnam glanced at Lord Redford standing by the wall, an untouched glass of champagne on a table beside him. "He's your father-in-law now and it is *frighteningly* unrefined to leave him to stew in his own juices! Go to him at once and make sure he is put well at ease!"

Ava glanced doubtfully at her new father-in-law. Lady Purnam gave her a bit of a shove with her elbow. With a heavy sigh, Ava walked forward. The duke did not acknowledge her as she approached, but stared sourly at the guests. He was, Ava thought, being terribly rude on the occasion of his son's wedding.

It wasn't until she was standing almost directly before him that he shifted his gaze to her. "Your grace," she said, dipping into a curtsy. "Are you unwell?"

"Unwell?" he repeated, surprised. "I am very well, thank you."

His gaze flicked over her as if she were a villager standing in his way. He really did disdain her, didn't he? "I am pleased to hear it, although there must be something that concerns you, sir, for you seem quite cross."

"I'm cross now, am I?"

Ava forced a smile. "I don't blame you in the least. It's not an ideal situation, to be sure."

"That, madam, is an understatement," he said, and turned his gaze back to the guests.

"Nonetheless, it is my wedding day, your grace,

and I would be very honored if you'd sit with me and try to smile at least now and again."

Her cheekiness startled him; he jerked his gaze to her and frowned. "Lady Ava—"

"—Middleton."

"I beg your pardon?"

"I am Lady Middleton now."

The duke blinked. And then, miraculously, he offered the barest hint of a smile. "Indeed you are."

"It could be far worse, you know," Ava said with a conspiratorial glance about. "I could be a dreadful bore. I would come to supper and bore you unto tears, and bear you dullard grandchildren."

Now the duke was smiling. "I must trust your word that you are not a bore, mustn't I?"

"I assure you I am not in the least. What I lack in finesse I always make up in knowing a bit of news about our closest friends."

Amazingly, the duke actually laughed and offered her his arm. "You must tell me all, Lady Middleton."

She slipped her hand into the crook of his arm. "For example, did you know that Lady Purnam was once a favorite of our new king?" she whispered as the duke led her to a table.

He squinted at Lady Purnam across the room. "I daresay I did not," he answered honestly, and turned back to Ava, anxious to hear the tale.

And Ava was so engrossed in the telling of it that she didn't realize her husband had joined them until the duke looked up and nodded curtly.

"Your grace," Middleton said, and put his hand to Ava's shoulder and leaned over to ask softly, "Are you quite all right?"

She smiled up at him. "I was just telling his grace

about Lady Purnam. She was once a favorite of the king's."

He looked at her as if he thought she had lost her mind, but straightened and exchanged a look with his father.

"A toast!" someone called out. "A toast, a toast!"

"Join me," Middleton said, and slipped his hand beneath Ava's elbow and pulled her up.

Lord Harrison was the first to step forward and gain the attention of the small crowd with his crystal flute of champagne raised high. "If I may, my lord," he said, bowing theatrically to Middleton's nod that he should continue. "I have been told that the secret to a long and happy matrimony is that you should never go to bed angry with one another—stay up and argue."

The guests burst into laughter, shouting "Hear, hear!"

"What do you know of marriage, Harrison?" Middleton scoffed.

"Absolutely nothing," Harrison said jovially. "The same as you, my lord." The crowd laughed again, and Harrison lifted his crystal flute in toast. "May your marriage be blessed." Middleton inclined his head and lifted his flute.

"Fools, the both of you," Stanhope said, and stepped forward, next to Harrison, and put a collegial hand on his shoulder. "Here, sir, is *my* best advice. Learn these four magic words and learn them well, and trust me, sir, they will smooth the roughest of roads with your beautiful bride."

Middleton laughed. "And they are?"

" 'You're quite *right*, darling,' " Stanhope said. Once again, the crowd laughed uproariously, Ava and

Middleton among them. But then the duke rose from his seat, and a hush fell over them. Beside her, Ava could feel Middleton's entire body stiffen as the duke turned to them and lifted his glass.

"A toast, if I may?"

"Of course," Middleton said instantly.

He looked at Ava. "To Lady Middleton," he said quietly. "May you find joy."

No one said a word—they scarcely even breathed. But then Lady Purnam, God bless her, shouted, *"Hear, hear!"* and the rest of the crowd followed suit, lifting their glasses and toasting Ava's joy.

Ava laughed, and glanced up at her husband. He was smiling, but it barely turned the corners of his mouth, and it certainly did not reach his eyes.

A few more toasts were made to their mutual happiness, and then Harrison stepped forward again, looked around the room, and said, "Now I think the time has come to leave the happy couple to one another's good company." And with that, he walked forward, threw his arms around Middleton and slapped his back heartily. He let go, grabbed Ava up and kissed her soundly on the cheek.

He looked at Middleton and winked. "Be a good husband, lad," he said sternly.

"I shall endeavor to do my best," Middleton said.

The duke was next. He looked at his son and said, "Best wishes for you both."

Middleton nodded. "Thank you, sir," Ava said quickly. Middleton extended his hand to his father. The duke looked at his hand a moment, and took it, but shook it and dropped it quickly before walking out of the room, obviously eager to be on his way.

Lady Purnam wished Middleton well, but as she

embraced Ava, she whispered ominously in her ear, "Have a care in everything you do, girl, for all of England will be watching."

"Ah . . ." Ava stammered, uncertain what to say to that. "Thank you."

Lucy hugged her, too, but looked at her sternly and said, "Your stepfather will not be happy in the least when he learns that you wouldn't wait for his arrival."

Ava smiled and shrugged. There was certainly nothing she could do for it now, thank the saints.

She said good-bye to Phoebe last. She took her sister's hands in hers and smiled.

Phoebe frowned. "I'm alone now. First Mother, then Greer, and now you," she said petulantly.

Ava squeezed her hand. "Aren't you the least bit happy for me?"

"Of course I am!" Phoebe exclaimed, and smiled through the tears that suddenly welled in her eyes. "But I am very sorry for *me.*"

Ava laughed and hugged her, and whispered in her ear, "Keep sewing. I don't know how long it shall be before I am given an allowance of any sort. And I won't be gone from you for very long, Phoebe, I promise you that."

"That's precisely what Greer said," Phoebe muttered, and when Ava pulled away from her, she saw the tears glistening in her sister's eyes. "I shall miss you dreadfully."

"Not nearly as much as I shall miss you," Ava promised, tears welling in her eyes, too.

"Oh there now, such maidenly tears!" Lady Purnam scoffed, and put her hand on Phoebe's forearm. "Come along, Lady Phoebe, I should like to arrive in London before nightfall, when murderers and thieves roam the streets."

Phoebe looked so forlorn that Ava grabbed her and hugged her fiercely once more. "I shan't stay away long," she said again, and let her sister go.

She and Middleton followed the guests out, and watched them being loaded into their coaches and carriages. Ava waved to her sister, waiting until Lady Purnam's coach—the last to depart—had pulled out of the drive, leaving her and Middleton the last two standing.

Neither of them spoke until Lady Purnam's coach had disappeared around a bend. Only then did Ava glance up at Middleton.

He was still squinting down the drive. "It's just the two of us now," he said.

Yes, it was just the two of them. Completely and irrevocably. She was struck with the cold reality of what would come next, especially when she looked at Middleton, who smiled thinly.

"It has been quite a morning, madam. I should think you'd like to rest before this evening's supper."

"But . . . I am not tired," she said, her belly tightening with trepidation.

He did not smile, just looked at her stoically. "I think you should rest," he said again, only more firmly. "I will see you at supper." And with that, he turned away from her, told Dawson to have the mare saddled, and walked into the house, yanking at his neckcloth as he went, leaving her to stand on the drive, utterly alone.

Her face burned with embarrassment, and she hesitantly started after him, making her way to her rooms, her head swimming around his abrupt dismissal of her, and the fear of what would come. She sat in her chaise, staring at the floor for what seemed hours, but when she finally stood to change from her wedding gown, she walked to the windows and looked out at the lovely landscape.

And there she saw him, riding away, reckless and full-bore.

A shiver shot through her—that man, who rode so fiercely, so utterly without discretion or even care for himself, would be in her bed tonight.

Sixteen

~~~~~~❧~~~~~~

Miss Hillier appeared in Ava's suite at seven o'clock to help her dress, but she was already dressed and waiting.

After Middleton's abrupt departure, she hadn't known what to do with herself, and to steady her nerves, she'd spent the afternoon going through her things, trying on different gowns Phoebe had made. She chose soft green brocade for supper, a gown Phoebe had embroidered with tiny little rosebuds that matched the silk rosebuds on the hem of the underskirt. The bodice fit low and tight across her bosom, which Ava had insisted to Phoebe was too revealing. Phoebe—whose mouth had been full of pins at the time—had rolled her eyes and continued on, undaunted.

Ava allowed Miss Hillier to help her put her hair up. When she'd finished, Miss Hillier stood back and smiled. "Ah, Lady Middleton, you're very beautiful," she said appreciatively as she looked at Ava. "It is plain to see why his lordship wanted you as his wife."

Ava could only hope that he wanted her—she wasn't certain given his demeanor on the drive, but she smiled at Miss Hillier and donned the garnet earrings that had been her mother's.

She might have liked to stay holed up there until Middleton came to look for her, but Miss Hillier seemed rather determined that she should join her husband before dinner in the green salon.

A footman was waiting at the door of the salon and opened it as Ava approached, bowing his head in deference to her. With a smile, she stepped across the threshold of the salon, but was brought to a halt just there, for the room was majestic.

Huge six-foot paintings of Middleton's ancestors lined the walls beneath a fifteen-foot ceiling. Gilded chairs upholstered in red silk were pushed up against the walls—it looked as if there were enough of them to seat four dozen people. On opposing walls, four mahogany commodes held enormous Oriental porcelain vases and amazing floral arrangements. The rug at her feet was thick and intricately embroidered, depicting an English forest complete with animals, wood nymphs, and someone on a horse.

"I have been remiss in inquiring . . . but I trust you found your suite to your liking?"

His voice startled her—she hadn't seen Middleton standing to one side of the marble mantel at the opposite end of the room. "I . . . yes. Yes, the suite is beautiful. Thank you," she said, and realized she was trembling again. Her husband—*husband!*—was wearing black knee breeches that fit him like a glove, a white silk shirt and waistcoat, and black coattails. His neckcloth was simply tied, the small gold pin holding it in place. His dark hair was brushed back and long over his collar, and his face clean-shaven.

He seemed even more handsome now than he had this morning—and a bit dark.

He casually gestured to a grouping of furniture

near the hearth. "I thought we might have a drink before we dine."

Ava couldn't possibly eat a thing, so she walked dutifully across the room. He met her at the grouping of furniture, took her hand, and paused to look at her gown. "How lovely you are," he said, and slowly lifted a smoldering gaze to hers as he brought her hand to his lips. "Very lovely indeed."

The way he looked at her, the quiet, assured way he spoke and held her hand made her feel slightly intoxicated, and she sat heavily on the settee to which he ushered her.

"What would you like?" he asked, motioning toward the sideboard. "A bit of wine, perhaps?"

Ava glanced at the decanters. "I think I would prefer something stout."

"Port, perhaps?"

"Whiskey?"

He smiled. "I don't believe whiskey is a suitable spirit for a woman's tender constitution, but by all means, if that is what you would like . . ."

"Please." At the moment, it seemed the only thing strong enough to buoy her. Everything felt different— *he* felt different somehow. She worried that he regretted their marriage.

At the sideboard, Middleton poured a small tot of whiskey for her, then one for himself, and brought them back, along with the decanter, to the settee where she was sitting.

He put the decanter on the table and handed her a tot, his fingers grazing hers with a certain familiarity. He sat, draped one arm over the back of the settee, and looked at her, watching her as she smelled the whiskey. Once, when she and Phoebe and Greer were all of sixteen or so, they had stolen a bottle of Lord

Downey's whiskey and drunk it. It had been years before she could stomach the smell of whiskey again, but today, she needed its calming effects.

"Are you unwell?" Middleton asked.

"Me?" she asked, startled by the question. "No . . . I am very well. I could not possibly be happier." The words, which she'd said a thousand times in the last few days, flowed off her tongue so voluntarily that they were essentially meaningless.

He, on the other hand, looked a bit tense. "Are *you* unwell?" she asked.

"Perfectly fine." With his finger, he stroked her arm, looked at her thoughtfully. "Here we are, then, Lady Middleton. Bonded together in connubial bliss until death us do part."

"My. When said *that* way, it sounds rather dire, doesn't it?" she remarked. "Do you regret it?"

"No," he said immediately. "Do you?"

Ava shook her head. "No," she said quietly.

"I think we both understand one another and what we've gained by this marriage, do we not?"

She nodded.

"But," he said, reaching for the ribbon of her sash, his fingers possessively brushing her breast as he did, "I rather imagine that should not preclude us from enjoying it." He lifted a darkly glittering gaze to hers. "Particularly the private privileges that come with being husband and wife," he added quietly as he tugged lightly at the ribbon.

Ava tried to smile, but she could scarcely even swallow. "Yes," was all she could manage.

He smiled then, his eyes creasing at the corners. "Drink," he said, nodding to her whiskey.

She looked at the tot, lifted it to her lips, closed her eyes and drank, and waited for the inevitable burn.

Beside her, Middleton chuckled. "You might find it more to your liking if you sipped."

"I shall never find whiskey to my liking, sir," she said hoarsely, and opened her eyes.

He leaned forward, poured a little more into her glass. "Try to sip," he advised, and held up his tot, clinking it against hers. "To many happy years."

"To many happy years," she echoed, and sipped the whiskey. It burned her lips, her tongue, and her throat. No, she decided, it was most decidedly better to swallow it whole than sip.

Middleton must have agreed, for he tossed his back.

Ava drank the contents of her tot. When she finished gasping for breath, and felt the calming effects of it begin to seep warm and thick into her limbs, she smiled a little crookedly. "Very nice."

He casually took the tot from her hands and put it aside. "I've not had time to personally show you about. Shall I give you a tour of the abbey?"

"I should like that very much."

Middleton took her firmly in hand, and Ava liked that—she liked the feeling of belonging with him.

Perhaps the awkward moment on the drive had been an aberration, the result of fatigue. Perhaps everything would be very nice between them.

Perhaps her nerves, now assuaged by the whiskey, would settle down.

But if anything, they grew worse. Their tour took more than an hour. Middleton pointed out the historical facets and where the monks had once lived, their cells now converted to servants' quarters. He showed her the west drawing room, which had once been a chapel, and the various wings and rooms and artwork that had been added through the centuries. Too nervous to focus on the art and architecture of the grand old abbey, Ava asked few questions about his revered family's history, and he told her very little.

In fact, Middleton became less talkative as the tour wore on. He just kept looking at her in a way that made her feel incredibly exposed. Her skin tingled with the intensity of his gaze, and Ava could scarcely think—her trepidation at what was to come growing more acute by the hour.

By the time they had returned to the salon, Dawson was waiting to take them in to dinner.

The smaller family dining room was a size that most would consider to be a formal dining room, large enough to seat two dozen. At the far end of the table, two place settings had been arranged. Middleton's, at the head of the table, and Ava's, to his right. Two footmen stood silently next to a large buffet, on top of which were six silver-domed platters.

Dawson held the chair out for her; Ava slid into it self-consciously. As accustomed as she was to formal dining, this seemed far more formal, and bigger. But Middleton gave her a smile and a slight wink as he took his seat. "A lot of pomp and circumstance to eat one fat hen, isn't it?"

She smiled gratefully at his attempt to put her at ease, but as Dawson poured wine, her nerves felt as if they were all but exposed, hovering just beneath the surface of her skin, ready to explode. She drank the wine and pushed her food around, her appetite completely crushed under her anxiety.

Middleton, however, didn't seem to be bothered. He made small talk as he ate, asked her about the sorts of things that amused her.

"I'm not certain I know what you mean."

"What sorts of things do you like to do? Besides

your charitable work, of course," he added with a devilish smile.

"Oh. Well. I suppose I like to read—"

"What do you read?"

"Novels," she said. "Popular novels, particularly."

"Ah. Stories of love and lust," he said, his gaze dipping to her lips as he reached for his wineglass.

"And the daily newspapers," she added quickly. "I particularly enjoy the *on dits*. Phoebe and I make a game of out of it."

"The sort of game that supposes which gentleman is in which lady's bed?" he asked, idly watching her.

Ava didn't answer—her face burned with the truth.

"Or perhaps you enjoy another sort of game," he suggested, his voice dropping to a low pitch. "Wondering which gentleman you would like to find in *your* bed?"

"Of course not," she said instantly.

Middleton smiled at her obvious lie but nodded gallantly. "I beg your pardon, madam. I did not know you, your sister, and your cousin were as chaste as that."

"We . . ." Her voice trailed off, and she cast her gaze to her plate. She tried to think of something witty and clever to say to her husband, but nothing came to her.

He smiled and picked up his fork. "What else amuses you?"

"Music," she said. "I like the pianoforte, although I play it wretchedly. Greer is the talented one among us. And I like dogs, I think. Not cats, especially, for they are rather aloof. But I enjoy seeing the dogs in the park. They seem friendly and exceedingly loyal. And, oh yes, I do enjoy a good walkabout."

"You shall have plenty of room to roam at Broderick Abbey."

She tried to picture herself walking around the grounds of Broderick Abbey, the lady of the manor, and the image brought a smile to her face. How absurd! Ava Fairchild, a marchioness!

"There we are, at last—a lovely smile," he said, smiling, too. "What amuses you at this moment?"

"The idea that I should be a marchioness. Or a duchess, for that matter."

"I suspect you will be a very good one. I have all faith."

"Your faith in me is very much appreciated, but very much undeserved." Before he could politely argue, she asked, "What amuses you, my lord?"

"Hmm," he mused, his brow wrinkled with thought. "I suppose horses rather than dogs, although I had a dog as a lad and I was quite fond of him. Hunting rather than walking. I do enjoy music. And reading, although I must confess I have never read a popular novel of lust and love," he added with a sly smile. "Perhaps we might indulge in one together."

Ava pretended to study her wineglass. "What was your dog's name?" she asked, avoiding any mention of lust or love.

"His name?" He grinned. "Doogie."

Ava laughed.

"What?"

"That is a *wretched* name for a dog."

"I beg your pardon?" he asked, feigning offense. "It is a perfectly suitable name for a cur!"

"It is perfectly suitable for a stableboy. Not a dog!"

"And who are you, madam, to declare what is a suitable dog's name?" he teased her. "I will have you know that I spent hours determining the perfect name for him. Now, then, to be fair, you must tell me the name of your childhood pet."

"I did not have a dog, I had a canary," Ava informed him. "And as there were three of us, the naming was not done entirely on my own."

"Very well, what did the three of you name your pet canary?"

"Buttermilk," Ava said, and smiled, pleased that he should laugh so roundly at that.

He asked about her childhood—Bingley Hall, the move to London after her father died and her mother remarried. She told him about her debut into society, and her presentation at court, and how she had accidentally spilled wine on the prince regent's velvet shoe at the ball afterward.

She talked at length about her mother. It felt good to talk about her; it helped to lessen her anxiety somewhat. And it was good to speak of her to someone other than Phoebe and Greer, to someone who had not known how lovely she was so that Ava could say it aloud. She even spoke of herself, and of Phoebe and Greer, too, of Greer's foray into Wales and Phoebe's despair that she'd been abandoned.

"We shall send for her once you are with child," he said instantly.

A flood of heat invaded her face, and Ava glanced down at her lap, feeling butterflies at the mere mention of a child in her womb. All the anxiety she had managed to push down suddenly rose up again. "Thank you. It would be good to have her with me."

He paused in his dining and looked at her. "Is something wrong?"

She shook her head.

He reached for her hand, covered it with his and held it for a moment. "Rest east, Lady Middleton," he said at last. "There are greater things in life to fear."

"I hardly fear children, my lord."

He smiled a little lopsidedly. "I was hardly referring to children."

Dear God. She could feel her heart thumping in her chest as he gazed at her, his eyes roaming her face, dipping to her décolletage, which she knew very well to be quite revealing, and then up again, lingering on her lips before giving her a roguish smile and letting go of her hand.

Ava's insides churned with anticipation and fear all at once. Yet somehow, she made herself pick up her fork. "And what of your childhood, sir?" she asked. "Where was it spent?"

He answered vaguely. His childhood, he said, was rather dull, spent in boarding schools and in Europe. His house in London was bought from his uncle, who was now deceased. Broderick Abbey was his seat, and while he didn't spend as much time here, he rather liked it here, and was trying to institute some agricultural changes that would earn a better yield from the land.

"And your father?"

He glanced up from his plate and regarded her suspiciously. "What of him?"

The chill in his voice startled her. "You haven't mentioned him."

"Why would I?"

Why? After the interview in his father's study, and the obvious animosity between father and son, he would ask why? Ava blinked. "I don't know . . . he just seemed so . . . *displeased* . . . about us," she reminded him.

Middleton looked at his plate. "I wouldn't bore you with the unpleasant history of my relationship with my father. You wouldn't understand."

"Of course I would," she retorted, ruffled by his dismissive response.

But Middleton sighed and gave her a stern look she'd never seen from him before now. "All right, then, here you are, Lady Middleton. He is generally displeased because I am not, nor have I ever been, the son he wanted. He considers me feckless and undeserving, for we are not cut of the same cloth, he and I."

"But how is that—"

"If you wouldn't mind, it is really neither here nor there," he said, cutting her off. "I've little enough to do with him as it is and I'd rather not discuss it." With that, he looked at Dawson. "You may clear these things away. Lady Middleton and I would retire now."

Dawson and the footmen instantly began moving. But Ava, startled by his quick decision and his black look, didn't move. Jared came to his feet and walked around to Ava's chair. He put his hands on her shoulders and leaned down, so that his lips were against her ear. "You look as if you are expected in the gallows, madam." He straightened up, pulled her chair back, and helped Ava to her feet. Then he took up the wine and the two glasses they had drunk from and nodded to the door. "To the gallows, then."

Ava stumbled slightly, but he caught her with his hand. "Relax," he said low and put a steadying hand on her back. Out they went, walking silently down the carpeted corridor, then up the stairs. Jared paused at the landing as she gathered her skirts in one hand. He took her hand in his and led her purposefully to the end of the hallway, past beeswax candles casting eerie light on silk-covered walls, past consoles boasting hothouse flowers, past closed doors and two chambermaids standing politely with their backs to the wall as the master and his wife passed.

When they reached a certain door, Jared's hand

dropped from her waist and he turned the crystal
knob, throwing it open, and then, standing behind
Ava, he gave her a gentle push inside.

The room was similar to hers, only larger. It was
painted the blue color of a spring sky, the carpet
Oriental and plush and the furniture thickly padded
and covered in leather. There was a dresser, atop
which were the accoutrements of a man—a pair of
gloves, a discarded neckcloth, a small purse, and a
heavy silver candelabrum. She could see into the
dressing room, too, where there was a basin, with a
leather strop and razor hanging nearby.

And then, of course, there was the canopied bed.
It was draped in dark green velvet, the bed covering
brocade and embroidered with dark green and gold
leaves. The canopy was hand painted, rising tall on
mahogany posters at the four corners, topped with
gold pineapples. A fire burned brightly at the hearth,
and someone had turned down the bed for his lordship.

The boots he'd worn to his wedding were at the
hearth, a silk dressing gown was draped over the back
of a wingback chair. At the windows, gold and dark
green drapes had been pulled to keep out the morning light.

Ava clasped her hands to her belly and glanced up
at the ceiling frieze—papier-mâché ropes slung from
urn to urn, a circle of pineapples in the middle.

She heard the door close and the snap of the lock
and turned around. Middleton had put down the
wine and the glasses and was pulling the pin free of
his neckcloth, which he placed on the dresser. She felt
panicked, watching him.

He regarded her warily as he yanked the neckcloth
free and tossed it aside, followed by his collar. "I

agreed to marry a woman who laughed easily," he said as he shrugged out of his coat. "But, madam, since our vows were taken, you have turned into a nervous little ninny."

He pulled open his shirt, and Ava caught a glimpse of the crisp hair that covered his chest. His dark hair was almost to his shoulder, his hazel eyes glinting dangerously, his face impossibly handsome. She watched as he unbuttoned his waistcoat, big hands moving lithely down the row of buttons, and she suddenly had a vision of those hands on her body.

"I must amend my earlier statement," he said casually, as if he were quite accustomed to disrobing before a woman. "Now you look rather appalled."

"No, I—I . . ." She glanced at his hands again as he dropped the waistcoat on a chair. She wasn't the least bit appalled, she was overwhelmed—completely and utterly overwhelmed by the sight of him. She felt almost light-headed with it, and the burn in her cheeks spread to her neck. Ashamed at her lack of fortitude on her wedding night, she dropped her gaze to the carpet.

She was uncertain what to say or do, her mind unavoidably on the moment she would become his wife in more than name. It was something she had long wanted to experience, in truth, but now that the hour was upon her, she did feel a little as if she were marching off to the gallows.

She wished for her mother, who often laughed about the master's bedroom. "I let him do what he wants, as long as he promises not to frighten the staff or the children," she'd laughingly said to her friend one day. Later, when Ava asked her what she'd meant by it, her mother had smiled and kissed her cheek. "When the time comes, I shall tell you what you must know. But for now, darling, I shall tell you this: Never fear it, never give it away, but never say no."

She didn't know Middleton moved until he was upon her, taking her in his arms. He put his hand to her chin and pushed her head back so that she could look into his hazel eyes. "I once escorted a woman in a coach who had no fear of me," he said, his gaze drifting to her lips. "I would have that woman back, if you please," he said, and buried his face in her neck, kissing the hollow at her throat.

"That woman," Ava breathed as his hand slid down to her hip, pressing her into him, "was a ridiculous, silly thing who knew of only kisses, but I . . . I—"

He raised up, took her jaw in hand, and kissed her mouth firmly before suddenly sweeping her off her feet and carrying her to his bed and depositing her in a heap on it. Ava bounced, caught herself, and tried to move off the bed. "I should—"

"You should lie there and stop building shadows in your mind," he said, and with a practiced sweep of hand, he pulled the pin that held her hair and watched it fall. "Fear will make the experience intolerable," he murmured, his breath tickling her skin, his eyes darkening. "Just relax, Lady Middleton, and allow me to ravish you properly."

Seventeen

~~~~~~~

Ava gasped and laughed with surprise all at once, stammering her reply, but Jared would hear none of it. This would be done—the gravity of what he'd done had finally sunk in. He'd gone to the trouble of marrying her for it, and he would take what he'd given his freedom to have.

"My lord—" she started, pushing lightly against him.

He covered her hand on his chest and shook his head. "No, madam, you will allow me this. I am your husband and you will allow me this." He moved over her, trapping her beneath him as he put his mouth to her bosom, his lips and tongue sliding over her flesh, into the crevice between her breasts.

She gasped again, but this time, it was the sound of pleasure, not fear. He could feel the heat of her body through her dress, the blood rising to the surface. He felt her hand timidly touch his hair, her body slowly rise up to his mouth, and suddenly, any anger or confusion or emptiness he had felt was gone. He felt nothing but his own need rising up, pushing at him, at his limbs and his cock and his brain.

He moved his hands up and down her body, over her shoulders and the swell of her breasts, down her ribs and waist to her hips, to her feet. He flipped off one of her slippers. And the other. And then his hand was beneath the hem of her gown, sliding underneath, running up her leg, to the top of her stocking, to the smooth skin of her bare thigh, to the slit in her drawers.

She sucked in a sharp breath when he touched her there; her hands gripped his shoulders, her fingers digging through the fabric of his shirt.

He grinned, moved his fingers deeper into her damp folds. "This is the woman I have known," he said huskily, moving his fingers against her, feeling her body heat. "A woman full of passion and desire for a man."

Ava closed her eyes, releasing a sigh of pleasure, and her head rolled to one side as his hand moved against her. The pleasure that her response evoked in him spiraled down to his groin. "A woman who is bold enough to want pleasure for herself," he whispered as he stroked her.

There were too many articles of clothing, too much between him and her flesh, and he sat up, yanking her up with him, his arms going around behind her back as he kissed her mouth, unhooking the buttons, loosening her gown. When he had at last unfastened the garment, he stopped kissing her and leaned back, looking at her green eyes.

She was smiling a little but her eyes were big as moons. He took some pity on her—here was a woman who'd never revealed her body to a man. He pushed her hair behind her ear, stroked her chin, and, holding her gaze, he put his hands on her shoulders and pushed the gown from them, down her arms, until it bunched at her waist.

Ava's gaze did not waver from his. She did not

blink, she did not look down, just kept looking at his eyes.

But Jared couldn't help but look at her body, and the desire began to percolate. "My God," he whispered. "You are beautiful . . . so beautiful," he repeated reverently, taking her in. Her breasts were full and straining against the fabric of the thin chemise, rising rapidly with each frenzied breath. Her waist was slender, tapering into shapely hips. He smiled appreciatively and pressed his lips to her smooth cheek. Her skin was baby soft and warm beneath his mouth, and she smelled so sweet, so feminine and sweet.

He moved his lips to her ear. "*Stand up*," he whispered.

Ava didn't move right away, but Jared did, reaching for her hand and pulling her up. She stood beside the bed uncertainly as her gown and chemise slid down her body. He went down on his haunches, slipped his hand beneath her foot and lifted it. She wobbled, but put her hand to his shoulder and allowed him to move first one foot, then the other, and remove the gown.

He rose up, pulled his fingers through her hair, so that the honey blond tresses spilled around her shoulders. She was beautiful, this wife of his; he could not deny it, and his body was raging for her. "Beautiful," he murmured, and leaned down, touching his mouth to hers.

"I feel a bit scarce of breath," she whispered.

"So do I," he responded honestly.

Her lips began to move beneath his, nipping back at him, shaping around his lips. The sensation of her response began to flow through Jared like molten rock. He straddled her legs and began to coax her into his body by caressing her spine. But something was missing. He abruptly lifted his head and groped for her hands, which were hanging at her sides, and put them on his chest.

"There you are," he said, and returned to her lips, slipping his tongue between them, into her mouth.

Ava surprised him then. Her hands went from his chest to around his waist, pulling him closer, as she rose on her toes to kiss him. Her breasts were pressed against him, her mouth open beneath his, and as he kissed her, his hand on her breast, Ava moved her hand to the front of his trousers, brushing his erection.

Her virginal boldness excited him. He lifted his head and meant to say something, but then Ava opened her eyes and smiled with such seductive innocence that if she touched him again—just *touched* him—he feared how he might react, how swiftly he might put her on the bed and take her without regard for her ignorance.

"*Jared*," she whispered.

Few women had ever dared to use his given name in such intimate circumstances, and he was astounded by his response to it. It made it all seem real—it *was* real—and the dam burst, flooding every part of him, hardening his cock to the point of aching.

Ava dropped her head back, exposing the creamy white skin of her neck to him. He put his mouth to her neck at the same moment he slipped his arms behind her back and crushed her to him. "I want you," he said against her skin. "I want to make you my wife." And with that, he twisted around, falling onto the bed with her, instantly moving down her body. He could feel her body pulse with his touch. His mind, his eyes, every fiber of him was filled with the scent and the feel of her. He was dangerously aroused and piteously desperate for her body, ravenous for a taste of her.

When he took her nipple into his mouth, Ava made a guttural sound, dragged her fingers through his hair, and pushed her body up to meet him.

Something primal and deep kicked Jared hard; blood was raging through him like a river, ripping through his veins. He had never desired anyone or anything so badly in his life. The need to fill her was so overpowering that he couldn't stop.

Ava was panting, her hands roaming his body. When her fingers flitted across the fabric that covered his nipple, he suddenly rose above her, ripped the shirt from his body, and pushed the boots from his feet.

Lying beneath him, her breasts rising with each furious breath, her maiden's innocence apparently gone, Ava gazed at him, brazenly taking in all of his naked chest.

Jared ran his hand down her shoulder, over her collarbone, her breast, down the smooth plane of her belly, and over the fabric of her drawers. He caressed her thigh, and as he looked into her eyes, he slipped a finger into the slit of her drawers, and Ava squirmed.

He slipped his finger between the wet folds of her sex.

"*Oh God,*" she moaned, tossing her head back, baring her long neck to him. Jared withdrew his hand, took hold of her drawers and pushed them down her body. When he'd discarded them, he kissed her belly, then moved farther down, his mouth brushing the spring of honey curls, inhaling her feral scent.

Ava was panting harder now, the bedding in her fists. Jared pushed her legs apart and put his hand on her.

Ava came up on her elbows and looked down at

him as she drew long breaths into her lungs. "What are you doing?" she asked.

Jared smiled and slipped his tongue inside her. Ava squealed and tried to close her legs, but he pushed them open with his hands. "No," he said. "You will allow me."

He put his tongue against her again, and Ava slid down, her fingers groping for his shoulders. As he began to lick her, she bucked and made sounds of pleasure that sent the blood pounding through Jared, engorging him. But he held on and explored her thoroughly.

Ava's response was explosive; she was moving against him, panting for breath, the little cries of pleasure coming quicker and quicker as she neared her release. He stroked her, sucked her, nibbled as if she were a delicacy until she found it, crying up to the canopy, her hands clasping at his head, her body moving uncontrollably against him and away, then against him again. Her response was so explosive, and her demeanor so unrepentant that he came dangerously close to finding his release with her.

He rose above her, steadying himself with one hand as he unfastened his belt, shoved his trousers down his legs and kicked them off. Ava never opened her eyes. She just lay there, breathing hard, one hand draped over her naked breast, the other tangled in her hair.

"Are you all right?" he asked as he moved between her thighs.

She smiled dreamily without opening her eyes. "Mmm . . ."

He laughed, pressed the tip of his cock against her. Ava's eyes fluttered open as he began to move slowly back and forth. Her body was so warm, so wet—he strained for patience; he wanted to be inside her. He lowered himself to one arm, smoothed her hair back from her damp brow, then kissed her gently.

"Give me your hand," he said softly, and guided her to feel him.

Her fingers closed around him; he covered her hand with his and showed her how to move her hand on him.

"Oh *my*," she whispered. "It feels a bit like silk on marble."

Jared thought it felt like something else entirely and closed his eyes, clenching his jaw against the pleasures she was giving him.

With her other hand, Ava began to explore the rest of his body. She was conscious of the feel of his spine, the corded muscles in his back, the ripple of flesh in his shoulders. At the same time, he caressed her shoulders, her arms, and the curve of her waist into her hips and lower, slipping between her legs again, touching the very tender core of her. Ava strangled on her breath and pushed deep into the feather mattress, but Jared shamelessly stroked her, urging her thighs open with little effort. He buried his face in her breasts, suckling them while his shaft brushed her abdomen and thigh, its heat burning her skin.

She flinched when he slowly slipped one finger inside her, then two, and gently forced her body to open. But when he moved over her, pushing her legs apart with his knee and leaning over her until his manhood brushed against the swell of her sex, she flinched again.

"Relax," he muttered, and guided the velvet tip to brush her sheath. She wrenched beneath him, reflexively looking for an escape from the invasion. "*Relax*," he whispered again, and slowly, gently, he entered her, pushing a little farther, and then a little farther again, before settling down around her to begin a delicate dance inside her.

He kissed her tenderly, catching her bottom lip between his teeth, swirling his tongue inside her mouth as he continued his exquisite assault. Her body opened to him so naturally, so instinctively, that she was astounded both physically and emotionally by nature's joining of a man and woman. His breathing, she noticed, was hard, as if he struggled to maintain control.

He lowered himself to her completely and carefully slid deeper into her.

And then he paused. His hand stretched out to where hers clutched the bedcovers, and covered it. With a soft groan, he lifted his hips and suddenly thrust forward.

The sharpness of the pain caught her by surprise, and she unconsciously cried out as her whole body tensed in anticipation of more pain. She heard Jared's hiss of breath and felt his grip on her shoulder tighten as he stilled inside her. "Dear God, I'm sorry, I'm so sorry," he muttered, tenderly stroking her cheek. "God forgive me, I never meant to hurt you."

Ava barely heard him; she had no idea what to expect now, and was afraid that more pain would come. Even though the initial pain was slowly subsiding, she feared what he might do next.

She shifted uncomfortably beneath him—but his lips brushed across hers, touching her cheek and temple while his hand stroked her hair. He began to move again, easy and slow, sliding into her depths and out again, moving with her until his hand tightened around her wrist. "Easy," he breathed into her neck, and repeated the movement, filling her with pain and pleasure all at once.

It was a magnificent sensation—the pleasure was overtaking the pain as he continued his even course of stroking her with his body, lengthening inside her. When his hand slipped between their joined bodies and began to stroke her, Ava choked on a cry of pleasure. As every muscle strained to surround him, his strokes took on a new urgency, and he gathered her in his arms.

"Hold me," he whispered. Ava put her arms around him and lifted her legs, wrapping them around him, too.

She felt as if she were soaring high above their bodies, the pleasure seeping into the space around them. And when she thought she could bear no more, she climaxed again, heard his low groan as he thrust into her one last time and shuddered.

He lay panting for several seconds before he lifted his head and brushed the hair from her eyes. "Are you all right? Are you in pain?"

All right? She was glowing. She had not known that the joining of a man and woman could be so physically liberating. She smiled tenderly and put her hand to his chin. "I am fine."

He looked at her for a long moment, his expression full of desire. He kissed her lightly as he eased out of her body and rolled onto his back, propping one arm behind his head as his breathing returned to normal. One hand tangled with hers, stroking her palm and twining with her fingers. He said nothing, but looked toward the fire. Ava rolled into his side, nuzzling her face in his neck, smiling contentedly when he gripped her hand.

Beside her, Jared was feeling very strange. That had been a truly moving experience—to take a woman's virginity sparked something deep and primal within him. It wasn't just sex, but something much more profound. It had left him feeling oddly possessive of her, and worse, oddly vulnerable, as if he'd opened a door on himself he'd never known existed and didn't know where it led.

He squeezed her hand, thought of the morrow, and the day after that, and the day after that—and slowly began to remember why he was in her bed at all. "When will you next see your courses?" he asked with all the finesse of a goat.

His question obviously startled her; she looked up, wide-eyed, and blushing. "I . . . I don't know in all certainty. A week. Maybe longer."

He said nothing more, just closed his eyes, holding her hand. Next to him, Ava shivered and pulled the bedcovers around her shoulders, then settled onto his chest, her eyes closed. He listened to the sound of her breathing, listened to it deepen as she fell asleep.

He couldn't sleep—he couldn't allow such tender feelings to stew. His thoughts were warring with his emotions, his common sense trying to convince him it had been an unremarkable coupling while his heart told him something different.

He glanced down, saw that Ava was asleep, and carefully extracted himself from the arm thrown across his middle, the shapely leg on top of his. As he eased out of bed, Ava rolled to the middle; he couldn't help but smile.

He donned a dressing gown, walked to the window, and looked out at the early summer night. *Jesus*, but he felt at sea. He'd always bedded whom he pleased without feelings of guilt or remorse. But with Ava, he was feeling so many things at once that he found it all rather daunting.

So daunting that he hardly slept that night, and

when he rose with the dawn the next morning, clinging to the edge of the bed where Ava had pushed him in her sleep abandon, he was determined that he'd not let another moment of raw sentimentality cloud his thoughts.

He had done what was required of him. Now he need only wait and see if he'd planted the necessary seed. Yet he could not shake the grip of something unnatural budding inside of him.

Before the sun was even in the sky, Jared Broderick had dressed and taken a horse from a sleepy stableboy.

When Ava awoke the next morning, she was alone in the bed. She sat up, using a sheet to cover herself, and blinked the sleep from her eyes as she looked around the room.

"Jared?" she called, but the name sounded foreign on her lips. She cleared her throat. "My lord?" she called out again, and rolled her eyes. That sounded entirely too formal after what had happened between them. Something profound *had* happened to her—something greater than the loss of her virginity. She felt sticky and sore, but she also felt incredibly . . . *alive*. That act, as painful as it had been, was also perhaps the most defining moment in her life. It was as if she had crossed some sort of invisible threshold, and the thought occurred to her that she might actually come to love Middleton.

She got out of the bed, taking the sheet with her and wrapping it around her body.

He was not in the dressing room. Nor was he in his private study. With a sigh, Ava returned to the bedroom and glanced around. She saw a pin box on his dresser and walked over to have a look. The pin lay on the top of the dresser, and in the box, she noticed, was a small, folded piece of vellum.

Ava picked up the vellum and opened it, expecting to see something like the bill of sale. But what she saw was flourished handwriting that made her heart twist in her chest.

My darling, the note started, and Ava's breath caught in her throat. She lifted her hand to her mouth.

> *Please accept this token of my love. It is a Celtic love knot, one that symbolizes everlasting love between two people. My hope is that you will wear it today and think of our future, and know when you hold it in your hand that my heart shall always be yours to hold.*
>
> M.

Ava's mouth suddenly went dry. She dropped the vellum like it was fire, then quickly folded it and put it back in the box where she'd found it and backed away. Yet she could not take her eyes from the pin, the love knot tied so intricately that it could never come undone.

The knowledge that Lady Waterstone had sent it to him to wear on his wedding day, had asked him to wear it and think of her, made her feel quite ill.

She stumbled away from the dresser, to the bed and the bloodstained sheets, and collapsed onto it as she tried to catch her breath.

Eighteen

～～＞く～～

Jared was in London by late morning. He bathed, met with Mr. Bean about settling a suitable allowance for Ava on her family, to be given at once, and then repaired to White's by late afternoon.

With the exception of the early morning, when he'd left his bride sleeping peacefully in his bed, her lips curled into a beguiling little smile in her sleep, Jared hadn't thought of Ava very much. As soon as he knew he had put a child in her belly, he would return to London permanently and that would be the end to these uncharacteristically soft and tender feelings he was having for her.

At White's, he was met by several curious looks, but none more curious than that of Harrison, who stared at Jared as if he'd seen a ghost when he joined him at their usual table. "Has something happened?" Harrison asked anxiously.

"No," Jared said with a laugh. "There were matters here that required my attention."

"Here?" Harrison asked, peering at him skeptically. "None that could wait, or be given your attention at Broderick Abbey? You just married yesterday, after all."

"Are you my bloody conscience?" Jared snapped.

Harrison smiled wryly. "No . . . I'd be a better conscience to you than the one you've apparently got."

He didn't need to be lectured about his *duty* by his old friend—he'd done his *duty*. But Jared didn't respond, just turned and ordered a round of whiskey. And Harrison's initial scorn didn't keep him from drinking or indulging in a few high-stakes rounds of cards with him, either.

Jared returned to Broderick Abbey the next afternoon, arriving only an hour or so before the supper hour. "Please tell Lady Middleton I am returned," Jared said as he handed Dawson his hat and coat. He could hardly avoid Ava, and he didn't *want* to avoid her. Quite the contrary—he actually enjoyed her company. He just didn't want to feel a deep bond to her.

"Her ladyship has asked that, if you arrived, you join her for supper at eight," Dawson replied.

"I shall, but I should like to wash and change my clothing before I meet her. Have a bath prepared, will you?" he said, and strode past his butler, taking the post a footman offered him on his way up to his suite.

In his suite, he went through the various letters. Most were from well-wishers on the occasion of his marriage. There were a few pieces of business correspondence as well, and an invitation to join Harrison's annual inauguration of the hunting season in two months' time.

Last, there was a letter from Miranda. That one Jared put aside without reading.

He strode to the bellpull and yanked it; a few moments later, a footman appeared. "Bring some clothing for my supper with the marchioness," he said, and poured himself a whiskey—which he seemed to be doing quite a lot these last two weeks, he thought numbly—and sat in one of the wingback chairs at the hearth.

As the footman disappeared through an adjoining door, Jared removed his boots and leaned back, propped his feet on the ottoman, his mind wandering to thoughts of how he might rotate the crops to bring a better yield.

But when the door to the dressing room opened, he caught the faint scent of perfume and glanced up; it was Ava standing there, holding his clothing in her arms. "What a pleasant surprise, Lady Middleton," he said, slightly taken aback that she would appear without introduction.

She said nothing, just walked to where he sat and put his clothes on the ottoman next to his foot. Then she folded her arms across her middle in a way Jared recognized as the universal symbol of feminine ire. No matter how sweet the smile, the devilish gleam in the eye and the fold of the arms spoke volumes.

He slowly gained his feet, standing a good six inches taller than his wife. "You are frowning, Lady Middleton. Is there something not to your liking at Broderick Abbey?" he asked. "Tell me and I shall have it repaired at once."

She looked quite surprised by that. She leaned toward him, chin up, and said, "You disappeared without a word."

He leaned forward so that they were looking each other in the eye and said softly, "It is not true I left without word, madam. I informed Dawson where I would be." With that he picked up his tot and walked to the sideboard to pour another whiskey.

"But you didn't leave word with me."

"You were sleeping. I did not want to disturb you."

"I can understand if you'd gone to Broderick, but *London*?"

He shrugged insouciantly. "I had business there. I often have business in London."

"Of course, but we were married only two days past."

"I am quite aware of when we married," he said irritably. He tossed the whiskey down his throat and turned to face her. "Commerce does not cease for weddings, births, or funerals."

"Oh . . . then it was something that couldn't wait?" she asked hopefully, and waited for him to confirm that yes, it had been something so terribly important it could not have possibly waited another moment—something so important that it would cause a man to leave the woman he'd wedded only the day before.

As that was very far from the truth, her question made him extremely uncomfortable and he sighed impatiently. "I will indulge your questions on this occasion, Lady Middleton, as we are fairly new to one another, but I do not like to be questioned so closely. I went to London so that I could set up an allowance for you and your family. I have now returned from London. But I often travel as business and obligations dictate. In fact, in a few days, I shall travel to Marshbridge to see about some cattle."

"To *Marshbridge*?" she echoed incredulously.

"Your lady's maid will arrive in a few days," he reminded her. "I am certain you will have much to keep you occupied, what with all that you must learn about Broderick Abbey. You will hardly notice my absence at all."

"But I will," she said bleakly, as if he'd just announced he was leaving for the Continent for an indefinite amount of time. "How long shall you be away?"

As long as is required to rid myself of these unnatural feelings. "I am uncertain," he said. "Two days. Perhaps longer."

She blinked, and looked at her hands.

He felt, of a sudden, rather tired and cross. "Shall I see you at supper?" he asked curtly.

Ava lifted her head, and the mildly irked look in her green eyes agitated him. Why did she look at him like that? They'd made their bargain—would she pretend now that she didn't know exactly what they'd agreed? Her womb for his name, nothing more than that. She seemed to have already forgotten it, was intent on shackling him from the very outset. He abruptly turned away from her. "I shall join you downstairs."

There was a moment's hesitation, then the sound of her leaving his room.

An hour later, Jared joined Ava in the salon. She had changed her clothes, and was wearing a cream-colored silk gown embroidered with dark green leaves that made her look a bit like an angel. Around her throat was a triple strand of pearls that matched those clipped to her ears and strung in her hair. He had thought her pretty once, but the more he saw of her, the more he found her to be uniquely beautiful.

She was pacing a little when he walked into the salon, oblivious to the two footmen who attended her. She jerked her gaze to him when the door closed behind him, her eyes quickly taking him in as she walked across the room to him. She dropped a very quick curtsy, and just as quickly, rose up on her toes to peck him on the cheek.

He smiled wryly. "Been in the whiskey again, have you?" he teased her.

"Not as yet. Should I begin?" she asked sarcastically.

He hated that look on her face; he wanted to see her sunny smile again. "You may do as you like. You won't mind if I have one, will you?" Indeed, one of the footmen was moving toward the sideboard as he spoke. He motioned for Ava to take a seat on the settee, and sat beside her.

When the footman had presented him with the whiskey, he held it up to her in silent toast. "A very lovely gown," he said, taking it in. "Quite fetching."

She smiled thinly and sat rather stiffly next to him. Neither of them spoke. His bride, always so exuberant, was very subdued.

"Does the abbey meet with your approval?" he asked idly, hardly caring of her answer, wanting only to break the cold silence that was enveloping them.

But she looked at him as if he were mad. "Very much, my lord."

He glanced at the arm of the settee. "Did Dawson look after you while I was away?" he asked as he plucked absently at the seam in the fabric.

"He did, indeed. Miss Hillier, too. She's very fond of you."

"And I of her," he admitted. "She was my nursemaid."

"Yes," Ava said, glancing away. "She said as much. She told me how you were five years before you could pronounce the letter *s.*"

He shook his head. Miss Hillier could drive him quite round the bend on occasion. "Did you have a nursemaid?" he asked for sake of conversation.

"Several. My mother couldn't seem to keep them

employed for very long. I suppose we were so terribly spoiled that no one could bear us."

He could well imagine the three of them torturing some poor nursemaid. "Spoiled?"

"Oh, dreadfully!" she exclaimed, and seemed to relax as she began to tell him tales, in great animation, of her life at Bingley Hall. It was odd, he thought, that a person could swear his devotion to a woman and know so little about her. The years at Bingley Hall were obviously her fondest memory, and he wasn't even certain where it was.

But at least the memory of it animated her, and he enjoyed watching her talk, her hands moving expressively, her green eyes glimmering with tales of what seemed a happy childhood. When Dawson announced supper, and he escorted his wife to her seat, she told him again of her mother's death and how suddenly it had come. His heart went out to her—his own mother had been gone a long time now, but he remembered that deep sense of loss, the hole in him that his mother's love had once filled.

"Oh dear," Ava said, dabbing at the corner of her eye with her napkin. "I beg your pardon, my lord . . . I don't know what's come over me."

He reached for her hand. "She was very dear to you, obviously."

She nodded, and when she'd regained her composure, she turned her attention back to her plate and took a bite of pike. "Do you remember your mother?"

"Of course," he responded. But he didn't tell her that his memory of her was fading more with each passing year.

"If I may . . . where is Redford?" she asked.

Just the mention of his father's estate and his childhood home caused him to flinch inwardly. "North," he said tightly.

"What was it—"

"It is nothing but a distant memory now that I really don't recall," he said, interrupting her before she could quiz him endlessly on a period of his life he'd just as soon forget.

She looked at him with surprise.

He could see that the tone of his voice had upset her—really, almost everything he'd done since marrying her—with the exception of bedding her—had upset her. He sighed wearily and put aside his fork. "Do forgive me, but I don't recall a particularly happy childhood. As you can imagine, my father was quite . . . *stern*," he added.

She asked nothing else, and they continued their meal in silence. It seemed to Jared to stretch into hours. He ate and thought of London, of the many things he would be doing were he there, and how he could not bear to wile away the days here in pursuit of some elusive domesticity.

When supper was finished, and the footman had cleared the last of the dishes away, Jared reached into his coat pocket and extracted a cheroot. He held it up to Ava. "If it offends you, I shall step outside."

"No," she said, shaking her head, and gestured for him to smoke it.

He lit it, exhaled a ring of smoke, and smiled at her. "You must be tired. If you should like to retire, then by all means, you must do so."

She smiled. "I'm not tired," she said. "I can stay as long as you like."

That was precisely what he was afraid of. Just looking at her now, her cheeks rosy from the dinner wine, her long, tapered fingers dancing on the stem of the glass, he felt a tug of desire to take her to his bed. And once again, that desire unnerved him, and put him on uneven ground. He didn't want to physically desire her at all, for that only made the situation more difficult.

He had determined, during the long stretch of day, that he would do his duty by her, but no more than that. How could he? Anything more would feed expectations, and the less they expected of one another, the happier they would both be.

He ground the cheroot out, stretched his hands on the table before him, and said evenly, "You needn't wait for me, Lady Middleton. There is some correspondence I must review before retiring."

She blinked, glanced uneasily at the footman. "Won't you call me Ava?" she asked softly. "Lady Middleton seems so . . . *formal.*"

"Ava," he said reluctantly. The formality served to hold her at arm's length, where he wanted her. "If you will excuse me, I have some correspondence I must review."

But before he could go, she shifted in her chair, closer to him, and leaned forward, obviously aware of the footmen. "But . . . but can't you see to it on the morrow?" she whispered. "I thought perhaps we might read, or—"

"It cannot wait," he said curtly.

Her disappointment was clearly evident, and it pricked him much more sharply than he cared to admit. After a moment, she sagged against the back of her chair and released a long sigh.

"Is something wrong?" he asked calmly.

"Not at all, other than I rather thought that as we'd only joined together in matrimony day before yesterday," she said, lifting her gaze to him, "we might spend at least a *bit* of time together."

He'd been so certain she understood their match, so certain she would be little trouble when she had what she wanted. Now he felt pressed to explain when he really couldn't explain himself at all because *he* couldn't understand what was happening inside him.

The situation perturbed him; he glanced at the two footmen. "That will be all," he said, and waited for the two men to quit the room. When they had gone through the pocket door leading to the next room, he turned an unwavering gaze to his wife and said, "I prefer we not discuss the details of our private lives before the servants, Lady Middleton."

"Private life? As we have not as yet established *any* sort of life, I do not deserve your admonishment."

His gaze narrowed. "We do indeed have a *life*, and it is none of the servants' concern."

Ava shrugged and looked away.

Women, he thought with an internal sigh. "Lady Middleton," he said quietly but firmly, "look at me."

She lifted her chin, just like a child, and refused to look at him.

"*Look* at me," he said again, his voice brooking no argument.

She glanced at him from the corner of her eye. He leaned forward, put his hand around her wrist, and held it tightly. "We had an agreement, you and I," he reminded her. "We agreed to further one another's ends."

"I understand—"

"I don't think you do," he interrupted. "We made a bargain that came with certain defined expectations for us both. Beyond those expectations, there is nothing more, and you should not wish for it."

"I hope you will forgive me for pointing out that you were far more charming before we married," she said, yanking her wrist free of his grasp. "I understood our mutual expectations, my lord, but I did not think we'd be complete strangers to one another."

He snorted at that. "We are no longer strangers, madam, and well you know it. But I would advise, for the sake of your happiness, that you do not ask of me what I cannot give. Do you understand? I can give you a name, and my protection, and extend that protection to your family, all in exchange for your bearing me a son. That was our tacit agreement and that is *all* I can give you."

Ava's green eyes went wide. She blinked, with anger or hurt or perhaps both. But before she could argue the point, he stood up, walked around the table to her, put his hand on her shoulders, and leaned down to kiss her cheek. "Sleep well, wife," he said, and walked out of the dining room.

Nineteen

~~~~~·×·~~~~~

Another sleepless night, and Ava was up just after dawn, staring forlornly out her window—which gave her opportunity to see her husband ride out on his brown horse as the sun was rising, his speed reckless.

She pulled her dressing robe tightly around her as she watched him disappear down the road. When she couldn't see him any longer, she walked back to her bed and flung herself on it. She'd never felt so lost, not when her mother died or Greer left. No, nothing had prepared her or warned her for the loneliness of marriage. She felt as if she were wandering aimlessly, seeking any direction.

This was most certainly *not* what she had bargained for. It was not what she'd expected, not what she wanted, and not something she thought she could possibly bear.

Granted, she'd been fully prepared to live a life separate from her husband—except for the relations they would have to produce children, obviously, and, all right, except for the fabulous routs she had dreamed of them hosting—but then again, she'd not expected to *feel* so differently about it all after her wedding night.

That was something her mother had neglected to tell her—that strong emotions would accompany relations with a man so handsome and dashing as her husband. Ava had never suspected she could feel so tender of heart that she would *need* to see him, need to touch him, need to bask in the warmth of his smile.

This was not the carefree existence her mother had touted. This was not pleasant, nor was it convenient. It was, in fact, quite painful. Ava felt like a fool, like a trollop who had carelessly and foolishly traded her happiness for wealth and social position.

Worse, she had absolutely no idea what to do about it and no one to help her. She could scarcely confide in Miss Hillier—she didn't know the woman, and besides, she clearly loved Middleton like a son. There was simply no one to whom she could unburden herself.

"Well, then," she said to no one, "you must endeavor to think quite hard on it, Lady Middleton."

She frowned at the sound of her new name. She found it distasteful when *he* said it, as if she were more a mistress than a wife, and hardly a mistress at that.

All the moping was making her restless. She'd never been one to mope, actually, and made up her mind she would not start now. A walk—that is what she needed. A walk to help her think.

She marched to her dressing room, where all her clothes had been pressed and put away by a staff so efficient that she was actually beginning to think that if she *did* do something entirely on her own, they would be highly offended. After rifling through the few gowns she'd brought, she found a serviceable, somber day gown.

At her solitary breakfast, Ava inquired of Dawson

if there were any walking paths to which he might point her.

He looked surprised by her question. "There are some walking paths, madam, but the gardens are much more enjoyable."

"Thank you, but I would prefer a good walk with sun and fresh air."

Dawson frowned lightly. "I would not think his lordship would want you to walk alone, my lady. Perhaps you might wait until he returns?"

Just the mention of his absence rankled Ava, and she abruptly stood up, smiled brightly at Dawson, and shook her head. "I think not, sir, for he could very well be gone quite some time. Days, even. I should like to walk today."

Dawson hurried after her to show her the path, pleading with her not to go alone. But Ava fit a bonnet on her head and asked, "What is there to fear, Mr. Dawson? Cows?" She laughed at her own joke.

"There is nothing to fear, Lady Middleton, but you might twist an ankle—"

Ava gestured for the footman to open the door. "I assure you I am quite capable of walking, and frankly, I think I do it rather well. I will be quite all right. Is there a chance I might stumble on a village or some such thing?"

"Madam," he said, clearly mortified, "you *cannot* mean to go as far as Broderick!"

"Can't I?" she asked airily, fitting her hands into her gloves. "How far can it be? Three, perhaps four miles? I shall return this afternoon. Oh do stop looking so alarmed, Mr. Dawson!" She patted his arm. "I assure you, I will be quite all right. Where is the path, then? To the east? The west?"

Mr. Dawson frowned and reluctantly pointed out the path.

Ava set out at a good pace, hoping a bit of exercise would help her. And if it didn't, Sally Pierce would arrive from London in two days. At the very least, she'd have someone to talk to. She might not agree with everything Sally said—probably nothing, really—but at least it would be better than the quiet that surrounded her now.

It was so quiet, in fact, and the air so still, that she heard the snap of a twig behind her. And then twice more. Having been the oldest of three, Ava knew very well the sound of being followed. She instantly suspected Dawson, and with a roll of her eyes, when the path turned, she ducked behind a tree, held her breath, and waited.

It was only a moment before the footman appeared, walking clumsily along, his shoes ill-suited to the forest path. "Here I am," Ava said.

The poor man cried out, clapped a hand over his heart. "I beg your pardon, milady," he said as he gasped for breath. "I didn't see you there!"

"Obviously," she said, stepping out from behind the tree. She stood before him, her hands on her hips. "Why are you following me, sir?"

The man flushed and averted his eyes. "Mr. Dawson said I should."

"And did he tell you to watch for roots and limbs and anything that I might stumble over and twist my ankle?"

He nodded sheepishly. "That," he muttered, "and robbers."

"Hmm," Ava said, and folded her arms, drumming her fingers against her arm as she considered him. "Are there robbers in this forest?"

"Not," he said with a sympathetic wince, "that I am aware."

"I thought not," she said with a sigh. "What is your name, then?"

"Robert, mu'um."

"Well, then, Robert, if you must walk with me, then at the very least, *walk* with me. I can't abide you sneaking about."

"Aye, mu'um," he said, and fell in beside her, stepping carefully as Ava walked easily through the forest.

They had gone only a little farther when a child's voice called out to them, "Halt! Who trespasses in the marquis' forest?"

Ava stopped and followed the sound of the young voice, looking up. There, in the crook of an oak tree, was a boy, holding a child's bow and arrow. It was the boy she'd seen at the wedding, the one who had been watching her as he stood apart from the others as they scampered for the coins Middleton tossed. He was well dressed, she thought, his clothes clean and well fitted. She thought he was the son of someone with a good living—a clergyman, or a lawyer, perhaps.

"Pardon, mu'um," Robert said gruffly. "He's a wee ruffian. I'll see to him," he said, and strode forward.

But the boy instantly pointed an arrow at him. "Have you his lordship's permit to cross these lands?" he asked imperiously.

"Come out of that tree, lad! Do you not recognize your marchioness?"

"Of course I do," the boy said. "I saw her married, same as you."

"Then wouldn't you assume, if she is the marchioness, that she has the lordship's leave to cross these lands?"

He seemed to consider the question a moment,

then shrugged, and hopped down out of the tree. On the ground, he looked to be seven or eight. He had a mop of thick dark brown hair and hazel eyes, through which he peered closely at Ava. "You're prettier up close," he announced.

The footman slapped the back of his head. "Mind who you're speaking to!" he said sternly.

Ava laughed and touched the top of his head. "Thank you, kind sir," she said with a playful curtsy. "Have you a name?"

"Edmond Foote, mu'um."

"Believe he belongs to the gamekeeper, mu'um," Robert offered.

The child looked too finely dressed to be the game-keeper's son. She smiled at the boy again—he was a sturdy young thing. One day he'd be a man as strong and tall as Middleton, she reckoned. "Mr. Foote, we're to Broderick. Would you care to join us?" Ava asked.

He squinted up at her and shook his head. "I'm not allowed in Broderick."

"No?"

He shook his head.

"I'm very sorry. We might have used your protection. If we have your permission, we will carry on."

"I'll allow you to pass," he said agreeably, and stepped back, bowing low. Ava laughed, and with Robert glaring at the boy, she walked on.

By the time she and Robert reached the small village of Broderick, she knew that Robert was an orphan, had been taken in by Middleton when he was a lad, and that he held Charlotte, one of the scullery maids, in very high esteem. Ava advised him that if he thought to marry her, to marry her because he loved her, and not to marry for the sake of convenience or situation.

Robert seemed confused by her advice. "Convenience, mu'um? I didn't know marriage was meant to be convenient."

"My point precisely," she said, tapping him on the arm. "It's not terribly convenient after all."

"Aye, mu'um," he said, dipping his head, but he still looked rather confused.

In Broderick, she stepped into a dry goods shop and chatted it up with the proprietor, who eagerly agreed to come to Broderick Abbey early the following week and show Ava fabrics for her sitting room, which she found cold and damp and very dark. Ava decided it was perfectly acceptable to order materials. After all, she would probably be alone and he had promised to provide for her every need.

At a confectionary, she admired the sweetmeats, but when the proprietor asked if he might wrap some up for her, she shook her head. "I'm afraid I haven't any money, sir," she said.

The proprietor looked at Robert. Robert stepped forward and whispered something in the man's ear. He instantly set about wrapping up the sweetmeats, and when Ava protested, he shook his head and said firmly, "Pardon, madam, but I *insist*."

"But I—"

"Your husband's name will do well enough, I assure you," he said, and with a broad smile, he deposited a wrapped bundle in her arms.

"You are too kind," Ava said, trying to juggle the enormous package, which Robert took from her to hold.

She and Robert started back under a glorious blue sky, munching on sweetmeats, laughing about the man they'd seen who'd had a row with a goat he was trying to bring to market. It was really a very pleasant day, and might have ended very well had Robert not very gallantly offered to get her some water from the stream and then fallen down the embankment, landing awkwardly, leaving his foot at an odd angle to his leg.

His ankle was, Ava determined when she managed to pick her way down the steep embankment, quite broken.

"You must go on, milady," Robert said, in obvious pain. "Dawson will have me head if you aren't returned at a proper hour."

"Nonsense, Robert. I will not leave you alone." She glanced up and noted it was getting late. "Surely there is someone close by I can summon for help?"

"The gamekeeper," Robert said through clenched teeth. "But he's fairly new to the abbey, mu'um, and I've not met him."

"Where can I find him?"

"The fork in the road, where we went right. If we'd gone left—"

"I know where it is," Ava said, and took the light cloak from her shoulders and put it over Robert. "I shall bring him at once. Don't fret, Robert." And with that, she scrambled up the embankment and ran down the path to the fork.

She found the cottage easily enough, but when she knocked on the door, young Edmond Foote opened it.

"Mr. Foote, we meet again, but under less pleasant circumstances," she said. "Where is your father?"

"Setting traps, mu'um."

"Then is your mother within?"

"She's in heaven."

"Oh dear." Ava glanced up at the sky. The sun had started its descent into late afternoon. "All right, then, young man, you are the one who must help me. You

must go to the abbey at once and tell Mr. Dawson
there has been an accident."

The boy's eyes lit up. "What *sort* of accident?" he
asked eagerly, coming out of the cottage to have a
look around, obviously hoping the accident had
occurred close by.

Ava clamped a hand on his shoulder to gain his
attention. "Edmond, listen carefully. The footman has
broken his ankle. You must go to the abbey and bring
help."

"But I'm not allowed at the abbey," he said, looking
very concerned.

Good God, was the child allowed anywhere but
the forest? "You have my special permission," she
said. "Now go at once."

Edmond glanced uneasily at the cottage behind him.

"*Now*, Edmond. I will speak to your father and tell
him that I demanded you go."

"Yes, mu'um," he said, and set out at a run.

"I will meet you at the fork!" Ava shouted after him.

Jared returned from his rounds to his tenants at
teatime, having determined that he should be more
accommodating to his young bride until she was
accustomed to their arrangement. But instead of finding her painting or sewing, or whatever it was wives
did to occupy their time, he found a rather frantic
Dawson.

In all the years of their association, he'd never seen
Dawson in such a state. "What is it?" Jared asked.

"It is Lady Middleton, my lord. She walked to the
village—"

"*Walked?*"

"I said that she shouldn't, but she insisted. I sent
Robert, the footman, along with her, but they've

been gone too long. Billy has just come back from the village, but could find neither hide nor hair of them."

The edge of panic nosed Jared. He would never forgive himself if something had happened.

He quickly strode outside with the intention of getting his mount and riding the walking path himself, but he was brought up short by the appearance of a boy on the drive. He knew the boy—of course he knew him. He'd seen him about the grounds, but he'd never seen him so close and was taken aback.

The boy looked frightened and was wringing his wool cap in his hands. "I know I'm not to come to the house, my lord, but the marchioness sent me."

"Where is she?" Jared asked, snapping out of his surprise. "Is she all right?"

"There's been an accident," the child said, and Jared felt his heart plummet.

He caught the boy by the shoulder and shook him, forcing him to look up at him. "What sort of accident? Is she all right?"

"She is!" he cried. "It's the footman! He's broken his ankle!"

Jared instantly let go of the boy and turned to the servants who had rushed outside to see what had happened. "Have Billy bring two mounts—he and I will go and fetch them."

One of the footmen began running, and Jared turned and looked at the boy, his gaze taking in his face—his dark red lips, the tilt of his nose. His eyes . . . *his eyes*. "Well done, Edmond," he said quietly, and the child's face broke into a gap-toothed smile.

By the time Jared and Billy found Ava and the footman, they had been rescued from the stream by the gamekeeper. Jared swung down from his mount, then helped Edmond down. Edmond had ridden in front of Jared, leaning forward, stroking the horse's mane along the way. The boy ran to his father, who instantly put a protective arm around him and held him close to his side.

"Mr. Foote," Jared said, acknowledging the gamekeeper. "Your son is to be commended for coming to the marchioness's aid."

The man nodded and glanced at Robert, who was gritting his teeth as Billy, Jared's longtime groundskeeper, had a look at his ankle. "I was setting traps for the boar," Mr. Foote said, "and I come across them, down by the stream."

Jared nodded and swallowed hard. "It would seem I owe you yet another debt of thanks," he said, but Mr. Foote shrugged and tightened his grip on his son.

Jared moved to Ava's side. The light was beginning to dim, but he could see her muddied walking gown and the thick strands of hair that had fallen loose from her bonnet. Robert was as gray as a winter sky.

Jared didn't say much—he couldn't seem to find his voice, either from relief that she was unharmed or anger that she'd come so close to harm. He helped Billy put Robert on the back of Billy's mount, then moved to put Ava on his horse. But she darted away from him, to the side of the path and a bundle he'd not noticed before that moment. She picked it up, walked back to his horse, and stuffed it into the bonnet that was hanging from her wrist.

He looked into her eyes; she smiled a little. "Sweetmeats, from the confectioner's shop. I hope you don't mind."

Still unable to speak without emotion, he shook his head, put his hands to her waist, and lifted her up, setting her atop the big gray he'd ridden. "Hold on to the pommel," he told her.

Ava shifted her bundle and held on to the pommel as instructed. Jared swung up behind her and put his arms securely around her, her bare head tucked beneath his chin.

He sent the bay trotting along the path. Billy and Robert would follow behind, but at a slower pace to keep the pain from Robert's ankle as best they could.

When they were a good distance from Billy, Jared said, "Lady Middleton, you are not to *walk* to Broderick."

"But I—"

"You may have a carriage take you, or you may ride horseback in the company of a servant. If you do not ride, I will teach you, but you are not to *walk*. Am I perfectly clear?"

"Perfectly," she said in a small voice.

He let another moment pass and asked her gently, "Do you ride?"

She said nothing for a moment; her hand went to the nape of her neck, as if she were somehow debating her answer. At last, she admitted, "I do not."

"Then I shall teach you when I have returned from Marshbridge."

She said nothing at all, but slowly sank back against him, her head on his shoulder, the warm weight of her against his chest.

He dropped one arm from the reins, slipped it around her middle, and held her tightly to him. He took in the rosewater scent of her hair, felt the softness of her body, and felt that little nudge inside him, just as he'd felt when Dawson had said she'd gone missing.

It was the edge of panic again, only a panic born of a different sort of fear entirely.

Twenty

~~~

Middleton did not come to Ava's suite that night, nor did he invite her to his, but the next morning, she was startled awake by him standing over her bed. She gasped and quickly pushed herself up.

He said nothing, just gazed down at her. He was dressed to go out, his cloak draped over his shoulders. He held gloves in one hand that he kept slapping into the palm of his other hand.

Ava pushed herself up a little farther and brushed the braid of her hair over her shoulder. "My lord?"

His gaze swept over her, from the top of her hair to the shape of her feet beneath the bedcovers. "Did you sleep well?"

"Yes," she said uncertainly.

He nodded and slapped the gloves against his hand again. "I'm to Marshbridge," he said. "I shall return in a day or two."

She nodded.

He smiled a little lopsidedly. "I am personally informing you," he added, and sat on the edge of her bed. He leaned close to her and looked her in the eye. "You are not to *walk* to Broderick, madam."

Ava sighed and rolled her eyes, but she smiled. "I

am very well aware of that. You've mentioned it more than once."

Middleton's gaze roamed over her once more. He lifted his hand, brushed her bare collarbone, then trailed his fingers into the gap of her nightgown, between her breasts. When he lifted his gaze again, it seemed to be simmering, and Ava suppressed a shiver. He looked as if he intended to speak, as if he *wanted* to speak . . . but he pressed his lips together, put his hand to her cheek, and kissed her.

Carefully, achingly, he kissed her.

Ava wrapped her hand around his wrist, sought to put her other hand on his chest. But Middleton stopped her by covering her hand with his and lifting his head. He said nothing; he stood, put his hand to the crown of her head, and caressed her hair. "Good day," he said, and strode out, his cloak snapping around his ankles.

When he'd gone out, Ava grabbed her pillow tightly to her, sank back into the feather mattress, and wished again that he would love her, if only a little.

All day long, Ava felt she was being watched by a chicken hawk. Wherever she went, Mr. Dawson or Miss Hillier seemed to be nearby.

Miss Hillier, Ava was learning, was a very disapproving woman. She kept rattling off all the things a marchioness would never do, such as walk to town. Or feed the chickens. Or tidy up her own room. Or inquire after a footman and his ankle, which, Miss Hillier assured her, was doing perfectly well.

It was as if Lady Purnam's spirit had come to reside in Miss Hillier.

With the constant watching after her, Ava felt trapped inside the enormous Broderick Abbey. It was old and drafty and quite damp, but worse than anything, there was absolutely no life there. It seemed as if everyone just toiled in their daily labors.

After luncheon, Ava walked outside. The day was warm and bright, and she wandered in the direction of the lake she'd seen the first day she had come to Broderick Abbey. It was near the entrance to the estate, she recalled, and indeed, she found it within a mile of the house. She stood at the edge of the water, breathing in the fresh air.

A flock of swans swimming furiously to the middle of the lake caught her attention, and she saw the reason for their distress: On the left bank was Edmond Foote. Ava lifted her hand high above her head and waved. Edmond waved back.

He was fishing, she realized, and she decided to have a look at what he'd caught. She walked around the lake, finally reaching him. "Any luck?" she asked as she made her way down to the water's edge.

"No, mu'um. I think my line is caught," he said, and tugged at the string. He started to move toward the water's edge, but Ava quickly stopped him with a hand to his shoulder.

"Your father would not approve of you going into the lake, young man. I'll fetch it for you," she said, and sat down on the rock next to him to pull off her stockings and shoes.

"You mustn't put bare feet in lake water, mu'um. My mother said cold water on cold feet will catch your death. Didn't your mother ever tell you so?"

She laughed as she rolled off her stockings. "My mother told me many things, but never that."

"Where is your mother?" he asked curiously.

"In heaven, like yours."

He regarded her thoughtfully. "Does she know you've been sent to Broderick Abbey?"

He made it sound as if she'd been sent against her will, but she smiled and winked at him. "In a way, I think she does."

"I think mine does, too," he said with a firm nod of his head.

Ava stood up, picked up her skirts so that her legs were exposed from the knees down, and waded into the lake. The water was clear but frigid, and she winced with each step. The fishing line had caught on some debris, and with a bit of a tug, Ava was able to free it, much to the delight of young Edmond. He pulled in the line as Ava waded back to the shore.

"Thank you, marchioness!" he said, picking up his bucket.

"Wait!" she cried, still wading in. "Where are you off to?"

"Home!" he shouted, and skipped off.

"That's a fine how do you do," she muttered to herself, and took a step, sinking into mud up to her ankle. Drat. She pulled her foot free and stepped out of the water.

"Good day!"

With a gasp, Ava inadvertently dropped her skirt and looked up. A woman in a very fetching riding habit was atop her horse, on the rise above the lake, waving a gloved hand at Ava.

"Oh dear God," Ava whispered, and glanced down at her skirt. The hem was soaked and stained brown now.

"Good day, good day!" the woman said again as she sent her horse down the slope. She was a dark-haired, blue-eyed beauty—the sort, Ava thought, that was often painted around London.

"May I introduce myself? I am Lady Kettle. My late husband's estate borders yours."

"How do you do," Ava said. "I am—"

"Oh my goodness, I *know* who you are!" she cried cheerfully. "I would have made proper introduction at your wedding, but I only just yesterday returned from Scotland."

"Ah," Ava said.

Lady Kettle's horse stopped just above Ava, and Lady Kettle smiled down at her, her gaze taking in Ava's gown.

"You will forgive me," Ava said hastily. "I was helping the gamekeeper's son free his fishing line."

"Who?" Lady Kettle asked, peering around the lake.

"The gamekeeper's son," Ava said, and glanced over her shoulder. Around a bend in the lake, Edmond had stopped to throw rocks at the swans.

"I wasn't aware the gamekeeper had a son," Lady Kettle said absently. "I hope you won't mind my intrusion, Lady Middleton," she said, turning her attention to Ava again, "but I saw your handsome husband this morning and he urged me to come and make your acquaintance."

Ava put a hand over her eyes to shield them from the sun as she looked up at Lady Kettle. "You saw him this morning?"

"Mmm, we breakfasted," she said, nodding, and at Ava's look of confusion, she flicked her wrist and said cheerfully, "Oh, I've known him for *ages*, since we were children. We were often in one another's company coming up."

Ava was still having trouble comprehending that her husband had left her this morning to breakfast with Lady Kettle. To breakfast with *beautiful* Lady Kettle.

"Oh, I mustn't forget, I've some medicinals from

the surgeon for your footman. They should ease his pain a bit."

"Oh," Ava said, trying to hide her embarrassment. "He told you of our accident."

"I heard of it in Broderick," Lady Kettle corrected her.

"You *did*?"

Lady Kettle laughed at her astonishment. "We are a small parish, Lady Middleton. Word travels very fast. Almost as fast, I suppose, as it does in London."

"How remarkable," Ava said, meaning it.

"Poor Middleton is quite worried about you. 'She walked all the way to Broderick,' " she said, mimicking him.

Ava tried to smile, but there was something unsettling about Lady Kettle. Perhaps it was that her husband found time to call and breakfast with her when he might have breakfasted with his wife. Perhaps it was that during their breakfast, he talked to Lady Kettle of his worry about his wife. Whatever it was, Ava suddenly felt very much the outsider.

"I thought to invite you to have a ride in the near future. The weather has been glorious and there are so many pleasing vistas around the abbey."

Of course Lady Kettle would know of the vistas around the abbey. Ava, on the other hand, was hardly allowed to walk to the lake unescorted.

"Would you like that?"

"I would," Ava said, but then remembered that her husband had yet to teach her. "That is, when my husband teaches me how to ride."

"You could have no better instructor. I speak from experience—he taught me," Lady Kettle said, and laughed gaily. "And he still insists on instructing me, even though I am an accomplished rider."

Ava's laugh sounded forced. She could well imagine that he had taught Lady Kettle. She was beautiful, and quite cheerful. And her riding habit, Ava thought, was to be envied.

"Well, then, I will leave you to your fishing, Lady Middleton. May I call again?"

"Of course."

"Thank you," she said with a smile. "I can scarcely wait to tell Middleton that we've met and I find you absolutely charming."

Ava smiled, folding her arms tightly across her, and hoped that Lady Kettle would at least leave out the part about her sloshing about in the lake. "Thank you. You are too kind."

"I look forward to a time we can come to know one another."

"Yes, that would be lovely," Ava said, wishing she'd never come to the lake, that she'd never taken off her shoes or her stockings.

Feeling at sixes and sevens, Ava put on her stockings and shoes and made her way back to the abbey, where the sight of a plain black coach on the drive relieved and rejuvenated her at once. *Sally!*

By the time Ava had reached the drive, Sally had climbed, rather lazily, out of the coach, put her hands to her back, and stretched backward. "Bloody awful road," she said as Ava bounced to a halt before her, just ahead of Dawson. She glanced at Ava's gown. "What have you done to your gown, mu'um?"

"I'm so glad to see you, Sally," Ava said, and threw her arms around her lady's maid to Dawson's complete shock, judging by his expression. She let go and turned to Dawson. "Might I introduce you to my lady's maid, Miss Pierce."

Sally curtsied. Dawson looked at her, then at Ava.

And the hem of her dress. "Very good, madam," he said, as if he didn't quite know what to say, and pointed a footman to Sally's bags. "I will show her to her quarters."

"In a moment," Ava said. "I should like a word with her first." She linked her arm through Sally's, tugging her along.

As they stepped into the abbey, Sally pulled back and let out a low whistle. "Quite grand, ain't it?" she said, her voice full of awe as she turned around in a circle.

"Quite," Ava said, and grabbed Sally's hand. "Come on, then—there will be ample opportunity to gape at it." She pulled Sally up the curving staircase, down the long corridor to her suite, opened the door, pushed Sally through, and shut it behind her.

"Will my chamber look like this?"

"I've no idea," Ava admitted. "Never mind that— thank God you've come, Sally."

"Oh?" Sally asked as she wandered about, her hands trailing across the smooth finish of the furniture. "What's happened, then? Hasn't your handsome man done his duty by you?"

Ava's blush made Sally laugh as she paused in front of a mirror to check her hair. "I don't believe it!" she exclaimed as she fussed with a curl. "He's not yet come to your bed?"

"Yes, of course he has!" Ava said adamantly, but instantly softened. "Only once, the first night. And then he went to London. And when he returned he said he had correspondence. And now he is in Marshbridge to buy a cow or some such thing."

Sally stopped her nosing about and looked at Ava over her shoulder, her brow furrowed. "He's left his bride to buy a *cow*? Hmm. I'd think a marquis would have someone to see to buying his cows."

She was missing the point. "I think, Sally, there is a bit of a . . . *problem*," Ava clarified.

"Oh," Sally said. She glided to the chaise before the hearth, and fell onto it. She pressed the tips of her fingers together and studied Ava thoughtfully over the tops of them. "You weren't missish, were you? A lot of crying and carrying on?"

"No!" Ava exclaimed.

"Are you quite certain?" Sally asked, her eyes squinting suspiciously at Ava. "You don't look as if you could bear hardship very well."

"I don't know what you mean by that," Ava said, offended, "but I swear it, I didn't cry. I . . . I rather *liked* it."

That earned a howl of laughter from Sally. "By God, I've never heard of a woman who liked her first time in a man's bed!"

"*Sssh!*" Ava hissed at her, and slapped her feet off the end of the chaise. She sat down, her face flaming—which Sally seemed to enjoy—and worked up her courage to ask Sally for her help. "You can tell me what to do, can't you?"

Sally thought about it a moment and then nodded. "Indeed, I can help you, mu'um. But you must do exactly as I say. And I won't abide a lot of speculation as to where I might have learned this or that. Agreed?"

"Agreed," Ava said earnestly.

Sally suddenly sat up, leaned forward, and took Ava's hands in hers. "Above all else, you must *never*—"

The knock at the door startled them both, and Sally quickly scrambled to her feet, inadvertently kicking Ava as she did.

Ava jumped up, too, and whirled around to the

door just as it opened and Miss Hillier came sailing through. She looked at Ava, then at Sally. "My lady?" she asked, her voice belying the look of displeasure on her face. "I understand your lady's maid has come."

"Yes, of course," Ava said. "Allow me to introduce Sally Pierce. Sally, this is Miss Hillier, the house-keeper." She said a silent prayer of thanks that Sally actually curtsied as she ought to have done.

"Good to make your acquaintance, Miss Pierce. Now, then, if you will come with me," she said, gesturing for Sally to come along, and then proceeded to do precisely what Ava suspected she would do—she took Sally to her chamber and to meet the other staff. With a roll of her eyes behind Miss Hillier's back, Sally dutifully followed along.

That evening, Miss Hillier came to tend Ava before supper. When Ava asked about Sally, she was told that she was settling in and learning the routine of the house. "She'll start her duties on the morrow," Miss Hillier said with a bit of a sniff.

"Very well," Ava said, disappointed.

"My lady," Miss Hillier said, clasping her hands at her waist. "If I may?" The woman looked very uncomfortable.

"Yes?" Ava said.

"It would not do to have a great lady befriend her lady's maid," she said, lifting her chin a tiny bit. "That is not to say a great lady wouldn't be *kind* to her lady's maid, and treat her well. But to *befriend* her—well it's just not done," she said with an adamant nod of her head. "It's not what is expected of a woman who will one day be a duchess."

This business of being a "great lady" was begin-

JULIA LONDON

ning to annoy Ava on many fronts, not the least of which was being constantly lectured by the house-keeper. "Thank you, Miss Hillier," she said stiffly, and turned her back to the housekeeper until she had left the room. Honestly, she despised the attitude that servants were somehow lesser beings, unworthy of her attention or esteem.

And really, if Miss Hillier knew where Ava had found Sally . . . Well. That was something Miss Hillier must never discover, or else she and Sally might both be booted out the front door.

Because of the rigid view of the world in that dreary house, Ava had a solitary supper in the dining room instead of in her rooms with Sally as she would have liked. After supper, she amused herself by wandering about the main floor of the house. She'd only seen the public rooms and was curious about what was behind so many closed doors.

With the candelabrum Dawson had offered her, she went from room to room, opening the doors, walking inside, peering at the lavish furnishings and velvet drapes and massive portraits. Really, the rooms all began to look somewhat alike. She imagined changing them up a bit, perhaps putting more comfortable furnishings in one, painting another a cheery color.

But it wasn't until she reached what was obviously Middleton's private study that she took a keen interest. This was where Middleton worked, she realized, and she stepped inside, closed the door, and holding her candelabrum high, wandered around.

She studied his collection of books. Most seemed to concern agriculture and banking. There was a smattering of fiction, but nothing that interested her. And there were several history tomes, most notably of the British Royal Navy, which she thought rather interesting.

Next to his desk was a silver tazza, a platter on a pedestal that held a collection of whiskey tots that looked to be quite old. On the desk was an ivory pen and inkwell, and a crystal paperweight with a small gold coin embedded in it. There was a tobacco box and another wooden box that held a stack of high-quality vellum. And there, on the edge of his desk, was a heavy silver tray that held the post.

There were a few unopened letters in the tray, which, she assumed, Dawson had placed there today.

Ava sat down in the tall-backed leather chair and put the candelabrum aside. She spread her hands on the desk, imagined him sitting here, engaged in any number of important business dealings. Her eye fell to the post again, and she picked up the small stack of letters and flipped through them.

They were all of a business nature, judging by their wax seals. But the last one was different. It was a woman's handwriting, the script of it heartbreakingly familiar.

The Honorable Lord Middleton, Esq., it read on the front. Ava slowly turned it over and looked at the seal. There, embedded in the red wax, were three letters. A large *W* in the center, with a smaller *M* and *P* on either side of it.

Lady Waterstone.

Ava dropped the letter in the tray as if it were poisonous, and carelessly tossed the other letters on top of it. First Lady Kettle. Now this.

On second thought, she dug through the post, fished the letter out, and stuffed it in her pocket. It was a horrid breach of privacy—but then again, Lady Waterstone had breached *her* privacy.

Ava stood up, arranged Middleton's desk just so, and then picked up the candelabrum and walked out, her heart pounding in her chest. She was not a thief. At least not until tonight, not until she realized that whatever she might have thought marriage would be, whatever she might have made of it, she could never accept another woman in her husband's bed. At his breakfast table, perhaps. But in his bed? *Never.*

Now she had to convince him of it.

The next morning, Sally woke Ava by throwing open the drapes and slapping the bottom of her exposed foot, which had escaped the bedcovers.

"Up with you," she said sternly when Ava whimpered. "They'll have my head if you sleep too long. Bloody rigid here, they are," she said, hands on hips as Ava tried to sit up. "Expecting me to clean and whatnot in addition to tending you!"

"Do they?" Ava asked sleepily. "I can speak to Miss Hillier—"

"Don't bother. She'll undoubtedly have me sent away before the day is gone—we had words this morning."

"*Sally!*" Ava cried, fully awake now. "Miss Hillier was his lordship's nursemaid! You can't go round angering her!"

Sally tossed her head and clucked her tongue as she dropped Ava's dressing gown on her lap. "Don't fret so! I'll be good."

Ava hoped that was a vow. She slipped into her dressing gown and stood up, stretched her arms high in the air, then walked to the basin, threw water on her face, and reached for a brush.

"*Ach*, but you don't look as if you've slept a wink!"

Sally observed. "God help you if your bed is as hard as mine. Like sleeping on river rocks, it is."

"My bed is fine," Ava muttered. "It's not that."

Sally stopped in the making of the bed and glanced up. "What?"

Ava sighed, pulled open her bureau, removed Lady Waterstone's letter, and held it up between two fingers.

Sally quickly crossed the room to have a look. "What's it say?" she asked Ava.

"It's addressed to Middleton. The seal is that of Lady Waterstone." When Sally was clearly unaware of who that was, Ava felt tears welling up. "She is his mistress . . . *yet*. And perhaps not the only one!"

"*Ooh*," Sally said, nodding sagely. "Come on, then, let's have a look at it," she said, gesturing for Ava to open it.

"*Read* it? I can't break a seal on a letter addressed to him!"

"Would you share him with a whore?" Sally asked flatly.

Ava shook her head.

"*Open* it," she said again.

Ava reluctantly took the letter and broke the seal and began to read.

"Aloud, if you please," an exasperated Sally insisted.

Ava drew a breath. "*My darling,*" she read aloud, and felt her belly clutch. She closed her eyes until Sally lightly punched her arm. She looked at the letter again and turned partially away from Sally. "*My darling,*" she repeated. "*I live in agony, counting the hours until I see you again. Every day extends unbearably long into the next—you know my disposition too well to not be aware how desperate I am without you nearby. The only pleasure I can seem to derive is to dream of what Providence will bring me when you are in London again. I have sacrificed for you, darling, and never will I be happy in this world if I cannot be with you. Please hurry back to me so that I will suffer no more. Faithfully yours, M."*

Ava angrily crumpled the letter. But Sally peeled it from her fingers and looked at the writing on the page. "Very well done," she said, and looked up, assessing Ava closely. "She's right cunning, this one—she knows how to speak to a man's ego. You must be just as cunning, mu'um."

"But I don't know how to *be* cunning!" Ava moaned, falling helplessly onto a chaise. "It's hopeless, isn't it? I shall lose my husband before I've even known him!"

"For the love of God!" Sally cried. "Will you give in so easily! You may as well deliver him to her with a pretty bow tied round him. Will you not at least *attempt* to have him?"

"I don't know how," Ava said morosely.

"Well I do," Sally said, and sat on the chaise next to Ava. She put one hand on her shoulder, forcing Ava to look up. "Now, mu'um . . . have you heard of the harem?"

"The what?" Ava asked dully.

"The *harem*," Sally said, leaning forward. "They've a way of moving that drives a man to madness," she whispered, and began to describe—in very graphic detail—how a woman in a harem conducts herself in the presence of a man.

Ava gasped, covered her hand with her mouth, and made sounds of shock as Sally talked. How Sally knew such things Ava did not want to know.

But she hung on to every blessed word.

Twenty-one

Jared returned to Broderick Abbey at dusk the next day, having cut short his trip to Marshbridge for reasons he wasn't entirely certain.

He asked for his wife, but Dawson told him she was engaged and, incidentally, would not be available to dine with him at supper, either, as her lady's maid had arrived, and there was some work that could not wait.

"Work?" Jared asked skeptically. "What sort of work?"

Dawson's face pinched slightly. "I wouldn't rightly know, my lord, but were I to venture a guess . . . I would note that quite a lot of trunks arrived along with the lady's maid."

"Ah," Jared said, and nodded sagely, knowing full well a woman's love of her things. "Well, then . . . did she say when I might be allowed the pleasure of her company?" he asked wryly.

"She did not, my lord. I could inquire—"

"No, thank you," Jared said with a small smile. "I shall inquire personally."

He retreated to his study and reviewed the post, but finding nothing remarkable, he adjourned to his rooms to change for supper. In his suite, however, he heard the faint laughter of women filtering in through the hearth. He paused to listen, but heard nothing more. He started to move again, but heard the distinct sound of laughter again.

He sighed. Apparently, he would have to speak with her. He had hoped that Ava had come around to the reality of their marriage and harbor no fantastic illusions about it, but he hadn't realized that she'd be traipsing off to Broderick on foot, or splashing about the lake, or carrying on with her lady's maid. Another burst of laughter, however, made him curious. He left his suite again and walked the length of corridor to the main door of Ava's suite.

There it was again, the laughter of two women. But when he rapped on the door, the laughter abruptly stopped. In fact, there was no sound at all coming from the room. He frowned and rapped harder. He then heard some muted sounds of movement, and had the distinct impression that someone was running in circles about the room.

He was just about to rap again when the door opened a crack. "Oh! Good evening! I beg your pardon, I was resting," Ava said, her eyes full of something that was most definitely not sleep.

"Were you?" he asked skeptically. "I swear I heard laughter."

"From me?" she asked, blinking innocently. "Oh yes—I was reading a book that is quite humorous."

"Oh?" he asked, knowing full well that she was lying. "What is the title? Perhaps I've read it."

"I rather doubt you have," she said as her fingers curled tightly around the door.

"Perhaps I have," he politely insisted. "What is the title?"

"Hmm. It's interesting," she said, her brows dipping into a slight V, "that a book so cleverly done should have such a difficult title to recall." She flashed a fleeting smile at him. "I trust that your journey was safe?"

He nodded.

"Very good. I hope you will forgive my absence at supper, my lord. I've read so much today that I've something of a headache."

"You've read as much as that?" he asked, smiling wryly. "Then perhaps you might join me later? There is something I'd like to discuss with you."

"Hmm . . . well. I had thought to retire early," she said, as if the thought had just occurred to her. "That is—if that's acceptable to *you*."

His eyes narrowed suspiciously. "Whatever you desire, Lady Middleton," he said, inclining his head. "Perhaps, then, on the morrow, we might have that riding lesson. Provided, of course, you've recovered from your headache."

"Yes," she said, her eyes lighting up. "That is . . . depending, on how I'm feeling."

"Naturally."

"All right. Well, then. Good day, my lord." She smiled and shut the door.

He was surprised, he realized, and disappointed there wasn't more.

He stood there a moment longer, listening for the laughter, but heard nothing. With a shrug, he walked back to his suite of rooms. But when he reached them, he heard a shout of laughter coming from Ava's rooms and shook his head.

He dined alone in the small dining room. As he ate, he saw a footman go by with a large tray and two silver-domed plates. "Where's he off to?" he idly inquired of Dawson.

"To her ladyship's suite, my lord. She is taking supper in her rooms with her lady's maid."

So much for her headache. Or retiring early. Apparently, he'd been relegated to dining alone. His father, for as long as he could remember, dined apart from his mother, unless there were guests. That irked him. It irked him that his wife was obviously avoiding him. Whatever their arrangement, she had no call to avoid him.

He finished his meal, then stepped outside to have a smoke. He liked the feel of cold on his face, and walked to the edge of the terrace that overlooked a small river that fed the lake. But when he turned back to the abbey, he noticed a movement at the far end of the wing where the master suites were housed. He paused and looked up at Ava's window. There was the glow of a fire and candlelight, but what caught his attention was a shadow on the wall that seemed to be dancing.

His gaze narrowed. Not only was she avoiding him, she was apparently having a grand time without him.

The feeling of disappointment surprised and confounded him. This was precisely what he wanted. That it should disappoint him in the least seemed ridiculous and hypocritical.

He shrugged it off and returned indoors, had a bit of brandy, and read awhile, and at a quarter to midnight, he decided to turn in.

He walked up the grand, curving staircase and headed down the long corridor to his suite, untying his neckcloth and opening his waistcoat. When he passed Ava's suite, he paused only briefly, heard nothing, and walked on.

In his rooms, he had barely divested himself of his

coat and waistcoat, had pulled his neckcloth from his collar and his shirt from his trousers, when there was a knock at the door. He sighed wearily—Dawson was nothing if not a very attentive butler, sometimes to the point of vexation. The man was probably apoplectic that Jared had retired before he could offer his services.

In his bare feet, Jared walked to the door, pulled it open—and was completely startled.

It wasn't Dawson at all, but Ava at his door, wearing a dressing gown loosely tied and holding a long strip of red silk. But what he noticed more than the provocative dressing gown and long strip of red silk was her eyes. Her green eyes were glittering, and it was a very stirring sight. "Lady Middleton, you deign to favor me with your company after all."

She chuckled low and abruptly reached up and shoved him in the chest, forcing him backward. She stepped over the threshold after him and quickly shut the door behind her, leaned up against it, and spread her arms wide, her fingers on the door frame, the scarf dangling from her hand. "I do, but on my terms, sir."

"Oh?" he asked, his eyes roaming her curves, "Have I given you leave to define our terms?"

She smiled, held up her arm, and twisted it slightly, so that he could see the gold bracelets she wore. "Must I have your permission?"

He didn't quite know how to answer that. He didn't quite know his mind at all at the moment. "Why didn't you join me for supper?" he asked.

Ava raised a brow. "Did you miss me?"

"That is beside the point," he said brusquely.

"Is it, indeed?" she asked low, and pushed away from the door, her shapely leg sliding out from beneath her dressing gown. A flash of gold on her ankle caught his eye.

"What—"

She boldly covered his mouth with her hand, tilted her head back, and smiled seductively. "Now which of us is the unhappy one?" she whispered, and pushed him backward.

Jared moved back, his legs bumping against the chair at the hearth. She reached up, put her hands on his shoulders, and pushed him down. He sat, his legs sprawled before him, watching her warily, his curiosity and his blood highly aroused.

Ava said nothing, but still smiling seductively, she began to move. It seemed strange at first, as if she were dancing to music only she could hear, draping the silk across him, following it with the trail of her fingers—but soon his mind and sight were preoccupied with very delectable parts of her body moving very sensually. Hers was not a dance he'd ever seen before. She moved with her hips, draping the silk over her arm, flinging it up, then draping it on him as her hips swung back and forth.

As his focus grew intent on the curves of her body, and she used her hands to skim her body suggestively, he became aroused. She twirled around him, reaching her hands high in the air and shaking her bottom, then twirled again, leaning over him, caressing his cheek with her hand while the silk draped across him, then she was up again, twirling, and frankly, driving him quite mad.

The woman, this innocent whose virginity he had claimed, was making him delirious with thirst for her. He was completely seduced, could not take his eyes from her. Yet when he would reach for her, she swayed away from him.

"*Ava*," he said, his voice surprising him with its hoarseness, and his hands, his skin, surprising him with the need to just *touch* her.

But she laughed at his desire, twirling around in a blur of red silk and flesh and honey blond hair before suddenly falling to her knees between his legs.

"*Jared*," she said, her breasts rising with the pant of her breath. She slowly leaned forward and pressed her lips to his chest, to a patch of skin visible through the slit of his shirt.

She might as well have burned him; his body seized with the sensation of her moist lips. He put his hands to her face, tried to draw her up, but she gripped his arms, pushed them away, and kissed him through the slit of his shirt again, the tip of her tongue flicking against his flesh as she slipped her hands beneath his shirt and moved them, light as a feather, up his torso to his nipples.

His pulse was pounding, keeping time with his throbbing cock. He closed his eyes, leaned his head back, and luxuriated in the light, ethereal touch of a woman's hand on his body. Her hands moved down again, flowing over his skin, to his hips, and moved like a feather across his erection. But there she paused, and through the fabric of his buckskins, she caressed him.

Jared sucked in his breath when she touched him; his head snapped up and he grabbed her arms. "Come here," he growled, moving forward, his hands cupping her face.

She shook her head. "Allow me this," she said, using his words from the first night they had lain together, as her hand cupped him. "I am your wife and you will allow me this."

Bloody hell, he'd allow her the sun, the moon, the

stars—whatever she might desire. With a groan of surrender, he fell back against the chair, his body on fire. Ava tossed the silk aside, and with both hands, she undid his belt, and opened the flap that scarcely contained the evidence of his passion. When his cock sprang free, Ava did not flinch; she drew a breath, leaned down, and closed her lips around the tip of him.

His blood turned to liquid fire. Jared grabbed Ava's head, tried to lift her, but she was steadfast and took hold of his hips, then slid the length of him into her mouth.

The tender flick of her tongue proved more than he could bear, and he abruptly sat up, took her face in his hands, and forced her to look up. Her eyes had a sultry, hot look to them. He reached under her arms and easily pulled her into his lap. Her dressing gown fell open, exposing her breasts to him, and he eagerly took one to his mouth as his hand sought the juncture of her legs.

He found it, hot and wet, the flesh swollen. Above him, he heard her ragged draw of breath, felt the tables turn. He was in control now. He held her firmly by the hips and moved her against his cock. Ava, his bride, his beautiful, sensual bride, gasped for breath above him. He moved her body, positioning her, and looked up at her face. She was flushed with excitement, her eyes glittering, and slowly, carefully, he slid into her.

She closed her eyes; her head fell back as she sank down on him, and she let out a long, deep sigh of pleasure. He moved gently in her, afraid to hurt her, afraid he might overwhelm her with the passion raging in him. But when Ava lifted her head and smiled down at him, he began to move with more assurance.

She began to move, too—awkwardly at first, but

then matching his rhythm. His hands sought her breasts, his mouth her skin, and when he thought he couldn't reach her, couldn't reach deep enough, he put one arm around her waist and surged up, taking them both to the rug at his feet. Her legs came up on either side of him; he slid deeper and harder, his hand between them, stroking her to the same explosive conclusion that was building in him.

Moaning, she moved beneath him, bucking against him until she found her release with one long, low cry. She grabbed him, her nails digging into his skin, her mouth on his shoulder.

He drove into her, felt the draw of his own release and shuddered his life's blood into her.

A moment passed as they lay panting. When Jared had finally regained his senses, he thought he might be hurting her and shifted, bracing himself with his arms. "Lie still," he murmured as he kissed her cheek. "I shall bring you a clean dressing gown."

"Mmm," she responded, stretched her arms above her head, and gave him a very sated, catlike smile. Jared kissed her lips, then stood up, pulled his buckskins up, and walked into his dressing room to find her a dressing gown.

But when he walked into his room again, Ava was on her feet, had wrapped her dressing gown around her, and had picked up the length of red silk.

He smiled. "Do you mean to dance again?" he asked, holding the gown out to her. "For if you do, lady, you might kill me."

She smiled lopsidedly, walked to where he stood, rose up on her toes, and kissed him soundly on the lips. "Good night, my lord."

He slipped his arm around her back and returned her kiss with one a bit more ardent. "Are you tired?"

She smiled. "Sleep well," she whispered, and moved out from the circle of his arms.

It confused him. He thought perhaps she meant to get in his bed, but she walked toward the door instead. "Wait!" he exclaimed, confused, before she opened the door. "Where are you going?"

"To my rooms," she said with a bright smile, and opened the door. "Good night."

He stood there, confounded, as she walked out, his body and mind still steeped in their lovemaking, still holding a dressing gown, trying to fathom what had just happened.

When Ava slipped into her room, she walked to the hearth and hugged herself tightly. She hadn't wanted to leave him. She had wanted so badly to stay, and she believed that he'd *wanted* her to stay. But she'd given Sally her word.

"You must trust me on this, mu'um," Sally had firmly told her. "If you give yourself to him and seem eager to do it, he will take you, but he will think of another. If you only share yourself with him when you please, he shall want you even more. He'll want you so desperately he'll be devoured by the want, mark me."

That sounded splendid, but still, Ava had wondered how Sally could be so certain.

Sally had laughed and called her naïve. "Mark me, Lady Ava," she'd said. "If you heed my advice, he shall come to you. Not the whore in London. *You.*"

Ava certainly hoped so, for after tonight, there was no place she wanted to be but in his arms.

Twenty-two

———✦———

J ared had a ravenous appetite the next morning, and
breakfasted alone, replaying the events of last night
over again in his mind's eye. When he'd finished, he
had the mare saddled and rode out, spurring the
young horse faster and faster, recklessly leading her
to jump over streams and fences, trying to shake that
interminable and peculiar feeling at the core of him. It
was a feeling of discomfort that seemed to grow in
him each day, feeling a little like there was something
too large inside his body.

When the mare was spent, he rode her easy back to
the abbey. As he neared the old castle ruins, he saw
the gamekeeper's boy standing high on a mound of
rocks, his wooden sword at his side. He'd often seen
the boy here, but he'd always ridden past. Today,
however, he sent the mare trotting up the hill.

As he neared the ruins, the boy jumped down from
the mound of rubble, his expression wary. Jared dismounted and tethered the horse and walked up the
hill to the ruins. As he climbed up to what had once
been the main floor of the castle, behind the lone wall
that remained standing, he could see a tin cup,
another wooden sword, an old saddle blanket that
was neatly folded to form a pallet, and a cloth, folded

and tied and undoubtedly containing bread and cheese.

It was, Jared thought with an aching twist of his heart, the same place he used to play as a child. He'd spent endless hours here, master of all he surveyed. When his governess came after him late in the afternoon, he returned to the abbey, where, at about the same age as this boy, he'd been master of the house before he even knew what that meant.

"King of the castle, eh?" he remarked to the boy, walking into the middle of what was left of the castle floor.

"Papa said I had your leave, milord," Edmond said, looking a bit like he'd been caught doing something he ought not to do.

Jared smiled. "You do indeed have my leave, lad. I'm merely curious as to what you're about." He glanced at the child and studied his face. "I often played here when I was your age." He looked around at the familiar pile of rubble. "I got bored of playing alone, though. Once, I insisted a footman accompany me so that I'd have someone to slay."

Edmond blinked. "I haven't got a footman, sir."

"No," Jared said, his smile fading. "I suppose you haven't."

"I don't mind being alone," Edmond said, absently swinging his sword at the ground. "I'm always king that way. One day I shall go to London where I shall have footmen."

Jared smiled and put his hand to the boy's head. "I have every confidence you will." He wanted to say more, to ask the child how he fared here at Broderick Abbey, if he helped his father in his work. But Edmond had found something on the ground to fascinate him—he was digging the point of his sword at whatever it was—and Jared realized he had no idea how to talk to a young boy. He felt inept, incapable of speaking the appropriate language.

He stepped back. "Carry on, then," he said, and turned, walking back to the mare. He had one last look at Edmond before riding off, but Edmond's attention was elsewhere.

Back at the abbey, Jared sought out Ava and found her in the blue drawing room. She was reading a letter, her head bent over a writing table, her eyes squinting.

"Good morning," he said.

She started, and quickly picked up the letter she was reading and folded it.

"What are you reading?" he asked absently as he strolled into the room, his eyes on her face.

Ava blinked, stuffing the letter into her pocket. "Nothing, my lord. Just a bit of old news," she said, and looked at him expectantly.

He kissed her on the cheek. "You weren't at breakfast."

"Oh, did you breakfast here?" she asked, her voice light. "I thought perhaps you had ridden to breakfast with Lady Kettle."

So Veronica had paid her a call as he'd suggested. "Not today," he said with a smile. "I ate entirely alone. *Again.*"

"*Hmm,*" she said, and glanced away.

"I think it a perfect day for riding lessons, madam."

She looked at the window and shrugged insouciantly. "I had thought to write some letters. I've not written Phoebe in several days. She'll be *desperate* to know how I am getting on, of course," she said, and glanced at him from the corner of her eye. "And I've *so* much to tell her."

What in God's name was the matter with her? "That can wait."

"Very well," she said with a sudden bright smile, and abruptly stood. "I suppose I could spare you an hour or so."

Spare him? She'd left him last night, and now she acted as if she'd rather be writing long and boring letters than spend time in his company. What in the devil was going through her mind? This wasn't his usual experience with women—normally, they were quite eager to spend time in his company. "How very kind of you," he drawled. "*Thank* you."

Ava began moving purposefully toward the door. "Shall I meet you in the foyer?" she asked, but she'd already sailed past him, was already walking out.

Jared watched her go, then put a hand to his nape and tried to work through what, exactly, went through a woman's mind at any given moment.

Fortunately, Sally was cleaning her room when Ava burst through the door, her pulse racing.

Not that Sally seemed to notice her exuberance, for she was quite cross. "Your Miss Hillier is quite the taskmaster," she snapped when Ava entered the room. "She had the gall to waken me this very morning and insist I clean your dressing room! At seven o'clock in the bloody morning! She's not very kind, that one."

"He's insisted on a riding lesson," Ava said, ignoring Sally's protests.

Sally dropped the pillow she was plumping and folded her arms over her middle. "What did you say, then?" she asked sternly.

"I said, 'well sir, I have some letters to write, but I suppose I might spare you an hour or so.' "

"Brilliant!" Sally cried. "Perfectly well done. Now go and be as charming as you can possibly be. Lots of smiling and touching, and be pretty with your words."

"Pretty with my words?" Ava echoed. "What do you mean by that?"

"Heaven help me," Sally muttered to the ceiling, then leveled a gaze on her. "I mean that you should *flirt*, mu'um. Tease him and make certain that he feels quite the king. A woman must always appeal to a man's ego, as it is every man's greatest weakness."

"Appeal to his ego," Ava repeated as she hurried into the dressing room to change into a dark green riding habit.

"Try and keep in mind," Sally said, stepping in front of Ava when she had changed and was hurrying out, "that you are reeling in a very big fish. He's much bigger and stronger than you, so you must reel *carefully* and evenly, for if you let the line go slack or pick it up too quickly, you'll lose him."

"You really do have a tendency to speak in metaphors, don't you?" Ava asked as she grabbed Sally's hand and gave it a squeeze.

"To speak in *what*?" Sally demanded, insulted.

Ava squeezed her hand again. "Never mind. I must hurry now," she said, stepping around her.

"God blind me, have you heard a word I've said?" Sally called after her. "Don't appear too eager!"

Ava walked slowly until she was out of Sally's sight. But the moment she was clear of her, she hurried down the corridor and the grand staircase, slowing again only when she could see the foyer.

From that point, she walked carefully down the steps, her posture erect, just as she used to do with Phoebe and Greer, when they would practice walking down the steps with books on their heads in preparation for the day they would be queen. They never quite worked out the details of how they might become queen but, nevertheless, they would be prepared to don the mantle when the time came.

When she reached the bottom step, Middleton appeared from the corridor on the right. In his riding cloak, he looked large and forbidding, particularly with his gaze as intent on her as it was. "There you are," he said quietly.

"Yes. Here I am!"

"If you are quite ready, then?" he asked, and held out his hand to her.

Ava put her hand in his, and cursed the tiny, enchanting little shiver of delight it gave her when he possessively closed his fingers around hers. "I must thank you, my lord, for taking time to teach me to ride. You're such an accomplished horseman that this must be very tedious for you."

"Not in the least," he said, smiling charmingly, and led her out.

When they walked outside into the bright sunlight, Ava's face fell. There on the drive was the brown mare she'd seen Middleton ride with such fury. And standing next to her, an old, swaybacked chestnut. She had no doubt the old bag of bones was intended for her, but he looked as if he had one or two hooves in the grave.

"Who is that?" she asked, squinting at the chestnut, held by one of two stableboys.

"Bilbo," Middleton said.

"He doesn't seem very sturdy on his feet."

"I assure you, he is. He'll be gentle with you."

She glanced at Middleton sidelong and thought the better of responding too pertly to that. "Where are we going?"

"The west fields. They are fallow and level."

Ava looked again at Bilbo, wondering if he could even make it as far as that. "Am I to *ride* him there?" she asked, stepping a little closer to Middleton.

"That was my intent."

She instantly shook her head and stepped even closer to her husband. "Please, allow me to ride with you," she said. "He's so big and . . ." *And old . . . !* "He's *frighteningly* big."

Middleton put his hand on her waist. "You mustn't be afraid." He then looked at one of the young hands from the stable and said, "Bring Bilbo to the west fields. Lady Middleton will ride with me."

With that, Middleton guided Ava to the mare and urged her to stroke the horse's nose. "You must be very careful," he said to Ava. "She's young and not fully broken."

"Oh," Ava said sweetly, "I'll be *very* careful."

He looked at her oddly, but then easily lifted her up onto the front of his saddle. He swung up behind her and put one arm around her middle. "All right?"

"All right," she sighed, and sank back against him. There was nothing quite like the security of being in Middleton's muscular arms, his hard body at her back. Truly, nothing in the world felt quite as safe as that.

As they rode out, Middleton pointed out some of the cottages belonging to tenants who farmed crofts of his land. And then he asked her how she found Broderick Abbey, if it was to her liking.

"Very much, my lord," she said, although she really didn't care for it in the least. It seemed too formal, too cold. "It's very . . . large."

He choked on his surprise. "It's *large*? Is that all you would say of it?"

"No," she said with a smile. "I might also say that it's awfully cold at night," she said, slanting a look at him. "There's a bit of a draft."

"A draft!" he said with mock indignation. "Then we must have the entire east wing brought down and put back up again."

"I hardly think *that* is necessary. I should think a bit of grout, or whatever it is you stuff in cracks."

"Then I shall have a mountain of grout brought round. No crack will go unpunished."

She laughed and tossed her head as Sally had suggested.

"Is there any way we might repair the problem of the abbey's size?" he asked playfully.

"I don't think so. Better to leave it large than ruin its appearance."

"Well, then . . . is there anything else I might do for you? Anything to make your time at Broderick Abbey easier?"

She shook her head and sank deeper into the curve of his arms.

He bent his head and touched his lips to the top of her ear. "It seems there is something on your mind of late, Lady Middleton. Something that, if I knew what it was, I might mend for you."

"I don't know what you mean."

"Perhaps," he said, his breath warm on her ear, "there is something about our arrangement that concerns you. If you tell me, I might repair it."

All thoughts of flirting coyly flew out of her head. She sat up and turned so that she could see his face. "Something that you might *repair*?" she asked, incredulous that he might think a marriage, or an adulterous love affair, for that matter, might be fixed up with a bit of grout and plaster.

But Middleton nodded and gave her a patronizing smile. "You seem to be a bit out of sorts."

"How so?" she demanded.

He tightened his hold of her and pulled her back against him once more. "You have seen fit to dine without me. And you left me last night," he said quietly. "And, furthermore, you didn't seem to want to come along this morning."

He had determined the rules, and now he would complain about them? How quickly she forgot Sally's caution to flirt and keep herself just beyond his reach. "All right, here you are: I thought we agreed we were suited for marriage."

Middleton's brows dipped into a frown of confusion. "We *are* suited, and we've set a perfectly acceptable arrangement—why aren't you happy with it?"

Ava heard Sally's voice in her head urging her to make light of it, to tempt his curiosity and leave him wanting more. And suddenly, perhaps for the first time, she saw the wisdom in Sally's words. The man took far too much for granted. She smiled devilishly and inclined her head demurely. "Of course I am *happy*—how could I not be? Far too often, marriage seems to be the cause of much misery. But as we have come together as the result of fortune and standing, and not silly feelings of love or companionship, or, apparently, even *felicity*, there is no reason we shouldn't be happy. I daresay we shall succeed handsomely, for we've no particular attachment to one another . . . have we?" she asked, peering up at him.

"No," he agreed, all too readily.

Her anger soared and her smile became brighter. "We should be very thankful, really, that we are so agreeable in this. The common marriage is much more complicated than ours. We shall suffer none of the uneasiness when we are apart. Or dream of one another. No, my lord, we shall sleep quite soundly."

He looked, she thought, far too agreeable.

Dear God, what had she done in marrying him? She turned away from him, sitting up, her back stiff, her body as far from him as she could possibly get on the back of that mare. "What a lovely day! The air is cleaner here, I think. Do you?"

"Yes," he said, but he sounded as if his thoughts were elsewhere.

Ava hardly cared—she was so flustered and angry she wanted to scream. It seemed almost savage that two people could come together and share such intimate and personal acts without feeling *something* more enduring than the need to "repair" whatever ailed her with plaster or money.

When they reached the west field, she jumped down before Middleton could help her. But when he dismounted and stood at his horse, looking so majestic and as if he didn't quite know who she was, she couldn't resist the feeling that was growing stronger in her each day. She could not look at him and not want to be with him. She couldn't see the smile in his eyes and not yearn to win his heart and possess it. So when he asked her to get on Bilbo, she complied.

She complained that she felt she was in a precarious position, but he smiled happily at her, melting her anger away with it, and told her she was doing marvelously well as he led her around a big circle like a child on a pony.

Yet he seemed so pleased that Ava might have gone on all day for the pleasure of his smile had not Lady Kettle arrived, riding hard across the field, reining to a perfect stop before them.

"Look who's riding!" she cried happily, and

allowed Middleton to help her down from her horse by putting her hands on his shoulders and laughing when he caught her at the waist and lifted her down.

He said something to her that Ava did not catch, and kissed her cheek. Lady Kettle smiled up at him so beautifully that Ava's heart clenched. *She was in love with him.* She could tell by the way her eyes sparkled when she looked at him, and the blush in her cheeks when she smiled at him.

When she had quite finished drooling over Ava's husband, Lady Kettle turned a bright and, all right, a beautiful smile to Ava. "You are doing very well, Lady Middleton!" she said. "I knew you'd find Middleton an excellent teacher!"

"Yes, he is," Ava said, trying to seem completely unaffected.

"Do you know that he taught himself to ride?"

"That's hardly true," Middleton said with a laugh. "I had many instructors when I was a young boy."

"But you *did*," Lady Kettle said, playfully grabbing his arm and turning her face up to him again. "Do you remember how we'd come up here to these very fields with that old gray, and you would ride round and round, practically falling off every time he swished his tail, until you could ride him with your eyes closed?"

Middleton laughed. "I suppose I do remember something like that. I am surprised you remember it as well, Veronica."

Veronica.

Ava didn't know what made her do it—maybe it was simply the use of Lady Kettle's given name. Or the fact that her husband and Lady Kettle were laughing and reminiscing like lovers. Whatever the reason, Ava chose that moment to ruin her ruse of not knowing how to ride just so that she might spend time with her husband, and kicked Bilbo in the soft part of his belly to send him bolting.

She heard the shouting behind her, but as Bilbo ran—surprisingly fast for his age with another well-placed kick—Ava laughed like the devil. She yanked the reins right, headed him into the forest, and heard the shouting behind her again as she leaned over the old horse's neck. When they had crashed into the thicket—which she hoped she made all the more exciting by shrieking—she reined Bilbo up, jumped off, and with a slap to his rump, sent the horse running again. She instantly dropped down, landing a little hard on her bottom, and then lay down on her back and squirmed about a bit before standing up.

She wasn't satisfied that she looked properly thrown, and picked up a handful of dirt and twigs and, wincing at the unpleasant necessity, rubbed them about her gown.

By the time Middleton reached her a few moments later, she looked, she thought, rather abused. He swept off the mare before he'd even reined her to a halt and strode forward so fast and so sternly that for a moment Ava feared him and took a step backward. But he caught her up in his arms, picking her up off her feet as he grabbed her and held her tightly to him.

"Are you all right? Are you harmed?"

"No," she said, her voice muffled against his shoulder, he held her so tightly. "A bit bruised, but I'm really all right."

He released his grip of her, grabbed her by the shoulders, and pushed her back, examining her face. "You're certain you're all right?"

She nodded.

"You didn't harm yourself?" he asked as he put his

hand to her chin and moved her head from side to side.

Ava shook her head.

He frowned slightly, put his hands on her ribs, pressed gently, then slid them down and around to her derriere as he watched her eyes. Ava blinked as he cupped her bottom, but said nothing. He moved his hands up her rib cage again to the sides of her breasts. "You seem no worse for the ride," he remarked, pressing against her breasts, letting his hands linger there longer than was necessary to ascertain if she'd been injured.

Ava swallowed. "I'm really all right."

He smiled a little crookedly and stroked her temple with the back of his hand. "And Bilbo? You didn't harm Bilbo, did you?"

"Bilbo?" she repeated. "No . . . he's . . . he's fine."

His smile widened, and he pulled her to him, wrapping his arms around her. "Come on, then, Lady Middleton. We've had enough riding for one day."

They emerged from the forest a few moments later, Ava securely in the circle of Middleton's arms atop the mare. The stableboys had easily caught Bilbo, who hadn't run very far at all, having seen a patch of grass to his liking.

"Dear God, are you all right?" Lady Kettle asked as she pulled up next to them, looking quite concerned. "You gave us all a fright!"

"I am. Thank you," Ava said, and pressed her cheek against Middleton's shoulder. "I'm just a bit tired, that's all."

"Do rest, Lady Middleton. That must have been very frightening."

Ava nodded that indeed it was, and smiled sweetly as Middleton bid Lady Kettle a good day and headed back to the abbey. Once, on the ride back, she thought she heard him chuckle, but when she looked at him, his face was full of concern. Twice, he put his hand to Ava's cheek and kissed her temple. At the abbey, he helped her down and pulled a twig from the shoulder of her habit. "Not to worry, Lady Middleton. In spite of today's setback, I think you will become a fine horsewoman."

"Really?" she asked hopefully.

He laughed softly and kissed her lips. "I am *certain* of it," he said. He put his arm around her shoulders and led her up the steps to the main entrance, and Ava might as well have been walking on air. But as they walked into the main entry, Dawson met them. He took Middleton's cloak and extended a silver tray. "The post, my lord."

Ava saw Lady Waterstone's letter on the very top, the distinctive curve of her handwriting burned like a brand on the back of her eyes. She glanced up and saw the recognition of the handwriting pass across Middleton's features, too.

"Put them in the study," he said, and glanced at Ava. "I will have the pleasure of your company at supper, madam," he said, his voice brooking no argument.

"Yes," she said tightly. "Of course." With a smile pasted on her face, she walked away, all the lovely, summery feelings inside of her gone and replaced by a cold blast of winter.

Twenty-three

A va walked straight to her suite, shut the door, and yanked the bellpull as hard as she could. And again. And every few minutes until Miss Hillier appeared, looking rather startled.

"Lady Middleton? Is everything all right?"

"Where is Sally?" Ava asked.

Miss Hillier pressed her lips tightly together disapprovingly. "I beg your pardon, my lady, but there is a rather indelicate predicament about which I must speak with his lordship."

Miss Hillier's expression alarmed Ava—something had happened to Sally. "*What* predicament?" she asked.

"I'd rather not say—it's rather vile. But it involved your lady's maid."

"Tell me, Miss Hillier!"

The woman's displeasure was pinching her face. "She was seen . . . *cavorting* . . . with one of the footmen."

"*Cavorting?*" Ava echoed, not understanding immediately. She pictured them running about the garden, playing at horse or some such foolishness.

But Miss Hillier narrowed her eyes and spat, "*Cavorting,*" in a manner that clearly relayed her meaning.

Lord God, Sally! Not here! Ava's mind raced—she made a tsk-tsk sound and shook her head. "You mustn't pay her attention, Miss Hillier. Sally is indeed rather flirtatious, but she's quite harmless, I assure you."

Miss Hillier's face was now a very deep red. "One can hardly term her behavior harmless. You must remember, Lady Middleton, that you are the wife of a marquis now. Your actions—or those of your servants—reflect on him."

Her actions? What of *his* deplorable actions? "I am well aware," Ava bit out. "But *you* must remember that Sally is from London. It's different there. What is improper here is often tolerated in London."

"Be that as it may, this is certainly not London."

The old battle-ax had no bloody idea how true that was. "No, it's certainly not," Ava calmly agreed in spite of her racing heart. "But might we give Sally a day or two to acquaint herself with the habits here before punishing her?"

Miss Hillier seemed to think about that for a moment. But then she shook her head. "I can't let that sort of behavior go unremarked. And I *must* mention it to his lordship. I've known him since he was but an infant. He's suffered so much in his life, and particularly at the hands of unscrupulous servants, that I take it as a personal mission to ensure nothing ever sullies his honor."

Suffered? He had no idea what it meant to suffer! And besides, Ava failed to see how Sally's indiscretions might dishonor Middleton in any manner, but it was apparent that she would get nowhere with his mother hen. "Very well," she said stiffly. "I will speak to my husband about this matter later. Now, then, will you send Sally to me?"

"I'm afraid I can't, Lady Middleton. She has been dispatched to the village."

"The *village*?" Ava cried. "What in God's name have you done, Miss Hillier?"

"I did not turn her out," Miss Hillier said icily. "I merely sent her home with the cook's daughter. She will have a roof over her head until Lord Middleton has made his decision."

Ava couldn't contain herself any longer. "I beg your pardon, but do you mean to imply that Lord Middleton will make a decision about who is to be *my* lady's maid?"

The witch actually looked surprised by the question. "Why, of course! Is he not lord and master of this house? Is he not the benefactor of all of us?"

"He is my husband, not the bloody king of England!" Ava cried. Her heart was pounding so hard that she could scarcely breathe.

Miss Hillier gasped; she was truly offended.

Ava put a hand to her heart and sank wearily onto the edge of her bed.

"Shall I help you dress?" Miss Hillier asked tightly.

"*No*," Ava said, shaking her head. "I will manage."

Miss Hillier wasted no time in leaving her room, which suited Ava very much. How had this happened? How had she gone from fairy tale to nightmare so quickly? She had to manage her way out, think what to do. In the meantime, she wished to God in his heaven that she could see her mother once more and tell her how wrong she was about marriage.

*   *   *

My darling, I wake every morning filled with thoughts of you. I spend my days walking about like the dead, intoxicated by the memory of you. My soul

aches to be near you, my heart is full of such love for
you that it sets my blood afire. . . .

The knock on his study door prompted Jared to
toss Miranda's letter in the fire.

It was Dawson, who bowed deeply as he stepped
inside. "I beg your pardon, my lord, but Miss Hillier
requests an audience."

"Oh?" he asked idly.

"It would seem there is a bit of trouble with the
new lady's maid."

That got his attention. "Show her in."

When Miss Hillier entered, he could tell from her
expression that she was very displeased. He was not
surprised, really, for Miss Hillier was often displeased—if the flowers weren't cut fresh daily, or a
portrait hung a little crookedly on the wall, she was
displeased. More often than not, she brought her dis-
pleasures to him.

He invited her to take a seat and tell him her woes,
which were, not surprisingly, quite long and minutely
detailed.

Later that evening, long after Miss Hillier had told
him of the incident involving Ava's maid, Jared's
thoughts turned to Ava. If Miss Hillier's suspicions
about the maid were true—and he rather suspected
they were, given the maid's behavior—he was
intrigued by how she had come to be in Ava's employ.
How could a young, naïve debutante—and Ava was,
in many respects, naïve—have managed to employ a
woman with questionable virtue?

He thought of the butler in Ava's house, a man
who was intent on opening and closing doors. And
the young man with the familiar face who had han-

dled Jared's horse the day he'd called on her . . . hadn't he seen him working in the public stables? Whatever the explanation, he was looking forward to supper when he might ask his wife directly. He suspected the answer would be highly entertaining.

That was the thing about Ava he most appreciated, he supposed—she was full of life, full of unconventional ideas and actions. She was unique, he was beginning to realize. An original. He could not imagine ever feeling stifled or feeling that the day was endless with Ava, as he'd felt with Lady Elizabeth.

"Supper is served, my lord," Dawson intoned from the open door of his study.

Was it as late as that? Jared glanced at the clock and noticed the time with some surprise. He'd been sitting in his darkened study for more than an hour, mulling over things. Women in general. Ava, to be precise.

His wife was waiting for him in the green salon, sipping a glass of wine. She came to her feet when he entered—but not anxiously, not as eagerly as when she'd first arrived at Broderick Abbey.

"Good evening, Lady Middleton."

"My lord."

He took the glass of wine a footman offered him, turned, and held it up in toast. "To a pleasant evening."

Her brows rose skeptically. She picked up her glass and held it out, like him. "To a pleasant evening." She drank, put her glass down, and clasped her hands behind her back. "I should like to speak to you about a very important matter," she said, her voice strong and clear.

Jared took a seat and crossed one leg over the other. "Would it be about your lady's maid?" he asked casually.

"Yes. My lady's maid. I should like her returned to me as soon as possible."

Frankly, Jared didn't care if her maid was here or in London or riding a star. He did not agree with Miss Hillier that a bit of foolishness with a footman necessitated her immediate dismissal. He did not condone such behavior, of course—at least not in public, where lovers risked discovery—but neither did he condone throwing a young woman to the wolves for one misstep.

What he chose to reveal to Ava, however, was something else entirely. He looked at the footmen and dismissed them with a nod. When they had quit the room, he looked at his wife and asked simply, "Do you condone such behavior?"

"Of course not. I will speak with her."

"And do you suppose she will heed what you say?"

"Of course!" Ava said, clearly agitated. "And I certainly won't require Miss Hillier's assistance in speaking to my maid."

Jared almost laughed. He knew very well how selfrighteous Miss Hillier could be. He idly swirled his wine around in his glass. "You are aware, are you not, that her behavior is insupportable."

Ava sat heavily on the settee across from him, her hands pressed together. "It *is* insupportable—I couldn't possibly agree more," she said earnestly. "Nevertheless, she is *my* lady's maid, and I should have the responsibility of speaking to her myself."

"I don't know," he said, toying with her.

Ava closed her eyes and sighed. Jared smiled.

"She is my lady's maid, my lord," Ava said. "She serves *me*—no one else in this house. I can't possibly do without her."

"Should I decide that she must be sent back to London, Miss Hillier will assist you."

Ava's mouth dropped open. *"What?* Send her back to London?" she cried. "No! How dare you?"

"Oh, I don't know," he said, quite enjoying himself. "It's rather easy, really."

Ava made a sound of angry despair, suddenly stood up, and began pacing in front of the settee. "I must admit, my lord, that I find this all very distressing. I cannot do without Sally—"

"Where did you find her?" he asked.

Ava almost stumbled. "W-what?" she asked.

"Where," he said clearly, "did you *find* her?"

She blanched. Turned one way. Then the other. Punched her hands to her hips and frowned at him. "Where does anyone find her lady's maid? Here and there," she said, gesturing to what he supposed was here and there.

"Aha. Here and there," he repeated.

She folded her arms across her middle.

He stood up and put his wine aside. "I suppose, then, that she served other ladies in London before coming to your service?"

"I suppose," she said, lifting her chin.

"Who?"

"No one you know, I assure you."

"You might be surprised, madam. I know quite a lot of people in London."

Her brows dipped into a V. "All right, then. She came to me from Lady Hartsford."

"Lady Hartsford?" he echoed with a laugh.

"Yes! Lady Hartsford!"

"She is deceased."

Ava blanched, then shrugged carelessly. "Which is *why*, my lord, I was able to employ Sally when I did."

He leaned forward and pinned her with a look. "Lady Hartsford died four years ago."

Ava didn't even blink. "It took quite a lot of time to settle her affairs. And really, why are you so concerned about Sally's credentials? Are you in need of a lady's maid?"

He chuckled and asked again, "Where did you *find* your lady's maid? Or your butler? Or your footmen?"

Her lovely face went from white to pink. "What difference can it possibly make?" she demanded, clearly flustered.

"Do you want her back?"

"Of course I want her back! What do you want me to say? That she came from a whorehouse?" she cried.

Jared laughed. "My, my, Lady Middleton. Such language is unbecoming. What else has Sally taught you? A certain, private dance perhaps?"

Ava groaned. "Just have her brought back, *please.*"

"I may," he said idly. "Provided you tell me where you found her."

Ava sighed wearily and closed her eyes for a moment. Then she opened them and looked at him directly, her green gaze piercing his. "A poorhouse, if you must know. She is a former harlot, duly reformed by the parish and the Ladies' Beneficent Society. Mr. Morris was a jeweler's clerk with very poor eyesight who lost his position. Our footmen? A pair of lamplighters, father and son, injured in a carriage accident. The boy who helped around the house came from the public stables, and merely had dreams of working in a house. We were very fortunate that he agreed to work for no wages."

Jared's smile faded. "No wages? I don't understand."

"It's quite simple, really," Ava said. "We had no

money. We had nothing but the roof over our heads. My mother left her fortune to my stepfather and he did not see fit to share it. So we did the best we could, finding servants who needed a roof, too, in exchange for working until we could pay them."

"And when might that be?" he asked, horrified that Downey had left them in such a state.

For some reason, the question made Ava's face turn pinker. "Well . . . *now*. Because I married you," she said quietly. "The allowance you've provided is very generous."

He blinked. Then burst out laughing. "Very well done!" he said.

"Then I will have Sally back to me?" she asked anxiously, her eyes sparkling with hope.

Jared shook his head. "You ask me to put a harlot in my house, Lady Middleton. I shall think on it."

"No!" she cried, throwing her head back with despair.

He put his hand on her elbow. "I shall think on it," he said again, and forced her around, toward the door.

"Where are we going?" she demanded with exasperation.

"To supper."

She muttered something under her breath, but allowed him to march her along.

In the dining room he helped her into a chair next to him, then took his seat, and nodded for Dawson to begin the meal service. Two footmen bustled around them, ladling turtle soup into china bowls and filling their glasses with wine. When they'd finished, they stepped back to stand silently along the wall.

Jared picked up his spoon and glanced at Ava, who sat with her arms folded, glaring at the soup bowl. "Will you sulk about your maid for the entire meal?"

She snorted—but then she suddenly looked up as if someone had just called her name, and graced him with a very sensual smile. "I do not sulk. But I do not care for the soup."

"No?"

"Mmm, no," she said, shaking her head. "It's rather tart. I prefer onion soup," she said, turning slightly in her chair to face him. "Do you like onion soup? Our cook in London makes the most delicious onion soup," she said, and began to talk about the merits of that soup. Jared smiled and nodded, and ate his turtle soup, completely uninterested in the many facets of soup . . . until he felt her bare foot on his ankle.

He glanced up; she was smiling wickedly. "I like it served warm," she said softly. "As warm as bathwater."

"Do you indeed?"

"Oh yes. I'm very fond of warm baths," she added, and the light shining in her eyes went deeper. "Long, warm baths. The sort in which one might luxuriate."

"Then I suppose you like the waters at Bath," he said, as her foot went higher on his leg.

"I've never been. But I should think I would like it very much."

"We must remedy that, madam. I shall take you to Bath so that you might"—his gaze dipped to the décolletage of her gown—"*bathe.*"

Her hand dipped to her cleavage; she drew a line up, then down again. "Shall I tell you what else I enjoy?" she asked as her foot caressed his leg.

"By all means."

"Soft beds."

"Ah," he said, nodding appreciatively, enjoying her efforts to flirt her maid out of him. He propped his arm on the table and leaned toward her. "Do you find your bed here very soft?" he whispered.

Ava smiled, leaned toward him, and whispered, "*Very.* Would you like to try it?" And then she sank back in her chair as her foot moved between his thighs.

He cocked a brow. "Is that an invitation?"

She shrugged playfully as her fingers brushed the flesh of her bosom.

He felt full of anticipation, loved playing this lover's game, and gestured for the footmen to pick up their plates, wanting to hurry the meal along. "Did you enjoy your riding lesson today?"

She smiled. "I would that I were more skilled. I dearly hope that you will continue to teach me."

His gaze dropped to her bosom, two creamy mounds of flesh exquisitely displayed in a pale blue satin. "It will be my great pleasure," he said, and winked at her as a footman cleared their dishes.

They spoke of inconsequential things for the remainder of the meal, Ava laughing softly at the things he said as her foot continued to dance. He pretended not to notice, just smiled and enjoyed her efforts to entice him. When the meal was finished, and the last of the dishes were cleared away, Dawson brought him a cheroot and a port.

"Thank you, Dawson, but I don't care for any."

"My lord, please do enjoy your port," his wife said, rising from her chair as a footman hurried to pull her chair out. She walked to the head of the table where Jared sat, let her hand trail his shoulder, and leaned down, so that her lips were next to his ear, and whispered, "You must give me time to prepare my soft bed for you."

That, he reasoned, would be worth the addition of one trollop to his staff. He took Ava's hand and kissed the back of her knuckles. "I will join you shortly."

He watched her glide out of the dining room, her hips moving seductively beneath a trim back, her hair simply but perfectly coiffed. How odd, he thought idly as she disappeared into the corridor, that a scant few days ago he'd wanted to avoid her company.

He finished his port, but decided to forgo the cheroot in favor of getting to his rooms more quickly. "That will be all," he said quietly to Dawson, who still attended him after the footmen had gone.

"Good night, sir," Dawson intoned as Jared strode out of the room.

A good night, indeed, he thought.

Just as Ava had anticipated, a half hour later, Middleton knocked on her door. She didn't answer, but moved deeper behind the thick velvet drapes that hid her. From a small space between the drapes and the wall, she could see the door open, and his dark head pop in, looking about the room. "Lady Middleton?"

"Come in," she called out to him.

He stepped inside wearing his dressing gown, his feet bare. He closed the door and walked into the middle of the room, looking for her. With a lopsided smile, he put his hands to his hips. "All right. Where are you?"

"I'm here, my lord. Please do sit."

He paused, looking directly at the drape she was hiding behind. "Sit?"

Ava moved deeper into the thick velvet drapes, and insisted, "*Sit*." She listened until she heard the slight groan of the overstuffed, chintz-covered chair at her hearth.

As she moved from behind the drape, she saw his head turn and said low, *"Don't."*

With only a slight hesitation, he settled back. "I must remark that you have an alarming way of changing humors. One moment you are cross, then inexplicably happy, and now, rather mysterious."

"Are you displeased?" she asked from a distance behind him.

"Not in the least. I am just curious to know what you are about."

"You shall know momentarily," she said, stepping carefully from behind the drapes. He was sitting, resting his head against the back of the chair. Ava moved quietly, carefully, until she was standing behind him. "Close your eyes."

He chuckled. "There. They are closed. Now what keeps you?"

She didn't trust him not to look and eased her way around the corner of the chair to stand in front of him. Indeed, his eyes were closed, and there was the barest hint of a smile on his lips.

Slowly, she lifted the épée she had taken from the great room, raised it high, then lowered it to rest on his shoulder.

The touch of the metal blade to his shoulder startled him; his eyes flew open at the same time he made a move to sit up, but she pressed the épée against him and shook her head. "I wouldn't, were I you," she said cheerfully, smiling as his gaze focused on the full length of her, taking in the silk chemise she wore and the fact that she wore nothing else.

He slowly sank back in his chair, his smile broadening.

Ava moved the épée to his fresh-shaven chin. Middleton showed no fear; in fact, he grinned. "You obviously esteem your maid, madam."

"I *do*," she said silkily.

"You are a woman with many secrets," he observed as his gaze skimmed her bare legs.

She moved the épée down to the gap in his dressing gown. "But I have no secrets, my lord. I only want my maid returned to me."

"That is not entirely true," he said as he lifted his gaze, first to her waist, and then to the open laces of her chemise. "How you came by your maid was a secret. And I think you have more."

She smiled, drew the épée down a little farther. "I have no more."

He looked down at the tip of the épée and grinned wolfishly. "I'll make you a bargain, lady. I will send for your maid at first light if you will confess your other secrets."

She laughed low, slid the tip of the épée down to the sash that tied his dressing gown. "You, sir, are in no position to bargain."

He laughed and held his arms out wide. "Oh, but I think I am." And then he moved so swiftly that she didn't have time to react. He easily pushed the épée away and caught it at the same moment he surged up. Startled by his sudden movement, Ava stumbled a bit, but Middleton caught her about the waist, crushing her tightly to him at the same moment he pushed her up against the wall. The épée fell to the carpet; an ottoman toppled onto its side.

"I do enjoy your games," he said as his gaze hungrily roamed her face. "*Quite* stimulating."

Surely not nearly as stimulating as she was finding him at the moment. His strength surprised her, as did the grace with which he moved and overpowered her in her game. He was strong, virile, handsome, and looking at her as if he could devour her in one bite. She squirmed, trying to release his hold of her and regain the upper hand, but he easily held on.

"Why do you struggle, Lady Middleton? Do you fear how I will extract your secrets?"

She laughed, and managed to get her arms between them, pushing hard against his chest. "I don't *have* any secrets."

"I think I will hold you captive until you confess," he said with a dark smile.

"There is nothing to tell," she said, and pushed him again, but she couldn't budge him at all.

"Isn't there?" He yanked at the sash around his middle and pulled the tie free with one hand. "If you don't tell me, I will disrobe you . . ." He paused, his gaze running the length of her body and back. ". . . and punish you by licking you here . . . and there. . . ."

Her skin was already on fire, her pulse already coursing blood through her body. She drew a sharp breath; he laughed, and put his hand to her cheek as if he meant to end their play. Ava smiled gratefully, turned her mouth to his palm—and bit the flesh.

Middleton yelped with surprise at the same moment she pushed hard against him and darted away. But he was too fast, catching her with one arm, bending her backward over a chair, his hazel eyes glittering with desire. "You should not have done that," he said. "Now you must pay for it." Holding the tie of his dressing gown, he grabbed her hands and wrapped the tie around them. His dressing gown fell apart, yet he hardly seemed to notice or care that beneath it he was quite naked and quite aroused.

Ava's heart raced as he pushed her against the wall with her hands bound, and put his face against her neck. She moved her head to one side so that he could better reach it, closed her eyes, and let the hunger for him seep into her pores. The man had the capacity to disable her—when he began to kiss her, when his hands began to roam her body, sliding in and out of its most intimate parts, she couldn't think, couldn't move, couldn't do anything but enjoy the ride.

He kissed her neck. *"Confess, wench."*

"There is nothing to confess," she said breathlessly.

He bit her neck. "Perhaps you might start by confessing that you are an accomplished horsewoman, and not the novice you would have me believe."

She gasped with surprise and brought her heel down on the top of his foot.

"Ouch," he yelped as Ava slipped away, running to the bed, her hands tied. "How do you know?"

"I saw you ride. Furthermore, you weren't thrown from Bilbo, or you would have suffered a bruise or a cut instead of the artfully placed dirt on your clothing."

Ava felt herself color.

He laughed, and pointed a long finger at her. "You may as well confess your other secrets."

"Why should I? I'm not the only one with secrets!"

He growled and lunged for her, and with a squeal of laughter, Ava hopped up on the bed to stand.

"What secrets?" he asked, eyeing her like prey.

"That you have a particular friend in Lady Kettle."

"That is no secret," he said, reaching for her foot, which Ava eluded by jumping from his reach. "She has been an acquaintance for years and is like a sister to me."

"I rather doubt Lady Kettle perceives it in quite

that way," Ava said, panting a little now. "And what of the riding?"

"The riding?"

"You ride like the wind, my lord."

"I never claimed to be a novice as you did."

"But when you ride alone, you ride as hard and fast as is possible. It's as if you are riding away from something."

Something dark passed over his eyes, just before he leaped for her, catching her and pulling her down on the bed with him. "It is time for your punishment, Lady Middleton," he said, and kissed her passionately.

In moments such as this, she was certain she loved him. That she felt this way, that she longed to feel his hands on her, longed to see his smile and hear his voice and lie in the comfort of his arms, made her heart take wing.

He moved down her body, his mouth leaving a hot, wet trail. She didn't object when he pulled the laces of her chemise free and pushed it open, exposing her breasts and torso, or when his hands grazed lightly over the same path his eyes took. His expression was ravenous, his hands warm and smooth on her skin. He raked his fingers through her hair, then lifted her bound hands and pushed them above her head.

"Just lie there," he said softly. "Lie there." He divested himself of the dressing gown, unabashedly standing before her, his body lean and muscular and magnificent. He moved on top of her, bracing himself with his arms, and began a very casual exploration of her with his mouth and hands.

And when he at last slid into her, long and hot, Ava closed her eyes and sailed on the cloud of sensual gratification as he pumped his blood into her womb.

When they had both climaxed, they lay together—

her hand, still bearing the silk tie around her wrist, lying carelessly across his chest, and his leg on top of hers. Her head rested on his shoulder while he stroked her hair with his fingers.

They said nothing, for they had, in Ava's estimation, passed the point where words would serve them. What she was feeling was too profound, too great for mere words, and she hoped, she prayed, that he was feeling the same thing.

But she dared not ask him, dared not let her heart be dashed to pieces.

Twenty-four

~~~~~>∼<~~~~~

The tide seemed to turn after that night, or at least it seemed that way to Ava.

He invited her along on his outings during the day, the two of them riding side by side. She had the opportunity to see him work, once alongside his tenants, when a small dam on a stream broke and had to be mended. He removed his coat and waistcoat and lifted large rocks along with the tenants to rebuild the dam.

She watched him help herd the cattle he'd bought in Marshbridge, ushering them out to a field on the north side of the abbey. She even tried to help by trudging behind with a big stick, until she stepped into a patch of questionable mud and ruined her shoe.

At night they would sit together in the study, she reading one of the books from his library, he poring over papers that, he explained to her, gave him an accounting of his money.

As to that, there was no end to his generosity. He was adamant that she have what she needed to support Phoebe and Greer—assuming, of course, they ever saw Greer again. According to Phoebe's latest letter, Greer had traveled deeper into Wales in pursuit of her family. Ava was very disturbed by it and asked

Jared one night, "What sort of lawlessness and disorder do you think is in Wales?"

He smiled. "The usual sort, I'd suspect."

"Oh *no*," she exclaimed, the furrow in her brow going deeper.

He laughed. "By that I mean not very much of it."

"*Ooh*," she said, greatly relieved.

Ava was pleased that he tolerated Sally, too, who had become quite chaste after the dressing-down Ava gave her.

"You're not pinching the bottoms of the footmen or anything as ill-advised as that, are you?" Ava asked one afternoon.

Sally clucked her tongue at her. "Of course not. If I'm to pinch, it's the cock I'm after."

"*Sally!*" Ava cried, whirling around so quickly that Sally lost the fold she was pinning at her back.

"What?" Sally asked innocently. "Don't you want to pinch the master's from time to time?"

Ava flushed and turned around. "Whether or not I do is very much beside the point. The *point*, Sally Pierce, is that you must be on your best behavior. You promised."

"Not bloody fair that you're the only one in this house to be allowed a bit of sport," she groused, but then grinned at Ava's reflection over her shoulder and winked.

Ava closed her eyes and sighed heavenward, but in truth, she did enjoy Sally's fresh view of the world, and moreover, she needed Sally. The woman had taught her many things about how to please her husband—even though she was constantly cautioning Ava that she was giving in to him far too easily.

"The moment the whore comes round, she'll catch him in her web again," she warned Ava one night when Ava waxed dreamily about her day with her husband, in which they had both joined in the binding of hay bales alongside the crofters.

"For pity's sake!" Sally exclaimed when Ava mentioned how very strong he was. "He knows he has *you* in his pocket, doesn't he? He'll think, Why, I've another empty pocket here . . ."

"Hush," Ava said sternly. "You don't know what you're saying."

But privately, Ava feared that Sally could be right. She couldn't seem to grow accustomed to Lady Kettle's frequent visits to the abbey, or the easy way she laughed with Middleton, or the way she looked at him. But at the same time, Ava had learned quite a lot from Lady Kettle about her husband. She had told Ava stories that had painted the image of a lonely boy, rarely with his parents, yet still under the thumb of a very rigid father. His childhood sounded rather bleak.

And there was the reckless riding that she couldn't understand. And when he worked, he worked to the point of exhaustion, doing more than any other man, often working fearlessly, without regard to his person. It almost seemed as if he didn't care what happened to him, and if he didn't care for himself, could he really care for her?

While her relationship with him had improved—they seemed to be getting along quite well, she thought—she couldn't help but feel that something was missing. Just when they would get very close, he'd be gone again, or his mood would grow dark and pensive. She often had the impression that he felt trapped in the moment, or the day. Or perhaps even the marriage.

Honestly, she supposed she really didn't know him very well at all.

Which was why she had come to dread the delivery of the post. She endeavored each day to reach it before Middleton. She had, in the last two weeks, snatched up two letters Lady Waterstone had penned, but fretted that more had reached Middleton.

The two she'd confiscated she read aloud to Sally, who lay on the chaise rolling her eyes, puffing out her cheeks, and making all sorts of disdainful noises.

But Ava did not see any letters posted to London in response. That kept the flame of hope alive in her.

Unfortunately, the flame was not as bright as she would have liked. She had noticed, over the course of time, that the marquis never used her given name. And she never used his, except in the privacy of their marriage bed. It was almost as if the use of given names between them was somehow too intimate.

That he wouldn't say her name began to gnaw at her. She began to count the number of times he referred to her as "madam" or "Lady Middleton." She counted the number of times she referred to him as "my lord" or "sir." It began to feel as if she were the maid sleeping with the master, never allowed the use of his first name, except in the most intimate of circumstances.

She stopped using his given name altogether, stubbornly determined that his name would not pass her lips until he loved her. Ava didn't care how long she might wait. It was as she wrote to Phoebe:

Sisters and cousins use given names. Why on earth wouldn't a husband and wife? It seems positively barbaric. As to barbarians, is there word from Greer?

It wasn't until the week of their departure for Harrison's estate and his annual gathering to mark the start of the fox-hunting season that Ava finally reached her limit.

It was a dreary night, cold and wet and a bit blustery, and given that she had a draft in her suite—"The crack in the wall is as wide as the Thames," she avowed—she had crawled into his bed that night for warmth. "How will you possibly hunt in such weather?"

"Ah, but that is half the fun of it," he said, putting his arm around her and pulling her into his side.

They lay silently for a moment, listening to the sound of rain on the windows, the crackle of wood burning in the hearth. Middleton wrapped her braid around his fist and after a moment, he asked softly, "Have your courses come?"

The question galled her. He'd asked it three times in the last two months, as if her fulfillment of that single function was the most important thing in the entire world.

"Two weeks ago," she bit out.

"Ah," he said, and damn him if he didn't sound disappointed.

Ava buried her face in his chest, but he put his hand to her chin and forced her to look up. In the firelight, his hazel eyes were dark in a way that she understood very well now, a darkness that always made her shiver with anticipation, a look that made her blood rush.

He knew it, too—he suddenly rolled her on her back, coming over her. He pulled the top of her nightgown open and pressed his lips to her throat. "Beautiful," he muttered.

She wanted to push him away, but she couldn't—she lit up so quickly with the touch of his hands, the pressure of his lips. Her blood warmed and moved, pooling in her groin, filling her with a desperate longing to be held and loved by him.

"My lord," she moaned as his hands found her breasts.

"Call me Jared," he uttered before turning his mouth to her breast.

Something caught in the beating of her heart, and the very warm feeling suddenly evaporated. "No," she said flatly.

He paused in his attention to her breast and glanced up at her face. "Beg your pardon?"

She roughly pushed him away, then pushed herself up to sit. "I won't use it because your given name is reserved for those you love and who love you. It's the same reason you never call me Ava."

He looked stung; he pushed up, too, swung his legs off the side of the bed and sat there, looking a little dazed. "By God, I don't know what you want at times," he said. "I don't know how to please you. I've tried to be good to you, I've tried to make things right when you feel they are wrong, yet you still find something to grieve. What do you want, *Ava*?"

She bit her lip, felt the sting of tears in her eyes, and blurted, "I want . . . I had *hoped* . . . that you would grow to love me."

He looked stricken; it was clear from the confusion on his face that he had no idea how to respond. It was just as clear that he wasn't going to give her any declarations of undying love, either. "Ava," he said, reaching for her hand. "My darling Ava."

It was the first time he'd used any term of endearment, and she heartened, turned toward him, and swiped at the tears with her fingers.

"Love . . . love comes with time," he said haltingly.

Her heart plummeted, and she actually felt a bit queasy. "Oh God," she said.

"It takes time and experience to develop," he added, looking awfully pained.

"Yes, I know that," she said, pulling her hand from his. "It's just that . . . it's just that I don't know how two people can be . . . like this," she said, gesturing vaguely to the bed, "and there be no stronger affection."

"But there is affection!" he insisted with a smile, and cupped her face with his hand. "I hold you in the highest esteem. I . . . I esteem you greatly."

He seemed to be fumbling for words, but Ava waited for more. "And?" she prompted him.

"And?" he echoed, confused as to what she wanted.

"*Oh!*" she cried, and scrambled off the bed, grabbing up her dressing gown.

"Wait," he said, holding his hand out to her. "Where are you going? Don't go—let's speak of this. If you want me to call you Ava, I will certainly do so, and of course you have my leave to use my given name—"

"I have your *leave*? Dear God, you haven't understood a word I've said, have you?" she gasped, tying the sash of her dressing gown around her. "You believe that this is about your given *name*?"

"But you said—"

"Yes, yes, I know what I said," she cried, gesturing wildly. "I wish I'd never spoken of it! My mother, rest her soul, was right! Marriage is nothing but a matter of convenience and fortune, and to want more from it is sheer lunacy!"

"What are you saying?" he asked roughly. "This marriage is rotten because I did not use your given name?"

"This marriage is rotten because it's not a *marriage*!" she cried. "It's a business arrangement!"

"*Yes,*" he said, his voice suddenly cold. "It is indeed a business arrangement because that is precisely what you wanted! I warned you, madam—do not ask of me what I cannot give you!"

Tears began to blur her vision. "Is it because you love someone else?"

"*No!*" he said, his voice full of exasperation. "I love no one."

"*Augh!*" she cried, and ran around the foot of the bed, trying to run past him, but Middleton caught her arm. "Let go!" she cried.

"You knew what this was!" he bellowed. "You knew from the moment we met what this was!"

"But it changed!" she cried, trying to yank free. "You cannot deny that it has changed!"

"Ava, listen to me," he said, grabbing her other arm and forcing her to stop squirming. "We are comfortable together. That's really quite good!"

She wrenched free of his grip and lunged for the door.

"Ava!" he shouted after her, but she had already run through the door, wanting to be as far away from him as she possibly could be.

Behind her, Jared stared at the open door, then turned and slammed his fist into the dressing room door. He knew precisely what Ava wanted, and he wanted nothing more than to give it to her.

He just didn't know if he could. He didn't trust his feelings and was far more comfortable with their arrangement.

Frankly, he'd been feeling quite lost of late. He enjoyed Ava's company in a way he would not have thought possible. He found her witty and smart, willing to help out where most women would not deign to lift a finger.

Ava's allure was in her bright, and perhaps somewhat naïve, outlook on the world. He found it utterly charming, a refreshing perspective from the way he'd come to view the world. He adored her spirit, he did. But he didn't know if he *loved* her, if he was even capable of it. He'd only loved once in his life, and that had ended disastrously. He had learned, a long time ago, that if one invested too much of oneself in another, someone or something could take it all away.

There was the preservation of the self in not falling in love.

Ava, he thought wearily, would learn it one day as well as he had.

Twenty-five

～～～

The next day, the rains had stopped and, according to Dawson, Middleton had ridden to Broderick very early. Ava was glad for it—she didn't want to see him until she had managed to find her way and a method of enduring her marriage.

She took a long walk, up to the old castle ruins. As it happened, Edmond Foote was there, brandishing a wooden sword. "Friend or foe?" he called down to her.

"Friend!"

He nodded, and carefully slipped his sword into a cloth scabbard he'd obviously sewn together.

"May I enter?" she asked from the bottom of the old castle walls.

He gave her a beautifully charming smile and bowed low, sweeping his hand grandly to the ruins. "My castle is yours."

She climbed up and saw that he'd been dragging rocks around to form the outline of rooms.

"Ah. You are rebuilding the castle, are you? I must be standing in the kitchen."

"You are standing in the *bailey*," he said, as if that were obvious from the outline of rocks.

"Oh," she said, and stepped over the rocks. "And now?"

"Now you are in the kitchen." He turned around and pointed to a place he'd marked with rocks. "That is the great room, where the king and his knights decide who they will kill," he said with relish.

"Ooh," she said, wrinkling her nose. "Giants and that sort of thing?"

For some reason, that made Edmond laugh. He tossed his head back and laughed loudly, his hazel eyes squinting with mirth. And in that moment, Ava knew why the boy wasn't allowed at the abbey, or in Broderick. She knew why he was a virtual prisoner of the forest.

And she suddenly hated Middleton for it.

Frankly, she was surprised she hadn't seen it before now, but the child was clearly Middleton's son. He had the same hazel eyes, the same mouth. And when he laughed, he looked just like his father.

Nevertheless, she was appalled by the recognition, horrified that Middleton had treated his son so abominably, and even angrier that a man of his position and wealth wouldn't do better by his son, illegitimate or not.

As she stood there, smiling and nodding as Edmond pointed out the rest of his rooms, she wondered if there was anything about marriage that could be recommended. For the moment, she couldn't possibly think of a thing.

On the following day, when Lord and Lady Middleton were to leave for Harrison's, Ava finally appeared (having claimed a headache at supper last night), dressed in a traveling gown, her bags in place, her lady's maid smiling provocatively. Apparently, Jared thought, his wife was ready to make the journey east.

Nevertheless, he approached her cautiously in the

event her mood changed as suddenly as it had two nights past. "You seem ready for a sporting weekend, are you not, madam—er, Ava?"

"I am indeed. *Jared,*" she said, her eyes narrowing slightly.

He almost smiled. If there was one thing on which he could depend, it was that Ava Fairchild would rebound from any setback, perceived or real, large or small. "Splendid," he said. "Then we may proceed. The rain has stopped and it looks to be a glorious day."

"*Doesn't* it," she said, and turned away from him to fit her bonnet on her head.

He watched her fussing with it. The thought occurred to him that he was proud of her, proud to present her as his wife. Only a few short months ago, he hardly noticed her at all. And now . . . now he wanted to touch her, to feel her skin. But he dared not—she looked as if she might punch him square in the mouth if he so much as thought it.

She slept for most of the journey until he woke her when they were nearing Harrison's estate. She came up with a start, wide-eyed and absolutely beautiful. She leaned forward to see out the window, then reared back, pinched her cheeks, smoothed her hair, and turned toward the window to watch the scenery. Jared didn't press her—he looked out the opposite window.

There were carriages everywhere, footmen running back and forth, gentlemen and ladies standing in the drive and walking up the entry steps.

His coachman barreled around the circle, coming to an abrupt halt before the doors as two liveried footmen raced down the steps of the house to assist in helping them down.

Jared descended first, and turned, one hand behind

his back, one hand held up to Ava. As he helped her out, Harrison appeared at the top of the steps and hurried down, his smile big and warm. Behind him, Stanhope chose to make a more subdued appearance by merely walking down the steps.

Harrison grabbed Jared in a big hug, squeezing tightly and clapping him soundly on the back, and remarked that marriage suited him very well.

Jared didn't bother to respond to Harrison, for his friend had already turned to Ava, grabbing her up in a bear hug, too, squeezing the breath from her by the look of it.

"Harrison, old chap," Jared said, putting a hand to his shoulder. "Please don't smother my wife."

With a laugh, Harrison let her go. "Lady Middleton, you are indeed looking quite healthy and happy in spite of the nuptials," he said with a playful wink.

Unfortunately, Harrison had no idea how true that was.

"And how do you find Broderick Abbey?" he asked.

"Too large," Jared said.

"And drafty," she added, her smile seeming forced.

Harrison howled.

Stanhope put his arm around Ava and ushered her away. "Allow me to rescue you from an ardent admirer," he said. "Harrison has reserved a special room for Lord and Lady Middleton, on the west side, so you'll be warm, and painted a bright yellow, so you will be gay. Francis will show you up," he added, motioning for Harrison's butler to see them up.

"Have a bit of a rest, why don't you?" Harrison suggested behind her. "We'll all gather for wine at eight, supper at ten, and the hunt will begin at day-break on the morrow. Middleton," he said, turning from Ava and winking slyly at Jared, "I've a horse the likes of which you've not seen. She stands fourteen hands high, is as broad as a river. Would you like to see her?"

Jared glanced at Ava, who shrugged. "I will be quite all right."

"You're certain?"

"Of course," she said, already climbing the stairs, Sally close behind her. Harrison's butler hurried to catch up to them, and Ava disappeared inside without looking back.

Harrison waited until she'd stepped inside before he turned, withdrew three cheroots from his pocket, and handed one to Jared, another to Stanhope. "I bought her in Madrid, just last year. Had a Spaniard train her for the hunt. She's unbeatable," he said, and gestured for them to walk to the stables.

Harrison had always been something of a horse-man—racing ponies, big grays to pull his carriages, steeds for battle in the event he was ever called to war—and he was no less enthusiastic about this hunter. Jared pocketed the cheroot and listened to Harrison talk about his new horse.

He wasn't exaggerating—the hunter was a beauty, and Harrison was positively giddy with glee as he stroked her nose. Jared appreciated horses—and especially good horses—but not as much as Harrison. He bored of the fawning after a few minutes of it and stepped back, admiring the other horses stabled there as Harrison captured Stanhope and continued his intricate review of the new horse.

As Jared looked down the stalls, his eye caught sight of a familiar shape, and he turned fully.

Miranda was watching him, smiling softly. She was wearing a riding habit, her long dark red hair braided down her back, her hat tipped at a jaunty angle. She was holding a crop in her hand, and tapped it against her leg as the corners of her lips curled up into a sultry smile.

He started to move—to where, he didn't really know—but Harrison's hand to his arm stopped him. Startled, Jared looked at Harrison and was surprised at the look on his face. "I didn't know she was here," he said. "I asked you here but to see my horse."

"I know—"

"No," Harrison said, shaking his head as he glanced down the stables at Miranda. "We've known each other since we were lads, eh?" he asked, shifting his gaze to Jared. "I wasn't aware she'd come with Westfall, or I certainly would have stopped her—"

"What?" Jared asked, having to force himself to focus on what Harrison was saying. "There is nothing more between us."

Harrison colored slightly. "It's none of my affair, Middleton—but I'm not party to it."

Jared was shocked. He and Harrison had been friends for years and never once, not once in all those years, had Harrison ever voiced his disagreement with something Jared did. For him to do so now pushed Jared under the surface.

Harrison obviously saw his surprise—he glanced sheepishly at his feet, then at Miranda from the corner of his eye. "I happen to believe a vow taken before God should not be broken. Say what you will, but I believe it." And with that he turned away from Jared and began to walk toward the stable doors, where Stanhope had already escaped. "Wine at eight!" he said over his shoulder.

Jared didn't respond—he was stung by Harrison's admonishment that he be faithful to his wife. He *had* been faithful, hadn't even thought of Miranda since he'd decided to wed Ava. Yet his very best friend thought very little of his integrity. But why shouldn't he? More than once, Jared had bemoaned the fact that marriage would limit his ability to bed whomever he pleased.

He glanced again at Miranda, a woman who, he'd come to realize, thought more of his title and money than she did of him. She was walking toward him, her hips moving seductively, her smile sultry, and all he could think was, what had he ever seen in her?

She stopped just inches from him and sank into a deep curtsy, her eyes never leaving his. She rose up, gave him a knowing smile, and shifted almost imperceptibly closer to him. "You look very well."

She looked older than he remembered, her skin a bit sallow. Not fresh. *Not Ava.*

"How are you faring?" she asked, her smile fading, her eyes searching his face.

How was he faring? He was miserable. He didn't really know who he was any longer. "I'm fine."

"I miss you terribly. I can't bear to be apart from you, Jared."

He recoiled at the sound of his name on her breath. She used it easily, as easily as he used hers—and yet he could scarcely bring himself to say Ava's name aloud.

Ava was right.

That simple act, that intimate knowledge should be reserved for those he loved, and he hadn't had the courage to admit that perhaps he truly loved Ava.

Miranda was smiling up at him now, her eyes full of hope. She glanced around the stables, as did Jared, and saw only a stableboy, brushing down a horse. "Perhaps we could walk," she said, moving closer. "Someplace we might be alone and talk?"

"There is nothing to say." He couldn't stop looking at her, trying to imagine himself with her. He couldn't understand why, since he'd been gone from London, he'd felt sheer joy some days and sheer despair other days. He couldn't understand how a few short months could change everything and feel like a lifetime.

"Have you received my letters? I wonder what you are doing every moment of every day . . . and night," she added, letting her gaze drift down his body.

Where he once might have enjoyed illicit banter, now he found it obscenely faithless to his wife.

"You remember our nights, don't you, my love? Or has she captured your nocturnal imagination?"

His blood began to rise with anger. "You have no right," he said low, "to inquire about the private affairs of my marriage."

Miranda gasped. And then she laughed, the sound bursting forth from her lips. "Oh my!" she cried, laughing. "Your *marriage*? She's a poppet, darling, a girl with a womb. She's not a *marriage*."

His blood began to pound at his temples, and he took hold of her arm, wrapping his fingers tightly around it. "Heed me, Miranda, have a care what you say."

"Darling, what has come over you? Have you developed tender sentiments for her? I couldn't blame you if you had, for she is very endearing. But she's not *me*, Jared."

"No, thank God," he agreed. "She is not you." He pushed her away and strode from the stable, his heart pounding with fury, his head aching.

Ava sent Sally away when Middleton made his way to their rooms, looking uncharacteristically grim and fatigued. She sat on the settee and watched him walk restlessly from the armoire to the basin and back again. Clearly, he was not in a jovial mood, nor did he feel like talking, for when she asked about Harrison's horse, the only thing he said was *"Splendid."* That was all. *"Splendid."*

After a half hour of watching him stalk about, Ava rose. "I shall go and have a look about," she announced.

He barely spared her a glance. "As you wish."

She wished—she definitely wished—and left him, walking down to the main floor where guests were still arriving and servants were hurrying about, carrying fresh linens and lugging portmanteaus.

Ava wandered into the main corridor, pausing as she went to admire the artwork to pass the time. When she came to the grand salon, she noticed three men standing about at the hearth drinking whiskey. When one of them happened to see her there in the door, he called out to her, "Lady Middleton! Come and join us, will you? Tell us how it is to be married to the Marquis of Middleton."

His two companions snickered unpleasantly.

"Thank you, but no," Ava said, and quickly walked on.

She was drawn by the sound of ladies' voices and came upon an inviting sitting room. Four women were seated before a crackling fire having tea. As she knew two of the women, if only casually, she felt that she'd at last stumbled into a bit of refuge, and entered the room smiling.

Lady Blanton, the first to see her, smiled when Ava asked if she might join them. "Of course, dear. Do be seated."

"Tea, madam?" a footman asked.

"Please," Ava said, and sat next to Lady Blanton on the settee.

"May I introduce you, Lady Ava? Oh! I do beg your pardon, I meant to say Lady Middleton," Lady Blanton said, nodding at the other women. "She's only recently married—aren't you, dear?" she asked, shifting her gaze back to Ava, her lips pursed in something of an odd smile. "I've not had the pleasure of wishing you happy tidings on the occasion of your nuptials."

"Thank you."

"It happened rather quickly, didn't it?" Lady Blanton continued. "I think the whole of London was caught unawares."

The other women perked up and looked curiously at Ava, obviously smelling a piece of scandal. Lady Blanton smiled sweetly, and Ava couldn't determine if she meant to make her uncomfortable or if she was merely, and rudely, curious.

Either way, Ava's skin began to crawl. "We did not see the point in a long engagement," she said.

Lady Blanton nodded. A woman across from her— one who looked vaguely familiar—cocked her head to one side and peered closely at her. "Are you not the daughter of the late Lady Downey?" she asked.

"I am indeed," Ava said, now wishing that she'd stayed in her room. Or Broderick Abbey, if not London altogether. Downey House—yes, yes, if she could only turn back time and never have married him! Downey House had an entirely different set of problems, but they hadn't seemed so heart-wrenching as did her worries now.

"Oh dear, how tragic was your loss! I was quite sorry to hear of her passing, for she was always quite cheerful."

"Thank you."

"How long has it been now? Scarcely a year, has

it?" she asked, glancing at Ava's crème-colored silk gown.

"*Ahem* . . ." Ava paused to accept the tea the footman offered her. "It has been more than a year," she said. The other women glanced at one another, then their teacups, as they clearly put together the fact that she'd married almost as soon as her period of mourning had ended. It was little wonder what they must be thinking.

If only she could tell them that she'd done it to survive, that she'd done it to make sure her sister and cousin wouldn't be married off to the first men to offer a home without regard for their character. But of course she couldn't explain any of that and had to endure their quiet disdain.

The women avoided her gaze.

Miserable, Ava sipped her tea. It had been a mistake to come here, a mistake to think she could step into society and pretend all was right. Her mother would have known what to do. Her mother would have laughed at these women, offered some pithy retort, and flitted off to regale another group. Ava possessed neither her mother's wit nor confidence nor fortitude, and she would have been better off to have crawled in a hole.

The conversation fell silent; there was nothing but the clink of china and the occasional indelicate slurp. After several moments of that, Lady Blanton put aside her teacup, folded her hands in her lap and smiled at Ava. "And where shall you and Lord Middleton make your home? In the country? Or in London, do you suppose?"

"London," she answered, grateful for the change in conversation.

"Oh how lovely for you. You may see your family

as often as you like. I find it is quite important to have such diversions as family close by. Then your husband may carry on with his business and you may carry on with yours."

"I wouldn't have it any other way," one of the women said, and the others tittered politely.

"As long as he has his club and his hunts and his *other* amusements, he is perfectly happy," Lady Preston said with a subtle wink.

The women tittered again. Ava tried to titter, but she felt nothing but weariness. Did *no* one marry for love? She put aside her tea, stood and walked to the tea cart to help herself to the finger sandwiches there, and noticed, with her back to the room, that the conversation had fallen silent again. She had the distinct impression there was a bit of whispering, but when she turned around, the women were sipping tea and looking at their laps.

This would be an intolerable weekend.

It wasn't until the evening hours, when Ava and Middleton—whose mood had improved slightly—descended to the grand salon for wine and supper, that Ava realized the true hell she'd stepped into.

It didn't help that two gentlemen instantly closed in on them the moment they appeared, pulling Middleton to the side to discuss something "terribly" important with him and unwittingly leaving Ava to stand awkwardly aside, a glass of wine in her hand. When she'd once pictured herself married, she'd imagined her life would be much the same as it had been up until now—she would attend social gatherings and flirt with handsome young men. And while she was attending a social gathering, and there were several handsome young men in attendance, she didn't have the heart for any of it.

The only thing she wanted was for her husband to love her. What made that wish so heartbreaking was that she was now convinced he was incapable of it. Were he capable of love, he would not have treated Edmond so abominably.

In an attempt to avoid meaningless conversation, she wandered across the room to admire a beautiful jade sculpture of a woman, and she was joined by another.

"Lady Middleton?"

Lady Waterstone's voice startled her so badly that Ava spilled a bit of wine on the carpet. She knew who it was before she even turned, but she hadn't known until this moment that she would be here, hadn't even *thought* of her being here, and felt horribly betrayed by her unexpected presence. "Lady Waterstone," she managed.

Lady Waterstone smiled and dipped a curtsy, acknowledging Ava's superior rank to her now. The woman was, Ava realized for the first time, classically beautiful, with dark red tresses and dark eyes and lips the color of strawberries. Standing beside her, Ava felt plain and nondescript and even a bit fat.

"Marriage agrees with you," Lady Waterstone said cheerfully. "You look lovely."

Ava glanced down at her old crème silk and thought she must look rather drab compared to the vibrant green that Lady Waterstone was wearing. "Thank you," she said softly.

"How delightful you have come!" she exclaimed. "I hadn't thought you would."

Why hadn't Lady Waterstone thought it, Ava wondered, instantly suspicious. Had they planned to meet here? Was she in the way of two lovers?

"Are you a hunt enthusiast?" Lady Waterstone asked, breezing past her last remark.

"No. I've never hunted."

"Oh? That's good," Lady Waterstone said with a sympathetic smile. "Blood sports can be quite disconcerting."

She imagined Lady Waterstone knew that better than anyone.

"It's just not a sport suited to the tender sensibilities of women," she added.

"Lady Middleton?" It was Harrison, coming around the jade sculpture to join them. "If I may, you should join your husband. We will be going into supper soon."

"Oh, Harrison," Lady Waterstone said with a flick of her wrist. "You do know how to snuff out a bit of good conversation. We were just chatting about hunting."

"Perhaps you might chat with me, Lady Waterstone, for I am desperate to hear your tales," said Lord Stanhope, appearing suddenly on the other side of Lady Waterstone. "You know I find your conversation utterly fascinating."

Lady Waterstone laughed. "My, my, I do believe I am being sequestered."

Stanhope gave her a cold smile and put his hand on her elbow. She turned to go, but hesitated, and put her hand to Ava's arm. "We'll have an opportunity to continue our conversation, won't we?"

"Miranda, you are single-handedly holding up the procession," Stanhope said with another very cool smile.

"I'm going, I'm going," Lady Waterstone said with a laugh, and glided away on Lord Stanhope's arm.

Ava glanced up at Harrison. He smiled so sadly that it struck her she was not the only one who guessed that her husband and his lover had planned to meet so soon after he'd married. The knowledge stunned her. She couldn't seem to move.

"Your husband is waiting," Harrison said softly, and put out his arm.

Ava took Harrison's arm and let him lead her to Middleton, who was still engaged in conversation with the two gentlemen, but who smiled warmly when Harrison interrupted them. He put a possessive arm around her, pulled her tightly into his side, and made a small jest that he must keep his eye on her lest he lose her to some of the young men in attendance.

The two men laughed at his joke, and Ava smiled as she ought, but she felt ill. She could feel a pair of copper eyes on her from across the room, boring a hole through her, and in spite of Middleton's arm around her, she'd never felt so cold in her life.

Twenty-six

❧

Jared had thought the evening would never end—it was interminably long, the laughter and gaiety grating after a time, the situation extremely uncomfortable.

He was aware of Miranda's constant attention, could feel her gaze follow his every movement, could feel it burn him every time he touched his wife.

He should have known she would come—he even felt responsible for it somehow. Perhaps if he'd answered her letters instead of burning them, demanded she desist in writing him. Perhaps if he'd never taken her as mistress to begin with.

He felt trapped by his own devices.

After the ladies had retired from supper and the men had enjoyed their smoke, the sexes were at last reunited. He'd hardly stepped into the room before Miranda cornered him. As she spoke to him, whispering her affection, attempting to share a laugh over Lord Frederick's desperate attempt at humor during supper, and very much pretending as if nothing had changed between them, he could not take his eyes from Ava. He didn't want to be rude, but he was acutely aware of the many looks in their direction, and simply walked away as Miranda was speaking, feeling all eyes on him.

Save one person—Ava did not look at him once.

How unfair it was to have put her in this position. How callous he was to have assumed that they would—both of them—live peacefully and without conscience in their arrangement. How bloody *stupid* of him to have believed they could.

He went to his wife and suggested they retire. She didn't seem surprised, nor did she hesitate to accompany him. They made their way out of the room, wishing a cheerful good night all around, then just as a newlywed couple would, they walked out of the room, their arms around one another.

Ava dropped her arm the moment the door shut behind them. They walked silently to their suite.

Sally was waiting for them—Ava excused her and asked her to return in the morning. As Sally left, Ava turned around. She looked dejected as she walked into the adjoining dressing room and quietly shut the door.

Jared sighed, kicked off his shoes, and began to disrobe. He'd undressed to his trousers when Ava emerged, wearing a nightgown. Her hair was braided loosely down her back. She said nothing as she walked past him and slipped in between the sheets, her back to him.

Jared stared at her back and the long golden rope of hair. He'd never imagined it would be like this. He'd never thought, on the day he'd so rashly proposed marriage, that he would be so wretchedly unhappy, or that someone as vibrant as Ava could be so unhappy.

His head had begun to throb with a massive headache, and he turned away from her, went to the dressing room, and completed his toilet. When he joined Ava in bed, he noted that she was pretending to be asleep. Her body was tense, her breathing shallow.

The wind had picked up outside; he could smell rain. The first crack of thunder confirmed it, and as the rain began to fall, the staccato sound of it on the paned glass windows soothed him.

Ava hadn't moved, but he knew she wasn't sleeping—he could feel the tension radiating from her. Ava Fairchild, who had so amused him with her unconquerable spirit, was lying beside him, the light in her gone out. He'd done that to her. He had doused that beautiful light.

"I'm sorry," he said gruffly, surprising himself by voicing aloud his thoughts.

She didn't move.

He put his hand to her forearm, where she had pushed up the sleeve of her nightgown, and began to caress it, her skin smooth as silk beneath his palm. "I'm sorry," he said again, and he was, sorry for everything, sorry for the light, for hurting her, for ever having proposed to her.

As the rain intensified, he moved his hand to her hair, tangling it in the loose braid, pulling free thick silken strands, pulling it completely free as he catalogued in his mind the myriad things for which he was sorry.

The rain beat a steady rhythm on the paned glass and the fire hissed at the hearth. He didn't know exactly when Ava turned to him, but she pushed her face into his neck and wrapped her arms around him. His body warmed with her reaction—blood spread through him, creating an inevitable whirlpool of desire.

Her breath was warm on his neck, her lips soft and moist. But there was something else, too, that he felt on his shoulder: tears. They scored him, left a deep gash where they touched his skin. They made him insane, made him feel restless, full of the discomfort that had plagued him these last two months. And as more tears leaked out of her eyes, each one of them scarred him deeper than the last, each one of them leaving an indelible mark.

He had to erase those tears, had to get them off his shoulder. He suddenly came over her, pinning her beneath him.

"My lord," she said, her voice full of weariness.

"Be still," he said roughly, and when she turned her head to one side, he took her chin in his hand and forced her to look at him. Ava stared into his eyes for a long moment, then closed hers; a single tear ran down her cheek. "*Ava*," he whispered, and licked the tear from her skin. "*Be still*," he said again, and began to kiss her.

The rain continued relentlessly but faded into distant noise, because suddenly, Jared was aware of nothing but Ava. His hands caressed her body, arousing her breasts, inflaming her skin, wiping the dampness from beneath her eyes, then slipping between her legs. When she feebly tried to resist him, he insisted with his hands and his mouth.

He stroked and caressed her, made her slick with desire, then retreated to more untouched skin, working to arouse her as much as he worked to rid himself of his feelings.

Ava's breath was soon ragged, her hands on him. When he pressed her onto her back and came over her, parting her legs, his cock pressed into her belly. He kissed her eyes, her nose, her lips, then continued moving down her body, kissing the hollow of her throat, the valley between her breasts, the cloth of her nightgown bunched at her belly, and down farther, his hands moving to her hips. Ava's knees came up and apart, and as he sank between her thighs, she gave a little moan of pleasure. He plunged his tongue into her, feathering her with little strokes, circling around, nipping and teasing her until she began to moan, her hands grabbing at bed linens. When she began to pant, he closed his mouth around her and drew her into his mouth, and brought her to a mercilessly powerful climax.

Her cry was strangled, her hips lifting to him as she climaxed. He gripped her until she was spent, then made his way up her body. When he had reached her head, he sank his hand into her hair, his fingers reaching for the back of her head, and he deliriously sank his cock into her with a long sigh of relief.

Her body was hot and wet, a slip of heaven. He moved recklessly inside her, his rhythm quickly gaining momentum as he began to feel his release nearing the surface. She writhed beneath him, seemingly as frantic for him to fill her as he was to do it. He grabbed a fistful of her hair, bit her shoulder, kissed her cheek, her mouth as his tempo increased. His heart pounding, he at last felt himself erupting within her, and buried his face in her hair, fighting to keep a cry of sheer pleasure from waking the house.

When he'd found his breath, he rolled to his side, taking her with him, holding her in his arms, feeling her breath hot and ragged on his shoulder.

He didn't know how much time passed before she slept, but still he held her, occasionally brushing the hair from her face. He held her that way until he slipped into sleep, too, feeling in that moment before sleep a deep, soul-searing contentment that he'd never felt in his life.

* * *

Ava was still sleeping when he left her the next morning, in the middle of the bed, wound up in most of the bedcovers so that he was awakened by cold. He rose and dressed quietly. He took one last look at her before he quit the room—she looked so pretty lying there, her face soft and relaxed in sleep, her hair wild about her, her lips slightly open.

He walked down to the breakfast room and joined the other hunters, who were already in fine form, making bets with one another and eager to be out.

Jared helped himself to eggs and toast, and took a seat at the table while Lords Resnick and Hammilthorn argued about the skills of their respective dogs.

A half hour later, they gathered on the west lawn, their horses anxious, the dogs restless. The air was fresh and cold after last night's rain—perfect conditions for a hunt—but Jared couldn't have been less interested. He wanted nothing but for this interminable weekend to end.

When the hounds were released, dogs and riders surged forward, crashing through thickets, tearing up the earth. When the hounds split, he led his mare to follow to the west, letting her have her head, outpacing the other riders as she sailed over rock fences and into streams. But the mare was brought up short in a stand of forest brush, the vegetation too thick for them to make their way through.

That was where Miranda caught him. "I was beginning to believe you were trying to avoid me, darling!" she said breathlessly, obviously exhilarated from the chase.

His horse, agitated from the ride and the sudden halt, tried to run, but Jared reined her harder, pulling her around in a circle until she'd settled. Miranda laughed gaily when he at last faced her.

"You'll miss the hunt," he said.

"I don't care," she said breezily. In the distance, he could hear the baying of the hounds, and he knew that the hunt had swung wide east. They'd never catch them now.

Miranda slid off her horse and reached up to stroke the mare's nose. "She's a beauty. Wherever did you find her?"

Jared didn't answer. He dismounted and pulled his horse away from Miranda's touch.

"*Darling!*" she said, offended.

He swiped the hat off his head, pushed his hand through his hair, and said wearily, "You have to *stop*, Miranda. It is fruitless. We are through, you and I."

She gasped. "Darling! How dare you say that after all I have sacrificed to be with you!"

"*Stop,*" he said firmly.

Miranda tried to reach for him, but he pushed her hand away. "Do try and accept what I am saying," he said as firmly as he could. "I do not love you. I *never* loved you. I do not want to be with you. I am married—"

"No!" Miranda cried, and suddenly threw her arms around his neck. "What you feel for her is compassion, and well you should, the poor thing! But don't confuse compassion with *love*, darling!"

He grabbed her arms and pulled them from his neck. "*Stop.*"

"Do you love her?" Miranda cried. "You scarcely know her! She is a plain little mouse! I *love* you, Jared!"

"No, you don't. You love my title, the fact that I will one day be duke. You love my fortune and the gifts I lavished on you. But you don't love *me*, Miranda. You never have. You've never really even known me."

"That's not true!" Miranda sobbed. "Is it her bed?" she demanded wildly. "Do you prefer her bed to mine?"

Furious, he grabbed her arms and shook her. "*Stop this now,*" he said through clenched teeth, and let go of her.

But Miranda launched herself against him and slid down his body, to her knees, and began to fumble with his belt.

"Dear God, *stop!*" he cried, appalled, and grabbed her by the arms, roughly lifting her to her feet.

Miranda's tears were flowing freely now, and she closed her eyes, sinking against him with a wail. "You may as well slay me," she sobbed. "I can't go on without you, Jared, I *can't!* I have devoted myself to you entirely, have given you my heart and soul, and I cannot bear to know that you will abandon what we had for a mere *child.*"

"I cannot abandon what never existed. We have been done for a long time, you know it very well. No letter, no display of tears—*nothing* will alter it. Don't pretend there was more to us than there was, Miranda. Set your sights on another man—but for God's sake, leave me be!"

She gasped, dragged the back of her hand across her mouth, and glared at him. "I *hate* you," she said vehemently. "Lord God, how I despise you!"

For that Jared was relieved.

They rode back at a rapid pace, Miranda trying valiantly to outpace him, but riding an inferior mount.

They were the last to arrive at the estate—the others were in the drive, milling about trading tall stories. When Jared and Miranda rode into the drive, he caught sight of Ava. She was standing at the top of the steps with some of the other women, watching him, her arms folded protectively across her middle, her expression grim. Miranda saw her, too, for she turned to Jared and said quickly, "There is your bloody little mouse, Middleton."

But his mouse, having seen them, had already turned and disappeared inside.

Twenty-seven

~~~~~~~~~~~~~~~~~~

Ava was the first to leave the impromptu gathering on the drive, escaping to her room, slamming
the door behind her as she entered.

"Hallo, what's this?" Sally called from within.

Ava yanked off her pelisse and tossed it onto a
chair as she sailed into the room where Sally was tidying up. "They returned *alone*, long after the others.
They didn't *hunt* anything in the woods but each
other, I'd wager."

Sally walked to the window overlooking the drive
and peered out. "Who is she?"

Ava was instantly at her side, pointing out the
woman in the russet-colored riding habit. They
watched her a moment until she turned around to
speak to someone behind her, and Sally saw her face.
"*Oh*," she said with a sympathetic wince. "She's quite
pretty, isn't she?"

"*Augh!*" Ava cried, and half crumpled to the
ground, catching herself on the sill before rising up
again and turning away from the window. "I can't
bear to watch it!"

"Ah, you poor thing, you," Sally said. "Don't you
know it yet, madam? Men are never true. If it's not
this one, it will be another."

It was such a wretched and sad thing to believe—what hope was there for any woman if no man was true? "Do you really believe it?" Ava asked Sally. "Do you really believe men are never true to women?"

Sally laughed as if that were a ridiculous question. "Of *course* I believe it. I've rarely met a man who didn't want a little from me, eh? And there are just as many fancy ladies about who want the same from their footmen. Oh, don't look so astounded! If you expect him to be faithful, you're a silly fool."

"I never said that I did," Ava snapped, and began to pace.

But she *had* said it—perhaps not in so many words, but certainly she'd implied that she wanted more than anything for her husband to love her and to cherish only her. She wanted it with a strength her mother would have found appalling and Ava herself found surprising. And if she couldn't have it, if she were faced with a lifetime of wondering who he was with, she thought she might very well perish.

"It's obvious to me that you want him all to yourself," Sally blithely continued. "I reckon it's obvious to him, too."

Ava stopped her pacing, put her hands to her hips, and glared at Sally. "Don't you have some maidish thing you should be about?"

Sally glanced around the room. "No," she said thoughtfully. "I think I've tended to all here."

"I am certain that you *do*," Ava insisted.

Sally caught her meaning and casually came to her feet. "Perhaps I do," she agreed, and left Ava to stew alone.

Ava stewed, all right. And she paced.

When Middleton returned to the room an hour or so later, she was sitting at the hearth, a book in her lap.

She glanced up as he entered and smiled thinly. "Did you enjoy your hunt, my lord?"

He gave her a quick once-over as he yanked roughly at his neckcloth. "Not particularly."

"Oh?" she asked, turning her gaze back to her book. "Didn't you find your fox? Or perhaps your fox found you?"

He stared down at her as she flipped the pages of her book, but she refused to meet his gaze. Without a word, he walked into the dressing room. But he returned a moment later, standing over her once more. Again, Ava refused to look up, waiting for him to speak. Except that he didn't speak. He just stood there, staring down at her, as if he expected *her* to speak.

She shut the book, put it aside, and looked up. His expression was full of strife, but more than that, as his eyes locked on hers, she realized that she was seeing pity in his eyes. Pity for *her*. Pity, no doubt, that she'd seen him with his lover and was hurt by it.

The realization knocked her off her feet and sent her mind reeling. It was a disgusting feeling, to be pitied, and she quickly stood up, managing to look him square in the eye without the help of her heart, which was staggering about in her chest, drunk with despair. "I want to go home," she said quietly. "I can't bear to be here a moment longer."

"We will leave at dawn's light," he said, surprising her. He turned and walked to the bellpull. "Ask for a bath when the footman arrives. I should like to clean up before supper."

Ava watched him disappear into the dressing room.

Something was wrong with him. Something was different, something that made her feel even a twinge of pity for him.

But for only a moment, until she realized how

absurd that was. He didn't deserve her pity—she wasn't the one with a lover. *He* was. Yet he still seemed deeply troubled, and at least she could empathize with him, for she was no stranger to the torment of being deeply troubled. Not of late, anyway.

True to his promise to leave early, Jared made sure the Middleton party was in the drive by eight o'clock the next morning, much to the dismay of their host.

"Are you certain you must go?" Harrison asked again as a footman settled the last bag on top of the coach.

"I'm sorry, but we must," Jared said. "I've a meeting in Marshbridge to buy some cattle and I dare not miss it."

He could tell from Ava's expression that she knew it was a lie. He'd told her himself when the cattle had come weeks ago that it was all the cattle he'd purchase this year. The land could not sustain more grazing than that.

"Ah, well . . . if there's nothing to be done for it," Harrison said, and smiled at Ava.

"We'll be in London in a fortnight," Jared added.

Again, Ava looked at him, her displeasure clear. Jared raised a brow and returned her look. He owed her no explanation—it was his prerogative to move his household to London. Furthermore, he was quite certain that no matter what he did, his wife would be sorely displeased.

That annoyed him to no end, primarily because he realized he actually cared that she was displeased. He *cared.*

At least Harrison seemed overjoyed by the prospect. "Capital news! I've missed you at the gaming tables."

"Not as much as I have missed your purse," Jared added with a thin smile as he handed Ava up into the coach.

As he moved to shut the door behind her, Ava suddenly put a hand out to stop him. "Wait . . . what are you doing?"

"Closing the door so you do not fall out during the course of the journey," he answered curtly.

Her eyes narrowed. "Do you mean to stay behind, my lord?" she asked, her voice cold.

Jared consciously curbed his reply. "No," he said quietly. "I will ride alongside on horseback. I thought that this arrangement might allow us both to find a bit of peace on the journey home."

Ava glanced at Harrison, then at Jared, and without a word, she moved back against the squabs, out of his sight.

Jared clenched his jaw tightly and closed the door behind her. He took the reins of his horse from the stableboy, and when he had mounted, Harrison called up, "Godspeed," and slapped the side of the coach, signaling the driver to go.

As the coach pulled away from the house, Jared paused to say good-bye to Harrison, and caught sight of Miranda standing in the drive in the company of Stanhope. They were dressed to go riding, but as the coach rolled by, Miranda's eyes were on him.

Jared spurred his horse and caught up to the coach without looking back.

When they arrived at Broderick Abbey, Middleton went directly to his study, closeting himself there for the rest of the day. That was just as well with Ava. She wanted to bathe, to wash the entire weekend away, and to write a letter to Phoebe.

In fact, it was the following afternoon before she saw her husband again, as he was returning from some sort of work that had soiled his clothing and put a bit of mud across his face. She was walking along the path when he rode up and began to trot alongside her.

"It's rather cool," he said as he slowed the horse to a walk. "Are you certain you ought to be about?"

"I'm quite all right."

"Mmm," he said, and he swung down, took his horse by the bit, and began to walk with her. "We are to London at the end of the fortnight," he said.

"So I've heard," she responded sarcastically.

He ignored her tone and said, "I should like to be in London before the rainy season. With enough rain, these roads are impassable."

Actually, that sounded quite nice to Ava—so far away from his bloody mistress and all the speculation about her marriage—but she remained silent.

"And if, by chance, you are with child," he said, slanting a look at her, "then it would be best if we were in London."

Ava stopped midstep. That angered her. It was all he cared about, whether or not he got his precious heir. After days of feeling like a forgotten wife, of wishing for something more, she lost her patience and composure. "That's all this is to you, isn't it?" she asked hotly. "I'm only a *vessel* to you."

Her remark obviously crawled under his skin, because his eyes were suddenly hard and cold. "You *are* a vessel, *Ava*. We are *both* vessels, you and I—I carry the seed to put in your womb. And lest you forget it, you *agreed* to be a vessel, so please do not take issue with my inquiry! I have a right to know!"

"I *will* take issue!" she cried. "I never agreed that the only thing you would care about is my womb."

"Madam, you knew very well what game we played—to pretend otherwise is beneath you."

"Did I really know what game we played? I certainly didn't know you had a mistress on our wedding day!"

"Oh dear *God.*" He sighed impatiently. "There is no mistress! I did not have a mistress on our wedding day, or *now* for that matter—"

"Perhaps you shouldn't leave your love letters lying about, my lord."

He paused; his gaze narrowed dangerously as her words sunk in. "You have been through my mail?" he asked incredulously.

"Yes!" she cried, throwing up a hand and marching on. "And I don't want to hear your pathetic lies!"

"*My* lies?" He caught her roughly by the arm and jerked her around to him. "I have *never* lied to you," he said through gritted teeth. "Let me never hear you say so again! I have been frightfully honest with you from the beginning, Ava—you cannot deny it."

"Honest? That's a lark!" she said disgustedly. "You pretended to esteem me!"

"Don't pretend your innocence! You wanted my title and my fortune, just like every other woman I have ever met in my life," he said through gritted teeth. "You were *desperate* for a match!"

"And you were desperate for an heir!" Ava retorted hotly. "Apparently, the only way you might sire a legitimate heir is through a deceit of feelings, for you are incapable of any *real* feelings."

That turned his expression so dark that she thought for a moment she might have gone too far. "You know *nothing*—"

"What of Edmond?"

The mention of the boy's name paralyzed him. He glared at her, his eyes filling with ire, his jaw rigid.

But Ava had gone too far to stop now, and stepped back, away from him. "I know he is your son, just as I know you are ashamed of him. It's why he's not allowed to the abbey or to Broderick, for fear that someone else might recognize you in him! How could you be so cruel? How could you deny your responsibility?"

His expression turned dangerously dark, and he clenched his fists. "On my life, you know *nothing*. And if you dare say to another living soul what you just said to me—"

"Dear God, have you no heart? Are you incapable of even the most basic of human feelings?"

"What in God's name do you want from me?" he suddenly roared. "I have given you all that you asked for! I have spent time with you, I have tried my best to be good to you, and yet you find fault! Mother of God, Ava, what do you *want* from me?"

"I want you to love me and no other!" she blurted, and whirled to the side as tears suddenly filled her eyes. She hugged herself tightly, and struggled for her composure as tears begin to slide down her cheeks. "I want you to love me because I love you so!"

His silence was suffocating. Everything seemed impossibly bleak all at once and she felt as if she had reached the end of her tether. She couldn't bear it another moment—her shoulders sagged and she let out a long, painful sob.

"Ava," he said, and reached for her, his hand on her waist.

"Dear God, I beg you, please don't condescend—"

"I am not condescending. I do hold you in the highest esteem—"

Oh God, here came the infamous *but*, to be followed by words that would most assuredly send her into seclusion, if not a convent for the rest of her life. Yes, that's what she'd do. She'd write Phoebe and tell her she was joining a convent because she had been humiliated beyond repair.

He grabbed her hand and brought it to his lips. "Ava . . . I will be painfully honest. I am conflicted. I have very strong sentiments about you, sentiments that might yet be love . . . but I find myself quite unprepared for it."

Her humiliation effectively sunk into deep-seated hurt like she'd never felt in her life.

"I don't know how to explain it to you," he said.

"You don't need to explain anything to me—I am not ignorant. You are not unprepared for love—you are incapable. Edmond and I know it very well."

He looked as if she'd struck him. He yanked the hat off his head and thrust a hand through his hair. "I will not dignify that with a response. You have no idea of what you are speaking. Can't you at least try and understand?" he snapped. "It's not as if ours was a love match from the beginning, is it? You pursued this match with a single purpose, and that purpose, I would submit, was not for me to *love* you!"

"But you made me think it was possible!" she tearfully insisted.

He looked unbearably sad, as if he'd lost someone very dear. "It was not my intent," he said quietly. "I assumed you understood."

Oh dear God. Dear God. Humiliation, despair, and now the ugly truth presented her a crippling blow. Tears blinded her, but she shook her head. "I cannot deny it, then," she said weakly. "I did not set out for you to love me. But then . . . then everything changed, and where I once feared being trapped by this marriage of convenience, now I fear unhappiness."

"Oh, Ava . . ."

"I feel it seeping inside the abbey, under the doors, through the windows, filling the entire house and surrounding us because you and I are so far afield from one another," she said, wrapping her arms about her.

"Maybe not so far afield as you think. Things have changed for me as well."

She laughed wryly. "But not quite as profoundly as they have for me, have they? You are conflicted. I am not. No," she said sadly, "I am astonishingly unconflicted."

His eyes said it all—he could not return her affection.

"So there seems nothing more to say . . . except that I cannot exist this way, my lord. I . . . *cannot.*" She looked away from him and began to walk, stumbling along, the path blurred by her tears.

"Ava!" he called from behind her.

"Please leave me be!" she shouted pleadingly, and began to run.

He didn't argue. He didn't follow. He let her go.

Ava walked for what seemed hours, each step heavier than the last, until it seemed she had dug a furrow in the ground as long and deep as the ache in her heart.

Twenty-eight

~~~~~~

In the days that followed that afternoon, the two of them existed just as Ava imagined her mother and her friends existed—in the same house, certainly, and with the required civility—but with very little physical contact between them.

Middleton rode out every morning, returning late in the day, usually covered in dirt or his boots caked with mud, and usually exhausted. Ava attempted to keep her mind from her troubles by playing games with Sally, much to Miss Hillier's dismay. Ava hardly cared—she would do anything to keep her mind off of him.

But it wasn't very easy. She thought of him constantly, listened for the sound of his horse in the drive. She longed to speak to him—or better still, she longed for him to speak to her, to tell her that he was no longer conflicted, that he loved her completely.

She felt like a silly girl with silly dreams.

One day, she received a letter from Phoebe reporting that the paper had carried an interesting *on dit* one day about a "certain" marquis and his new wife who had journeyed to a country estate for a bit of a hunt, and what should the marquis snare but his mistress? And furthermore, Phoebe, wrote, the *on dit* speculated that there was a rift between the newlyweds, given their hasty departure.

Marvelous. Now all of London shared in her misery.

Middleton came to Ava's rooms twice during that fortnight, and both times Ava's resolve melted. All it seemed to take was his touch, and she was lost. They hardly spoke during these moments, just reached for each other, taking solace in their physical longings. Their hearts could not seem to exist as one, but their bodies and their passions were perfectly matched to one another.

At least Ava believed that was so. She couldn't possibly have known that after Jared's heart had been reduced to mush, he despaired that it would ever grow again.

But much to his genuine surprise, it *was* growing, slowly but surely knitting itself back into one piece. And that piece, as fragile as it was, was wrapping its roots around Ava.

Every morning he rode out just to put some space between them, just so he might think, might learn to understand himself before he hurt her more. When he returned home, it was Ava's face and bright smile he longed to see, the same smile that had captured his imagination the first time he'd met her.

In fact, the irreverent Ava had returned to him, sitting with him every night at supper, pretending not to care in the least what he thought of her. One night, for example, she complained that the abbey was bereft of any good books.

"I've a library full of them," he informed her, surprised by her declaration.

"I've seen them all," she said with a flick of her wrist. "I suppose if one actually enjoys Shakespeare or Jonson, they might consider it quite nice."

"And you don't enjoy Shakespeare or Jonson?"

Ava rolled her eyes. "I am not a bluestocking, my lord. I much prefer the secular. *Modern* novels."

"I will make certain the next time we are in London that I purchase many *modern* novels for the Broderick Abbey library."

She shrugged. "As you wish. I really don't have time to read, what with the redecorating of the green salon."

He ignored the incongruency of the conversation. "The green salon?"

"Mmm," she said, fitting a bit of sorbet on her spoon. "It's quite dreary. Far too many portraits of positively ancient people, and the décor is really rather feudal."

"How odd," Jared remarked, shaking his head at the offer of sorbet from the footman. "The furniture is French. I had it on good authority that it is the sort of furniture currently sought after in all of the finest salons."

Ava snorted. "I suppose, if one prefers that sort of look."

He smiled. "Please do as you like. You are mistress of Broderick Abbey."

"Thank you," she said, inclining her head sweetly. "I ordered some new fabrics from a tradesman in Broderick and put it to your name." She smiled at him. "I hope you don't mind."

"Not at all," he said, and meant it. As far as he was concerned, there was no limit for Ava. Whatever she needed to make her happy, whatever would stop the unhappiness from, as she said, seeping in under the doors and through the windows to swallow her whole, whatever would bring that sparkle back to her eye he'd do. To the extent he was capable of doing it.

Certainly he knew what might make her happy—
and if he didn't know it, he was reminded of it on
those occasions he visited her bed. The way she held
him, the way she moved with him, the way her
mouth hungrily sought his—it was obvious to him
that her feelings for him had not changed, no matter
how hard she might pretend that they had.

But his predicament of not being able to fully commit himself to her body and soul—*What was it he
feared?*—continued to drive a wedge between them.

He tried to mend some of his mistakes. He tried to
see Edmond more often, to insinuate himself into the
boy's life, but it was quite clear that the boy loved the
man he believed to be his father. Jared was, he realized, six years too late with his efforts.

He hadn't even known of Edmond's existence
until the boy was three years old. As a young man of
twenty, he'd fallen in love with Martha, Edmond's
mother. She might have been a servant, but Jared had
loved her. *He had, hadn't he?* Honestly, he didn't know
anymore—but he suspected that if he'd truly loved
her, he would have searched for her when she left
him.

He never knew why she'd left him—but he'd been
naïve enough to believe that she hadn't loved him
and had feared for her employment and reputation,
just as Miss Hillier suggested. It wasn't until three
years after she'd left that he found out the true reason
for her departure—he had put a child in her, and Miss
Hillier had discovered it.

Of course Miss Hillier had told the duke, and the
duke had sent Martha away, threatening to take the
child she carried if she ever revealed her lover's iden-
tity. When Jared had discovered the ugly truth, he'd
forced Miss Hillier to tell him where the duke had

sent Martha and, ignoring his father's threats, he'd set out to see her.

But it was too late. The boy—*his* boy—thought Mr. Foote was his father. Mr. Foote, a kind and generous man, had married Martha and given her and her bastard child his name. And Martha, Jared's beloved Martha, professed to love Mr. Foote. She had begged him to go away, to leave them be, to give her his word he would not tell Edmond who he was.

Jared had left quite shaken, uncertain about what to do.

The only thing he knew for certain was that he must confront his father. But the duke was characteristically furious with him for going to Martha and Edmond and unearthing what he called a "blight" on the duchy. He had threatened Jared with destroying the boy by telling him that Mr. Foote was not his father. Jared had understood how painful that would be to the little mop-haired boy he'd seen, and had been swayed by his father's threats.

But now, he couldn't help believe that if he'd *truly* loved Martha in the beginning, things might have turned out differently.

He didn't hear from Martha again until last year, when she wrote to him as she wasted away from consumption, begging him to give her husband and Edmond a home. Of course he'd done it—it was the very least he could do. But when his father had heard of it—the gossip among the servants was ceaseless— he had come to Broderick Abbey to see for himself, while Jared had been away in London. Unbeknownst to Jared, the duke had threatened Mr. Foote, promising to see him impressed into the Royal Navy and his son sent to God knew where if the boy was ever seen about Broderick or the abbey, for there was a resemblance between him and the marquis.

Mr. Foote had taken the duke's threats to heart.

When Jared had learned of his father's vicious threats, they had argued most bitterly, but as usual, to no end. Since then, Jared had been quite uncertain about what to do. He wanted to know his son, but he would not take the boy from the only father he'd ever known—that seemed to him the height of cruelty. And when his father threatened to have Mr. Foote impressed, Jared was even more uncertain. He believed his father capable of such action and poor Mr. Foote lived in fear of it.

So he had let the matter simmer, indecisive as to the best course of action. He wanted to take part in his child's life, but he could not see how to do it without causing pain to them all.

Yet he had, in these last few months, begun to question his own moral character. And it was his uncertainty as to his true moral character that kept him distant from Ava.

As a result, her appearances at the supper table grew less frequent. Worse, she seemed to feel quite uncomfortable in his presence when the two of them were alone. Yet he would hear her laughing in her rooms, would see her and Sally together in the gardens on some mornings, and he'd long to be with her.

But Ava held him at arm's length—except in her bed. There she hid nothing from him, unabashedly released herself to him—and then seemed to regret it with increasing intensity the next morning.

"He's there again," Sally remarked one morning as they walked in the garden. "He's there, just now, watching you," she said, peering up at Middleton, standing at the window in his study, looking down.

Ava would not look up. "No doubt he is about to sit and pen a letter to his beloved," she said sarcastically.

"In truth, I've not seen one letter dispatched to her," Sally said.

"And how would you know, dear? You don't read, remember?"

"I don't read," Sally said with a sniff, "but I know what her name looks like—I've seen it quite enough times."

"Perhaps he posts his letters privately through a footman, or through the estate agent who comes here."

"And perhaps he doesn't," Sally said with a cluck of her tongue. "You are determined to see the devil in him, aren't you?"

"I'm determined to survive. And as soon as we return to London, I am to my old home, my stepfather be damned. I refuse to live in Middleton's house."

Sally shrugged and looked up at the sun, closing her eyes. "You might be slicing off your nose to spite your pretty face, mu'um."

Ava snorted at that.

"Suit yourself," Sally said with a sardonic smile. "Suit yourself."

Frankly, Ava wished Sally would suit herself and go inside and leave her be.

She wished the whole world would go away and leave her be. Everyone but the selfish and perfidious marquis whom she could not stop loving—and he was the only one who *did* leave her be.

But that night, when he informed her they would be leaving for London the day after the morrow, she understood the world would not go away. If anything, in London the world would close in on her as all eyes turned to the newlyweds who had left a country party early because of the appearance of his mistress.

It was the sort of sordid mess that used to make her and Phoebe and Greer clamor for the *Times* every morning with the hope of reading something quite titillating.

Twenty-nine

~~~~~~~~

They arrived in London just before sunset. As the carriage rolled down Oxford Street, Ava fit her hands in her gloves, straightened her bonnet, and said, "If you please, my lord, I should like to be taken to my stepfather's home."

"I'll have a carriage take you on the morrow," he said with a bit of a yawn.

Ava folded her hands in her lap, her mind made up, prepared to do battle, and stated firmly, "I should like to go *now*, my lord."

"Ava," he said wearily. "It is too late to go calling."

"I don't intend to call," she said softly. "I intend to reside there."

Her declaration caught him by surprise. His hand froze in the straightening of his neckcloth. "What do you mean, *'reside'* there?"

"Exactly as I say. I intend to reside at my stepfather's house."

Slowly, Middleton lowered his hand, his expression perplexed. "Might I ask why?"

"Isn't it obvious?"

"The only thing that is obvious to me is that you are my wife, and therefore you belong in my house, not your stepfather's."

She gave him a withering look. "Perhaps you've forgotten that you are conflicted, sir. I merely intend to make it easier for you."

"Deserting your marriage doesn't make anything easier for me," he snapped.

"You have such gall to say that *I* am deserting my marriage when *you* never fully entered into it. Will you now hold me against my will?"

His eyes narrowed coldly, but he reached up, pulled open the trapdoor that allowed him to speak to the driver, and gave him the direction of Ava's stepfather's house.

And he continued to stare at her until the coach pulled in front of the Downey town house. As a footman jumped down from the coach and ran up the steps to announce Ava's arrival—it was part of the protocol surrounding her new status as a marchioness—Middleton's frown darkened. "You are making a rather grand mistake, wife. Have you no care for the scandal this will cause?"

"It can be no worse than the scandal in marrying you," she said briskly. "The mistake I made was in assuming that marriage was somehow prescribed by a set of rules. In believing that if I followed those rules, I would have all that I need."

"And don't you have what you need? Do you want for anything? Your sister and cousin—do they want for anything?"

"You know very well what I mean. I do not have what I need to be happy. I can't possibly be happy in your house. I am rattling an empty cage."

His face darkened and he suddenly leaned forward. "Ava . . . there is something I need to tell you."

The door swung open; Ava heard Phoebe's squeal of delight and reached for the door opening. Thank

God! She didn't want to hear how conflicted he was, how he hadn't come to love her, but he hoped to in time. "Good-bye, my lord."

"For God's sake, if you will just listen—"

"I believe we've said all there is to say," she said, and took the footman's hand and climbed down.

Phoebe instantly accosted her, throwing her arms around her, pressing her face to Ava's bonnet, jumping up and down. "You're home, you're home!" she cried happily, then reared back, grabbed Ava by the shoulders, and peered closely at her. "You don't look the least bit different. Lucy said you would look quite different somehow."

Ava forced a smile. "I haven't changed in the slightest," she insisted. "I'm still the same Ava."

Sally snorted at that as she lugged a couple of bags past Phoebe and Ava.

Ava wrapped her arm around Phoebe's shoulders. "Come, then, I want to read Greer's latest letter," she said, and tried to force Phoebe to walk inside.

"But what of Middleton?" Phoebe asked with a laugh, pulling back. "I should like to meet my brother-in-law now that he's been forced to live with—"

"Lady Middleton!" Lord Downey called sternly from the door, his hands on his thick waist. "I would have a word with you if you please!"

"He's going to Middleton House," Ava said, and ignored Phoebe's cry of alarm as she went to greet her long-absent stepfather.

She never saw the carriage roll away, but she heard it, and in Lucille's arms, she closed her eyes tightly shut to keep the tears from falling.

Middleton House was, Jared thought, quite empty and cold. There was not a redeeming thing about it as far as he could see—each room seemed stark and lacking any warmth. Just like him. Just as he was missing Ava, so was every room. She'd removed herself from him, and just like that, pieces of himself were removed from him, a little more every day until he worried there'd be nothing left of him at all.

He'd known for a while—days, maybe—that he loved her, truly loved her, and that he couldn't be without her. Unfortunately, she wouldn't listen to him. He'd waited too long, had allowed the hurt to boil over and seep into her bones.

Once he'd spoken to his father—who was in Scotland hunting at present—he would tell Ava everything. How he'd not been able to sleep because he missed her so, how he didn't care if she ever bore him a child as long as she stayed close to him. How he'd wanted to tell her what was in his heart, but given the circumstance of their marriage and some unfinished business, he'd not believed he could. How he would do anything—*anything*—if she'd only come back to him.

He'd already sent a note to his father requesting an audience when he returned at the end of the fortnight. He'd already bought the expensive diamond bracelet he would give Ava when he went to fetch her from her stepfather's house and bring her home. He'd done everything he must to commit himself fully to Ava and their marriage and their life together. He was ready. He was ready to love her, completely, unconditionally, solely.

Phoebe had questioned her endlessly as to why she had not returned to her husband's house while Lucy flitted around preparing for the soirée that Lord Downey, having determined he owed no dowry to

Middleton for having taken Ava from his hands, insisted on hosting to welcome the happy couple back to London. That, and to begin the husband search for Phoebe.

"I can't possibly understand why you are not in his house," Phoebe said. "There is bound to be talk."

"I don't care," Ava said flippantly as she read the morning *Times*.

Phoebe thumped her on the shoulder.

"*Ouch*," she exclaimed, glaring at her sister.

"What happened?" Phoebe demanded.

"Best you sit for it, mu'um," Sally sighed as she flipped through the pages of a fashion plate, sprawled along the divan.

"As for you, Sally, I think there is a bit of dusting in the library that requires your immediate attention," Phoebe said with a strength Ava had never really noticed in her sister before now.

"Dusting!" Sally exclaimed. "That's for the chambermaid to do!"

"Precisely. And as you may recall, we do not *have* chambermaids, so *any* maid may be required to do it." Phoebe pushed Sally's feet off the divan. "And I would like a private word with my sister, if you please."

"All right, all right," Sally said grumpily, and went out.

Phoebe shut the door behind her and locked it just to be safe.

Ava tossed the newspaper aside and dug a gown Phoebe was working on from its hiding place in a cupboard. She held up a beautiful gold brocade glittering with tiny sequins—perfect for Parliament's reduced autumn season and all the festivities that went along with it.

"Do you like it?" Phoebe asked, wrinkling her nose.

"Like it? It's beautiful, Phoebe."

"I thought it was perhaps overly adorned."

"No, it's beautiful."

"Put it on," Phoebe said as she picked up her sewing basket.

Ava squealed with delight, turned her back to Phoebe so that her sister could unbutton the gown she wore, then slipped out of it and pulled the gold one on.

"Now," Phoebe said, as she fussed with the shoulders of the gown. "I will have your answer—a *truthful* one. Why have you abandoned your husband?"

"You know why," Ava said as she admired herself.

"No, really, I don't, and I am quite perplexed by it."

Ava leaned down, picked up the *Times*, opened it to the society page, and read aloud: "The hunter becomes the hunted: A certain bit of hunting that began at the country estate of a popular viscount two weeks past has continued in town. Now it would seem the hunter has been caught in a zoo by the hunted, a lord of the highest order. The widowed hunter never had a chance of escaping, according to reliable sources."

Ava tossed the newspaper aside. "There you are, Phoebe. He has a mistress."

Phoebe snorted. "As do most of the married men in this town. Why should that have you so over-wrought? You expected no more or no less when you married him."

"*Why?* I will tell you why, Phoebe. Because I simply cannot bear it."

"Why on earth not? Everyone does."

Ava jerked around, knocking Phoebe's hands from her shoulders. "I'm not everyone, Phoebe," she snapped. "I can't abide it."

Phoebe replaced her hands firmly on Ava's shoulders and forced her around to the mirror above the hearth. "You love him," she said, and yanked the dress so tight that Ava wheezed. "Don't you? For all your talk of convenience and fortune, you *love* him," she said, and yanked the gown even tighter.

A tear slipped from Ava's eye, slid down her cheek, off her jaw, and landed on the flesh of her breast. "*Yes*," she whispered.

"Good," Phoebe said with a smile, and put a little slack in her dress. "Do you remember what Mother used to say? That a marriage is made for convenience and fortune, and rarely is it inspired? Well, Ava, darling, your marriage is inspired. You are a fool if you don't grab it and hold tight."

"And if I hold on to it, he will wound me endlessly. Were it a *true* marriage of convenience, I'd not be slighted in the least. *That* is what Mother meant for us to learn."

"Rubbish," Phoebe said as she attempted to button the gown. "I rather think even Mother would have been quite happy to think that perhaps, just once, love might conquer convenience." She pulled the dress again and sighed. "The country air must do you well. I can scarcely button you," she said with a bit of a grunt as she struggled to fasten the dress.

When Phoebe had managed to button Ava, she looked at her sister's somber reflection in the mirror, slipped her hands around her, and hugged her tightly. "If you love him, Ava, then you must go to him."

"*No*," Ava said, tears in her eyes. "He doesn't love me."

Phoebe sighed wearily. "You've always been uncommonly stubborn, haven't you? If he doesn't love you now, he will in time. How can he not?" She squeezed her sister affectionately and let her go. "Wait there while I fetch a bit of chalk," she said, and walked across the room to dig through her sewing basket.

With her back to Ava, Phoebe couldn't see Ava examine herself in the mirror and the tight fit of a gown that would have, a mere month ago, fit her perfectly. Or see Ava put her hand to her belly and squeeze her eyes shut.

Phoebe didn't see the second tear that slipped from Ava's eye when she realized, with not a little helplessness, that her suspicions must be true—she was carrying his child.

On the night of the grand Downey soirée, Lord Downey would not leave Ava be. "Where is the marquis?" he asked excitedly. "I've an exciting proposition for him that he cannot possibly refuse!"

"I don't know," Ava said wearily, feeling a little ill. She'd sent word to him about this wretched event and had received his reply that he would come. And he did come—in the company of Harrison and Stanhope, both of whom looked as if they'd had too much whiskey. He stood to one side.

But he was tolerant of her stepfather—Ava knew, because Downey cornered her later, his little eyes blazing. "He's agreed to give my venture serious thought!" he said eagerly. "*Serious* thought!"

And she supposed he was tolerant of her, for he danced with her.

He asked her in front of several ladies, knowing full well she could not cut him and cause more talk than was already circulating. As it was, the ladies were eyeing them closely, waiting for the first crack in the façade.

When they stepped onto the dance floor, Middleton took her in hand and said, "Stop looking as if you will perish with disgust at any moment."

She looked away.

"*Look* at me," he commanded her. "They will think we are arguing if you don't, and I, for one, am sick of the speculation."

Ava looked at his neckcloth.

"I've missed you," he said simply.

Her heart wrenched; she lifted her gaze to his hazel eyes and swallowed the bitter taste of tears in the back of her throat. "What, as busy as you've been at the zoo? I don't see how you possibly might have missed someone as insignificant as me."

He sighed, bent his head, and looked at her closely. "Are you unwell?" he asked.

There were the tears again, always the blasted tears since she'd missed her courses.

"Ava . . . what's wrong?"

"What's wrong?" she said, blinking back the tears. "The very thing that has been wrong from the beginning."

"God," he said, stealing a glance around them. "Please don't do this here. Not now."

"When would you prefer that I do it?"

He sighed again, but said nothing. They danced on in silence, his hand warm on her waist, his shoulder firm, wide, and strong beneath her hand. She didn't want to miss him, but she did. Terribly.

At the end of the dance, he kissed her hand and looked at her as if he meant to say something, but then pressed his lips together. "I am leaving now."

"Good night," she said, and as much as she wanted to ask him to stay, she wouldn't. She preferred to cling to whatever shred of pride she had left.

A full two weeks had passed since their return to London—two interminably long and tense weeks.

The *ton* was growing restless with rumors, too, he knew—there were little whispers in the gentlemen's club, vague *on dits* in the society pages. Even Harrison had asked him bluntly if he and Ava were estranged.

"Only temporarily," Jared had responded.

Harrison frowned. "What of your father's Autumn Ball? I rather imagine he won't brook an argument between you and Lady Middleton for everyone to see."

"There is no argument," Jared lied. "Nothing more than a young woman adjusting to married life. Lord and Lady Middleton will attend the soirée as required."

He left it at that, preferring not to tell Harrison about his audience with his father that very morning, only a day after his arrival from Scotland, in which his father had berated him for having mucked up his marriage before it had even begun. As if he needed to be told that. As if he hadn't berated himself a thousand times over.

"You are a disgrace, gallivanting about with your mistress before you've put your seed in your wife's belly!" he'd blustered angrily, assuming what everyone else had assumed.

It was interesting, Jared had blandly observed, how everything with his father seemed to surround the heir. How sad, he thought, to be so driven by something over which one had absolutely no control. What a miserable existence for the old goat.

"Have you nothing to say for yourself?" his father demanded at the sight of Jared's little smile.

"Nothing, other than I am amazed at how quickly you have gleaned the gossip, having only just arrived in town. And how ironic I find it that you would fault me for doing exactly as you did."

That clearly surprised the duke. "I beg your pardon?"

"You kept a mistress, or a series of them, throughout your marriage to Mother," he said calmly. "Why would you fault me for doing the same?"

His question, which he'd thought so straightforward, caused his father a near fit of apoplexy. "You are a *vile* man," he said low. "How *dare* you!"

"No, Father . . . the better question is, how dare *you*? You have disdained me since I was a boy. Perhaps I deserved it—I hardly know or care any longer. But I have done as you've wished—no, as you've *commanded*. I have married a woman with the pedigree you require. And if we give you your bloody heir, I shall be very happy for it. But frankly, I scarcely care if Ava ever bears me a son." Because he loved her. He *loved* her. "Furthermore, I want you to set aside part of the entail of Redford for Mr. Edmond Foote so that he will always be provided for."

"Who?" the duke asked.

Jared's fist closed. "My son. *Your* grandson," he said tightly.

"You are mad! You've done well enough by him as it is. You've installed the boy and his father at Broderick and given them an income in spite of my warnings—"

"It's not enough. It can never be enough. I want him protected by the grandeur of your name," Jared said simply. "And if you don't set aside part of the entail for him, I shall tell the world how you sought to destroy a young boy's world by taking his father from him in a most unscrupulous manner."

"I didn't take you from him!" the duke said angrily. "He was never anything to you!"

Jared let that dagger sink into his heart for a moment, then said, "I didn't mean me, unfortunately.

I was referring to your threats to tell a young boy that the man who took him in when he was an infant, the man who ignored the fact he had been sired by me, was not his real father in order to force me into a marriage. Furthermore, you have threatened a decent, Christian man with ruination for having given your grandson a name. Do you have any idea how cruel that was?"

"Honestly—"

"And do you realize, sir, that Mr. Foote has done what you and I have never been capable of doing?"

"I don't know what you mean."

"He is a father, in every sense of the word. That is a function that has escaped us both. It is too late for me to be a father to Edmond, and I daresay, too late for you to be a father to me. But by God, I will ask Mr. Foote if there is *some* role I might serve in my son's life, and I will, at the very least, provide for that child and Mr. Foote, and Edmond's children."

The duke gaped at Jared.

"Oh, and one last thing," he said, almost casually. "There is no mistress. I ended it with Lady Waterstone when I asked Ava to marry me. Unlike you, I could not take one woman to wife and bed another—it destroys people."

His father, he noticed, looked pale, but Jared didn't care. He stood up. "Ava and I will be happy to attend your Autumn Ball on Friday," he said. "Thank you for the invitation."

For the first time in his life, Jared left his father's house feeling quite unburdened. He hardly cared what the duke thought of him. He hardly cared if he disowned him or planted roses in his arse. The only thing Jared cared about was bringing Ava home.

The sooner, the better. He felt like an empty cage without her.

And to that end, Jared asked his driver to take him to Clifford Street. He had a call to pay.

The butler opened the door to the Downey house almost as soon as Jared released the brass knocker. "Yes?" he asked politely, his face showing no recognition of Jared.

"Lord Middleton calling for Lady Middleton."

"Have you a card?"

A *card?* Jared snorted. "I would assume that Lady Middleton does not need a card from her husband."

A silver tray appeared in the butler's hand and he put it out to Jared all the same. "I'm to take a card to her ladyship, sir."

Jared sighed, supposed that the jeweler's clerk hadn't quite learned the finesse of butlering even yet, withdrew a card from his pocket, and placed it on the silver tray.

The butler seemed very pleased, judging by his beaming grin. "If you'd wait here, milord," he said, pulling the door open so that Jared could step inside.

Jared did as the butler asked and stood patiently in the foyer as the butler trotted off to hand over the card. A few moments later, Morris returned. "She's not receiving, my lord."

The wench. Middleton smiled. "Like hell she's not," he said politely, and began to walk in the direction Morris had just come.

"No, no!" Morris cried, rushing after Jared once he'd recovered from his surprise. "You can't go in, milord! She's not *receeeiving!*"

But Jared walked on, opening one door and then the next, stumbling across Downey in a small study.

"I do beg your pardon," he said to the stunned Downey, and shut the door.

"My Lord Middleton!" Mr. Morris cried frantically. "Allow me to at *least* introduce you properly!"

The door to the small study banged open and Downey rushed out, his eyes wide with consternation. "I told her she had to go, my lord!" he said frantically. "I've not sanctioned her stay here! This won't affect your agreement to hear my proposal, will it?"

"Lord Downey," Jared said, frowning darkly.

"Yes, sir?"

"Shut your gob," he said, and looked at the butler. "If you're to announce, be quick about it."

Morris hastily opened the door and stepped inside. A few moments later, the door opened again, and Jared noticed the dew of perspiration on the poor man's brow. "Very well, sir," he said with a low bow, and opened the door wider, stepping out of his way.

Jared strode past him into the room, his eyes immediately locking on Ava. Then her sister. And Miss Downey. And the ever-present Sally. Frankly, he could not recall a more vigilant lady's maid than Sally.

He ignored them all, looked directly at Ava. "Good afternoon."

"Good afternoon, my lord. Thank you for calling, but I am not receiving today."

"Oh, but I think you are," he said evenly.

"*Oh,*" Sally said, her brows reaching her hairline.

"Oh but I'm *not,*" Ava said. "My sister and I were just reviewing our accounts."

"Perhaps the accounts can wait, as I shall be paying them. And besides, madam, your husband needs a word."

"Husband," she said with a bit of a smirk.

"*Oh my,*" Miss Downey said, exchanging a stunned look with Sally.

He didn't care how angry or hurt she was, he would not tolerate her insolence. "A word, Lady Middleton," he said sharply. "*Alone.*"

"I beg your pardon," she said with a flick of her wrist, "but I—"

"We were just leaving," Phoebe interrupted, frowning darkly at her sister as she gestured for Sally and Miss Downey to stand.

Ava exclaimed at the betrayal and gaped at her sister hurtfully.

"Come on, then, Lucy," Phoebe said sternly. "His lordship would like a word with his *wife,*" she said with a firm nod for Ava. "Come on, then—you, too," she said to Sally, and extended her hand, took Sally's firmly in hers, and with her free hand on Miss Downey's back, pushed them all to the door, forcing the butler out, too, as well as Lord Downey, by their exodus at three abreast.

When the door shut, Jared turned to look at Ava, who was staring back at him defiantly. So defiantly, in fact, that he noticed her skin had a certain glow about it. "You're beautiful," he said helplessly.

She put up a hand and shook her head. "Just . . . what do you want?"

"To see my wife. To hold her again."

She rolled her eyes, turned away from him, and stalked to the sideboard, where she poured a glass of water for herself. "Now that you've seen me, you can leave."

"Ava!" he said commandingly. "You will cease acting so missishly. I've come to tell you that my father is hosting the annual Autumn Ball and we are expected to attend."

"Oh how grand!" she exclaimed to the ceiling. "I suppose I should pretend that all is perfectly all right between us and smile happily when you steal a kiss from your mistress in some dark corner? Or better yet, on a private terrace. You seem to know where all the private terraces are," she said, setting the glass down with a *thwack* against the sideboard.

"Good God," he said, his exasperation mounting. "I told you—there *is* no mistress! There has never been a mistress!"

"Please spare the lies, sir. I will not attend."

He struggled to maintain his composure. "You may not decline, Ava."

"How can you insist on *anything* from me?" she cried. "Haven't you taken enough? And now you would take me into your father's house and make a laughingstock of me?"

"A *laughingstock*? I would take you into my father's house as my *wife*!"

But Ava wasn't listening. "You think I am a girl, a mere child whom you may make a fool!" she said, waving her hand at him as she turned in a frantic circle. "I don't care what sort of bargain you think we struck, sir, but I will not be your wife in name only!"

"You can't say that you have been my wife in name only," he said angrily. "Frankly, you can hardly claim to have been my wife at all these last two weeks."

"Why should I pretend? The moment you are alone, you rush into someone else's arms," she said, picking up a newspaper and flinging it at him. "Your friends have made certain it is printed in the morning newspapers!"

"That's a lie. I—"

"I will not be held hostage to this marriage by vows we took in vain!"

"You *wanted* those vows!" he angrily reminded her. "You pretend as if your motives were pure!"

"I hardly know what my motives were," she said adamantly. "But God knows how I have regretted my lack of deliberation many times over!"

He bristled, put his hand on his hips, and glared at her. "Ava, listen to me. We may have taken vows in vain, but everything has changed—"

"Yes, everything has changed! I don't want to be married to you. Will you please accept it? *I don't want to be married to you!*"

The tremor of anger in him was turning to white fury. This was not how he had envisioned this meeting—he had imagined telling her everything, that he could see only her, think of only her, feel only her in his heart. Yet the vile way in which she spoke to him now made a part of him wish he'd never met her.

Unfortunately, he *was* married to her, and she to him. But that did not mean he had to remain in her company. He crossed the room in two strides, took her arm, and held her close so there would be no mistake. "You may not *want* to be married to me, but madam, you are, and you *will* attend my father's ball. If you think to defy me, I will carry you bodily. Do you quite understand me?"

"Ha!" she cried to the ceiling. "Now you will dictate to me where I must go and *when*? Very well, sir, I shall attend. But I will not be timid when your mistress presents herself."

His rage bubbling over, he clenched his jaw against the curses that were rising up in his gullet, and let her go. Silly woman. Stupid, *silly* child. She would one day regret her harsh words, but at the moment, he was too angry to care if she did or not. He let go, turned on his heel, and strode for the door.

"There is one more thing I would say before you rush off to meet your lover," she said acidly.

He closed his eyes and tried to summon his composure.

"You have your wish," she said behind him, her voice breaking a little. "I am carrying your child."

He felt that thing in him burst. That impossibly large thing in him that had made him so uncomfortable these many weeks suddenly burst. He gripped the door handle, his mind trying to absorb that wonderful—and wretched—news. A moment or two passed before he was able to speak, and he slowly turned to face her, his heart wrenching at the sight of the tears in her eyes.

Lord God, how he'd hurt her. "You are certain?" he asked quietly.

"Yes, *yes!*" she cried heavenward. "I am certain! You shall have your heir! You may toss poor Edmond aside like so much rubbish, but you will have your legitimate heir."

His heart was breaking. He could *feel* it breaking. "You have your wish as well," he said quietly, and reached in his pocket and withdrew the diamond bracelet he had intended to give her as a gift. "I did encounter Lady Waterstone at the zoo shortly after we arrived in London, but quite by accident . . . at least on my part. I suppose she followed me there. But therein I told her, unequivocally, that there is no one for me but you. And there hasn't been anyone but you in months. I told her that I love you. Desperately so."

"W-what?" Ava tearfully stammered.

"I can't say why I feared it or why it has been so hard to admit . . . ," he said, and glanced up, into her lovely pale green eyes. "And there is so . . . *much* about Edmond you do not know. But I love him, Ava.

And I love you. I love you so much that I am astounded by the depth and breadth of it. I think of nothing but you. I dream of you. I *yearn* for you."

It felt as if his knees were buckling, and he braced himself on the back of a chair. "I ache for you, Ava. There is a hole in my day, a hole in my heart when you are away from me. I am nothing without you. It's what I've been trying to tell you," he said, and tossed the bracelet onto the chair and walked out, completely spent.

Thirty

Ava felt quite ill the next morning, but couldn't be entirely certain if it was her pregnancy or the turmoil she felt about Jared.

Her illness tipped Phoebe to her condition, however, for she found Ava crouched over the basin and handed her a cool clean cloth. "Are you carrying a child?" she asked bluntly.

"Yes," Ava said, and sagged into a chair and closed her eyes.

"That's *marvelous*!" Phoebe squealed.

"No, it's not," Ava said.

"Ava! You will not sully this with your anger! It's marvelous!"

Ava laughed wryly. "It's not my anger that sullies it, Phoebe. It is my stupidity," she said, and opened her eyes. "He came here to tell me that he loved me. But I railed at him, Phoebe. I made quite an ass of myself."

Phoebe laughed.

"It's not the least bit funny," Ava complained as Phoebe helped her to sit.

"Yes it is. You can be rather dramatic when you are of a mind. You've had a lover's tiff, nothing more."

"And you are the expert," Ava said with a snort.

"I would do at least as well as you," Phoebe said with a sniff.

Ava couldn't argue. "What am I to do, Phoebe? He was so angry when he left! I've never seen him so angry!"

"I don't know, exactly," Phoebe admitted. "But I should think three heads are wiser than one."

"What do you mean?"

"I mean, darling, that there is more than one rule for hunting a man who will be a duke, and I rather suspect if we put our minds to it with Sally, we shall discover it."

"Oh dear, *no*," Ava said. "I'm far too humiliated!"

"That is precisely the reason we must confer," Phoebe said, and pulled her up. "My only regret is that Greer is not here to help us. She always has such a wise head," Phoebe said.

"Me too," Ava sighed, and together they went off to seek counsel.

Jared spent a miserable two days before his father's ball second-guessing himself, wondering when he'd become so damnably soft.

He'd been such a fool, such a bloody fool. The entire business of love had never been his forte, and why in God's name he'd ever thought he could manage it . . . Well. He'd not make that mistake again. The next time a woman captured his heart—if ever—he'd head to Broderick Abbey and bury himself in work.

Unless, of course, *she* was there. In which case, perhaps he would walk into the Thames until the water covered his head and he could see no more, hear no more. Feel no more.

But she was carrying his child.

He thought about that a lot. He marveled at the miracle of it, wondered how he grew inside her, how his arms and legs developed. Or perhaps it was a girl, like Ava. Blond and pretty and far too irreverent for her own good. He'd missed the miracle of it with Edmond. He'd not miss it again.

Frankly, now that he'd unleashed the beast of love, he feared he'd never be able to rein it back in. He could only hope that he and the beast and Ava would find a comfortable way to exist with one another.

Yet at the moment, the wound was quite raw, which was why he sent a driver for her the night of the ball with strict instructions she was to be carried bodily if she thought to demur. The footman recoiled in horror when he said it, but Jared stepped forward so that they were nose to nose and explained to him very carefully that he'd not have a position in his household if he disobeyed him.

He dressed slowly, almost lethargically. He dreaded any evening in his father's company, but this evening—he didn't know if he could even bear it. To see her now, when the rift between them was so deep? His heart felt in danger of disintegrating completely. He felt so numb he wasn't certain that it hadn't already.

Phoebe finished winding the gold beads through Ava's hair that matched the beads sewn on the gold gown. On her wrist, Ava wore the diamond bracelet Jared had tossed on the chair. When she had finally picked it up that day, she had noticed that it was engraved on the inside. *From J.B. to A.B. Hearts entwined will never grow apart.*

She had cried like a baby.

And the gown she wore—well, Ava was often in awe of Phoebe's talent, but this was unbelievably beautiful. She felt like a princess.

So too in awe, apparently, were Lucy and Sally, who stood to one side, wide-eyed, staring at Ava as if they'd never seen her before.

"What?" she cried, terrified that her pregnancy was already noticeable.

"Oh my dear, you are *beautiful*," Lucy said.

"Really?" Ava asked as she turned one way, then the other in the gold gown, noting how each little bead caught the light and made her gown appear to glitter.

"It complements your complexion," Sally said, nodding thoughtfully, but eyeing her critically. "Yet there seems something a bit off, doesn't there?"

"There does?" Ava asked fearfully, peering at herself in the mirror.

"Mmm," Sally said, and she, Lucille, and Phoebe stared at Ava.

"What is it, then? You'll drive me mad with all the gaping!"

"Aha," Sally said, smiling a little. She stepped forward, sunk her fingers into Ava's bosom, and yanked the gown down to indecency.

Ava and Lucy shrieked.

"You're absolutely right," Phoebe said, nodding approvingly. "Just a hint of bosom."

"A *hint*?" Ava cried. She moved to pull the bodice up, but was stopped by the shrieks of Phoebe and Sally.

"Leave it, you silly goose!" Phoebe chastised her, and pushed the shoulders of the gown down a bit. She and Sally stood back to examine her. "Oh, Ava," she said, tears in her eyes. "You're absolutely ravishing."

A knock at the door interrupted anything Ava would have said to that, for Mr. Morris had appeared and said, "A carriage here for you, mu'um."

The four women looked at one another, and then suddenly started talking at once, gathering the matching fur-lined cape and her gloves. When they had at last secured all of her belongings, Ava took a deep breath, smiled brightly at them, and the four of them trooped to the foyer.

On the way down, they passed Lord Downey hovering at the door of his study. He frowned as the four of them went by. "I have yet to understand why I wasn't extended an invitation!" he shouted after Ava.

They ignored him.

In the foyer, a Middleton footman met Ava, bowing deeply when she appeared, and held the door open for her.

"Where is Lord Middleton?" Ava asked, peering past him, into the night.

"He said you were to meet him there, my lady," the footman said, bowing again.

Ava's heart sank. She had hoped to speak with him on the way to the ball, to apologize for her behavior, to tell him she loved him, too. What a horrible mess she'd made of things!

"Ah," she said, forcing a smile for the footman. "Well, then. I suppose we ought to be about it."

"Yes, mu'um," he said, and strode ahead of her to open the carriage door.

Ava lifted the hood of the cape over her head and smiled weakly at Phoebe. "You promise you'll come as soon as possible?"

Phoebe grabbed her and kissed her cheek. "As

soon as I make a small repair to my gown. Now remember, darling. *Humility.* I know it's not something with which you are very familiar, but you really must try."

"Thank you, Phoebe," Ava said wryly. "I shall walk off to learn my fate knowing that my sister does not believe me to be capable of humility."

"I don't think you capable in the least," Phoebe said as she gave her a little push toward the door. "Astonish me."

And with that, Ava walked out into the night to try and inch her way back into her husband's good graces.

At least a thousand beeswax candles had been lit, if not more, for the annual Redford Autumn Ball. The glow of all that firepower could be seen several city blocks away. If there was one thing Jared could say about his father, it was that he never spared an expense.

He trudged up the steps, smiled thinly at his father's butler, and stepped inside. "Shall I announce you, my lord?" the butler asked as he nodded at a footman to take his coat, hat, and gloves.

"I rather think not. I'll just sneak in, if it's all the same to you."

"As you wish, my lord," he said, bowing low. "I announced Lady Middleton earlier."

The mention of her name caused his heart to skip a beat. He nodded and walked on, stopping to greet the many acquaintances, smiling and flirting as he always did, his heart completely numb.

The ballroom was, predictably, very crowded. Mistletoe hung from every doorway, and from the six candelabra that hung over the dance floor. A quadrille was in progress, and he watched idly as men in black tails stepped around richly colored skirts, remembering a night like this that now seemed a thousand years ago, when he'd flirted with Ava as they'd danced a quadrille. He moved along the wall, stopping for a bit of champagne, speaking with friends.

He had yet to see Ava; he assumed she was off sulking somewhere. But he could see his father reigning over the festivities at the far corner, seated in a thronelike chair. He was bent over the arm, speaking to someone Jared could not see.

He hardly cared.

He walked on, watching the dancers, watching the crowd for any sign of Ava. Or Phoebe, for that matter, as Ava surely would be close by. The thought occurred to him that perhaps she was ill, what with her delicate condition and the crush of dancers, the heat—was that possible? What he knew about enceinte women was negligible, but he thought they tended to be ill quite a lot. The idea made him panic a little, and he looked around more intently.

Ironically, it was his father who pointed him to Ava, for he had moved just enough that he could see his father more clearly, could see him laughing, which to Jared was nothing short of astounding—he could remember only a handful of times he'd actually seen the duke laugh. But he was laughing now, his face creasing with his smile. Jared was so startled that he moved closer to see what good soul could make his father laugh.

Ava.

It was Ava seated prettily next to his father, looking as radiant as he'd ever seen her. She was holding a fan that he recognized as having belonged to his mother— of course it did, as it bore the ducal seal of Redford.

She was fanning herself, her eyes shining bright, her lips moving as she rattled on about something.

The sight confounded him—his father and Ava had scarcely even met, and even then, not under the best of circumstances, but there they sat, like a pair of old friends. *A pair of old friends.* His first thought was that they had joined together in their disdain of him. He could imagine them chatting up his faults, having a laugh at his miserable expense.

He was suddenly striding forward, his mind racing ahead to what he would say.

But as he neared, his father caught sight of him and suddenly stood up, then quickly lent a hand to Ava, who also stood, smiling brilliantly. And then his father shocked him, almost knocked him to his knees. He smiled at Jared, extended his hand as if he meant to greet him. In fact, when Jared reached him, he was uncertain *what* his father meant by it, and was somewhat stunned when his father took his hand and clasped it warmly. "Son," he said, "allow me to be the first to offer my sincerest congratulations."

Jared looked at Ava. Ava smiled nervously. "I beg your pardon?"

His father dropped his hand, but continued to smile. "No need to be coy. Your lovely wife has told me all."

"All?" he echoed, his eyes darting to Ava. Behind her father, she shrugged lightly and smiled a little.

"Yes, all. What a fine husband you are and, of course, the news of my grandchild."

Jared could not have been more shocked if the sky had fallen. "A good husband," he repeated dumbly.

"You've made me very happy," the duke said. "Here now," he added, putting his hand on Ava, and drawing her forward. "Your wife has waited to dance with you."

Everyone was watching as Ava stepped forward and put her hand in the one Jared offered. He leaned over and kissed her cheek. "Good evening, Ava."

"Good evening, Jared," she said softly.

How remarkable it was that the sound of his name on her lips would cause his heart to take flight so quickly. "They are a playing a waltz," he said to her. "Can you dance? I mean . . . are you *able* to—"

"Of course," she said, her smile dimpling her cheeks. He kept staring at her, at the pale green eyes that had so captured his imagination one spring night almost two years ago.

Ava laughed. "Did you mean to dance *this* waltz?"

He smiled, led her onto the dance floor, and swept them into the rhythm, yet he couldn't take his eyes from her face. "I thought I'd never hear you say my name again," he admitted softly. "Now I understand why it was so important to you."

She sucked in a breath, surreptitiously looking around. "I am . . . I am so dreadfully sorry," she blurted. "I had no idea I could be such a shrew. You were right all along, you know. I knew what we'd agreed, but I was unprepared, and I couldn't help falling madly in love with you."

He squeezed her hand, saw the bracelet she wore, and smiled. "I understand," he said, turning his gaze to her green eyes, her rosy lips. "For it happened to me, too. I never thought for a moment that I could actually . . . *love*. Not like this. I love you, Ava. You were right—I truly am an empty cage without you."

She smiled; her eyes sparkled up at him. "Truly?"

"Truly."

Her head fell back with a glorious laugh. He twirled her around, watching her.

"Can we make it a marriage, do you think? I mean a *real* marriage, an inspired marriage and not a convenient one?"

"We can make it all that and more. When," he asked, glancing at her middle, "will there be three of us?"

"Summer. When the jasmine and larkspur bloom."

The joy swelled up in him and filled his heart. "There is so much to say, Ava, so much to tell you— about Edmond, about me, and how it all came to be."

"I want to know it all," she said, smiling, her green eyes glistening with joy again. "But it must wait until we are home tonight, don't you agree?"

Home. She was coming home. An enormous weight was lifted from his chest.

"But now . . . they are watching us," she added.

"Who?" he asked absently, smiling down at her, the world only a distant noise to him, now.

"*Everyone,*" she said on a laugh. "After what has been in the newspapers . . ."

He glanced around, saw the many heads turned in their direction, and laughed. "I should have warned you, sweetheart, there will never be a moment's peace. Their eyes will be forever on us, cataloguing every move, every breath we take. It is a hazard that comes with being the heir to a duke."

"I don't care," she said happily. "As long as I have you, I don't care."

"Well, then," he said with a wink. "Let us give them something to titter about, shall we?"

"What?"

He twirled her to a stop in the middle of the dance floor, wrapped his arms around her, and kissed her.

She laughed against his mouth, but she curved into him the way she did when she desired him, and he couldn't bring himself to stop kissing her until Harrison tapped him on the shoulder and whispered that they were causing quite a stir.

Two mornings after the ball, a courier arrived at Middleton House with several boxes. Inside were toys and baby clothes. "A gift from the duke," Jared said, and as Ava exclaimed as she opened the boxes, Jared tried to wrap his mind around his father's new demeanor. It would take him a while to trust it—if ever—but it was a welcome relief.

A few days after that, a maid brought toast, coffee, and the morning edition of the *Times* to the master suite at Middleton House. She knocked on the door, slipped inside, deposited the tray, then slipped out again.

Ava made Jared get out from under the covers to fetch the tray, which he did completely naked, much to her delight. When he returned, they huddled together, sipped the coffee, and read the newspaper together. When at last they turned to the society pages, Ava squealed with delight at a small headline: *"The Hunt."*

She took the paper from Jared while he munched on a piece of toast and read aloud: "It would seem that the hunting season has come to a decided close, and the fox has once again outfoxed them all. While the whole of Mayfair may well have believed the fox was losing ground to the widow, it was the lamb who threw the hounds off course and captured him completely, according to observers who witnessed the capture at a recent ducal ball."

Ava laughed and turned a beaming smile to him. "I caught you," she said, tapping his nose with her finger.

"Frankly, madam," Jared said, "we haven't played that game in a while." He tossed the newspaper one way, the toast the other, and the fox gathered the lamb in his arms. "Catch me again," he said against her mouth, and his beautiful wife laughed.

Thirty-one

~~~

"**D**earest Ava and Phoebe, I regret to inform you I have not as yet learned what has happened to my family. I despair of ever knowing but Mr. Percy cautions me to be patient."

"Blast it all, this Mr. Percy!" Phoebe cried, shaking the letter she was reading at Ava.

"Go on, read it!" Ava insisted.

"*Last evening, we dined at the home of Sir Blanmouth, and I was persuaded to play billiards after supper. I am surprised to have won a round. Mr. Percy said I am naturally inclined to billiards, but did not recommend I take it up as an occupation. I assured him I will not.*"

"Dear God, she's playing billiards!" Ava moaned. "What is next for her, do you suppose? Gambling?"

"I scarcely think it is as dire as that, darling," Jared smilingly assured her before turning back to the book about knights and knightly battles he and Edmond Foote were perusing. Edmond and his father had recently come to London to call on a man young Edmond now believed to be a distant uncle, Lord Middleton.

"Go *on*, Phoebe, read the rest of it!" Ava insisted.

"*I suppose I will have to travel on if I am to have my answers.*"

Phoebe sighed irritably. "Do you suppose she

could, at least once, bother to say *what* questions she must have answered?" She continued reading: "*I should think another month and I will be home, although Mr. Percy has warned me that travel can be quite slow this time of year due to the rains. I shall write again soon. My love to you all, and particularly, to my future godchild. Fondly, Greer.*"

Phoebe put the letter down and looked at Ava. "*Who* is Mr. Percy?" she cried to the rafters.

"I don't suppose we will know until she deigns to come home," Ava said soothingly, and patted her sister's hand.

FINALLY
A WEBSITE
YOU CAN GET
PASSIONATE
ABOUT...

Visit
www.SimonSaysLove.com
for the latest information
about Romance from Pocket Books!

READING SUGGESTIONS

LATEST RELEASES

AUTHOR APPEARANCES

ONLINE CHATS WITH YOUR
FAVORITE WRITERS

SPECIAL OFFERS

ORDER BOOKS ONLINE

AND MUCH, MUCH MORE!